Wedding Bell Blues

Susanne Matthews

Copyright © 2018 Susanne Matthews

ISBN-13:978-0994898333
ISBN-10:0994898339

DEDICATION

To everyone who has ever believed in magic and mermaids or searched for treasure: May all your fantasies come true.

CONTENTS

ACKNOWLEDGMENTS

Books are never written in a vacuum. ***Wedding Bell Blues*** is no different. It got its start in **Tuesday Tales**, a weekly blog created and sponsored by Jean Joachim. Each week, Jean provides a word or picture prompt that must be incorporated into the story. That's where this book was born. Many thanks to Trisha Faye, Vicki Locey, Tricia Andersen, Flossie Benton Rogers, Jillian Chantal, Karen Gino-Gatti, Davee Jones, and last but not least, Jean Joachim for their invaluable advice and support. I would also like to thank Christy Newton for taking the time to beta read this novel. Your comments and insights were invaluable. Finally, my sincerest thanks go to my cover artist, Melinda De Ross who created and designed such an incredibly beautiful cover for this story. Your talent never ceases to amaze me.

CHAPTER ONE

"Give it a rest, Carla. We're here," MJ said, her chin raised. She pushed a strand of her mouse-brown hair behind her ear.

"We're supposed to meet with the realtor at two, but I want to show you the school and the house first." She made a right turn onto Sycamore Street, and then a left onto Pine. "Once you see how perfect it is, you'll agree it isn't a dumbass move."

"Right." Carla crossed her arms over her baby bump, lips tightly compressed. "The area isn't as rustic as I thought it would be," she admitted, twisting her mouth to the left.

MJ smiled. "It's a nice neighborhood. There's the school." She stopped in front of the imposing two-story, red-brick building with polished oak doors with large brass handles glittering in the sunshine. "You would love the gym. It was added two years ago."

"I still think you're crazy. An elementary school that looks like a convent is the last place I would picture you. I don't get it," Carla said, shifting in her seat. "Snotty-nosed kids? Winter yard duty? Why?"

"I wanted something different—a complete change," MJ answered, her lips pursed. "There was too much drama in my life last year. I don't want to deal with broken hearts and mean girls."

Carla burst out laughing. "And you think teaching second grade will get you away from it? Good luck. Between my son and my two eight-year-old nieces, there's more angst than on a soap opera. It's all about drama at that age."

"You're exaggerating, but even if you aren't, I'll figure it out.

1

Regardless, it'll be better than living through another minute of the Mark and Melena show."

She clamped her jaw shut to stop herself from going down that road. M and M had already caused her more than enough grief. She put the car into drive once more.

"Anyway, when I spoke to the principal last month, he said the owner would hold the house for me. I'll be able to walk to work. Think of the money I'll save on gas."

"Whatever," Carla said, folding her arms across her chest again in her 'I don't believe you for one minute' gesture. "Where is this fantastic house of yours?"

"Just down this street. On Elm."

"Elm Street?" she shrieked. "You're moving into a house on Elm Street?" She crossed herself. "Have you lost your flipping mind?"

MJ bit her tongue to stop herself from laughing. "I intend to decorate it to the hilt for Halloween. I'll take off my glasses, dress in black, and hand out treats from a cauldron." At Carla's look of horror, she giggled. "Relax. Freddy Kruger doesn't live next door. You're going to love it."

"Right, and I'm looking forward to eighteen hours of hard labor, too." Carla clenched her lips so tightly they were white.

"Here it is." MJ pulled the car to the curb, turned off the engine, and opened her door. "What do you think?"

Carla got out of the vehicle, stretched her back, and turned toward the house. Her eyes widened, and her jaw dropped open.

"Oh my God. It's gorgeous," she exclaimed, crossing the street without waiting for MJ.

Locking the car, MJ hurried to join her on the sidewalk.

"What did I tell you? When I drove by the first time I was here, I knew I was destined to live in this house. I could almost see Papa on the veranda and hear Mama calling me in to dinner." She swallowed the lump in her throat. "The landlord is charging me twelve hundred a month plus utilities. I wouldn't have gotten a broom closet for that price in New York City, and you know it. Good things are going to happen for me, Carla, you'll see."

She nodded. "If this house is anything to go by, you could be right."

MJ took a deep breath, grateful her asthma wasn't bothering her despite the heat and humidity here. The house looked even better than she recalled. The lawn had been cut and the fieldstone walk re-laid, not a single weed in sight. Elephant hostas decorated the base of the veranda on which sat a couple of gliding lawn chairs separated by a brass and glass table. How nice of Mr. Newton, the landlord, to provide those homey touches.

In front of the house, the sixteen-foot blue spruce in the center of the lawn had been trimmed, the skirt raised, and crushed white stone laid all around the trunk.

"I thought you told me the place was a little run down," Carla interrupted her perusal of her new home.

She frowned. "It was. The landlord must've spruced it up. The veranda, shutters, and garage have all been repainted, and the windows have been washed. I didn't think he would go to that much trouble for a tenant. Come on. I'll take you around back. I haven't seen the yard, but according to the principal, there's a deck and a place for a garden. Maybe I'll plant tomatoes or something."

"You? Gardening? Hah." She snorted. "You killed an air fern, not to mention a cactus."

MJ ignored her comment, opened the gate, and stepped into the backyard. Carla stood in the open gateway behind her.

"Holy crap! That's one hell of a nice landlord you have."

MJ stopped in her tracks and stared. As with the front, someone had done extensive landscaping back here. The lawn had been mowed, the garden planted, and a hammock hung between two stately red maple trees. The deck had been stained and sported a gas barbecue and a patio set. She admired the brand-new dog house, the largest one of its kind she'd ever seen.

Dog house? That couldn't be a dog house. It had to be a utility shed.

Before she could take a step back, a huge animal came tearing around the side of the house. Carla reacted by screaming and slamming the gate shut, locking MJ in the yard with a dog, at least she thought it was canine, heading right for her.

Her heart hammered. She had the wrong address. This perfect house wasn't the one she was supposed to rent.

Before she could raise her arms to shield herself, the enormous dog ran up to her and knocked her to the grass with his greeting. His large tongue bathed her face, including her designer prescription sunglasses, making it impossible to see anything clearly, and he barked out a welcome. If she weren't so terrified, she might have enjoyed this doggy's exuberant greeting. She liked dogs, really she did. She just preferred them a hundred pounds lighter and three feet shorter.

"King, get over here," a man called sharply. The animal licked her one last time before turning to obey his master.

Damn!

She sat up. The barrette holding her hair in place had gone flying, her frizzy hair exploding out of it. Glancing down at the enormous muddy paw prints on her white blouse, one on each of her breasts, she groaned.

"I'm so sorry, ma'am," the man said, squatting beside her.

His words were a red flag to an angry bull. People called her mother "ma'am," not her. She wasn't *that* old.

"He's still a pup and a little too friendly. I just got him last week." He chuckled.

"That's a pup?" The words burst out of MJ's mouth. "What the hell kind of dog is it?"

"He's not a purebred, but most of him is Irish wolfhound," the man answered as if he were the injured party. "By the time he reaches his adult size, he may stand seven feet tall on his hind legs. He's more than half-way there now. I rescued him from the animal shelter. His previous owners hadn't expected him to get this size either. Are you okay?"

"Do I look okay?" she retorted through gritted teeth, her cheeks burning. "I could've been killed by that monster. You need a warning sign on your fence. Is a dog that size even legal in the city?"

"Look, lady. Calm down," the man ordered. "King may be big, but he's harmless. Now, does anything feel broken?"

"No," she replied grudgingly. Her pride had suffered more than her person, and that was a miracle. "Your pet dinosaur, and maybe you should rename him Dino, just knocked me down and stepped on me, not to mention gave me a bath."

Between the hair in her eyes and the blurry glasses, she couldn't see the man clearly, but his sexy voice, strangely familiar, grated on her taut nerves.

"Hey, don't go all offended maiden on me," he answered, an

edge to his caramel-smooth tone. "I'm not the one trespassing. The gate was closed, and I know the latch works. Here, give me your hand." Standing, he reached down to help her up.

MJ accepted the proffered hand and stood, but not before a powerful jolt of awareness ran through her. Shaken by the strength of her reaction to this man, she let go of his hand as soon as she could.

"Thank you." That was the least she could say. He was right. She was the one in the wrong.

"MJ, are you okay?" Carla's panicky voice came from the other side of the gate. "Should I phone the police?"

"No! I'm fine," she answered before Carla called 9-1-1 or something equally humiliating. "It was just a dog."

"*That* was a dog?" Carla asked, opening the gate and poking her head into the yard. "I've seen smaller horses." She stared at the man next to MJ and paled. "Holy shit."

MJ frowned and turned around. The dog was sitting quietly beside its master. She pushed her hair off her face ready to apologize when she realized what had left Carla speechless. This was a thousand times worse than Freddy.

Kill me now.

It had been fifteen years, but there was enough of the boy in the man that she would've recognized him anywhere. What the hell was he doing here in her house? He was shirtless, wearing only a pair of baggy shorts, and the man didn't have a six pack—hell no. That was at least a twelve pack. His chest was covered with a fine mat of dark hair that didn't quite hide the puckered, circular scar on his left pectoral, and his left leg was crisscrossed with fresh scars. He was a little older, a little taller, tanned a delicious golden brown, and more muscled than he'd been as a teen, but there was no mistaking the man staring down at them as if she and Carla were aliens. She smiled and swallowed what little saliva she had.

"Hello, Paul. It's been a while," she said, her voice cracking on the last word.

The man's frown deepened, creasing his eyebrows, accentuating his chocolate-brown eyes where curiosity replaced annoyance.

"Do I know you?" he asked.

If ever there was a time for the ground to open and swallow her whole, it was now.

"Of course you do," Carla piped up. "It's Marilyn Jean."

Where was a bolt of lightning when you needed one?

At his continued confusion, MJ huffed out a breath. "It's me—MJ? Kid? Ron's little sister? The pest?" He couldn't have forgotten her that completely, not when he'd meant the world to her, even if he'd been oblivious to the fact. She removed her Jackie O sunglasses.

His confusion turned to shock, and incredulity played across his face. The man's eyes almost bulged out of his head.

"Son of a bitch. Kid? Is that really you?" he asked slowly, his gaze raking her from head to toe before settling on her paw-marked breasts.

She fought the urge to cover her chest and swallowed. "The one and only," she answered with a false bravado her brother would've appreciated.

"You've gained weight." He smiled, eying her up and down once more, further adding to her desire to vanish. He shook his head. "You've changed."

"No shit, Sherlock." Carla guffawed. "I'm Carla Balducci—Hunter now. Do you remember me?" she stuck out her hand.

"Yeah. Kid and her trusty sidekick." He shook Carla's hand and then focused on her again.

Did he really think she was fat? The man was gorgeous, way more attractive than she'd ever imagined he would be. The long, black hair she recalled had been cut military short, but the style suited him. Her fingers itched to run through it, and she fisted her hands at her side lest they fly up of their own volition.

"What's it been? Fifteen years? It's great to see you, but what are you doing here?"

"The house," she stammered. "I came to look at the house. I thought it was the one I was going to rent, but I've obviously made a mistake. Mine must be farther down the block. I didn't know you lived here. Sorry for trespassing." She was blabbering. What the hell was wrong with her? Maybe these baggy pants made her look fat.

He grimaced and shook his head. "Right house, I'm afraid, but it isn't for rent anymore. I made the owner an offer he couldn't refuse, bought it, and moved in a couple of weeks ago." He shrugged. "Is your husband with you?"

"She's not married," Carla supplied. "Are you?"

"Am I what?" he asked, his brow furrowed once more, his eyes focused on MJ's face.

"Married," Carla repeated the word.

MJ fisted her hands at her side. If Carla opened her mouth again, she would kill her. It would be justifiable homicide. No jury of single women would ever convict her.

"Carla, for God's sake," she whispered through clenched teeth.

"I'm not," he answered.

Her friend grinned. "Great. Then you two can get to know one another again."

"I would like that. So, you'll be working down the street. Mr. Newton mentioned a teacher had been interested in the place."

"More than interested," Carla piped up again before MJ could answer.

Couldn't the woman keep her damn mouth shut?

"She thought it was a done deal. Now, she's got no place to live and … Ouch! Why'd you kick me?" Carla bent and rubbed her shin.

"Did I?" MJ bit off through gritted teeth, glaring at her. "My foot must've slipped on the grass."

"Come inside," Paul said, staring at her mud-stained shirt. "The least I can do is give you a cold drink and let you clean up. If I'd known company was coming, I wouldn't have watered the grass." He led the way up onto the deck and into the house.

The kitchen was just the way she'd imagined it. The new matching range and refrigerator were white, no doubt to coordinate with the built-in dishwasher. The above the range microwave oven looked unused. On the counter sat a variety of small appliances, including the latest in food processors her mother would have loved. Four oak bar stools stood on one side of the large, granite center island. This kitchen was every cook's dream.

"Can I get you a glass of water?" he asked, closing the screen door to keep King out of the house. "I've got beer if you prefer."

"Water for me," Carla said, pointing to her stomach. "Bun in the oven, and all that."

"Beer's good," MJ answered, glancing down at her blouse once more. "I'd better clean up."

"Bathroom's down the hall. Same floor plan as your old place.

Help yourself."

Nodding, she stepped out of the kitchen. The living room and dining room, both painted a light brown and trimmed in white, were empty other than the appliance boxes stacked in the corner and the gas fireplace which must've replaced an older wood-burning one. He might not be married, but a bachelor didn't buy a house like this. So where was his main squeeze?

She entered the bathroom, painted light blue, with brand new white fixtures and white trim, and locked the door behind her, leaning against it for support. White towels? Definitely not a bachelor pad.

Slipping down the door, she sat on the floor and let reaction and disappointment take over.

Paul Davis. He and Ron had been inseparable and always in one kind of trouble or another. In fact, Paul had probably spent as much time at her house as at his own—maybe even more. Between them, they'd made her pre-teen and early teen years hell. But, in spite of all that, he'd been her first love, as painful as the experience had been.

She'd worshiped him. He'd been her hero, coming to her rescue more times than she could count, but the rest of the time, he'd treated her the same way Ron had, as if she were his kid sister. He'd called her Kid—he probably didn't even know her real name. Mama had been the one to hold her in her arms when Ron had told the family that Paul had moved away for good—gone without even saying goodbye.

If she were honest, every boy she'd ever dated had been measured against her memories of her brother's long-lost friend, and sooner or later, all of them had been found wanting.

Letting out a deep breath, she sighed. Tears slipped down her cheeks. More bad luck. When would it stop? She was a good person, damn it. She tried to do the right thing, but the Fates never gave her a chance. It was as if she were cursed. What was she going to do now?

Over the years, especially those months after he'd left, she'd dreamed of running into Paul again, but it had generally involved a crowded ballroom and her in a wispy evening gown. He'd see her across the room and hold her gaze as he moved toward her, pushing the beautiful women out of his way until he took her into his arms. "Once upon a Dream," the song she loved from *Sleeping Beauty,* would be playing, and they'd step onto the dance floor, moving as one. He'd bend his head toward hers and—that's when she would wake up.

The man she dreamed of resembled the tall, lanky eighteen-year-old she recalled, not the sexy man she'd just met, and in her fantasy, he always remembered her, unlike the reality of today, and he *never* told her she was *fat*! That thought put steel into her backbone. What was she doing crying, sitting on the jerk's bathroom floor? Fifteen years ago, the son of a bitch had broken her heart and now, he'd shattered her fantasies and destroyed her dreams of living here. Damn him!

Why the hell hadn't the realtor or Mr. Newton called? No doubt they'd expected her to go to the realty office before showing up at the house. That's what a normal person would've done, but not her.

She stood, walked over to the sink, and turned on the tap. Unwilling to ruin one of the pristine facecloths, she used toilet paper to clean her face and then tried to wipe away the mud, making everything worse instead of better. When the mirror revealed nipples visible against the wet fabric of her blouse and bra, she smacked herself in the forehead.

Can't I get a break? Just one?

Using the blow dryer she found under the sink, she aimed it at her chest, letting the heat repair the damage. A few minutes later, convinced this was as good as it would get, she opened the bathroom door and cringed at Carla's laughter. More than a little nervous, she walked into the kitchen. What other secrets had her friend given away?

The twosome stood beside the stove tasting whatever was in the pot. She had to admit, it smelled delicious, just like her mom's fasolada. Come to think of it, there were other aromas in the house that made her mouth water.

Paul turned toward her and gaped.

"Sorry about your blouse," he said, scowling. "I'll replace it if you want to take it off."

MJ's cheeks heated at the image her mind created of the two of them buck-naked on the kitchen isle, humping like bunnies, in a scene reminiscent of *Bull Durham.*

As if he'd read her mind, Paul reddened. "I mean Carla says you've got a suitcase in the car, so you must have another top to wear, or I can lend you a t-shirt. You can change your blouse, and I can give it back to you in a few weeks when you move up here."

"That isn't necessary," she said. "It's not really *that* bad…"

"Are you insane?" Carla cried, her eyes huge and filled with disbelief. "Yes, it is. You can't go to the realtor's looking like that." She pointed to MJ's chest. "They probably have air conditioning there, too."

MJ glanced down at the nipples projecting from her breasts and quickly folded her arms over them. She looked up and saw Paul staring and wanted to kick him. Why did guys' eyes always zero in like that?

But the look on his face confirmed one thing. She stood a little taller.

Fat my ass!

MJ sighed. "Fine. I'll change if you think I have to."

Carla nodded. "Let me get your bag."

Once Carla left, Paul handed her the beer, forcing her to uncover her damp, mud-stained chest. MJ lifted the can to her mouth and guzzled half of it.

"So, Carla said you're moving up here because you wanted a change. I would've thought you married with a houseful of kids by now. How's Ron?" he asked as if there was nothing wrong.

Swallowing a burp that would have rivaled anything her brother might've made, she nodded. Apparently, Paul could gawk at her nipples, appreciate what he saw, and yet dismiss any sexual tension between them just like that; whereas, she was hornier than she'd ever been.

Some things never changed. So much for her *femme fatale* fantasy.

"Ron's fine," she answered, trying to be as nonchalant as he was. "He married Lucy Montroy. They've got three-year-old twins."

"Your mother must be thrilled. I'll bet she enjoys fussing over them as does your dad."

MJ swallowed, trying to hold back the tears so damn close to the surface these days.

"He would've adored them, but sadly, he died eight years ago."

She swallowed. "Mom dotes on the twins, but now that Ron's job took him to Buffalo, she doesn't get to see them as often as she did."

"I'm sorry, Kid. I know how close you were to your dad. He was a great guy. And as far as Ron moving away, that sucks."

"Mama certainly thinks so, and believe me, I hear about it regularly, as well as the fact I haven't given her any grandchildren." She raised the can to her lips once more.

"Speaking of your offspring, how come you aren't married? You must be what? Almost thirty?" He chuckled. "Doesn't that make you an old maid or something?"

Fighting to keep her temper in check, she squeezed the beer can, releasing the pressure only when she felt it dent in her hand. First, he said she was fat, and now, he'd called her an old maid. If she could, she would punch him, but King, who was watching them through the screen door, would probably break in and rip her throat out.

"Thirty-one last month, but who's counting? Never met the right guy, I guess. I'm not the only one who hasn't tied the knot. There's still Antonia, Maria, and Lena."

"Antonia's the one with the…" he rubbed his upper lip with his finger. "I remember her. She started shaving before half of the guys in our class did. Nobody messed with her."

"She's got a great personality." MJ winced. Describing a girl that way was the kiss of death.

Could this day get any worse?

CHAPTER TWO

MJ almost jumped for joy when Carla returned and handed her a small overnight bag. Chitchatting with Paul had been unnerving, especially when he seemed fixated on her chest.

"I'll be right back."

Paul had called her an old maid, a fat, old maid at that, but hadn't been able to keep his eyes off her boobs. She closed the bathroom door and pulled at the blouse, ripping off one of the buttons. Fighting not to give in to her disappointment and frustration, she removed her bra and replaced it and the blouse with the black tube top with the built-in bra she'd brought with her.

Dressed decently again and more than a little nosy, she looked around and saw that the house's bedrooms had been repainted. The smallest room contained an easel and art supplies and was a soft shell-pink. Dismay filled her once more. This couldn't be Paul's studio.

The door to the master bedroom was shut. He was only wearing shorts. Had they interrupted something? Maybe his girlfriend, the one who'd chosen the pink paint and white towels, was in there waiting for him to get back to bed. Why else would the door be closed?

Jealousy, stronger than anything she'd felt over Mark, speared her, and she shook her head. So what if he had a dozen women in that room? It was none of her business.

Glancing at her watch, she hurried back into the kitchen. "I hate to drink and run, but we'd better get going. I'm supposed to meet with the realtor in twenty minutes. If I had a lick of common sense, I would've called before I left Stilton, but you know me—jump in with both feet before checking the depth. If I had, I could've spared us both this." She gestured at the kitchen.

"I'm glad you didn't," he said, smiling. "And, as I recall, that day at the lake, Ron jumped in first." He took a swig of his beer. "You know, if you can't find anything today, you're welcome to stay here until you do. I've got more than enough space."

MJ almost choked on her last mouthful of brew.

"If you're working down the street, it would be perfect for you."

Carla burst out laughing. "And what would your neighbors think of that?"

MJ's libido was doing handsprings. If he offered to have her stay with him, there couldn't be a woman in that bedroom. She visualized getting to know Paul, in the biblical sense, in every room of the house.

"Get serious, Carla. MJ might as well be my sister," he said and shook his head. "I spent as much time, if not more, in her house than I did in mine. The offer stands." He turned back to her, a friendly smile pasted on his face. "Think of me as your second big brother. The rest of the furniture arrives on Wednesday. If you want a place to crash until you find yours, feel free, and if it works out, I won't mind the company." He shrugged. "I'll be out of town until the last week of July. You could house sit for me. King's friendly. You couldn't be in safer hands."

Thoroughly dejected, her girlish dreams in ashes at her feet, she mustered every ounce of dignity she possessed.

"Thanks for the offer, Paul, but Carla's right." She licked her lips. "Working for the diocese has its drawbacks, and the morality clause from hell in the contract is just one of them—not that I live the life of a Kardashian or anything—but living here, with you..." She was blabbering again. "I might think of you as a brother, but others wouldn't. Don't worry about the blouse. I'll take care of it." Handing him the empty beer can, she smiled, hoping she didn't look like a hungry barracuda. "Unfortunately, I won't be here until the end of the month either, so I can't help you out while you're away, but I'll tell Ron and Mama that I saw you. Maybe we'll run into one another sometime."

Hopefully, when I'm driving the car, and you're in the road in front of it.

The murderous thought surprised her. Ashamed of herself, she turned and headed out of the house with Carla scrambling to keep up.

Tossing her small suitcase back into the trunk, she slammed the lid shut with more vehemence than necessary. As soon as Carla was in the car, MJ didn't even give her time to buckle up before pulling away from the curb.

"What the hell's wrong with you?" Carla asked. "You were downright rude."

"Was I?" MJ swallowed her pain. "I didn't mean to be. It was past time to leave, that's all. Besides, his girlfriend was waiting for him in the bedroom."

"What are you talking about?" Her brow furrowed into her trademark 'are you nuts?' expression. "He lives alone. He told me so."

"Just because he lives alone doesn't mean he *was* alone, or that he plans to stay that way. The small bedroom is painted pink, and the bathroom towels are white—not that I was snooping. You smelled those cookies and tasted whatever was cooking on the stove. A bachelor doesn't cook and bake for himself, nor does he paint rooms pink."

Carla laughed. "Point taken. Hank freaked when I suggested we paint the bathroom pink. Since Rod's at my mother's, no doubt he'll have a stack of empty pizza boxes in the recycling when we get back, and we're only gone overnight. By the way, it's bean soup. Paul claimed he'd made it according to your mother's recipe. It's even better than your mom's, but don't tell her I said so."

"You can rest assured I won't. Everything he does is great," MJ spat the words out, her upper lip raised at the left corner. "It always was."

* * *

Paul stood in the living room window watching the car disappear up the street and frowned. Seeing Kid today was the last thing he'd expected. He'd recognized her the moment she'd taken off those sunglasses. There was no way in hell he'd ever forget her incredible eyes. They were a pale aquamarine with a deeper ring of the same color edging the outer iris. They reminded him of sand beaches and warm seas, and he'd never seen any others like them.

Turning back into the kitchen, he lifted his beer to his mouth and finished it, tossing the empty into the recycling bin along with hers.

Kid had been a vital part of the best times in his life, the times he'd hoped to recapture here. She'd been almost sixteen the last time he'd seen her. Pale and fragile, she'd reminded him of an angel, but looks could be deceiving. She'd grown a tough skin, forced to stand up to the bullies even when it brought her more trouble than she needed. He'd tried to make things easier for her; after all, she'd been his sister as much as Ron's. He shook his head. Kid. Hell, she was no more a kid than he was an elephant.

Her father had called her his wild, Greek-Irish rose. She still had that pale peaches and cream complexion, but her cheeks had burned brighter when she'd noticed King's pawprints on her breasts. With that curly hair, petite and curvy the way he preferred his women, the hard-on he'd gotten when she'd come back from the bathroom in that blouse, her nipples standing at attention, had yet to subside. No matter how many times he kept reminding himself that she was Kid, his body refused to accept it. Trying to keep his mind out of the gutter while he talked to her had been a feat worthy of sainthood.

What the hell had he been thinking offering to let her move in? Thank goodness Carla had seen the danger in that. There was no way the neighbors would accept that there wasn't any hanky-panky going on. Hell, he wouldn't believe it either. If Mama Summers knew what he was considering, she would emasculate him with a kitchen knife, and Ron would beat the living shit out of him and be done with it.

Guilt washed through him. He hadn't given a thought to the teacher who'd expected to move into this house. Buying it out from under her had been a dirty trick, but he'd been desperate. While he'd painted the living room, dining room, and kitchen in modern colors, he'd insisted on coming as close to the way the house had been for the two small bedrooms. He'd painted hers, the room where he now spent his evening hours drawing, a blush pink, the closest he could get to the color he remembered, but the green one where he'd spent so many hours avoiding the reality of his own family life was that same shade of green again.

Instead of the beige that had been in the master bedroom, he'd gone with the palest shade of turquoise. He hadn't realized why until today. In all these years, his memory of her eyes hadn't faded one damn bit.

He sighed, walked over to the stove, and stirred the soup. A couple of the guys from the base were coming over later to watch the ball game. It was just as well he wouldn't be alone tonight because the urge to follow her right now was as strong as any he'd ever had. Since his plan had been to recreate the happy times in his life, having her around would make that easier. In the last week, now that he had King and the house, there'd been fewer nightmares, and that meant his plan was working. As the doctor had warned, the Fourth of July had been difficult, but he'd managed. The healing had begun.

Now that he knew Kid would be living in Watertown, he owed it to Mama and Ron to watch out for her. He could offer to take her to dinner now and then, maybe help her get her place fixed up, but before he did either of those things, he needed to stop thinking with the wrong head and smarten up. Keeping an eye on her was the brotherly thing to do. Unfortunately, the last thing he felt right now was brotherly.

"You didn't make a very good first impression either," he said to King. "That's not the way to greet ladies when they come calling. I should take the cost of her new blouse out of your kibble allowance."

Reaching into the fridge, he grabbed another beer and headed outside to finish the grass. Would he ever be able to get the image of her nipples out of his head? Probably not, but then again, did he really want to?

* * *

Twenty minutes later, MJ stared at Duncan Phillips, refusing to look at Carla who had her "I told you this was a mistake look" firmly in place.

"You can't be serious?" First Paul had stolen her house out from under her, and now this. "There *has* to be something available for August—an apartment, a cottage, a trailer, anything," she begged.

"I'm sorry." The overweight man, large sweat stains at his armpits, mopped his brow with a plaid handkerchief. "Watertown doesn't have a lot of rental units at the best of times. I'll have a small house over on Henderson come November first. It's yours if you want it."

Since the air conditioner wasn't working, the realty office was barely cooler than hell, and Mr. Philips was chomping at the bit to get out of it.

"Something may come on the market in September, but the best I can offer you now is a long-term rental at a motel. The White Wolf was renovated and insulated last year. It goes for ninety a night. You might be able to talk him down to half that if you're staying more than a month." He shrugged.

"A motel?" Carla squealed, moving away from the photographs of cottages for sale. "You can't live in a *motel*." She turned to the agent, every one of her Italian features glowering. "And you're sure there isn't anything else?"

The man swallowed. "There might be a room in one of the houses used by Supportive Housing—"

"No," MJ interrupted, almost choking on what he'd said, but refusing to give in to the despair she felt. "I don't need a room in a halfway house, thank you. Lots of people stay in motels or hotels when they transition between houses. Even though I haven't seen it, the place on Henderson sounds good. In the meantime, the motel will be fine."

Carla's eyes bulged out of her head as she mouthed, 'are you frigging nuts?'

MJ ignored her and turned to the agent.

The big man smiled, his nicotine-stained teeth matching two of the fingers on his right hand. His eyes were full of commiseration as he wiped his brow once more, the damp cloth barely absorbing the moisture.

"I'm sorry the house on Elm didn't work out. If something else comes up, you'll be the first to know, and of course, if you decide you want to buy..."

"Thanks," she smiled, trying not to inhale too deeply. "Will you contact the motel and see if you can get me something for the duration? The last thing I need is to lose that, too."

"Of course. The owner's a friend. I'll put in a good word for you." He reached for his Smartphone.

While Carla hit the washroom again, MJ paced. Damn Paul Davis. This was all his fault. Essentially, she was homeless, and Mama would blow a fuse when she realized it.

"I'm sorry. The best I could do was get you into one of the motel's long-term rooms starting the second week of August. Those have kitchenettes," Duncan said, stepping closer to her and turning off the cell phone he'd been using. "The good news is he's prepared to let you have it for nine hundred a month. The motel's popular with cross-border shoppers. I'll keep my eyes open, but I wouldn't bet on anything better coming up between now and then." He handed her a card. "Here's the address if you want to check it out. It's just outside town."

"Thanks. I might as well take a look."

Tuning out Carla's diatribe, wishing she were a witch and could summon a lightning bolt out of nowhere to end her misery, MJ keyed the address into the GPS. She leaned back against the seat.

"One of these days, your impetuous behavior will be the death of you," Carla finished.

"Fine," she said, giving in and slamming her right palm against the steering wheel. "You're right. I'm an idiot. I should've made sure the house was still available before I signed the contract with the diocese, but it's done, and I'm out of options. It's the motel room or a park bench." MJ gritted her teeth, fighting not to give into the tears just below the surface.

Before long, she pulled into the motel's crowded parking lot. The place looked better than a couple they'd passed along the way. There was a pool and a few women sat around it, wearing bikinis smaller than the band aids she wore on her blistered heels. Mercifully, Carla didn't say anything.

More depressed than ever, MJ reversed out of the parking lot.

"Are you sure you didn't know Paul Davis was here?" Carla asked, startling her.

Stunned, MJ stepped on the brake and turned to the woman beside her.

"Where in the world would you get an idea like that?"

"If you did, all of this would make sense," she answered, one eyebrow cocked. "Fifteen years ago, you would've followed him to the ends of the Earth. Did you see him walking that horse when you came up for your interview? Is that why you're behaving like a complete and total moron, willing to stay in a motel that probably rents rooms by the hour?"

"You can't be serious. The man didn't even recognize me." Her lower lip trembled, and she fought to tamp down her disappointment.

"But you recognized him, and so did I." Carla scrunched up her nose. "Strange that he just happened to be in your house."

MJ turned to her, her chin jutting out in defiance, too angry and upset to respond.

Carla stared at her a few moments.

"Okay," she said at last. "Maybe you didn't ... Neither of you could've faked that struck dumb look on your faces, but you would be better off with him than in that motel—gossip or no gossip. Did you see the bimbos out by the pool? If they're cross-border shoppers, I'm a unicorn."

"Maybe they're sun worshippers," she mumbled, beginning to drive again. "As far as Paul goes, the last thing I want, or need, is another big brother."

"Don't knock it. Big brothers can come in handy. I have five of them, remember? You'll be alone here, and he looks like the right kind of person to call in a jam. Did you see those abs? While there might have been a woman in his bedroom, he did say he's not married. It's a small town. You're bound to run into him, but try to be cavalier about it if you do. Whatever you do, don't stalk him like we did as kids."

MJ stopped for a red light and turned to face Carla, all of the pain and embarrassment of the afternoon coming back to her.

"Stalk him? We did not stalk him," she said with all of the dignity she could muster. "We followed because we wanted to do whatever he and Ron were doing. Believe me, Hell will freeze over before I call him for anything."

"Whoa!" Carla pulled back as if she'd been struck. "You're overreacting. You caught him off-guard. That's all. You used to worship the ground he walked on. No need to cut off your nose to spite your face. He did offer you a place to stay—"

MJ clenched her fists and if she could have, she would've stomped her foot. "He was just being *brotherly*," she spat the word, unable to ignore the bad taste it left in her mouth. "Look, I'm sorry I got mad at you, but I'm really disappointed, and I want to forget all about that house and Paul. Let's get back to the hotel and get settled, and then we need to go shopping. You have to promise me never to breathe a single word of this humiliating afternoon to anyone."

"But MJ," Carla said, her brow furrowed in confusion. "Knowing Paul's here would calm all your mother's fears about you moving to Watertown and being at the mercy of who knows what. And you did say you'd say hello to Ron and your mother for him…"

"I lied. I have no intention of letting anyone in my family know I saw Paul. He didn't keep in touch for a reason, and there's no point in changing that. You know the way my mother is right now …. She's so damn anxious for me to get married ... If our friendship means anything, you have to swear never to mention his name to anyone."

"Have it your way," Carla said, her lip pulled up on one side. "But you're making a mistake."

MJ swallowed some of her bitterness; after all, Carla wasn't to blame for this fiasco. "You think so? I don't. If I never see him again, it'll be too soon."

"You aren't making sense. You're too worked up—"

"Really? He doesn't recognize me, he insults me, and steals my damn house from under me—what am I missing here?" MJ cut her off and let go of the steering wheel, pointing the index finger of her right hand at Carla. "If it makes you feel better, as God is my witness and since I can't summon demons or whatever to help me out of a jam, if a major disaster occurs, I'm in dire straits, and he's the only one who can help me, I'll turn to him for assistance. Satisfied?"

"Not really, and you shouldn't swear to God if you don't mean it, and never mind that nonsense about calling up demons, but it'll have to do." She sat quiet for a moment, and then turned back to look at MJ. "Did you say you need to go shopping?"

MJ licked her lips. "I'm taking a vacation before I move here."

"You are?" Carla asked, her face suddenly animated. "I wondered when you said the end of July because I thought you were leaving next week. Well, I hope you're going to one of those hedonistic places where gorgeous men wait on you hand and foot. There's bound to be some hunk there who'll make your body sing. I can't see Mark ringing too many of your bells in the sack."

MJ swallowed. "Don't be crude. Actually, Mark has a lot to do with where I'm going." She took a deep breath and stared at the road ahead. "I'm going on my honeymoon, and there's absolutely nothing you can say that will change my mind."

Carla opened and closed her mouth several times, but no sound came out, reminding MJ of a fish in an aquarium.

"Oh my God! Marilyn Jean Summers, you're insane."

The shrill pitch of Carla's voice made her ears ache, and MJ winced. She'd known her best friend would make a big deal of it which is why she'd waited until now to bring it up, but someone had to know where she was going in case of an emergency.

"First this crazy move, then agreeing to stay in a tawdry motel, and now this?" Carla shook her head side to side hard enough to give herself whiplash. "You've gone over the edge. You can't go on a honeymoon—you're not getting married—and you certainly can't go on a honeymoon by yourself," she cried.

"Why not?" MJ asked, suddenly calmer than she'd been all day. "Lord knows it's cost me more than anyone can imagine. Besides, a honeymoon is just a criminally expensive vacation, and I paid for the damn thing; ergo, I'm going. I've had enough disappointment to last me a lifetime. I'm not giving up anything else." She signaled and turned into the hotel parking lot.

"You do realize you'll be on a plane alone," Carla said, undoing her seatbelt as MJ parked the vehicle.

"I've been on planes by myself and survived," MJ mumbled. Why did Carla always have to hit on the sore spots?

"Don't you realize how dangerous it is for a woman to travel alone, especially to some unknown island in the middle of nowhere?"

"It's in the Caribbean, near Martinique, subject to all French laws and customs." She popped the trunk.

"What if you break a law?" Carla asked. "You could end up on Devil's Island."

MJ laughed and got out of the vehicle.

"Don't be ridiculous," she said, huffing out a breath. "That penal colony closed almost sixty years ago."

Carla hurried out of the car.

"Fine, but with your complexion, you'll fry, or someone will mistake you for a zombie. They practice voodoo down there. You could wake up with a stake in your heart."

"You're full of good news, aren't you? Stakes in the heart are for vampires, and if I had one, I doubt I would wake up. Be reasonable. Everything will be fine."

"So you think, but they speak French there, and *you* don't." Carla glared at her and crossed her arms as if that was the end of it.

Reaching into the trunk, MJ pulled out her small bag and Carla's larger one before slamming the lid closed.

"Since the resort caters to international tourists, I'll bet someone there speaks English. If I have to, I'll point at whatever I want or mime it. According to the brochure, printed in English, all your dreams come true on Paradise Island."

"You mean your nightmares. I don't know why anyone would want to go to a jungle island in the first place, let alone someone who's afraid of water and has asthma."

"It's tropical rainforest, not jungle, and my asthma rarely bothers me when I'm near the ocean." MJ picked up both bags and led the way into the reception area. "And it's not that I'm afraid of the water exactly. I just don't like it when I can't touch the bottom and stand up."

"Hah! I've seen the look on your face when you get splashed. It's the same as the one on the face of the Wicked Witch of the West in *The Wizard of Oz*."

"You're exaggerating again. I'm not likely to melt if I get wet."

"Fine, but don't you listen to the news? They've got snakes, lizards, and all kinds of insects there. They've even got killer bees in Trinidad and Tobago."

"Good thing I'm not going to Trinidad then," MJ said, rolling her eyes, letting Carla's wild imagination have its say. "Let's get checked in and get something to eat. There's a bowl of chocolate ice cream out there screaming my name. As you always say, chocolate fixes everything."

Not that anything could this time.

CHAPTER THREE

MJ stood at the railing of the resort's passenger ferry letting the drizzle soak her. She rolled her eyes. With her luck, she would probably catch pneumonia, spend the next ten days in bed, and listen to Mama and Carla's "I told you so" for the rest of her life.

Sighing, she shook her head. This was the twenty-first century. Despite Carla's dire predictions, lots of women traveled alone and had wonderful trips, coming home intact with all their eggs and organs right where they were supposed to be, without any danger of being sacrificed to volcanoes, zombified in voodoo ceremonies, or kidnapped by pirates—although if a Captain Jack Sparrow lookalike wanted to take her captive, she might surrender.

Last evening, on what should've been her wedding night, she'd consoled herself with room service and a large bottle of wine. After opening at least three dozen messages from friends and cousins showing the lucky couple, she'd flung her cellphone across the room, shattering it. Eventually, she'd realized that had been a mistake and had contacted Carla.

"Fine. I'll let your mother know you dropped your phone, but you've got to keep that Greek-Irish temper of yours in check, MJ. It's going to get you in trouble."

Staring out at the water, she huffed out a heavy breath. Somewhere out there, the man of her dreams waited for her. All she had to do was find him. She removed her glasses. There was so much mist on them, she couldn't see through them anyway.

A vision of Paul the way he'd looked last Saturday, half-naked, his body slick with perspiration, filled her mind, obliterating the stormy seas. He'd looked good, but she would die before she threw herself at him. A girl could only take so much rejection, and she wasn't going to grovel to any man ever again—not even men who looked like Greek gods.

The ship bucked the waves as it slowly crossed the distance between Martinique and Paradise Island. Ten miles seemed a lot longer by boat than by car. Her stomach roiled. She hated flying and had taken her medication, but with more turbulence than usual, it had been the worst flight of her life. While she didn't usually get seasick, it seemed this boat ride would prove the exception. If she were going to toss her cookies, not that she had any since there hadn't been a crumb to eat on the plane, she would rather do it overboard than in the crowded lounge.

Pursing her lips, she looked out at the horizon, but with the rain and without her lenses, there was nothing to see.

"Are you alright, miss?" The deep voice startled her.

She turned around. She didn't need her glasses to tell her this was the bearded crewman who'd checked her ticket when she'd boarded, the one with the nasty scar on his cheek. What had Carla said? Kidnapped by pirates?

The man leaned against the gunwale beside her and exhaled a plume of smoke she realized came from cannabis, not tobacco.

"It's dangerous for a landlubber to be up here alone in this weather."

MJ smiled, her lips compressed.

"I'm not feeling too well. I'll probably vomit all over myself shortly, and it seemed like a good idea to do it here rather than in there."

He chuckled. "How considerate of you since I would be the one to clean the mess. Have a drag. It'll settle your stomach." He turned and offered her the joint.

"No, thanks," she said, looking up at him. "I don't ... you know."

He stared at her, mumbled something she didn't understand, moving closer to her, invading her space.

Had she insulted him?

She tried to swallow, but her mouth was dry.

"No problem. Your kind rarely does."

Her *kind*? What did he have her pegged as? Some prissy, tight-assed bitch?

"Jack Crowder," he offered his empty hand.

"MJ Summers." She reached for it, her hand limp in his. Why the hell had she given her real name? Probably because it was plastered all over her luggage.

"You've got gorgeous eyes, MJ Summers," he said. "They remind me of these waters on a calm, sunny day. Beautiful and mysterious. A man could drown in eyes like yours."

MJ's cheeks heated.

Give me a break.

"Thanks," she said. "Nothing special about them—they run in the family."

She really needed to corral this imagination of hers. The man was flirting with her. Why was that so hard to believe? Hadn't she hoped for a single man here? It wouldn't be the first time her dreams didn't turn out the way she wanted them to. She put her glasses on and smiled, her mouth lifted to the left.

He grinned, lifting his hand to push her hair back behind her ear.

It took everything in her not to bolt.

"I'll bet they do."

There was something in his eyes that made the hair on the back of her neck stand on end. Carla's warning about organ harvesters reared its ugly head.

He finished his joint, leaned over to toss the butt into the water. The boat hit a wave that sent them crashing into one another, and MJ was sure her stomach was about to empty. She groaned.

"Don't like being on the water, do you?"

Hanging her head farther over the edge of the gunwale, careful to keep her feet firmly planted on the deck, she stared down into the water.

What the hell? Was that her reflection? It couldn't be. Someone was staring back at her!

Before she could say anything, a door opened.

"Jack," a younger crewman called. "You'd better get in here. The captain's looking for you. If he finds out you were up here smoking..."

"Keep your shirt on. I'm coming," the man answered, his face fixed on the water, too. Had he seen the face?

He turned to her. "Don't lean over too far. In these swells, we might not be able to fish you out. I'll see you around."

Not if I see you first.

"Thanks. I'll be careful," she said, grateful for the reprieve.

He tipped his cap to her and followed the younger crewman below.

While he wasn't the first person to comment on her strange eye color and wouldn't be the last, something about the way he'd looked at her, as if he was appraising her, creeped her out.

She shook herself, and peeked over the edge once more. Nothing but sea green waves topped with white foam. Great. Now she was hallucinating. Closing her eyes, she practiced her slow yoga breathing. As long as she didn't fall overboard, she would be fine.

Ten minutes later, the raindrops splattering her head stopped, and she opened her eyes, gasping as the island materialized out of the mist, almost like she imagined Jules Verne would've expected his mysterious island to do. As she looked up, she saw the sun peeking through a break in the clouds to illuminate the top of the volcano from which the island had grown.

The wind dropped, the seas calmed, and the dark clouds were breaking up. She smiled. Her vacation might not have had an auspicious beginning, especially when she'd boarded the ferry with visions of *Gilligan's Island* and the *Minnow's* maiden voyage going through her head, but things were looking up.

"I'll have fun, damn it, if it's the last thing I do. Markos Theopolis, eat your frigging heart out."

* * *

Paul sat at the bar drinking a bottle of *Bière Ambrée*. He'd sampled all the local brews since his arrival on Tuesday, but couldn't decide which one he preferred. As far as the geography and accommodations went, the place was perfect.

Unfortunately, the island wasn't meant for a bachelor alone. It was crawling with couples of every size and shape. Young couples, obviously newlyweds, older couples on what must be their second honeymoon, and there were even some he'd mistaken for mother and son or father and daughter. Good thing he hadn't hit on the young brunette the other night.

A whistle shrieked, and several couples rose. The boat taking them back to Martinique was due shortly. Paradise Island guests arrived and departed every Tuesday, Thursday, or Saturday, depending on the length of their stay. Once he'd realized the truth about the place, he'd tried to get an earlier flight out, but no such luck. His name was on a cancellation list, and unless they called, he was stuck at Honeymoon Central for another ten days. It wasn't as if there was nothing to do, but it was finding someone to do it with that was the problem.

Lucette, a gorgeous Creole girl with café au lait skin and the darkest brown eyes he'd ever seen, stopped in front of him.

"*Une autre bière,* Paul?" she asked, collecting his empty bottle.

"Sure. Make it a *Blonde* this time."

Within minutes she returned and poured the opaque ale into a frosted glass and set the glass and the bottle on the bar in front of him.

"Are you anxious for the treasure hunt?"

"Thanks." He emptied the glass he held and handed it to her. "Not really. It isn't my kind of thing."

"Since the resort opened, several people have found Spanish doubloons in the water surrounding the island."

"Seeded no doubt to make this whole extravaganza more appealing," he answered. "They probably aren't even real." He shook his head.

She frowned. "They were all authenticated. The museum in Saint Pierre bought them."

"I'm sorry, Lucette, I didn't mean to insult you or anyone, but television producers have been known to sweeten the pot to increase ratings." He shrugged. "I wouldn't have come here if I'd known there was going to be a televised treasure hunt." He raised the glass. "I was looking for a little peace and quiet." Just not quite so much solitude.

"But how could you not know?" she asked, her brow furrowed. "The treasure hunt was announced last year before the resort opened. The legend of Capitaine Lacorneille is as old as the island itself. The captain angered Ovine, the sea witch, and she called up a great storm. The men rescued from the *naufrage* spent the rest of their lives here. Few ever set sail again."

"A sea witch? You're kidding, right?"

"*Non.* The waters around our islands are full of magic and mystery."

Witches? Magic? He didn't buy it. He sipped his beer. There was usually a rational explanation for everything.

"That storm; if there was one, was probably just one of the annual hurricanes, but who was brave enough to rescue the crew?"

She shrugged. "Most believe it was *les sirènes,* but some think it was the Kalinago."

"Sirens? As in mermaids? I doubt that, although there are a lot of dolphins around and they've been known to save people from drowning. But as far as the natives go, weren't they cannibals?"

"*Mais non.* The Kalinago, also known as the Caribs, traditionally kept the bones of their ancestors in their homes, believing that their spirits would protect them. The Europeans did not understand. You may be the one to find the treasure, since your destiny is here."

The knowing glint in her eyes raised goosebumps on his skin. He shifted uncomfortably on the stool.

"I believe a man makes his own fate," he said, slightly discomfited by the direction the discussion had taken. "As far as finding the treasure, like I said, it isn't my thing. I didn't know about it since I bought the trip second hand." He chuckled. "It seemed like a good idea at the time."

She smiled, her eyes lighting up at his words. "And now?"

He shook his head. "Now, not so much." Raising his glass once more, he took another mouthful of beer. "You say people found doubloons? I thought Lacorneille was transporting stolen Incan treasure."

"Ah, but a pirate can have more than one treasure in his cache," she said and winked.

"This island and the waters surrounding it should be treasure enough for anyone."

"True," she agreed, wiping down the bar. "But many people want what they cannot have. Copies of Capitaine Lacorneille's maps are in the reception area with his notes. Because of the reference to mermaids, most people have searched the island for caves, caverns, and grottos. Monsieur Leroux plans to focus his search on the waters between here and Martinique itself. It has been many years since one of the sirens has been seen in these waters."

"People have seen mermaids?" He shook his head and smirked. "Maybe they had one too many, no offense."

"*Non.* My grandfather saw one when he was a boy."

He shook his head. "I'm sure he thought he did, but we all know kids can have vivid imaginations." He held up his hands in a placating gesture. "Don't get me wrong. I wouldn't mind diving for mermaids myself, and if one of them finds her way into the lagoon, I promise to be friendly. As far as the treasure goes, the hunt only lasts three days. As long as no one takes it too seriously, it should add a little zing to the adventure."

The trouble was that the thought of riches could make men do stupid, dangerous things.

Lucette cocked her head to the side. "My *grandmère* is *quimboiseuse.* She says you are where you need to be."

Paul swallowed the mouthful of beer he'd taken. "You mean you're descended from a voodoo witch? Should I be nervous?"

"You make a joke," she said, giggling softly. "*Grandmère* is not a witch; she's a priestess. She tossed the bones last night and saw you."

"Her ancestors' bones?" he asked, choking on his brew.

"But of course. They've been passed down for many generations. According to *Grandmère,* you will not be alone tonight. The sea brings you your heart's desire, but you must be strong and brave to keep it. She's never wrong."

"I don't want to rain on your grandma's parade, but I really don't believe in that stuff. I've already got whatever I need, and as far as strength and bravery go, I survived my stint in Afghanistan. I've got the perfect house, this great big dog to keep me company, the car I've always wanted, and I go back to work at a job I enjoy in August."

"But what about love?"

Love wasn't in the cards—or rather the bones—for him. Love was for fools and men who hadn't seen and done what he had.

The bar phone rang. Lucette excused herself to answer it.

Paul took a mouthful of beer. Kid's image forced its way into his mind, something that had happened several times this week. How many sketches had he made of her since that day? Some of them would get him into hot water with Ron and Mama, that was for sure. He shook his head. No, the next ten days would be as long and lonely as the last four had been.

Lucette's grandmother was a voodoo priestess? Big deal. He'd heard about the native religions practiced on Martinique and the other islands—everyone had seen a movie or read a book with zombies in it. *Live and Let Die* was still his favorite Bond film, and not only because of Solitaire, the tarot card reader, who reminded him of MJ. While he didn't believe in voodoo, magic, and mermaids, he'd seen and heard enough not to insult those who did. If Lucette thought her grandmother had some kind of power, who was he to dispute it? People were entitled to their own beliefs. If she wanted to worship a tree, a stone, a fish, or a bunch of old bones, so be it.

He yawned. The thunderstorm last night had made it hard to sleep, but it had cleared in time for the snorkeling activity he'd signed up for this morning.

Taking another mouthful of beer, he smiled at Lucette. If she wasn't married, he could spend time with her, but the last thing he would want to do is piss off her voodoo-practicing grandmother. What he should do is go back to his bungalow and laze around there for the afternoon, but he didn't feel like being alone right now. Despite what Lucette thought, he knew damn well that, unless her priestess grandmother could conjure up a mermaid for him, he would be alone tonight and every other night he was on the island.

He reached for his beer, pleased to see some of the new guests had arrived and were coming into the bar. Even if no one talked to him, it was nice to have people around. In the army, you were never completely alone, and if you were, you could bet your ass you were in trouble. He nodded at a couple who acknowledged his greeting.

"Hi. Noel and Lindsay Mitchum," the man said extending his hand. "Are these seats taken?"

"Paul Davis. Help yourself." He shook his hand and moved over to let the older man sit next to his wife. The woman seemed upset about something, and Paul wondered what could have happened so soon after their arrival.

"Thanks." Noel took the seat Paul had vacated, and his wife sat beside him. "Nice place, isn't it?"

"It's gorgeous. Calling it Paradise Island wasn't just an advertising ploy. The place is damn near perfect."

As long as you aren't alone.

* * *

Shifting from one foot to the other, MJ stood at the end of the line waiting to get off the ferry. She'd donned her Jackie O sunglasses once more and couldn't wait to feel solid earth beneath her feet. As far as that crewman and the face in the water went, that's what she got for staying up late, having too much wine, and watching that crazy pirate movie.

The vessel bumped against the pier, and MJ caught herself before she careened into the man in front of her. He and his wife had been arguing for a while now. The last thing she wanted was to have him pissed off at her, too.

Glancing at the shore, she could almost visualize Ricardo Montalban and Hervé Villechaize waiting just beyond the trees to welcome her ashore, and if they had a tray of tropical cocktails? Well, she would have one of those, too. This might not be *Fantasy Island*, but the brochure did say all her dreams would come true.

When it was her turn to get off, she hoisted her backpack travel bag onto her shoulder and, much as she would rather not touch the crewman, she reached for his outstretched hand.

"I hope you're feeling better. Enjoy your stay on Paradise Island," he said, a knowing glint in his eyes.

"Thanks. Where's my suitcase?" she asked, pulling her hand away as soon as she could.

"All the luggage will be taken to the resort shortly. The staff will make sure your bag's delivered to your room." He pointed to the roof of a large house set among the trees. "The reception desk is in the main building. Just follow the path, but watch your step. The jungle can be treacherous."

Goosebumps puckered her skin.

Rainforest, you jerk.

She handed him a two-euro tip since that's what everyone else had done. "Thanks for the advice."

She stepped off the gangplank and took a deep breath, refusing to let the man's sinister words get under her skin.

It was much warmer and far more humid on shore than it had been at sea. Her hair had dried in the warm breeze and was a mess of windblown curls, reminding her that she should never have gotten it cut and bleached in the first place … something else Carla and Mama would complain about when they saw her.

Walking at a relaxed pace, she followed the others along the white crushed stone path lined with electric torches. According to the brochure, there was a fishing village at the base of the island's volcano. It hadn't erupted in more than a hundred years and didn't show any signs of doing so in the near future, as she'd assured Carla. The odds of being tossed into it were zilch.

The clouds were nearly all gone, and everything would dry up in no time, easing the mugginess in the air. Nearby, plants steamed in the sun and birds chattered as they flew from branch to branch above her, almost as if they were welcoming her to the island. Removing her jacket, she stuffed it in the outside pocket of her backpack. She smiled smugly. Things were definitely looking up. Despite Carla's dire predictions and visions of disaster, she'd made it here in one piece. The crewman's warning rang in her ears once more, but she dismissed it.

The well-maintained path between the thriving tropical vegetation gave way to a lush green lawn in front of a plantation house that could have served as the backdrop for *Gone with the Wind*. Taking a deep breath, MJ absorbed the scent of the multicolored tropical flowers bordering the lawn and the house.

Climbing the three steps to the wrap around veranda, she noted couples enjoying lunch *al fresco*, and her stomach grumbled reminding her once more that she hadn't eaten today. She tugged the heavy backpack into position and entered the air-conditioned reception area.

The ceiling was at least twelve feet high and huge rattan fans circulated slowly. Here and there, luxurious chairs and sofas were arranged in conversational groupings. Bellhops, in green pants and plaid shirts, pushed carts of luggage through the foyer ahead of arriving guests. Large tropical plants and strange flowers added to the exotic décor giving the impression the inside of the mansion was part of the outdoors. A poster on a freestanding easel showed a life-sized pirate with a chest full of treasure at his feet. The man looked vaguely familiar, but the text was in French and the few words she could make out made no sense.

"May I help you?" A young woman, dressed in a white blouse

edged in French lace that set off her deeply sun-bronzed skin, smiled. Her brightly colored green, yellow, and white plaid skirt matched her headdress, a kerchief tied in a series of elaborate knots.

"Yes, you can, Rosette," she said, reading the woman's nametag. She removed her sunglasses and exchanged them for her regular ones, their slight tint masking the color of her eyes. She pulled the confirmation letter out of her backpack and handed it to the receptionist.

The woman tilted her head to the left, her eyes wide.

"You are alone. Madame?" She made it sound like a crime.

"I am," MJ answered raising her chin.

The woman nodded and keyed the information into the computer. She frowned.

"I am so sorry, Madame Summers, but according to my records," she said in heavily accented English, "this reservation has been changed, and the room reassigned. Let me get the manager. He will know what to do."

"That's impossible," MJ hissed. Her lungs tightened. This could *not* be happening.

"Please, you have to check again," she begged, keeping her voice low. "I did *not* cancel the reservation." Why the hell would she be here if she'd done that?

Her heartbeat increased, and it felt as if the amount of oxygen in the room had been cut in half. Not even Carla with all her "what ifs" had come up with this possibility. MJ glanced around the busy lobby. No one seemed to be paying attention to her, but the eerie feeling that someone was watching her wouldn't go away.

"Calm yourself, *Madame*," the woman pleaded, drawing her attention back to the counter. "I am sure it is just a computer error. Please, let me call Monsieur St Louis. He will know how to handle this." The receptionist picked up the phone and spoke rapidly in French.

Despite her four years of high school French, MJ didn't understand a word of it. Breathing was more difficult than it had been, and she coughed. What the hell was she supposed to do now?

CHAPTER FOUR

"Madame Summers?" asked a short, heavy-set, middle-aged man in a Madras jacket that matched the receptionist's skirt.

Balding, he'd moved the part in his hair to just above his left ear in what was surely the largest comb-over she'd ever seen. He didn't look at all like the mythical Mr. Roarke, and the last of her hopes this would end up being a vacation like she'd watched on *Fantasy Island* evaporated.

"Madame Summers?" he repeated.

Who the hell else would be standing here on the verge of collapse?

Like the receptionist, his English was heavily accented. Under the jacket, he wore a dazzling, white shirt and plaid tie. His pants were the same deep green as the green in the plaid. His chocolate skin accentuated the brightness of his shirt.

She drew in a shaky breath. "Yes, I'm MJ Summers," she answered. "I understand there's a problem with my reservation."

Her heart hammered, and her palms were wet. Her breathing was faster than it should be with the danger of hyperventilation a distinct possibility. She could still feel those mysterious eyes on her and noted the large number of people milling around. Didn't they have someplace to be? Cold sweat trickled down her back adding to her discomfort.

"I am so sorry, Madame Summers. I do not know how this happened, but the reservation was changed four weeks ago.

Usually, we double check these things and send out an official notification..."

He continued talking, but MJ felt the room start to spin. She grabbed the counter to prevent herself from falling. First, she was homeless in Watertown, and now she had no place to stay here.

"Emile," the man shouted beside her although he sounded as if he were miles away. "*Une chaise pour madame, vite!*"

A chair materialized beside the desk, and MJ plopped into it before she disgraced herself further. The receptionist handed her a glass of water as if her problem was dehydration instead of mortification.

Draining the glass, MJ closed her eyes. Maybe this was just a dream—a nightmare conjured up by the flight from Hell. When she gazed around once more, the scene hadn't changed, although the number of gawkers seemed to have increased. How could this have happened? Her brain couldn't make sense of this latest disaster, and her lungs were quickly finding it impossible to filter the oxygen from the air. She rubbed her forehead.

"I am very sorry, Madame," the manager said, forcing her to accept the horror of what was happening. "Obviously, we have made an error, but unfortunately, there is nothing I can do to remedy the situation right now. I'm afraid you are stuck here for the moment. The boat to Martinique has left and will not return until Tuesday."

Panic bubbled inside her. "There must be some place I can stay. Is there another room available somewhere else on the island?" she asked, trying to suppress her fear.

"*Hélas*, the resort is completely booked, and it is the only one on Paradise. We may be able to get one of the fisherman to return you to Martinique, but first, you must have a place to stay. Rosette will see if we can find you a spot in a sister hotel in Fort-de-France or Saint Pierre, but I am not optimistic. This is our busiest time, and with the treasure hunt, even the few spaces in private homes in the village are booked."

"Seriously? I thought it was off-season," she said. Hadn't Carla said something about hurricane season starting in early July?

The manager smiled at her, the look on his face the same one her father had worn when she'd said something particularly naïve, spoke rapidly in French to the receptionist, and then turned to her again. "Any season is the season for love, but with Monsieur Leroux's treasure hunt this week ... Perhaps if you would move over here while Rosette sees what she can find."

Treasure hunt? Had Mark mentioned a treasure hunt? He'd insisted on these dates, but she'd assumed it was so that they would have a month to get settled in the new house—another one lost to her.

MJ nodded and moved aside to allow the last few people to register. Poor Monsieur St Louis was almost as upset as she was, and strangely, seeing him that distressed calmed her. She glanced at the rest of the couples who'd been aboard the boat. Were they all treasure hunters? Many of them knew one another. Was it common for friends to honeymoon together?

As they finished checking in, seemingly staring at her as if she were some kind of alien, she fought the childish impulse to stick out her tongue at them. Would there be an empty room once they were all registered? Ten minutes later, Rosette came back to the manager's side and spoke quickly in the patois that might as well have been Chinese as far as MJ was concerned. He frowned, asked a question, nodded at her quick answer, and turned to MJ again.

"Rosette has found you a room in a small bed-and-breakfast in Saint Pierre, but they can only put you up for six days. You'll be well-taken care of by Dubois and his wife, and the resort will cover all of your costs. Sadly, the room will not be available until Thursday. Rosette will ask if one of the staff members can put you up for a few nights. Someone may be willing to let you sleep on their sofa. I would let you use mine, but my mother-in-law is sleeping there." He shrugged his shoulders in classic Gallic fashion. "If we cannot find you a place, you can sleep on one of these," he said, indicating the lounge furniture, as if the possibility of something so completely humiliating was a great offer. "Most of the guests breakfast in the privacy of their rooms and bungalows. You would not have to get up before six when the staff come to clean."

And what do I do? Shower out by the pool and dress in the bathroom? Wonderful, just frigging wonderful.

She smiled at him, fighting the tears she refused to shed. "Thank you. If you can get a fisherman to take me back, I'm certain I can change my flight and get an earlier one." She swallowed. There was one thing she needed to know.

"When did you say the reservation had been changed?"

"Four weeks ago."

"I see." She smiled. "Can you check to see if Mr. and Mrs. Markos Theopolis have arrived?"

He nodded to the receptionist who went to the computer. "Are they friends?"

"In a manner of speaking," she lied. "We work together."

"Then you could sleep on their sofa," the manager said brightly.

Before she could answer, Rosette looked up.

"I am sorry, Madame," she said, a half-smile on her face. "Monsieur and Madame Theopolis will not arrive until Tuesday."

The manager asked her a question in French.

She shook her head and said something equally incomprehensible.

He frowned. "I thought we could let you use the room, but it is unavailable."

She fisted her hands at her side, her nails cutting into her palms, and tried to smile, certain all she managed was an evil grimace.

The dirty, rotten, low-down, two-timing, scheming son of a bitch.

The messed-up reservation had nothing to do with the resort, and everything to do with that cheating, scum-sucking bastard.

"Thank you. I appreciate whatever you can do on my behalf." MJ said, suddenly calm in her fury. Even her breathing relaxed. She would vent her anger when she was alone, and God help the pillow she would pummel, wishing it were Mark's face.

She pictured meeting M and M on the beach, maybe watching them sitting in the gazebo she'd noticed, waiting to be called to one activity or another. When no one was looking, she would murder them and toss their bodies into the water for the sharks to eat. Then she would gladly move into their room—her room—and enjoy what was left of her vacation. Someone might even give her a medal for ridding the world of the dirty rat.

Where are Carla's mob connections when I need them?

She stood, pulled her bag back onto her shoulder, and turned to the manager.

"I need a drink. Where's the bar?"

"Right through those doors. Order whatever you want. Please let me express once more how sorry I am that this has happened."

"Well, it isn't really your fault. Glitches happen."

Especially when that rotten son of a bitch is to blame.

Unless she killed the bastard and got caught, this would remain her little secret. She would find a place to hide for the next couple of days until she could get back on the ferry. Taking a deep breath, she smiled at the frazzled manager.

"Thank you for whatever you can do."

"Rest assured, I will discover how this unfortunate mistake occurred and ensure it does not happen again. Rosette is confident she can convince someone in the village to take you in. She will come and find you when she has."

MJ nodded and, with all the dignity she could muster, walked toward the beautiful antique wood and iron doors that looked as if they belonged on one of those sailing ships from the sixteenth century, captained by a dashing pirate like the one pictured on the poster in the lobby.

Right now, she needed a drink, the stronger the better. As she moved forward, that feeling of being watched returned, and her temporary calm vanished. Her hand trembling, she pushed the door open. She needed to keep it together a little while longer.

Inside the lounge, couples sat enjoying drinks, some alone, some with others. Over at the bar itself, only three of the six stools were occupied. A man sat at the far end next to Lindsay and Noel, the couple who'd befriended her in Saint Pierre while they'd waited for the ferry. She would gladly reimburse them the full cost of their vacation if she could sleep on their sofa rather than in the lobby or with strangers.

Thinking things looked less bleak, she hurried over to the bar and stopped suddenly when the man on the last stool stood. The oxygen in the room vanished, and the panic she'd managed to stave off in the reception area flooded her. Her oath to Carla flashed through her mind. God, she really was cursed.

The man turned and looked up, confusion and surprise etched on his face. "Kid? Is that really you? Wow! Do you ever look different."

"Paul," she whispered, amazed that she could even make a sound. "Fancy meeting you here."

He wore white shorts, a black and white striped golf shirt, and sandals. He'd shaved since the last time she'd seen him, and if anything, he looked even sexier than he had. She swallowed, trying to catch her breath.

"Do you know one another?" Lindsay asked, but MJ was too shocked to answer her. She just nodded.

"Yeah, we're old friends," Paul said. "Nice hair. I almost didn't recognize you."

Lindsay frowned. "Really?"

"What are you doing here?" MJ managed to croak.

"I'm on vacation, remember? I mentioned it last week," he said.

Had he said he was coming here? Carla would never believe she hadn't followed him if he had.

"The new look suits you. So, do blondes have more fun?" His gaze raked her up and down as it had done when he'd recognized her in his yard.

The room began to spin once more.

"Shit," she said before her knees gave out on her, and she melted to the floor.

* * *

Stunned, Paul set his glass down in time to grab Kid before her head hit the stone tiles. What the hell was she doing here and where was her companion?

Her breathing was strained, and she was pale, far paler than he'd ever seen her. Considering how wan her normal complexion was, that wasn't a good sign. Carla had said she wasn't married, but he hadn't asked if she had a boyfriend.

"Do something," Lindsay yelled at him. "My God, I knew something was wrong."

"Look, lady, if I knew what to do, I'd do it," he growled.

He placed Kid on a chair someone had brought over to the bar.

Lindsay glowered at him, her face all puckered up and angry, her teeth clenched.

"Whatever you did to this poor girl was a dirty, rotten trick. You should be ashamed of yourself."

"Now, honey. I'm sure Paul didn't mean to upset her," Noel said, trying to calm his wife whose indignation on Kid's behalf was impressive.

Her face was red, her hands clenched into fists, and if the chair hadn't been between them, he had no doubt she would've kicked him. Kid stirred, stopping Paul from telling the woman he had no idea what she was talking about.

He squatted awkwardly beside her. Lucette's words echoed in his head. He didn't believe in that hocus pocus, but what in God's name was Kid doing here?

"Welcome back. Are you okay?" he asked.

She nodded, but struggled to breathe, and he remembered her asthma. Judging by the color of her and how rapidly the pulse at her throat seemed to be throbbing, the stress of whatever had happened could lead to a full-blown bout and that would be the last thing she would want.

Reaching for her hand, he gave it a friendly squeeze, trying to ignore the heat pulsing through him at this slight touch. He'd felt the same jolt of energy, almost a sense of recognition when he'd helped her up after King had knocked her down.

"*Excusez-moi, pardon*," the manager said, his accent heavy, as he pushed his way through the gawkers surrounding them. "Give them some room, please. Monsieur Davis," he said. "Is Madame Summers ill? Did she fall?"

"No, I didn't fall," she answered softly between pants, embarrassment evident in her voice. "I got dizzy, that's all. I didn't eat this morning, and with the excitement … my asthma … I'll be fine, really I will."

The staff moved everyone, including Lindsay and her husband, away from the bar in an effort to control the situation. Paul was grateful since it meant no one could overhear them.

"Where's your inhaler?" he asked.

"Front pouch of my backpack. Tell them to leave, please," she pleaded. "I'll be okay if they just all go back to doing what they were."

Paul handed her the asthma pump.

She shook it, took a puff, waited, and then took another. Within minutes, her breathing eased and her color improved.

"Feeling better?" he asked, exchanging the inhaler for a glass of water.

She drained the glass and returned the empty tumbler.

"Thanks," she murmured, glancing around. "Can we get out of here?" Her gaze begged him to make it possible.

He nodded. "Sure thing." He turned to the crowd pressing in closer once more. "She's okay. Her asthma had a little trouble adjusting to the climate," he said, wondering again where her partner was.

"You and Madame Summers are acquainted?" the manager asked quietly.

"Yes, we are," he answered, reading both concern and relief on the man's face.

"*Parfait!* Madame Summers can stay with you instead of sleeping in the lounge. I will take care of everything."

"Why would she sleep in the lounge? That's preposterous," Paul said, noting the look of horror on her face.

"Because she does not have a room, and unfortunately, the ferry has gone. We have tried to find a fisherman to take her back, but the boats are all out for the day, and once they return, it will be dark. Her partner did not arrive with her, but I am sure she can contact him to meet her in Saint Pierre."

Paul turned and looked sharply at the woman seated in front of him, noted the tears edging her eyes, and smiled down at her. He would've done anything for her fifteen years ago. Well, it looked as if Grandma was both right and wrong.

Partner? A woman as beautiful as MJ would have someone in her life. There was no way she would've gotten married in a week, but maybe she and whoever she was with were engaged. That's the only way Mama Summers would ever accept her only daughter on a honeymoon island. It looked like he wouldn't be alone tonight after all. The least he could do was let her sleep on his couch, although whether he would get any sleep with her in his room was a toss-up.

"Not a problem. I've got lots of room. Can you have lunch for two sent to my bungalow? I think we'd better feed her before she gets dizzy again."

"I will have Rosette arrange it immediately," the manager answered and rushed away as if he were afraid Paul might change his mind.

"Feel well enough to walk or should I carry you?" he asked.

The color Kid had lost flooded her cheeks. "I can walk, thanks. Let's just get out of here."

Shouldering her backpack, he emptied his beer glass and set it down on the bar.

"I told you," Lucette said and winked.

"What was that about?" she asked, indicating Lucette with her head.

"Nothing important. I'll tell you later."

"Are you sure you're okay?" Lindsay asked, stepping between them as if she were a referee in a boxing match. "I don't know what's going on here, but you don't have to go with him if you don't want to."

The scowl on her face would've killed a weaker man.

"Please, it's not what you think," MJ said, turning to look up at him, her gaze conveying her apology. "Everything's fine. Paul and I are old friends. Seeing him here came as a surprise, that's all. I'll talk to you in a short while and explain everything. You don't have to worry about me, I promise."

He had the distinct feeling Lindsay shouldn't hold her breath for that explanation, but he was determined to hear it.

"If you say so," Lindsay answered, sounding no more convinced than he was. "But if you need anything, call. We're in bungalow thirty-six."

"It's okay. Paul's come to my rescue before."

Lindsay nodded, her lips pursed. "If you're certain..."

"I am. I couldn't be in better hands."

"Are you ready?" he asked, not at all comfortable with the hero worship she'd just heaped at his feet.

She licked her upper lip and swallowed.

"I'm on your side, Kid," he whispered, with what he hoped was a 'please trust me' smile on his face, determined to do whatever he could to fix this problem for her.

She nodded, and he led her across the lounge and back through the reception area. The few people still standing around the desk eyed them curiously.

"This way." He took her elbow. The current of electricity flowing between them surprised him and he let go of her arm.

"That's the dining room," he said, indicating the doors in front of them. "There's entertainment after the meal. The spa is upstairs."

"I don't expect I'll use the facilities while I'm here," she answered, disappointment heavy in her voice.

"Why not?"

"I just plan to keep a low profile, that's all. I've had enough excitement for one day."

"Point taken. I might get a massage before I go. I haven't had one since I was on liberty in Germany."

He opened the door and escorted her out onto the path that led to his bungalow. The hot, humid heat was intense after the coolness of the building.

"Tell me your room is air conditioned," she begged, swiping at her brow.

"Yeah, all the buildings have AC. The ceiling fans in the lobby are just for show."

"I noticed them earlier. How far from the main building is your bungalow?"

"Not far, maybe fifty yards? It's just through these trees. The humidity won't be as bad later, and the heat's more or less what you would find back home at this time of year. My place is on the water, so there's a cooling breeze most of the time."

"Sounds good," she said and ran her hand through her damp hair, tumbling the golden curls, and looking sexier than ever. "I'll just stay there until I can leave. I'm really sorry about this. I hope your girlfriend won't be upset. You probably should've asked her before you agreed to put me up for the night. I'll do my best to stay out of your way."

"Hey, don't sweat it. What are big brothers for? And you don't have to worry about upsetting anyone. I'm alone on this holiday. Having someone to talk to for a few hours will be a pleasant change."

She swallowed and chewed her lower lip, the action sending heat straight to his crotch.

"I hope you have something alcoholic in your room? I need something stronger than water. It's been a hell of a day so far."

Paul chortled uncomfortably. "I'll bet it has, and I don't know half of the story. There's a fully stocked bar in the bungalow, but before I give you any booze, any chance you're pregnant?"

MJ gaped at him, her mouth opening and closing as the fury built in her eyes.

"What in hell made you jump to that conclusion?" she asked, knuckle punching him on the arm.

"Ouch! That hurt. You did. You said you didn't eat this morning, and you just fainted."

"I didn't eat this morning, jackass, because the flight left at six, and I expected to get fed on the plane."

"Another casualty of the war on terrorism, but you did faint," he answered in his own defense.

"Fine. Probably low blood sugar, but I can guarantee I'm not with child. For your information, Carla hasn't fainted once because she's pregnant. Now, if you don't mind, I really want to get out of the heat and have a drink."

He shrugged, but kept his mouth shut. She was mad enough to spit nails as it was. A strong drink might not be a bad idea.

CHAPTER FIVE

Angry and more humiliated than she'd been last week, something she wouldn't have even thought possible, MJ followed Paul along the walkway, watching her backpack bounce along on his shoulder.

How could her savior turn out to be as big a jerk as the man responsible for this mess? So much for thinking life was going to improve. Wait until Carla and Mama heard this. She would never live it down.

Once she got to Paul's room, she wasn't leaving it again until it was time to board one of the fishing boats. If worse came to worse, and she had to stay until Tuesday and the ferry, she would have to find a way to get from there to the dock unseen. Maybe with a big hat and sunglasses.

Could she appeal to Mark's better nature? Doubtful. He didn't have one. No, this was his revenge, and there wasn't a damn thing she could do about it. By now, her situation was most likely the talk of the resort, and that wouldn't end today. How many others had jumped to the same conclusion as Paul? If Mark got wind of that ... How was she going to get herself out of this mess?

She sighed. The sun had dried most of the lush tropical plants and the rich scent of exotic flowers perfumed the air. She could hear birds in the canopy overhead, and couldn't imagine a more beautiful place. Now that she was accustomed to the warmer air, she realized it wasn't as bad as it had been.

Paul slowed his pace , allowing her to catch up and walk

beside him.

"I'm sorry if I offended you," he said. "I didn't mean to. I'm glad you're here, even if you aren't. The guy who sold me the vacation package didn't tell me this was a couples' resort." He frowned. "When Carla said you were single, I should've realized you would have a boyfriend or fiancé."

Before she could think of anything to say, the path veered left, and she yelped.

"Holy shit! What the hell is that? Is that a dragon? They have dragons here?" she screeched, trying to climb up on Paul's shoulders and join the backpack.

He laughed. "Calm down, Kid. It's not a dragon, it's just an iguana. It won't hurt you. It eats nothing but plants and leaves. Even the bugs are safe. These are quite domesticated. See, it's even got a collar."

"What difference does a frigging collar make?" she asked, moving behind him, using him as a shield against the monster. "I've seen iguanas, and they're green, not gray like that one, and they definitely are *not* that big."

"This *is* a green iguana, but its color fades to a greenish gray as it ages. I'll admit it's larger than most specimens you've seen, but it's harmless. Right now, that poor little guy is as warm as you are, and that's why he's so pale. He's heading into the undergrowth to cool off. If you see him tonight, he'll be much darker in color."

"*Little* guy? Are you frigging nuts? If I met that thing alone on any night, I would have a coronary," she said, offended by the smirk he tried to hide, more determined than ever to stay inside the room. "What is it with you and overgrown animals? You've got a horse-sized dog and now this, this … dinosaur. That sucker's at least four feet long and has to weight fifty pounds, and you expect me to believe it eats plants?"

"Twenty tops," he said, his lips pulled in, his shoulders quaking. "His ancestors ate plants and look at the size of those." Paul used his foot to nudge the reptile out of the way and send him back into the trees. The animal disappeared into the bushes.

MJ eyed the brush suspiciously, not convinced the monstrosity was gone, but unwilling to go looking for the lizard—if that's what it really was. If she weren't so upset she might see the humor in the situation, but doubted it.

Paul started walking again, and she hurried to catch up to him.

"Some of his ancestors were meat-eaters, and who's to say he won't morph into an omnivore when salad isn't enough to fill him up? I didn't realize this island would be like the Galapagos Islands—they left that out of the literature."

Paul burst out laughing. "Welcome to Paradise, Kid. I forgot how much fun you could be. Having you around for a few days will be terrific." He turned and walked on.

"Comic relief," she mumbled. "Great, just frigging great." She shook her head. "Are there any other larger than life specimens I should know about? Monster spiders? Bird-sized mosquitoes? Giant stone heads?"

"I don't know about spiders or any other bugs," he answered, his face serious, but his eyes twinkled with humor. "I plan to visit Saint Pierre harbor to look at a gigantic head tomorrow. Since you're sticking around for a few days, you can join me. The tour leaves midmorning, and we'll be gone most of the day. Apparently, there are mermaids in the waters surrounding this island, too. I haven't seen any, but who knows, maybe you will."

MJ swallowed, the image of the face in the water resurfacing in her mind. She shuddered.

"No, thanks. I have enough trouble with real-live monsters without dreaming up mythical ones."

Paul laughed. "Have it your way, but I doubt people consider mermaids to be monsters."

"Why not? According to the myths I taught, sirens purposely sank ships."

"I prefer the Disney version—pretty little redheads who fall in love with humans." He shrugged. "So, where's the boyfriend, and how come you don't have a room?"

"It's just one of those modern miracles. The computer canceled my reservation," she answered, trying to be blasé. Hopefully, he wouldn't ask too many damn questions. "They've found me a place in Saint Pierre, but it isn't available until Thursday." She was a dismal liar at the best of times, and given the situation, concocting a lie on the fly to explain everything and save face was a feat way outside of her area of expertise.

But that all-day trek to Martinique sounded promising. If she could leave here before Mark arrived, it would be her word against his, and since Mama thought she was in Watertown, the only other person who would know the truth was Carla. She could skip out on the tour and get herself to the airport. The sooner she got back to the United States, the better.

They stepped out of the trees, and MJ drew in a sharp breath. "Oh my God, it's gorgeous."

"It is," he said, but he wasn't looking at the bungalows, he was staring at her, and the way he was examining her made her feel strangely exposed.

"Come on," he said abruptly. "We're in number six. Over this way. I need a drink, too, and then you can tell me what really happened, because you just said 'my' reservation and that they'd found 'me' a room. I know why I'm alone, Kid, why the hell are you?"

She stopped, too angry to walk and talk at the same time. "Don't use that tone with me, and my name's not Kid. It's MJ," she shouted, stomping her foot and glaring at Paul, her hands fisted on her hips. "I'm not a child anymore. I *had* a damn reservation. I sure as hell wouldn't have come out here without one. It's not as if I'm stalking you, if that's what you're thinking."

His stunned gaze bored into hers, and she dropped her eyes first.

What in God's name made her say that?

She took a deep breath. Could things get any worse? Relaxing her stance, she clenched her fists at her side, and bit her lower lip. She had to stay calm or else she'd have that asthma attack for sure, and more drama was the last thing she wanted. He may have stolen her house in Watertown, but what had happened here wasn't Paul's fault. She shouldn't take her frustration out on him. He was just trying to help her, and his question deserved an answer, even if it was going to humiliate her. As he'd said, *what else are big brothers for?*

"You may still think of me as the pesky kid who followed you and Ron around, but I'm not stupid, even if it does look that way right now." She hugged herself as the last of her anger evaporated, replaced by shame for never having suspected Mark would be malicious enough to humiliate her this way. "I didn't expect anything quite like this. First, the canceled reservation, then, you think I'm pregnant, dinosaurs crawl out of the brush, and now this," she indicated the lagoon. "The only thing missing is a big rock and your Disney mermaid sunning herself on it, combing her hair with a fork. It's like something straight out of a Hollywood movie, and I'm the butt end of the joke." Tears brimmed her eyes, and she swallowed.

I won't cry.

"No matter what's happened, things can't possibly be that bad. For the record, I'm well-aware of the fact you aren't a child. I'm not blind."

She chose not to comment on his observation and took a good look at the pod of stilted bungalows, using the few seconds to pull herself together.

The series of eight huts were linked by a boardwalk and all faced the lagoon, four per side, ensuring maximum privacy. She followed Paul up the wooden pier leading to number six's back door.

He slipped his key card into the card reader. The light turned green, and he opened the door, holding it open for her to precede him inside.

She stepped into the bungalow, barely holding her emotions in check.

"So this is how the other half live. Impressive."

No wonder Mark wanted to come here. This degree of luxury was right up his alley.

"Apparently, the resort only opened a few months ago," Paul said. "Make yourself at home."

Everything about the interior of the bungalow was sleek and modern. On her right, a door led to what must be the bathroom. The sleeping area, dominated by the largest bed she'd ever seen, occupied most of the left side of the room.

"I've got beer, scotch, rum, and fruit juice," Paul said breaking into her musings.

"Rum and fruit juice, please." She'd hoped for a tropical drink earlier. Might as well have it now.

"Coming right up."

MJ's gaze followed Paul as he moved around the bed to the lower right side of the room where the eating area was located.

There was a built-in wet bar, a small fridge, as well as a table and two chairs. On the counter sat a top-end, single brew coffeemaker. Crossing the floor, she stepped into the sitting area, with its luxurious sofa and matching overstuffed chair, and gasped. What she'd thought a rug from the doorway was a thick Plexiglas floor. She looked down at a small reef around which flitted colorful fish. Her stomach churned. How deep was the water?

"Wow. This is fantastic. Is it safe to stand on?"

"Yeah, it's about ten inches thick. You should see it at night. It's lit up. I must have spent an hour watching the fish play around the reef—didn't see any mermaids though. I tried to figure out how many different species there were, but since I couldn't identify them..." He shrugged ... I bought a book in the gift shop this morning. It's on the table, next to that pamphlet about Captain Lacorneille and his treasure."

She returned to the eating area and reached for the glass Paul handed her.

"My bed, I assume?" She indicated the sofa behind her.

"I don't mind sleeping on the couch if you would rather have the bed," he answered.

"Don't be silly—your room, your bed."

He shrugged. "Whatever floats your boat." He dropped her backpack onto the chair next to the sofa. Walking back to her, he smiled. "Have you called whoever Mr. St Louis said you were going to meet? I'll gladly talk to him and swear to behave myself. After all, we're practically family."

MJ scrambled for something to say, but her mind was blank. Practically family? That was a low blow.

Paul frowned. "MJ, where's your boyfriend?"

MJ looked around the room, realizing there was no way out of this. "I don't have one," she said softly. "I was engaged, but I canceled the wedding. This should've been my honeymoon, my perfect vacation." She burst into tears, yanking off her glasses and dropping them onto the table. "I'm such a fool."

* * *

Paul stared at the woman weeping in front of him, those incredible eyes awash in tears, and whatever anger he'd felt evaporated.

"Geez, Kid, I mean MJ, the last thing I wanted to do was

make you cry. I'm sorry," he stammered, reached for the glass she was holding, set it and his beer on the table, and pulled her into his arms.

He'd done this once before, almost eighteen years ago, when tragedy had struck the Summers's house for the first time, and the family dog had died. She'd been inconsolable, and nothing had made her feel better. He'd known what it was like to hurt like that. At fifteen, he'd had almost all his hopes and dreams broken, along with a few bones, by someone he'd loved. Eventually he'd given her a stuffed dog that had made her smile again. Somehow, he didn't think a stuffy with a cheap cut-glass collar would help this time.

Murmuring what he hoped were soothing words, he patted her back. He was amazed at the way her body fit against his, almost exactly the way it had back then, as if their bodies had grown in proportion to one another.

A good ten minutes later, he noted her crying had eased, and she was sup-supping now. The worst of the tears might be over, but he didn't think this would be the last of them. He knew he should let her go, but she felt good in his arms and didn't seem in a hurry to move out of them. She hiccupped again, and he smiled.

"Better?"

She looked up at him, her eyes still glassy, nodded, but didn't speak, nor did she move away. Now that she'd stopped weeping, his body was taking note of the soft mounds and curves in his arms and reacting much as it had a week ago, especially when she seemed to be nestling closer.

"Sorry about the waterworks," she said, pulling out of his arms a few moments later—just in the nick of time as far as he was concerned.

He sat down and guzzled half of his beer, the table hiding his body's response to her.

"I don't usually cry. As Ron likes to point out, I'm too cold-hearted for that, but I think coming here and ending up in this mess was the last straw." She picked up her drink.

"Want to tell me about it?"

She sniffled and then took a mouthful of the rum he'd given her. "Not really. I wasn't even going to tell you that much, but I couldn't think of a convincing lie."

"It can't be that bad," he said, his eyebrows creased in concern. Why would she need to lie? "This is a nice place."

"Yeah, but it's your place. Well, you'll only be stuck with me for the night. I'll go with you in the morning and make my way back to the airport. That way I can get the next available flight home."

He frowned. "Why don't you tell me what happened? I tried to get an earlier flight out of here myself, and believe me, there's nothing available."

"That figures," she said, throwing up her hands in frustration. "I hate it when Carla's right. I should've listened to her."

"Your mother couldn't have been too happy about it either," he added, knowing how protective Mama had been of her only daughter.

MJ's cheeks reddened, and she looked guilty as sin.

"You didn't tell her you were coming here, did you?" he guessed. "My God, MJ, what were you thinking?"

"I'm a thirty-one-year-old woman," she answered, fists clenched at her side. "I don't need my mother's permission or anyone else's to go on a vacation. I was thinking I would relax and enjoy myself. Mama thinks I'm in Watertown."

He stared at her. "Are you telling me no one knows you're here?"

"Carla does," she said, a hint of defiance in her voice. "But I swore her to secrecy."

"Of all the bone-headed things to do. If your mother doesn't hear from you for ten days, she'll be worried sick. Didn't you think of that?" He didn't know why he was so angry.

"I'm not heartless," she exclaimed, her cheeks bright red. "I was going to call her. I just wasn't going to tell her where I was."

"Why the hell not?"

Her eyes glistened, her fury gone as fast as it had appeared, but he wouldn't let her off the hook that easily.

"I may be an adult, but sometimes my mother treats me like a child."

"When you pull a stunt like this, she has every right to."

He wanted to shake her. What she'd done could've been dangerous. He knew women traveled alone, but after what he'd seen in the past twelve years and what he'd learned as a police officer, scenarios of the kind of things that could've happened rushed through his mind.

The color in her cheeks deepened. When had she gotten so beautiful?

"I should've moved out years ago, but after Papa died, she was so lost, and then Ron got married ... If I'd told her what I planned to do, she would've had my Uncle Nick lock me in his basement and called the priest over to pray for my soul."

"Considering how things have turned out that might not have been such a bad idea."

She blanched, the accusation in her eyes reminding him of a puppy who'd been kicked.

"I'm sorry I bothered you," she said, her face a stoic mask. "Maybe sleeping in the lounge isn't such a bad idea. I'll get my things and get out of your way."

He ran his empty hand through his short hair. "Stop. I'm sorry. I'm sure you had your reasons for doing what you did, but you're in a hell of a mess now."

"And you think I don't know that? You may consider yourself my big brother, but no one, not even you, can fix this."

The phone rang, startling them both.

"It must be the front desk," he said, walking over to the nightstand. "I suppose it could be your friends worrying about you, too."

He picked up the handset. "Hello? ... Yeah, she's right here. It's for you."

Handing her the phone, he stepped over to the wet bar and poured two fingers of scotch into a glass. "I'll be out on the deck."

She might not think he could fix this, but one thing was for sure, there was no way he would leave her on Martinique. He had a duty to Mama and Ron and would keep MJ safe if it killed him.

* * *

Lifting the handset to her ear, MJ spoke. "Hello?"

"Madame Summers, I have an international call for you," the operator said. "One moment."

"MJ?" Carla's worried voice came through the line.

"Yeah, it's me? What's up?" she asked, trying to sound blasé, despite the fact her heart was beating a mile a minute.

"What's up?" Carla screeched loudly, forcing MJ to pull the

phone away from her ear. "Do you have any idea what time it is? I've been worried sick."

"Everything is fine, Carla," she lied and chuckled softly. "They do have clocks here. It's just after one. What's the problem?"

"The problem? You promised you would call the moment you checked in, and that would've been almost an hour ago according to the itinerary you gave me. I've been worried sick."

"I didn't call because I haven't checked in," she answered, trying to keep her voice light.

"Why not?"

"The room isn't available until after four." Four days, but she didn't need to know that.

"Why did it take so long for them to find you?" Carla asked, her voice laced with suspicion.

"It's a big resort. I'm just having a drink with a friend. I'm fine. Relax."

"Male or female?" Interest replaced irritation in her voice.

"Not that it matters, but male."

"Get out of here. Are you telling me there are single men there?"

"That's exactly what I'm saying."

"Is he there with you?"

"He is." Well, he was sort of. "This place is absolutely gorgeous, everything I expected and so much more. As soon as I get settled, I'll message you on my tablet—"

"Not so fast. I'm paying for it so give me a few deets. Is he good looking?"

"Yes."

"Rich?"

MJ looked around the room, knowing it would've cost way more than the package she'd chosen, and he'd just bought a house. "Possibly."

"What kind of answer is that? Never mind. And you're sure he's alone."

"Oh, yes. He told me so. He bought the vacation from a friend, not realizing what kind of place it was."

Carla laughed. "Then you must be manna from heaven, but girl, you've got a big problem."

MJ dropped onto the bed. There was no way Carla could know about the reservation, so what else had gone wrong?

"What do you mean?"

"I was watching *Louis James Live* this morning, and he had Antoine Leroux, the salvage diver, on his show."

MJ scrunched up her nose. "How does that affect me?"

"Your mom watches that show, doesn't she?"

"Never misses an episode."

"Well, the man's on his way to Paradise Island to look for Lacorneille's ship. He should arrive Wednesday. Louis James is going to air daily segments on the treasure hunt and the resort. Plus, my cousin Louise told me that for their honeymoon, Mark and Melena are going on a treasure hunt. I've scoured the Internet, and the one on Paradise Island is the only one happening next week. That means they've got to be going to that resort, too. What are you going to do?"

Crap.

Lacorneille's ship? Who the hell was Lacorneille? Paul had mentioned the name. She glanced around the room and saw the brochure.

A televised treasure hunt? That bastard Mark must've known about this. The last thing she needed was to end up in a background shot, because no matter how brief the glimpse would be, Mama would recognize her and so would he.

No wonder the pirate on the poster had looked familiar. He was Louis James, one of New York's most popular morning show hosts. Come hell or high water, she needed to be out of here before he and his crew and the irksome duo arrived. She just needed to convince Paul that she'd be safe on Martinique until she could get a flight home.

"Earth to MJ. Are you still there?" Carla's voice brought her back.

"Yes," she answered impatiently. She needed time to put things into perspective not have more problems heaped on her. "Thanks for the head's up, but this is a public place, and I have as much right to be here as they do. As for the treasure hunt, well, I'll find a way to keep a low profile. Listen, I've got to go—he's waiting." Her voice sounded calm enough she should get an Oscar for this.

"I thought you would be more upset," Carla said, the suspicion back in her voice.

MJ chuckled. "I'm kind of busy right now. Don't worry. I'll stay out of their way, and since I have no intention of joining any treasure hunt, I'll be well away from the cameras. If I do get in the odd shot, with my designer sunglasses and sun hat, no one will recognize me."

"If you say so, but I have a bad feeling about this. I warned you not to go," Carla said, as if she'd somehow anticipated this latest disaster.

"Carla, I'll be fine." MJ crossed her fingers. "Now, I really do have to hang up. I'll message you later."

"Be careful."

"Always," MJ said, before hanging up the phone and draining the last of the rum in her glass.

"I see your call's over," Paul said, coming inside. "Can I get you another drink?"

"In a few minutes," she answered, chewing her lip.

Paul furrowed his brow. "You're upset. Is everything okay at home?"

"Yes, it's fine. How did you know it was home?" she asked, one eyebrow raised.

He chuckled. "No magic there. The receptionist said it was an international call."

"It was Carla checking on me to make sure I was still in one piece. She wanted to tell me there'll be a television crew here from *Louis James Live*. It seems some salvage diver is going to look for treasure, and Louis James is televising it."

"Yeah, Lucette, the bartender, mentioned it earlier," he said, pouring himself a glass of ice water. "Apparently, Lacorneille's hold was full of cursed Incan treasure and Spanish gold when his ship sank. Legend says some of his men were rescued by mermaids and settled here. Ovine, a pissed-off sea witch, was responsible for the storm." He shook his head and laughed. "Hard to believe people still tell those crazy stories, but this treasure hunt seems to be causing quite the stir. Louis James arrives Monday, I think, and the treasure hunt runs for three days after that. Apparently, the whole thing was planned a year ago, before the resort even opened. How come you didn't know about it? You booked the vacation."

Pursing her lips, she frowned. Witches and mermaids? What next? Zombies and voodoo ceremonies? She shivered, that "someone's walked over my grave feeling" catching her by surprise.

"This place wasn't my choice," she answered, wanting to ground herself in the here and now. "I just made the reservation when he told me to."

"Well, having a television crew around should make for interesting times."

"That's the last thing I need," she answered, the acid in her stomach warring with the rum she'd consumed. "Mama watches that show religiously, and despite the makeover, she would recognize me."

He pursed his lips and nodded, but didn't say anything.

"I know I'm imposing, but I need a shower. Do you mind?"

What she really wanted was time alone to examine her options—not that she had many.

"Help yourself." He drained the water in his glass and refilled it. "The bathroom's through there. Take your time. There's a clean robe hanging on the door."

The idea of sitting in this room, wearing nothing but a bathrobe, brought back the thoughts she'd had of wild sex in his kitchen, images that had played over and over again in her dreams this past week.

"Not a problem," she said. Why was it suddenly so hot in here? "I've got a change of clothes in my backpack. I won't be long."

She picked up her bag, went into the bathroom, closed the door behind her, and leaned against it. Chuckling softly, she shook her head. Hadn't she been in this man's bathroom cleaning herself up only a week ago? How ironic. Here she was in the most romantic place she'd ever seen, with a man she'd secretly worshipped years ago, probably the sexiest man alive, and he thought of her as his kid sister, and a damn foolish one at that.

On that depressing note, she moved off the door and scrutinized the room. This bathroom was the size of her bedroom in Stilton. On the left, there was a large double shower, on the right, a sunken tub, easily big enough for two, and in front of her, a marble bowl sink and counter, next to a toilet and bidet.

Fluffy white towels were folded on a shelving unit between the shower and the door. She opened her pack and removed a short, jersey, strapless sundress and clean underwear. Putting her small baggy of cosmetics on the counter, she stripped off the wilted capris and flowered tank top, and grabbed her anti-frizz shampoo and conditioner. Stepping into the shower, she turned on the faucet, let the cool water wash away her tiredness, and sighed. Things could probably be worse, but she couldn't imagine how.

CHAPTER SIX

Paul stood where MJ had left him and drained the last of the water in his glass. He wasn't a frigging saint, for God's sake. How the hell was he supposed to ignore the idea of her buck-naked in the shower, lathering her body with the bar of soap he'd used this morning?

He looked over at the king-sized bed and groaned. The sound of running water did nothing to dispel the image in his mind. If anything, it conjured up shower scenes from any number of X-rated movies. After pouring another shot of scotch, he went outside.

The deck was designed to assure its occupants of their privacy. There was a patio set and two umbrella-covered, rattan lounge chairs separated by a small glass-topped table. Five steps led down to the water level. He'd gone in for a moonlight swim last night and had slept like a baby until the rain had started. Tonight, rain or no rain, he doubted he would get much sleep.

He heard the water shut off and turned back to the railing. Keeping his body under control was going to be damn hard. Like it or not, the extremely sexy woman in his bathroom was Ron's sister, not another notch for his belt, and she needed his help. How had a place like this managed to screw up her reservation?

Thoughts of another girl flooded his mind. He shook his head. MJ wouldn't get shot on his watch, but would she be safe with him?

He finished his scotch, hoping it would erase the memories

before they took hold and dragged him into the darkness once more. The doorbell rang, and Paul reentered the bungalow, ignoring the sound of the hair dryer in the bathroom. Doorbells made sense since a lot of the guests spent time on the deck and probably wouldn't hear knocking. He opened the door.

"*Votre repas, Monsieur.*"

"Bring it in," Paul said.

The waiter, dressed in white pants and a white shirt with a plaid collar, pushed the linen-covered cart into the room.

"Where would you like to eat?" he asked.

"How about outside?" The farther they were from that bed, the better.

"Of course," the waiter answered, wheeling the cart through the bungalow and out onto the deck. He quickly set the patio table, leaving the extra dishes on the cart next to an ice bucket with a bottle of champagne in it.

"Would you like me to pour?" the man asked.

"No, that's fine. We'll take care of it."

"Very well. Monsieur St Louis asked me to tell you your dinner reservation has been changed to eight."

"Thanks." Paul tipped him and turned to watch the water once more.

"Wow. This place just keeps getting better, doesn't it?" MJ asked, joining him.

Paul gripped the railing for support, certain his fingers would leave a permanent imprint in the wood. Any lingering memories of Kabul vanished. MJ's hair glistened in the sun, its loose, golden curls tumbling to the edge of her shoulders. The turquoise, strapless dress she wore, the color an almost perfect match to the dark rim of her irises, reached mid-thigh and hugged her body like a second skin. Around her neck hung a silver chain with a turquoise stone—one of those new-age crystals. His eyes followed the line of the dress down her sides to its short hem and the long, naked legs exposed beneath it, all the way to the strappy wedge sandals on her feet. Desire, unlike anything he'd known, flooded him. This might be Ron's sister, but she was everything he'd ever dreamed of in a woman and more. If she were anyone else, he'd pick her up and carry her to that bed. He shook his head.

Don't go there.

"Nice dress." he said, nodding in appreciation.

"It doesn't make me look fat?" she asked, putting on her sunglasses.

"Where the hell did you get that idea?" She wasn't fat; she was perfect.

"From you," she answered, the pain poorly hidden in her voice. "It's the first thing you said to me."

"I did no such thing." God, he would've remembered making such a crass remark, and it certainly wasn't true.

"You did," she accused.

Reaching for a glass of water on the table, she bent forward.

His eyes focused on the turquoise-covered cheeks of her ass. What the hell did she have on under that?

She turned back to look at him. "You said I'd gained weight."

"I didn't mean you were fat," he stammered, recalling the comment. "I meant you'd filled out ... Let me take my size twelves out of my mouth. You are..." he searched for the right words, "just what the doctor ordered. I can't think of anyone I would rather have here with me right now." And he meant it.

"Thanks. I'm sorry I'm not going to get the chance to enjoy this place."

"Why not? You've got almost four days."

"Let's just say it's been an expensive lesson, one I could've done without, but hey, it is what it is."

"Things will work out, you'll see." He reached for one of the pencil-shaped breadsticks on the table, needing to keep his hands occupied, lest they reach for her and pull her into his arms.

"I doubt that. I can't get over how beautiful it is here, and you're right. It doesn't feel as hot or as humid now."

"The breeze helps," he answered, looking out at the water once more, every delectable inch of her imprinted in his memory.

"Did you order champagne?" she asked, coming up to stand beside him, the floral notes of her cologne tantalizing his senses.

"Nope, but the manager must be apologizing for this mess. We have the second seating for dinner tonight, too, which means we'll have a better table for the entertainment." He moved away from the railing and lifted the bottle out of the ice bucket. "Dom Perignon. I'm impressed."

After expertly popping the cork, he picked up one of the flutes provided, filled it, exchanged it for her water glass, and then poured himself some of the wine.

He raised his drink. "To old friends."

"Cheers," she said, clinking her glass on his.

She took a sip. Her eyes lit up as a grin split her face.

"This is fantastic."

"Be careful. It can have a hell of a kick. A champagne hangover isn't pleasant."

"That's the last thing I need," she groaned. "I made a big enough fool of myself in the bar earlier, hence my decision to stay here until I leave." She sipped her champagne. "This is quite the place, isn't it? I don't think I could imagine a more romantic getaway if I tried."

"Yeah, but the place loses something when you're alone." Was that really his voice sounding so needy?

She reached for a breadstick, drawing his attention to her backside once more.

"I suppose it would. Are all the units like this? My new digs certainly aren't this large."

He swallowed. "I'm not sure about the other rooms, but I'm glad you found a place to live. There didn't seem to be much choice when I was looking."

"The pickings were slim, but I'll manage."

She took another mouthful of wine, stared out at the lagoon, and sighed. Was she seeing the beauty of it? He didn't think so.

"MJ, I want to help you, but I have to know exactly what happened before I can do that. I need the truth, Kid, all of it."

She turned away from the water and bit her lower lip. Given what she was wearing, the gesture cut through him like a hot knife through butter.

Her stomach growled loudly. "Sorry about that, but I'm starving. Can we eat first and talk later?"

"Sure, but you'll tell me everything?"

She held up her hand as if she were swearing an oath in court. "Every last sordid detail, scout's honor. I'm not proud of any of this." Sitting down at the table, she placed the linen napkin in her lap. "What have we got?"

He lifted the covers.

"That's *vichyssoise*—I love that soup—but that can't be

lobster."

The crustacean had been cut in half, the meat removed from the tail, shredded, and mounded on it again for easier eating.

"It looks like giant shrimp," she said, "another larger than life specimen, like your dog and that iguana we met earlier. Where are the claws?" she asked, using her fork to prod the shell.

He shook his head and laughed. "Sorry to disappoint you. I had nothing to do with the size of these critters. They're called spiny or rock lobsters, and they don't have large claws. The tails are really the only part people eat. The dipping sauce has rum and jerk spices in it. I had some in an appetizer last night."

She picked up a forkful of the flesh, dipped it in the sauce provided, and tasted the tender meat. Swallowing, she slowly licked her lips.

He almost choked on the saliva in his mouth.

"That's incredible. Better than drawn butter. It's probably a good thing I'm not staying. I would gain ten pounds." She picked up her spoon and started to eat.

They were almost finished the first course, and while Paul managed to tamp down his desire and describe the things he'd done since arriving and those he still planned to do, he couldn't contain his curiosity any longer.

"Feel like telling me what happened now?"

"I don't know where to start," she admitted, setting down her spoon.

"How about why you called off the wedding?" he suggested. That had obviously been the turning point.

She shrugged. "Why not? Long story short, I caught him with another teacher in my office at school, and believe me, they weren't marking papers. I kept my mouth shut about what I'd seen—I do have my pride—and told everyone I'd decided that it wouldn't work between us. His story was the opposite."

"You did the sensible thing. If a guy can't be faithful before the wedding, he won't be after."

"It gets better," she said, stabbing at the lobster. "They got married last night, with the reception at Athena just as I'd planned it."

"And the bride agreed to that? Doesn't she have any backbone?"

"Not as far as Carla's concerned," she giggled. "She refers to her as the *Stepford Wife*."

He chuckled. "Not my kind of woman. If there wasn't a wedding, why come on the honeymoon?"

"Because I paid for it," she said, her hand trembling slightly. "He wouldn't let me buy the cancelation insurance—claimed it was bad luck. I decided I deserved to get something out of this mess, but he's taken that away from me, too. He's bringing her here on *my* honeymoon."

"You're not making sense, sweetheart. How the hell can he do that?"

"Don't patronize me," she said, her mouth tight, her back ramrod straight. "I've had enough of that lately to last me a lifetime."

"I didn't mean to be patronizing." He put his hands up in surrender, but whatever fight she had went out of her as quickly as it had appeared.

"I'm sure he called the resort, canceled my reservation, and rebooked a room in his name. The manager thinks it's their fault, but I asked. They're arriving Tuesday."

"It could be a computer glitch. This is a popular place, and you did say it was his choice not yours."

She shook her head. "He did this alright. Mr. St Louis said the reservation was changed four weeks ago. That's when he tried to buy the package from me for three thousand, which was five grand less than I paid for it. I told him that since I'd paid for the damn thing, I intended to use it myself, and it wasn't for sale. He called me a cold, vindictive bitch, among other things, and told me I would regret my decision."

"It's still circumstantial, but it does sound damn convenient. How are you going to prove it?"

"I'm not. I'm going to get off this island, hopefully with my pride intact, and pray I never see him again," she said, emptying her glass.

Paul's mouth gaped open. "You're not seriously going to let him get away with it?"

"I am. What *can* I do? It's his word against mine."

She took off her sunglasses, her eyes shimmering with unshed tears.

"I can't face him, Paul." She sighed, and her shoulders slumped. "Plus, if he discovers I spent the night here with you, he'll put his own nasty little spin on it. Mama will be mortified." A single tear slipped from the corner of her eye and dribbled down her cheek. She swiped at it. "I never expected him to pull a trick like this."

"It happens more often than you think." There had to be something he could do. "If it'll make you feel better, I'll punch out his lights for you," he offered, even though it would probably be for his own benefit.

He refilled their glasses, needing to keep his hands busy.

"It probably wouldn't help," she admitted, gesturing with the fork she'd picked up once more. "Knowing him, he would charge you, and I would feel badly seeing you tossed in jail."

"That wouldn't be good for my career either. So, who is this paragon you almost married?"

"You know him," she admitted. "Markos Theopolis."

Had he heard correctly? It couldn't be. She was way too smart to get involved with that jerk.

"Not Markos, the Achilles Heel?" Paul asked, his fork paused halfway to his mouth.

"One and the same," she admitted.

"How the hell did you get involved with him?" he asked, unable to hide his contempt.

She huffed out a breath. "I know what you're going to say—a leopard never changes his spots, but when Mark joined the school's staff, he was different. Ron didn't buy it, but Mama had been to a fortune teller who'd told her I would be getting married within two years. She was convinced he was her answer to prayer."

Paul rolled his eyes. "Only is she was praying to the devil."

MJ stabbed at him with her fork. "You can't imagine what it was like. I was almost thirty and unmarried. At that point, I could've brought home Attila the Hun, and as long as he had his own teeth, a heartbeat, and a penis, she would've been happy."

He bit his tongue, fighting not to laugh at her.

MJ's cheeks blazed. "Sorry. Forget I said that. When Mark wants to, he can charm the birds out of the trees, and Mama was more than ready to be charmed. I was blinded by his bullshit, too. Carla couldn't stand him."

"Not surprising. He picked on her cousin to the point where the guy tried to off himself."

Her eyes grew wide. "I didn't think it was that bad. Anyway, Ron was dead-set against the relationship. He's the only one who didn't give me grief about the break-up."

"Your mother might want to see you married, but there's no way she would tolerate that kind of behavior in a son-in-law," he insisted.

MJ pursed her lips. "Maybe, but I didn't tell her the real reason I called off the wedding. At the moment, she's more concerned about the possibility I'll end up an old maid. Even *you* mentioned my age, and the fact I'm unmarried seems to be some kind of sin."

He winced. Had he really been that big an ass? "My bad. Would you like to kick me?"

She giggled. "I thought about it last week, but I was afraid your dog would come through the screen and make minced meat out of me."

Paul laughed. "That big guy is a real pussy cat. He chases the squirrels in the yard, and when he's got one cornered, he runs away from it."

"Poor squirrel. Oh God!" She grabbed the turquoise crystal pendant she wore. "Carla suggested I sell the vacation on eBay. Can you imagine what might've happened if I'd done that? The only thing I can do is suck it up, take that boat in the morning, and camp out at the airport until I can get a flight home."

Paul shook his head. There was no way he would let Mark get away with this. He had to convince her to change her mind, but how?

"Explain something to me," he said, trying to think of a way to fix this mess. "Why do you think Mark would've gone to so much trouble to get this particular vacation? I understand he was pissed—even fifteen years ago, what Markos wanted, Markos got—but what he's done, if you're right, is a crime. He stole eight thousand dollars from you and used your identity to do it. That could land him a year or more in jail, which would most likely cost him his teaching credentials, and he would still be required to make restitution."

"What do you mean?" Her eyes narrowed.

"Well, by canceling the reservation, he implied he was you, which he wasn't, and did it without your consent. That's identity theft and fraud."

"What are you? A lawyer?" she asked, her head cocked to one side, her nose scrunched up.

"No, but I know how the law works."

She frowned. "I hadn't looked at it that way. As far as wanting this particular vacation, no doubt the treasure hunt's the reason. He was always watching television shows about that kind of thing or spending hours online in one chat room or another. Last summer, he was looking for El Dorado in the Superstition Mountains in Arizona." She started eating again. "All he got was sunburn and snakebite. Somehow, he must've found out about Leroux because when we were discussing the wedding, he was adamant the honeymoon had to be here on these exact dates."

Paul shook his head. "He always was a greedy son of a bitch." He smirked. "I've got an idea. Don't leave. Stay here with me, and we'll join the treasure hunt. Finding the cache would be the best payback you could get, and if we can get him to own up to what he's done, we'll get your money back, too. I'm a police officer, MJ. I know exactly how to nail his ass."

MJ's mouth gaped open. "Join the treasure hunt? Are you frigging nuts?" she cried. "I'm trying to hide from him, not piss him off more."

"Think about this," Paul said, his voice more animated than earlier. "They won't be here until Tuesday, which means since he would've known the ferry schedule, he expected you to suffer and be humiliated all weekend." He smiled and reached across the table for her hand. "This is fate. You aren't going to believe this, but according to Lucette's grandmother, this is my destiny."

"I don't understand," MJ said, her brow puckered. "What does the bartender's grandmother have to do with any of this?"

"Her grandmother's a *Quimbois* priestess. That's the nature religion practiced on Martinique. The woman apparently threw the bones to see what I was doing here."

"Seriously? Tossing bones sounds like some black magic ritual, something Callie Henderson would've accused me of doing when we were kids." Picking up her fork, she stabbed the lettuce in her salad.

"Callie Henderson is an idiot with a big mouth, but you have to admit this is one hell of a coincidence. Apparently, the woman's never wrong. Not only did she say I wouldn't be alone tonight, she claims I'm here to get my heart's desire."

MJ put down her fork. "That's just the blurb from the brochure."

He chuckled. "Maybe, but here you are."

She removed her glasses, her gorgeous eyes filled with confusion. "I don't understand."

Paul reached out and took both her hands in his. "Who knew my heart's desire was to help out a friend and get even with a jerk who'd made so many people miserable fifteen years ago?"

She pulled her hands away and stood. "I'm sorry," she stammered. "I need to go to the washroom."

He watched her go, his brow furrowed. Maybe she'd eaten too quickly. He leaned back. Markos Theopolis. If anyone needed to get what was coming to him, it was that asshole, and if it kept MJ here, so much the better.

* * *

MJ wet a facecloth and pressed it to her cheeks to keep the tears at bay, trying not to smudge her eye shadow or smear her mascara. For a second, she'd been on top of the world, but then Paul had spoken again and disabused her of that notion. His heart's desire? Of course, that wasn't her. How could it be?

Until last week, they hadn't seen one another in fifteen years, and it was highly unlikely he'd fallen head over heels in love with her—hell, he hadn't even fallen in lust. He still called her Kid, for God's sake.

Her new-found fascination with the man had to be based on her old crush and the fact she hadn't had sex, even disappointing sex, in more than seven months. Coupled with the emotional turmoil of this latest disaster was his attempt to come to her rescue. Paul was only offering to do this because he hated Mark and wanted to get back at him for the things he'd done to others. He felt sorry for her, and if there was anything she didn't want, especially from Paul Davis, it was pity.

The word of a *Quimbois* priestess? Wouldn't Carla have fun with this? That voodoo religion had been one of the excuses she'd used to try to talk her out of taking the vacation. Damn it. Why hadn't she listened?

Carla would be the first to buy into the premise of a fated

encounter and kindred spirits out to right the wrongs in this world. She would love the irony, too. MJ couldn't share his house in Watertown for fear of gossip, but apparently ten days in a romantic bungalow in the Caribbean was no problem.

Reality slapped her in the face. Once they confronted Mark, how would they keep him from blabbing this "secret rendezvous" to the world? Mama still didn't know she was here, and she would never be able to evade the camera crew for a week—especially not if they joined the damn treasure hunt as Paul suggested. No, this idea wouldn't work; in fact, it would make things worse.

MJ wiped her face and washed her hands. As much as she might want to stay here, it couldn't happen. Sighing once more, she went out to finish her lunch.

CHAPTER SEVEN

"Sorry about that. Something didn't go down right. I hate to say it, but your suggestion won't work," MJ said, resuming her seat. "While Mama and Ron know you, and if we say nothing happened, and I slept on the couch, I'm sure they'll give us the benefit of the doubt, but what about everyone else? Mark will find a way to spin it, and I'll come out of this looking like a slut or worse."

"He'd better not make a comment like that, or he'll be chewing his food on its way out," Paul said, his brow furrowed, his eyes mere slits.

She giggled. "Now, that would be worth seeing, but as I said before, he would have you charged."

Reaching for his hand, she fought to ignore the tingling she felt at the slight contact.

"Not only does this place have Wi-Fi, there's going to be a television crew here, and if we join the treasure hunt ... Mark will tell everyone back home that I'm shacked up with a stranger, and he'll let gossip and innuendo do the rest of the work for him. It may be the twenty-first century, but there's a morality clause in my contract. What are the odds no one in Watertown watches that television show? If one person recognizes me, it could cost me my job." She shrugged.

"I'm not a stranger, but considering how long it's been since I left Stilton, I see what you mean. I'm not ready to give up on this plan yet. There has to be a way to make this work."

"I really don't see any other option. If I had my own room, maybe, but like this?" She shook her head. "What happened to you after you left Stilton?"

"Not much." He used his chin to indicate she should eat. "When I graduated from police academy, I joined the state police, but after 9-11, I enlisted. I've spent the last twelve years in the army."

"Are you still a soldier? I should've picked up on that with the nifty haircut and your mention of liberty."

He shook his head and chuckled, but she didn't sense any humor there.

"Nope, but it'll take a couple more weeks for everything to be signed, sealed, and delivered. As for the hair, how long it gets will depend on how gray it is."

She chuckled. "A little gray on a man makes him look distinguished."

He screwed up his face. "Is that a euphemism for older than dirt?"

"No, silly," she said and bit her lip to keep from laughing at him. "It's the truth. It implies wisdom. Besides, you're only three years older than me. So, why did you leave the army?" She reached for her glass once more.

"My last tour was a rough one," he answered, shrugging, but his shoulders were stiff. "I decided I should get out while I was still on the right side of the grass."

"Don't even joke about something like that," she cried, the passion in her words surprising her, the thought of him lying dead on the road, filling her with pain. "Think of how hard that would be on your mother."

"Mom died of cancer five years ago." He raised his glass and took a drink. "Don't look so sad. I'm alive and I have just about everything a man could want. I bought that house because it reminded me of yours and the good times I had there."

"That's why I wanted it, too," she confessed, not wanting to dwell on the fact it was no longer hers. "What kind of stuff did you do in the army?"

"The usual stuff, but I also worked with dogs. It's one of the reasons I wanted one of my own."

"You certainly ended up with a big one. Where is super pooch?"

"He's in the kennel at Fort Drum."

"What are you going to do now?" She forked the last of her lobster salad into her mouth.

"Try to forget what happened in Afghanistan," he said soberly. "No one who goes over there is ever the same afterwards. I'm one of the lucky ones. I get to go back to work with the state police in August."

He stared into space, his face a tragic mask. Where was he?

"Paul?" she asked softly.

"Sorry," he said, obviously pushing bad memories away. "You became a teacher."

"Yeah, nothing heroic about that. I've taught geography and English at Stilton High for the past five years."

"But the school near my place is an elementary school. How does a high school teacher end up teaching little kids?"

"It was the only thing I could find," she admitted. It was so easy to talk to him. "I didn't want to move to New York or another big city. Staying in the state meant I didn't need to requalify."

He nodded. "You found a place to live ... where?"

"It's in the north end of town," she answered. "My new digs aren't as nice as yours, but I can look for something else next year." That skirted the truth a bit, but there was no way she would tell him about that ratty motel.

"You know, I can still renovate the basement and rent it to you when we get back," he said, standing and moving the soup bowls, salad plates, and lobster platters back onto the serving cart, putting a fancy French pastry in front of her. "I can seal it off from the main house and give you a separate entrance. That would put a stop to any gossip. It wouldn't be that hard, really."

"Don't worry about it. I'll be fine." Living in the same house would be impossible, even with a separate entrance.

"Well, think about it. It's really too bad we can't work this out. We would have a wonderful time." He reached for the last of the champagne, dividing it between the two glasses.

"I'm sure we would," she answered, unable to keep the longing out of her voice. "I doubt I would try diving, given the way I feel about the water, but I would love a chance to try my hand at deep sea fishing."

Paul nodded. "When Lucette mentioned the treasure, I wasn't interested, but now ... If Louis James and Antoine Leroux are ready to invest time and money in this, he must believe it exists. And then there's Mark. I don't think punishing you for standing up to him would be enough to have him put his future on the line. You can't let him get away with this. When I get back to Watertown, I can help you bring charges against him. He's stepped over the line this time. He needs to pay for his sins."

MJ shook her head. "I don't know about that. As far as charging him, I'm sure he's covered his tracks. No one disrespects the great Markos Theopolis. He always gets what he wants, and what he wants now is to break and disgrace me, which he's basically done."

"Bullshit," he cried, making her jump with his sudden fury. "He's only got the power over you that you give him."

"I wish you were right," she said, "but it isn't just me. When this gets out, Mom will be devastated." She pushed her dessert plate away and stood. "I can't eat another bite."

"Coffee?" Paul asked, his earlier anger gone. "Or would you prefer tea?"

"Coffee's fine, as long as there's cream or milk and sugar."

"There's cream in the fridge and sugar on the counter."

"What about all this?" She indicated the dirty dishes.

"We can keep the fruit and the cheese for later, someone will come and collect the dishes in an hour or so. I'll get the coffee."

She sighed. It really was too bad his idea wouldn't work. Paul was the real deal, a man who'd put his life on the line for others and now was determined to help her. The problem was the more time she spent with him, the more she was afraid her heart would get battered again, and she couldn't risk that.

* * *

Paul entered the bungalow to make coffee, feeling better than he had in months. Just being around MJ was good for his morale, but the fact she wasn't going to stay was probably for the best. The Achilles Heel would jump at the chance to humiliate her, and the last thing Paul wanted was to give the jerk ammunition. Deciding to keep the vacation and come here without telling her mother might not have been the smartest choice she'd ever made, but she didn't deserve more grief because of it.

If only they were back in the States. This had all the makings of a first-class sting operation, and he'd been involved in plenty of those. Ideally, MJ could stay on the island, enjoy her vacation, protect her reputation, and Mark would get what he deserved. It was a shame they couldn't figure out how to pull it off. He would enjoy getting to know the grown-up version of the only girl who'd ever mattered to him—even if it had been as his best friend's sister.

Selecting the coffee cups, he turned on the coffee maker. He'd bought a similar one for the house in Watertown, pleased to be able to drink coffee that wasn't like tar most of the time. One of his buddies had joked his fiancée, a girl he'd met through pen pal letters, could do anything but brew a decent cup of joe. He grinned.

"That could work."

Maybe it was more of that *Quimbois* magic at work, but this idea was brilliant. All he had to do was convince MJ to go along.

Once the coffee was ready, he carried the small tray with two cups, cream, and sugar out onto the deck.

"Listen, I have an idea," he said, setting the tray down on the table. "What if we were engaged?"

"You're asking me to marry you?" she squeaked.

"No." Damn, that hadn't come out right. "I mean I want to pretend we're engaged," he said, sweat trickling down his spine. "It would legitimize our relationship and allow you to stay here with me. Lots of engaged couples vacation together. I remember one of your Greek cousins and her fiancé went back to Greece to see her grandfather."

She shook her head vigorously, her hair fanning out around her. "No one would believe it—Mark certainly wouldn't—and neither would Mama. It's been fifteen years. People don't see one another for the first time after that long, fall madly in love, and get engaged in a matter of days. It might work that way in books and movies, but not in real life. Besides, Mama was devastated when I broke off the engagement. I can't get her hopes up and dash them again."

"But this could work," he answered. Why couldn't she see how perfect this plan was? "Your mother might be angry with you, but jerks like Markos Theopolis need to be taught a lesson. The resort must've sent out a written confirmation when the change was made."

She frowned. "The manager said something about that, but knowing Mark, he would've found a way around it. He's counting on me being too ashamed and afraid to go after him."

"Which is why you have to do just that." Paul pounced on the idea. "The only way to put a stop to bullying is to confront it. I've done enough undercover work to know you can convince people of anything if you've got the right bait."

"I can't imagine any scenario where Mama wouldn't be crushed by something like this. I may have lied about coming here, but this is different." Her lips were pursed, her arms crossed tightly.

"Think about it for a minute. How will Mark's lies about you make her feel?" he asked. "You've said it yourself, once he realizes you're here, he'll be like a kid in a candy shop spreading his malicious gossip." Seeing the confusion in her eyes, he warmed to the topic. "He'll destroy you and her in the process, and while you'll be in Watertown, she'll be in Stilton, getting it from both barrels. We can stop him once and for all."

"I don't know…" She rubbed her arms, her mouth a thin line.

"Listen to me, MJ," he coaxed. "We've got him trapped. He probably expects to find you here, cowed and humiliated, chomping at the bit to get off the island, but you won't be. You'll be with me, ready to stand up to him. As soon as he owns up to what he's done, we'll tell your mother the truth—all of it—and I'll take the blame. Let me help you. Let me put an end to this bastard's tricks once and for all."

"I'm not sure," she said, her brow drawn. "I don't want to see Mama hurt, but it looks as if she will be, no matter what I do. Carla was right. I should never have come here."

"But you have. That can't be changed now."

She nodded. "Convincing people we're a couple in love … I don't see any way they would believe it."

"Hear me out and then decide. You and Mark broke it off in January, and I take it, other than the argument over the reservation, you really haven't spoken to one another."

"That's right. I avoided him as much as I could."

"And, let me guess; you didn't date much."

"Much?" She snorted. "Try not at all. Carla and Mama both tried to fix me up, but I refused. As far as Carla was concerned, Mark won since I was the one in solitary confinement."

"Then that makes this even easier. He moved on; who's to say you didn't?"

"I just told you. I was a hermit—I went to work, to church, and home."

"But you've got a computer, right?"

"Yeah ... Where are you going with this?" Her eyes narrowed as her forehead creased once more.

"I have an idea that would put Markos Theopolis's nose out of joint and might get him to admit to what he's done."

"Go on."

The interest in her voice was all the encouragement he needed. He grinned.

"Lots of people who've been hurt are reluctant to disclose the fact they've let someone else into their lives. Would Carla be willing to support a white lie if it upset Mark?"

"Carla would walk on hot coals to get even with him. She offered to contact some of her less than stellar relatives and take him out for me. I only talked her out of it when I pointed out I'd be the prime suspect."

He guffawed. "Good old Carla. You have to admire her spunk. As much as I hate the creep, I wouldn't want to see you spend the rest of your life in prison either. No, my idea keeps Mr. Theopolis very much alive."

"You've sucked me in," she admitted, adding cream and sugar to her cup before raising it to her lips and sipping. "What have you got in mind? Not some online dating thing, I hope. No one would believe I would do something like that."

"No *Couples R Us.com*, I promise, but I have a feeling this would be something even your mom would accept. I've been in the army for twelve years. You would've been nineteen when I enlisted. Have you heard of the Adopt-a-Soldier pen pal program?"

"Of course," she said, setting down her cup. "My college roommate had one. Her brother was in the army and talked her into it. She wrote to him at least once a week." She reached across the table and touched his hand. "If I'd known you were a soldier, I would've written to you."

"I thought you would. Here's what I have in mind. This will definitely work, MJ. You'll see."

Paul smiled. This would keep her with him for the rest of the vacation. Was it smart to have her around considering the way she affected him? Probably not, but at the moment, it seemed like the best idea he'd had in a long time.

* * *

"And I'm sure your mother would accept that," Paul finished his explanation, a smug grin on his face.

MJ stared at him in wonder. Pen pals. It sounded so simple, so plausible. One of the girls she'd known at school had actually married hers.

"Why wouldn't I have mentioned I was doing this before now?" she challenged, needing to find holes in this scenario.

"Let me think … Maybe when we first started corresponding, you were afraid Ron would accuse you of chasing after me like he did when you were a kid. I'm not sure how Mama would've reacted."

MJ felt the heat in her cheeks. Mama wouldn't have been happy. She'd known about her crush and how heartbroken she'd been when he'd left.

"As far as Carla goes, you said it yourself—she's as big a gossip as anyone, and if the idea was to keep it a secret ... Mark probably would've had a fit if he found out. He didn't share his toys or play well with others, and I doubt that's changed."

MJ choked on the mouthful of coffee she'd taken.

"That's an understatement. If he'd realized I was exchanging emails with you, he would've had more than a fit," she said, shaking her head. "He was insanely jealous."

"More like possessive. Believing you were doing something like that will really put his nose out of joint." He rubbed his hands together. "Let's ice this cake. Over the years, we corresponded maybe every couple of months, but while I was in the hospital in Germany and later in rehab, our relationship grew deeper. I told you I was moving to Watertown and asked you to marry me. Talk to Carla. Get her to play along. She can swear to the fact you were both in my home."

MJ chewed her lower lip once more and looked away from him.

"What?" he asked, his brow furrowed.

"Convincing Carla I knew you were there won't be that hard," she admitted. "She was positive I did, and I had a bitch of a time assuring her it wasn't true. In the end, I'm not 100 percent sure she believed me, and if she knew you were coming here, especially after I was so adamant about keeping the honeymoon..."

"That plays right into our hands." He paced the deck, his excitement contagious. "While you were changing, I mentioned that I was going to a new Caribbean resort. If we can figure out a way to make her add two and two and come up with five, it'll be all over Stilton in no time."

"How would I explain lying to her? Believe me, she'll zero right in on that point."

"Well, since I wasn't supposed to get back to the States until July fifteenth, and you really had no idea I'd bought the house, it would be understandable. You could say I wanted to surprise you."

"You certainly did that," she admitted. "But you didn't recognize me."

"Maybe I did, but was just playing along since we were still keeping our relationship secret."

MJ blew out a breath, twisting her hands together. "You're really good at lying, aren't you?"

He shook his head. "I'll never lie to you, MJ, you have my promise on that. This is all window dressing—setting the stage. I've run more than twenty of these sting operations. People believe what you want them to believe. Think of a magician. He doesn't really make that rabbit appear and disappear, nor does he saw that woman in half. He just makes you think he did. Smoke and mirrors, babe, smoke and mirrors."

She looked down at the lower deck. "How deep is the water here?"

"Less than four feet. You can stand without any problem. I'll never forget how terrified you were that day at the lake."

She shuddered. "Ron thought he was helping me overcome what he still considers an irrational fear. It's the only time both Mama and Papa ripped him a new one." Sobering, she glanced at him. "But deep down, I knew you wouldn't let me drown."

Paul's gaze met hers. "I would never let anything happen to you." He cleared his throat. "I should've asked this earlier. I know he hurt you, but do you still love Mark?"

"Love him?" she spat the question, her arms gesturing wildly, almost knocking her empty mug off the table. "Only a masochist would still care for a man who's done what he has, and while I may be a lot of things, I'm not one to wallow in pain and beg for more. I never realized how easily love could turn to hate until now. He used me, humiliated me, and destroyed all of my dreams, and I don't think I can ever forgive him for that. There's nothing I would like better than a little payback."

"Then, let's get it. I'm sure the manager will agree to help out. What Mark did could've given the resort a black-eye. This will be a breeze. Undercover work is all in the details. When we're out and about, we'll behave the same way as any other couple here—we'll hold hands, be affectionate—we don't have to overdo it, but it has to look real. Do we have a deal?"

MJ looked at his outstretched hand and debated whether or not she'd completely lost her mind by even considering the idea. She raised her gaze to meet his once more. "You're really serious about this? You'd go to this extreme to help me? Why?"

"I'm sick of seeing the bad guys win. You're my friend, and in my world, friends take care of friends."

"Let me think about it," she said, reaching for his hand.

He covered it with his other one. Heat engulfed her. She desperately wanted to say yes, but hadn't acting impetuously gotten her into this mess in the first place? She could easily be jumping out of the frying pan and into the fire. Either way, she was afraid she was about to get burned.

MJ finished her second cup of coffee. She had to be crazy to even be considering this.

"Regardless of what you decide, I really should know your full name," Paul said. "I must've heard it at some point, but I'm ashamed to say I don't remember it. What does MJ stand for?"

"Marilyn Jean Summers. The only time anyone seems to use it is when they're annoyed with me."

"Marilyn."

The way the word rolled off his tongue made heat pool in her stomach.

"I like it. Marilyn," he repeated the name as if he were tasting it. "It's a great name. Why didn't your parents use it?"

"I don't really know. It's my grandmother's name. Maybe two Marilyns in the house was too confusing. Do you remember her? She had an apartment in our basement. She died just before I graduated from high school."

"Yeah. She made great stew."

MJ laughed. "You *would* remember that. That was when you and Ron had hollow legs."

"We were growing boys." He opened his eyes wide, feigning innocence.

"Yeah, right." She shook her head and chuckled. "From the amount you two ate, you both should've ended up ten-feet tall. As far as my name goes, it's one of those family hand-me-downs. I did a search on it and in Hebrew it means longed-for child, but it also means rebellious. I did find an obscure reference to it as the star of the sea."

"I like that one. The color of the water here is almost the same as the color of your eyes. I tried to capture that shade so many times..."

The heated look he gave her threatened to have her combust on the spot.

Hiding her embarrassment, she chuckled. "Really? You spent hours drawing my eyes? That's a stretch." She shook her head. "These damn things have caused me nothing but grief. I've been called a witch, a zombie, even a child of the damned after some stupid movie." She tried to swallow her bitterness and failed. Even that flirting crewman had mentioned her eyes. "Worst pick-up line ever actually belongs to a guy I met at university. He asked me if these were really my eyes."

"What did you say?"

"That I'd borrowed them from a corpse at my uncle's mortuary. The look on his face was priceless, but I never went out without tinted contacts or lenses after that. I used to pray for brown eyes like Carla's."

"God, I would've loved to have seen his face, but I've always found your eyes fascinating, and if people can't see that, then they're nuts. Their shape and color are something I could never forget about you—not that I forgot much. If you hadn't been wearing those sunglasses, I would've recognized you instantly."

MJ licked suddenly dry lips. She'd never forgotten anything about him either, but this wasn't the time to tell him that. Her emotions were jumbled enough without tossing that into the mix.

Instead of commenting, she stared out at the aquamarine water once more. Were her eyes really that shade?

"What did the Achilles Heel call you?" Paul asked, reaching for her empty coffee cup.

She frowned. "I don't think he called me anything. Isn't that silly? In front of the students, it was Ms. Summers, but when we were alone, he didn't use a name for me—he just ordered me around. It was just do this, or do that. He must have called me MJ at some point, and he had choice words when I broke off the engagement and refused to sell him the vacation, but I'm positive he never used pet names or terms of affection. Thank God for that. The last thing I would want to be called is cupcake or dumpling."

Paul burst out laughing, his eyes crinkling in amusement. "If you agree to be my fiancée, I promise never to call you food names, but I like Marilyn, although I'm sure MJ and Kid will slip out once in a while."

The mention of her nickname brought back reality. This would be make-believe, a pretense to get the creep who'd treated her so badly. A sting operation. A police investigation. Nothing more. She had to remember that.

CHAPTER EIGHT

The doorbell rang.

"I'll get it," Paul said, jumping up.

He moved into the bungalow, grateful for the opportunity to be alone for a moment. What had started out as a way to get even with Mark for everything he'd ever said and done in the past had changed. His heart hammered, and his palms were slick with sweat. This would be either the best thing he'd ever done, or the biggest mistake he'd ever made.

"Yes?" he asked, opening the door to a concierge.

"Monsieur St Louis has sent Madame Summers's case," the man said, placing the blue suitcase inside the room.

"Thank you."

Before he could pull a couple of euros out of his pocket, the young man was gone.

"Who was it?" MJ asked, coming up behind him.

"The concierge with your suitcase. Looks like you have everything you need now. So, what will it be? Flight or fight?"

He crossed his fingers behind his back, the way he used to do as a kid when he wanted something he wasn't sure he would ever get.

Licking her lips, she nodded. "I'll fight, but you'd better hope your *Quimbois* witch knows what she's doing; otherwise, this will be a disaster."

Paul grinned. He'd just won the prize.

"Or the best thing that could happen. Lucette assures me Grandma's not a witch. She's a priestess, descended from the island's original settlers, one of the men who survived the shipwreck. Who knows? This could bode well for the treasure, too." He winked. "Remember what the brochure says. While being rich beyond the bounds of avarice isn't something I've considered, all your dreams come true on Paradise Island."

Were her dreams, the ones she claimed Mark had destroyed, that different from his?

He picked up her case and placed it on the bed.

"If you're okay, I'll go and see the manager now. The sooner he knows the truth, the better. The last thing we want is for someone to get fired over this. Why don't you unpack while I'm gone? When you finish, you can meet me in the bar, and we'll hang around the pool for a couple of hours. Don't worry. It has a shallow end. We can figure out how to break the news to your mother and Carla and contact them later, but the sooner we do, the better."

"I guess."

She didn't sound convinced. He would have to work on that before she contacted her mother. With that long face, she looked more like a condemned prisoner than a happy bride-to-be.

"How long will you need? I doubt my conversation with Monsieur St Louis will take more than half an hour."

"That should be plenty of time."

"I haven't put anything in the tallboy on the left, and there's still lots of room in the closet. "I'll change before I go." He grabbed a swimsuit out of the top drawer of the other dresser. "You won't need to bring a towel with you," he said, grabbing a Yankees' cap off the nightstand. "They've got some by the pool, but bring your hat, sunglasses, and sunscreen. The roof is retractable, and the afternoon sun is stronger than back home. I don't want to see you turn into a lobster on your first day here."

"Neither do I." She held up the large can of spray-on sunscreen she'd just removed from her suitcase. "I came prepared."

"SPF 50? Should work. But we'll still keep a close eye on your skin."

He walked over to her, put his hand on her shoulder, and gazed into her eyes. Energy coursed through him, making him feel alive, but the serious look on her face worried him. She could still back out of their deal, and that was the last thing he wanted. His eyes focused on her lips, slightly parted in a nervous smile. What more could he say or do to convince her to take a chance on him?

Unable to stop himself, he brushed his lips across her brow and pulled away before he moved down to her tantalizing lips and ruined everything. He didn't miss the surprise in her eyes. Well, she'd better get used to it because being affectionate was a critical part of his plan, and this was one sting he intended to enjoy.

* * *

Paul sat in the chair across from the manager. "There you have it. Marilyn knows the resort wasn't to blame for this mix-up. Please don't give anyone grief over the matter. I'm sure your staff did everything exactly the way they should have."

Raymond St Louis frowned and steepled his fingers, his two index fingers rubbing up and down against his chin, although he looked far less angry and upset than he had when Paul had first arrived. The heavyset man leaned back in his leather chair. Like everything else in the office, the seat was designed for the occupant's comfort. The resort wanted its staff to be happy in their work, but at the moment, its manager looked anything but.

"This is not the conversation I expected to have with you, but you have no idea how pleased I am to hear this ... not for the sake of my staff, but for Madame Summers." His scowl belied his words. He pursed his lips. "We keep excellent records here. My accountant tracked down the change to the reservation. I was going to have Madame Summers arrested as soon as she set foot on Martinique."

Paul exploded out of the chair, slamming his fist on the desk. "Arrested? What the hell for?"

"Calm yourself, sir. I wondered if you were involved, but that didn't make sense. Scam artists are the bane of many resorts these days. Here. Let me show you why I jumped to that conclusion."

Paul walked around the massive desk. The computer screen was open revealing the email transactions for room thirty-nine, dated four weeks ago. He began to read.

Stepping back, he returned to the front of the desk, but couldn't sit, too angry at this latest turn of events.

"So that's how the conniving bastard did it. He didn't cancel the reservation; he had it transferred to his name." Paul shook his head.

"There was also a telephone conversation, and then the confirmation letter was sent out as you can see. Would you like to hear the phone call? Perhaps you will recognize the voices."

"Maybe. Let's hear it." Paul dropped into the chair, too furious to say anything else. When Mark did show up at the resort, it would take every scrap of self-control he had not to strangle the son of a bitch.

"Paradise Island Resort, *bonjour*. How may I be of assistance?" the disembodied voice of the receptionist spoke.

"My name is Markos Theopolis. I have a reservation, or rather my former fiancée has. The confirmation number is 358296."

Mark's voice was like nails on a chalkboard, and raised Paul's hackles.

"One moment, please." Soft music played until the woman came on the line again. "The reservation is in the name of MJ Summers, monsieur. To make any changes, I would need to speak to Madame Summers."

"She's right here."

"Very well. How may I help you?"

Mark chuckled. "It's nothing too difficult. We just want to change the reservation from her name to mine. We'll be married by then anyway."

"To do what you ask, I require confirmation from Madame Summers."

"Of course," Mark said, and Paul could hear the smugness in his voice.

"Hello?" The voice was low and throaty, hesitant and unsure, but definitely not MJ's voice. They probably wouldn't even need a voice print analysis to use the tape in court.

"Madame Summers?" the receptionist asked.

"Yes."

"I understand you wish to change the name on your reservation. Is that correct?"

"Yes."

"*Ce n'est pas un problème.* To confirm the identity, I require the credit card number you used."

The woman rattled off the number from an American Express card.

"And the CVI?"

Three numbers came through the line.

"*Alors.* The reservation in the name of MJ Summers has been canceled, and the room reallocated to Markos Theopolis with the charges for the room left on the existing card. Is that correct?"

"Yes," the woman answered once more.

"Is there anything else I can do for you?"

"Yes. Can you make a note that we won't be arriving until Tuesday, and we have to leave Saturday?" Mark asked.

"You do realize while your stay with us will be brief, we cannot refund you any of the money you've paid? I am sorry," the receptionist said.

"I know, but we'll be there for the treasure hunt, and that's what counts—not that the rest of the honeymoon isn't important. Will you send confirmation of all this?"

"*Mais oui.*"

"Then you need to change the email address and land address," he said, giving his own information.

Monsieur St Louis ended the playback.

"There you have it," he said. "Our parent company in France requires that all calls be recorded for the safety of our clients as well as our staff. Based on this, I believed Madame Summers was playing some kind of trick to get a free vacation." He rubbed his chin. "There is nothing I can do to Monsieur Theopolis and his associate since he has not broken any laws here on Paradise, at least not yet."

Paul was so angry, it was hard to keep his temper under control. "Well, I can assure you he's broken quite a few American ones." Paul ran his left hand through his hair. "I'm a New York State police officer. I'll see charges laid as soon as I get stateside. This is my problem now."

"*C'est abominable,*" Monsieur St Louis said, leaning forward. "That a man could stoop so low as to do such a thing…" He shook his head. "Madame Summers is to be commended, but regardless I intend to keep a close eye on Monsieur Theopolis. Rest assured, none of the staff will be chastised, but it does tell me we overlooked the possibility that such a thing as a broken engagement could result in a fiasco like this one." He shook his head, but not one hair of his steel-gray comb-over moved. "What will Madame Summers do? It is a shame to let the man get away with this and lose out on something she has paid for."

"He's not going to get away with it, I can guarantee you that, but with your permission, Marilyn will remain as my guest."

Monsieur St Louis nodded. "That is not a problem. It is hard to understand what would make a man stoop so low as to try to humiliate the woman he once loved."

"I doubt Markos is capable of loving anyone but himself; however, I believe the treasure hunt is at the root of all this. MJ and I have no intention of causing any trouble, beyond making sure Markos is as uncomfortable as he can possibly be with our presence here, and if by some stroke of luck we find Lacorneille's treasure ... Enough said." He frowned. "Because of the man's vindictive nature, MJ and I will pose as an engaged couple. The last thing I want is him smearing her name and her reputation."

The manager leaned back in his chair once more, his face a mask of disgust. "I would like to do whatever I can to help. The man is a cad and may see through a pretend engagement, which is a fabrication." His eyes narrowed. "I may have a way to prevent such a thing from happening and protect Madame's good name—at least until you have laid your charges."

Paul's eyes narrowed. If he could find a way to change that possibility and guarantee MJ's reputation, he'd jump at it, and hopefully so would she. He still expected her to change her mind at any minute.

"What do you suggest?"

"My brother-in-law is here for the treasure hunt, too. He's a *notaire publique*. He can write up a marriage contract for you and Madame Summers."

"A marriage contract? Whoa!" Was the man crazy? MJ would never agree to that. "Isn't that a little drastic? MJ doesn't want to marry me; she just wants to be able to walk out of here with her reputation intact and get some semblance of justice from Mark."

The manager chuckled. "Even if you wanted to, marriage between you and Madame Summers here on Paradise Island is not possible. We have strict residency requirements, but if the two of you were to sign a marriage agreement, you would be legally bound to one another, and the paperwork would legitimize the relationship."

"Would this contract be binding in the United States? Like I said, MJ doesn't want to marry me."

"*Mais oui*, but let me explain," the manager said, his grin reaching from ear to ear. "On Martinique as in France, marriage is a civil matter. Couples choose the type of marriage they want and sign the agreement. The wedding itself, a *noce civil* recognizing the contract, takes place afterwards. If the couple wishes to wed in a church, it's the third step. In your case, once you return to the United States, you would simply see a lawyer and void the contract." He shrugged his shoulders.

"And your brother-in-law would draw up one of these knowing we planned to dissolve it?"

"Who can see the future other than Lucette's *grandmère*?" the manager asked, holding up his hands, palms up.

Did everyone on the island know about the *Quimbois* prediction?

"My brother-in-law is a romantic, but a realist. If he knows this is a police matter, he will do his part."

"Let me run it by MJ. This has potential," Paul answered and nodded, more than a little taken with the idea. "If she's agreeable, when could your brother-in-law draw up the document?"

"Tomorrow morning before you leave for your visit to Saint Pierre. I will add her name to the passenger list."

"Do you keep a record of all of your guests' activities?" Paul asked, not sure whether or not he should feel offended at being watched so closely.

"The resort never has more than one hundred guests, and it is my duty to make sure they are all as safe and happy as they can be." He chuckled. "In your case, as you can understand, a man alone on what is essentially an island for lovers was cause for concern. I needed to know what you had in mind. Germaine said you were here to help another and that your arrival was predestined. I do not argue with the Fates or Germaine, even when I have doubts." He smiled once more.

"Germaine?" Paul asked.

"Lucette's grandmother. We set great store by her abilities. I asked her to throw the bones for you."

Paul chuckled and shook his head. "Well played. I guess you need to keep your guests safe in whatever way you can."

"*Mais oui. C'est la vie*, and today..." He shrugged. "Should

Madame Summers agree to your proposal, the resort has a handsome selection of rings in the boutique. I'm sure there would be something there to suit her. A ring adds another layer to the charade, *n'est-ce-pas?*"

"Good point. Thank you, sir. I appreciate your help, and I know Marilyn will, too."

"*Très bien.* I'll speak to the staff. No one will discuss the circumstances of her arrival. As for the guests, I doubt many of them realized what happened earlier, and we can remind those who do to stay hydrated to avoid dizzy spells. Once the events start tonight, they will be far too preoccupied to think of anything else."

"What happens tonight?"

"It was Monsieur James's idea to showcase this as a honeymoon resort, so we agreed to a mock wedding to be shown on American television. This will be explained to the guests before the second seating for dinner tonight. All their names will go into a basket, but I will make sure yours are not added. It might complicate matters, *non?*"

"It certainly would." Paul glanced at his watch. He'd been here longer than he'd expected. "I'd better get going. Marilyn is meeting me in the lounge. I don't want to leave her there alone."

"Very well. I will make sure copies of everything I have shown you are available for you when you leave. As a thank you for sparing the resort from what could have been an embarrassing situation, I am going to upgrade your vacation to our gold key package." He handed Paul a brochure. "Not all of the rooms on Paradise Island are as luxurious as yours. Monsieur Theopolis will get what he is entitled to and no more."

"Then, if Marilyn agrees to this plan, I'll gladly accept your offer since that alone will put Mark's nose out of joint. He hates to see anyone get more than he does."

Chuckling, Monsieur St Louis stood. "Some of my ancestors came from France, the land of love, while others were torn from their African homes. I may prefer to make love, rather than war, but I understand the need for such, and know that revenge can be sweet at times." He extended his hand to Paul. "On Paradise Island, we say all your dreams can come true."

"I'll talk to MJ." He reached out his hand to shake the one the manager extended. "Thank you."

"The pleasure's all mine, Paul, and call me Raymond. We are allies in a just cause."

Paul nodded. It looked like the manager was a good man to have on his side. Now, all he had to do was get MJ to agree.

* * *

"Paul, where is your friend?" Lucette asked as he approached the bar. "I hope she's recovered?"

"She's fine now; as a matter of fact, she's unpacking."

Lucette grinned from ear to ear. "Voila, just as *Grandmère* said. You are no longer alone. This makes you happy?"

"It does." In fact, he was far happier than he could remember. "She should be along soon."

Paul turned to watch the doorway. Within seconds, the wooden doors swung open and MJ stood there, worrying her lower lip as she'd done earlier. She'd replaced the sexy tube dress with an even shorter navy and white striped one. Despite his best efforts, he couldn't stop himself from admiring her long, tanned legs. Since when did girls just over five-foot-tall have legs that seemed to go on forever?

The moment she spotted him, her face relaxed, a grin replacing her worried look. His heart skipped a beat.

"That was fast," he said as she reached the bar. "I expected it would take you longer to settle in. You did settle in, right?"

"Yes," she answered, removing her sunglasses and reaching for her tinted lenses inside her bag. "Although I'm still not convinced this will work. I didn't really bring all that much since I figured I would spend a lot of time sitting on the beach or by the pool."

He released the breath he'd held and turned to the bar. "Lucette, I would like you to meet Marilyn Summers, the answer to your grandmother's prophesy. Lucette's grandma saw you coming."

MJ laughed. "Really? I'd like to know what else she's seen. Hello, Lucette." She held out her hand. "My friends call me MJ. Paul's the only one who calls me Marilyn, although he used to call me Kid."

"But he does not see you as a child any longer," the woman said softly, staring at her. Paul saw the way MJ shifted her stance before putting on her tinted lenses, her hand trembling. Her cheeks were pale once more.

"What's the matter?" Paul asked, pulling her to him.

"It's nothing."

Lucette blinked. "My apologies, Madame. I did not mean to upset you. I've heard of the eyes of the *sirènes*, but I have never seen them. They are even more beautiful than I thought they would be. Please, may I see them once more?"

MJ frowned, her cheeks redder than they'd been moments ago. "You want to see my eyes again?"

The woman nodded.

"I'm a little sensitive about the way people react to them," MJ explained before removing her glasses. "What are *sirènes*?" she asked mangling the word.

"*Sirènes* are mermaids," Paul answered. "Did you have any trouble getting back here?"

"No," she said, covering her eyes once more. "Thankfully Hercules wasn't anywhere to be seen."

"Hercules, who's Hercules?" he asked, confused by the name.

"He's that dinosaur-dragon creature you laughingly refer to as an iguana," she explained. "Anything that big needs a name, right?"

He pulled her closer and hugged her, laughter bubbling up inside him. God, she was good for him—like the dog and the house. She would keep the darkness away. He would be happy with MJ in his life for a while—the longer the better. The idea of the marriage contract suddenly appealed more than it had. If he could prolong their engagement, maybe she would come to know him as someone other than Ron's friend and he could build on that.

"I should've guessed you would name him after a Greek hero."

"Would you prefer Sreng or Cú Chulainn?"

He stifled a laugh. "Maybe not. I've never heard of them, but I'll take your word they were Irish heroes. Hercules it is."

"*Alors,* you met one of the resort's mascots," Lucette said placing cocktail napkins on the bar in front of them. "They're large, but quite harmless. They aren't native to the island. During a particularly vicious tropical storm about thirty years ago, a few of them drifted across the water from their homeland. Since Paradise Island has a lot for them to eat and none of their natural enemies, they grow quite large. Did the one you saw have a collar?"

"It did," MJ said, nodding.

"Then most likely, its name is on there. The next time you see it, have a look."

"You mean those things let you touch them?" she asked, her eyebrows raised in disbelief.

"*Mais oui*; they enjoy being petted. There's one near the village my uncle named Anselme. He's so domesticated, the children play with him all the time. They attach him to their wagon and he gives them rides. Now, would you like something to drink, Madame?"

"You should try one of her rum concoctions," he offered, wanting her to relax and enjoy herself.

"Why not? And a glass of water, please."

"Very well, and for you, Paul?" Lucette asked.

"I'll have a beer. Make it a Blonde." He winked at MJ and watched the faint blush tinge her cheeks once more. "I seem to prefer them."

Lucette chuckled softly. "As you should. Will you sit here or go out by the pool?"

"I think we'll sit over there for a while," he indicated a table apart from the others.

While he had no intention of telling MJ how close she'd come to going to jail, he wanted to broach the idea of the marriage contract. He should probably take her back to the bungalow to do it, but he didn't mind having the men who'd given him dirty looks the last couple of days realize the most beautiful woman in the room was his.

Besides, spending too much time near that bed could wreak havoc despite his best intentions.

CHAPTER NINE

"That's fine by me," MJ agreed, smiling at the bartender, wondering what the manager had told Paul that had him looking like a kid who'd been promised a new puppy. "I'm easy." Realizing the implication of what she'd said, she changed the topic. "You were right about the humidity. It didn't feel that bad on the way over, but I was so afraid of meeting the lizard, I wasn't really thinking about it. Actually," she admitted, licking her lips nervously, "I was wondering about a snake big enough to eat that lizard."

Lucette placed their drinks on the bar in front of them and smiled. "The few snakes we have on Paradise Island are tiny, no bigger than earthworms." She raised her hand. "Sit wherever you like; Félice will be on duty shortly to serve you. If you have a chance to visit the village, I know *Grandmère* would be honored to meet you. She knows far more about the mermaids than I do. We consider them blessed, like angels. To resemble one the way you do must be a great honor."

"It certainly hasn't felt that way to me," MJ answered, and he sensed her pain, reminded of the teasing she'd mentioned.

Lucette frowned. "That is a shame. Here, you will get the respect you deserve. In the meantime, if you need anything else, just let me know."

"Thanks," Paul said, tossing a couple of euros on the bar. He turned to MJ. "Let's go over to that corner."

"It's incredibly beautiful here," she said, sitting in the rattan chair and taking a mouthful of the drink Lucette had given her. "Wow. This is good and dangerous." She chuckled. "You can't even taste the rum, and considering I've already had my fair share of that champagne, I'd better be careful. If I'm not, I may fall face-first into my dinner tonight." She set down the glass and leaned closer to him. "Lucette really believes mermaids exist, doesn't she?"

"Yeah, and I don't think she's the only one. It's hard for me to understand how anyone can, but I'm long past questioning people's beliefs. If it makes her happy to think half-fish, half-women are floating around out there, who am I to rain on her parade?"

"I guess. As a child, I believed in a lot of things, including mermaids. Growing up and losing that naïveté stinks." She took another sip. "It's like Christmas without Santa Claus. The magic is missing." She sighed. "What did the manager say? He won't fire anyone, right?"

"No, he won't. You can rest easy on that," Paul said, taking a swig of his beer. "He would like to see Mark pay for what he's done since it could've had a negative impact on the resort. As a thank you, we've been upgraded to gold key guests, which involves preferential treatment and makes this an all-inclusive stay for us. As far as Mark and his wife go, they'll be given what's due them, but nothing more. Apparently, all things are not created equal on Paradise Island."

MJ chuckled. "Knowing that is almost as good as getting my money back. Mark was annoyed when I chose the mid-range package, but he would never fork out the kind of cash I paid or what your bungalow cost. Seeing you get things he can't will annoy him. He thinks he's entitled to the best even when he doesn't pay for it."

"You mean seeing *us* get preferential treatment," Paul said, his eyes glowing with excitement.

MJ shook her head. "Maybe, but I'm still not convinced this fake engagement will work." She couldn't conceal her disappointment. "I keep thinking about all the things that can go wrong."

"The manager has an idea that might help."

"The manager? What could he possibly do to assist us and keep

Mark from guessing the truth?" she asked.

"This place, like Martinique itself and a lot of the other islands, adheres to French marriage laws," he began, gesturing with his hands the way Carla did when she was excited.

MJ listened patiently to what Monsieur St Louis had told him, unable to believe what he was saying.

"You want to sign a contract that says we're really getting married?" The implications of such a thing were huge. "Wouldn't that be fraud, the same as what Mark has done?"

"No." He shook his head. "The man who'll prepare the contract will know it's a police matter. In fact, we could add an additional protection to our plan by keeping up the charade after we get back. When the time's right, we'll find a lawyer and have the contract dissolved. We can say we had second thoughts since this really is a spur of the moment idea, and by then, you'll have laid charges against the Achilles Heel, and everyone will finally know what a stellar human being he isn't."

"Or what a complete fool I am," she mumbled, taking a large mouthful of her drink and swallowing her pain along with the rum. "It's a great idea, but I can't help being Negative Nelly here. Once we dissolve the contract, Mama will be devastated, and Mark will get wind of it and open his mouth, putting his own dirty little spin on it, especially if I humiliated him, and the charges don't stick. If it got back to the diocese, I'm not sure a temporary engagement would save my job."

She would love to stay here with him and pretend she'd found Prince Charming and her own happily ever after, but fairytales were for kids, not jaded old maids like her, and there was nothing *Quimbois* magic could do about that. She would enjoy the rest of today and tonight, and then convince Paul the only smart thing to do to spare them both more embarrassment was for her to get off the tour boat in Saint Pierre, get to the airport, and catch the first flight home. They would have one night in paradise, and she would remember it for the rest of her life.

Glancing over, she watched Paul's expressive face as he wrestled with everything she'd said. He set down his beer and smiled at her, reaching for her hand.

"Then, I guess we'll have to get married," he commented so matter of factly, she thought she'd imagined it. "We'll just ask your mother to keep it small."

For a second, she couldn't breathe, and then she threw back her head and laughed so hard she snorted, tears filling her eyes.

"You rat," she said, punching him on the arm. "You had me going there. Now I know you're pulling my leg. I'm Greek and my mother's only daughter. You have seen *My Big Fat Greek Wedding*, right? There's no such thing as a small Greek wedding." She swiped at the tears of laughter on her cheeks. "Paul, I appreciate your offer, more than you'll ever know, but I can't break Mom's heart with a fake marriage. Besides, what about your girlfriend?"

"What girlfriend?" he asked, his eyebrows meeting as his brow creased deeply.

"The one who was waiting for you in your bedroom the day I was there. The door was closed, and you were half-dressed. I assumed we'd interrupted something." Her cheeks heated at the admission she'd snooped.

"The only thing you interrupted was yard work. I was half-dressed because I'd been cutting the grass. The door was closed to keep King off the bed. Believe me, there wasn't any girl in there, nor has there been."

"I'm sorry," she said, knowing she was probably red enough to resemble the French flag considering the white and blue stripes she wore. "I have a bad habit of jumping to conclusions. As Carla puts it, it's a predisposed condition brought on by my Greek-Irish genetic material."

"I'm not joking, Marilyn. Let's do it. Let's get married."

She stared at him. Had he lost his mind?

"But you need to understand something," he said, his voice low and solemn. "While I really like you and think we could be great together, I don't believe in love."

The words were like a slap in the face.

"I don't even know what love is," he continued before she could speak, the words wrenched from somewhere deep inside him. "I was engaged to a woman two years ago, but she broke it off by sending me a 'Dear John' letter in Kabul and a copy of her wedding announcement. Was I hurt? Sure, but by then, I'd been expecting the shoe to drop. My father claimed to love my mother and made her life a living hell. Alcohol can't excuse all of his mistakes. He cheated on her, beat her, slapped me around until I was old enough to hit back, and then walked away from us as if we were nothing but the garbage left on his tray at a fast food restaurant. When Mom died, I sent him a letter, he sent me back a note thanking me and asking for her death certificate to claim his official status as a widower. He never even showed up for the funeral. I don't know where he is, and I don't give a damn one way or another."

"I'm sorry, Paul," she whispered. Empathy for the child, now a man, who'd grown up feeling unloved and alone, filled her. "I never knew. No wonder you preferred our house. I'm sure your mother loved you—"

"Did she?" he asked bitterly, not letting her finish what she was going to say. "Then she had a hell of a way of showing it. Why didn't she protect me? A lot of people knew what went on in our house. Your parents did. In fact, they're the only ones who ever tried to help. The last time your mom patched me up, your dad went to see my old man. He didn't lay a hand on us for weeks after that visit, but then, he packed up and left us with nothing. That was harder on Mom than anything else he'd done. You wondered why I never said goodbye, why I never called. I was ashamed."

"You aren't your father. I'm sure you would never do what he did."

"You don't know that," he spat the words fueled by anger and pain. "Genetics tells me 50 percent of me comes from him, and I have no intention of passing those genes along. I've seen more marriages fall apart than stay together, and good men died over there because they lost whatever they thought they had here. Your folks were the exception to the rule. They never judged. They made me feel like I belonged. Like I mattered. It wasn't love, but it was respect and understanding, something I appreciate."

MJ bit the inside of her lower lip, her heart going out to him in his pain, wishing there was something she could say to make him understand that she knew he wasn't his father no matter what his genes said. He'd already proven that in more ways than one.

"I can't give you love, and I know you don't love me, but I respect you. If we have to, we could make it work in the short term. In a year's time, if you want out, or you find someone to love, we can look into an annulment. I know that's the only thing that would sit right with your mother. Because of the speed with which we're doing this, and the fact that I have no intention of giving you children, which I believe the church says I have to do, we should be able to get one. If worse comes to worse and we can't, then we'll get a divorce. Either way, the house will be yours free and clear, and we'll have dealt with the Achilles Heel."

"Paul, I need to think about this," she said stunned by the raw pain in his voice. "It's an incredible offer, but…"

"Do you like me?" he asked, his eyes filled with concern as if her answer really mattered to him.

"Of course, I like you, but this isn't the marriage proposal I envisioned. To me, marriage is supposed to be forever. I screwed up once …"

"I'm sure Theopolis was all hearts and flowers and look how that turned out for you," he said, his voice dripping sarcasm.

Tears brimmed her eyes at his harsh words. She lifted the glass of ice water Lucette had given her with her cocktail and drank deeply. He was right. Mark had made a grand production of it, and it had all been a lie. Besides, this wasn't a marriage proposal. It was a business proposition.

"I'm sorry. I shouldn't have said that," he said, hanging his head. "The last thing I want to do is hurt you." He looked up, his gaze meeting hers. "You deserve far better than either Mark or me, but this is what I'm offering. I'm talking a year, maybe two. Who's to say it won't last longer than that? Marrying for love is a fairly new concept. For centuries, people got married because their parents arranged it. They solidified peace treaties. Women married men they'd never seen for security and companionship. I won't lie to you. I get lonely, and while King's great, he's a lousy conversationalist. I'm offering you security, companionship, a house to live in, respect, and admiration. It may not be what you expected, but the offer is sincere. This would be a real marriage, MJ, not a fake one or a sham, but it would be a marriage in name only."

MJ watched his face as he spoke. He was putting himself out there, hoping she would understand his sincerity, but she saw the insecurity he tried to hide. He was afraid she would reject him. What he said made sense, but could she accept his offer? She wanted love, children, and the whole damn dream, and she wasn't getting any younger. He was offering her a watered-down version of the future she'd imagined fifteen years ago when she'd written her name—MJ Davis, Marilyn Davis, Mrs. Paul Davis—over and over again in her diary. The only one who'd ever seen the signatures had been her mother. She swallowed her sorrow.

"I need to use the Ladies' Room. I'll be right back."

She escaped into the bathroom, needing to pull herself together before she made what could be the biggest mistake of her life.

Entering the deserted room, MJ sat on a rattan stool in front of the mirror, more confused than she'd ever been. Paul had offered to marry her—marry her—just to save her reputation and keep her mother from suffering the embarrassment Mark was sure to heap on her if he could. What kind of man offered to do that?

The kind of man her father would've wanted her to marry—one with integrity. She shook her head. As Confucius said, "Before you embark on a journey of revenge, dig two graves." Sure, she would get her tropical vacation and get even with Mark, sully his reputation, maybe even get him arrested, but at what cost?

What she needed to do was make one of her infamous lists of pros and cons. On the pro side, she could write protecting my reputation, a place to live, companionship with a man I admire, a big dog ... but on the con side she would have to write no love, no sex, no children, annulment or divorce down the line, and heartache—lots and lots of heartache. No one would win this game.

Paul was a hero, a man who'd suffered both as a boy with what must have been a terrible home life, and as a man in the hellhole that was the war zone. He wasn't pulling his punches. Could she do the same? She wanted love in her life and a family. Would it be worth the price of forsaking that dream to get her revenge and keep her honor intact?

She would probably regret it, but something good had to come out of this mess she'd created with her impulsive behavior. Paul deserved to know love existed, and that if anyone merited love, it was him. Regardless of how long or short their relationship would be, she could use that time to show him how wrong he was about himself.

"I gave him a piece of my heart years ago," she said softly, staring at her reflection. "He might as well have the rest of it now."

Turning away from the mirror, she pasted a smile on her face and returned to the lounge.

"It could work," she said, dropping back into her chair, "but only if we can sell Mama on how long we've been a couple." She licked her lips. "Since we're baring our souls here, there's something you need to know—the one thing that would make her believe this." Choosing her words carefully, she gave up her deepest secret. "When you left Stilton, I was heartbroken. I had such a crush on you, and you didn't seem to even know I was alive. If she thought you'd cared for me, too, but hadn't said anything because of what was then a huge age gap, she might believe it was a second chance at love thing," she finished lamely. She put up her hand to stop him from speaking. "I know there's no love involved, and I grew out of my crush—hey, I was all set to marry the Achilles Heel, remember? If she thinks we're in love, it'll be easier for her and Ron to buy. If they accept it, so will everyone else. If the engagement contract is sufficient for a while, we can leave it at that, but if it isn't enough for the diocese, are you really ready to go through with the whole shebang involved with a Greek Orthodox Church wedding just to save my reputation?"

"I'm willing to have it written into the contract," he said, surprising her with the vehemence in his words.

She stared at him, watching his face for a sign that he was baiting her, but as Carla would've said, he was a serious as death.

"It's a good plan," he continued, seemingly at ease with the whole thing while she was a mass of twitching nerves. "Everybody loves a happy ending and considering how much time I spent at your place, it's believable. I even argued with Ron in favor of letting you tag along a time or two, especially after the dog died."

"After Sparkles died, you were my hero. I still have that stuffed animal you gave me and the drawing you made," she admitted.

He smiled. "I'm flattered. I would've expected that pooch to have been tossed out years ago."

"Thrown away? Never," she said, horrified he would even think such a thing. "It's one of my most prized possessions. In fact, it was one of the things we fought about before I called off the wedding. Mark didn't want me bringing any of my junk to clutter his home."

"What a jerk. His home? I thought it would have been your

home, as in the two of you." He chuckled. "I did see that movie, by the way, laughed until I cried. I'd have to be baptized, right? Naked with oil and water, like your cousin the last year I was in Stilton?"

"No! Well, oil and water yes, and they perform an exorcism at the door of the church, absolving you of all your sins, but you get to wear white shorts. Only babies and toddlers are naked."

"Absolved of all my sins—I doubt that—but as long as my family jewels aren't on display like your little cousin's were, I should be able to handle it. So, Marilyn Jean Summers, will you marry me?

Taking a deep breath, she reached out to shake his hand.

"I will."

* * *

Paul jumped up, hurried over to MJ, and lifted her high into the air, spinning her around and drawing the attention of every person in the room, but he didn't care. She'd said yes, and that was all that mattered.

Depositing her on her feet, he kissed her quickly to seal the deal.

"Come on," he said, taking her hand in his.

"Where are we going?"

She panted out the words, and he looked at her, afraid her asthma was acting up again. Her wide-eyed gaze implied he was insane. Maybe he was.

"We have to go shopping." He grinned so broadly, his face hurt. "You need a ring."

"Don't be silly," she protested, her breathing returning to normal even though her cheeks were red. "I'm not big on jewelry," she continued, licking her lips. "A lot of women don't wear engagement rings."

"Well, any fiancée of mine does," he replied, jutting out his jaw, well-aware of the fact it wouldn't seem real, even to him, unless she wore his ring, and he wanted this to be real for as long as it would last. "Besides, Mark and your mother will expect you to have a ring, and you know it. So, let's go pick one out."

"Fine, but can we make it something simple, please?" She reached for her drink and finished it. "I really don't want a gaudy ring like the one he gave me. Melena has it now."

"Was it a family heirloom?" That might explain passing the ring along.

"No, just something modern, and ostentatious." She shrugged.

"And Melena was satisfied with that?" he asked, unable to accept that any woman would be happy with a 'used' ring.

MJ nodded. "I guess so. She certainly flashed it around enough, and she did use my wedding plans, too." She chuckled. "Maybe Carla's right about the *Stepford Wife* connection."

Paul was glad to see that smile on her face and hear her laughter. He'd been terrified she was going to change her mind.

"But to be fair, I hated the ring and wouldn't wear it to work, so no more than a dozen people knew it had been mine."

"Let's forget all about the robot and the heel until Tuesday and go see what they have in the boutique." He tucked her arm in his and led her out of the bar into the lobby. "Raymond said Rosette can open the showcase for us."

"Raymond? You're on a first name basis with the manager?"

"Let's just say we have something in common." He wasn't going to let on what that was if he could help it.

"You were pretty sure of yourself, weren't you?" she asked, her eyes troubled once more.

"No, I wasn't presuming anything," he assured her, "but I'd hoped you'd agree to the marriage contract. I hadn't anticipated going beyond that."

He licked his lips. How could he make her understand that while this might not be the future either one of them had considered, it could be a good one. Loneliness was a monster that ate at your soul, bringing with it ghosts to ravage your sanity. Together, they could defeat the beast.

"The more I think about going through with the wedding, the better it feels. We'll have a wonderful vacation, and Mark will get what's coming to him and never hurt anyone again. Plus, you'll be able to live close to the school in the house you wanted all along. This will be a 'win-win' situation, you'll see."

"What about Melena? I mean, she isn't my favorite person, but I feel she's just a pawn in this. It really isn't her fault. Knowing Mark, the only thing he really cares about is her family's money. Carla suggested he might've knocked her up to get her to marry him. He didn't even propose until the end of May. Six weeks later, they're having the wedding I planned." She exhaled heavily and shook her head. "Apparently, her father's a big shot in Philadelphia, but knowing Mark, he would've realized he could get everything I'd ordered at a discount. That probably would've impressed the man. No matter how rich a person is, they're always keen to save a buck."

Paul swallowed the words he knew pointed to the woman's involvement in what had happened to MJ.

"Maybe she'll realize for herself what a jerk he is, and dump his ass." Although the fact she'd been complicit in his betrayal of MJ didn't bode well. He lifted MJ's hand to his lips and kissed her knuckles. "Let's go look at those rings." The last thing he wanted on MJ's mind right now was Mark.

"*Bon après-midi*, Monsieur Davis," Rosette said, as they reached the desk. "Madame Summers, Monsieur St Louis tells me you have found a place to stay. That is good, although my aunt was willing to take you in."

Paul frowned. She made MJ sound like a load of laundry drying on the line.

"How may I help you?"

"Raymond said you could help us pick out an engagement ring," Paul answered.

She smiled, but her eyes were narrowed. "I did not realize you were a couple. Monsieur St Louis told us very little other than the fact your lack of a room was not to be mentioned. Congratulations."

Rosette spoke rapidly to one of the other girls behind the desk and walked around it. "Our rings are of the highest quality. If you'll come this way?"

She led them through the boutique, past designer garments, shoes, and purses.

"Do you have a stone preference?" the woman asked, unlocking the showcase, removing two trays of rings, and setting them on the counter.

"Whatever she likes," Paul interjected before MJ could ask to see the least expensive rings. He wanted her to have the best, and it would be hers to keep when and if they parted ways—he liked the idea of "if" better than "when."

"What about that one?" He pointed to the ring that had caught his eye. The band was narrow and held a circular stone, blue-green in color. Surrounding the unusual gem were deep blue sapphires intermingled with diamonds, which gave the gemstone a pale aquamarine color, similar to the shade of MJ's eyes.

"Monsieur has exquisite taste," she said, looking at him, her eyes narrowed once more. "The platinum setting is a fitting canvas for this rare pale green sapphire. It's called the Star of the Sea."

"The Star of the Sea? Really? I thought all sapphires were blue," MJ said, staring at the ring, obviously captivated by it.

"Sapphires come in many colors, although it is true the most common are blue, like those surrounding this one."

She picked up the ring and tilted it—the center stone now looked teal.

MJ gasped.

"The jeweler who cut the stone did so in such a way that the ring changes the intensity of the color with movement. Does it not resemble our waters? According to the ancients, green sapphires bring good luck while teal ones denote fidelity."

Paul reached for the ring and slipped it onto the third finger of MJ's left hand. It was a perfect fit. Fate or *Quimbois*?

"What do you think? It's even named after you—well, sort of."

Rosette tilted her head to the left, her eyes scrutinizing them. The intensity of her gaze discomfited him.

"It's beautiful," MJ breathed, the words barely audible, her eyes fixed on her hand. She raised her head and gazed at him. "It must cost a fortune. I can't let you spend all your money…"

"Let me worry about that." He kissed her knuckle and the ring. Raising his head, his gaze captured hers. "It was made for you. We'll take it, Rosette. Charge it to my account."

"Very well, Monsieur Davis." She angled her head to the side, her smile closed-lipped. "I hope you will be very happy together. Such unions as yours are rare."

He furrowed his brow. "I'm sorry."

"I meant two people finding themselves like you have. You each arrived alone and now are bonded. It is very romantic."

Paul chuckled. "It is, isn't it?"

Did MJ ever feel the same way?

"Thank you," she said, her bright eyes still on his. "It's the most beautiful ring I've ever seen."

He swallowed nervously. Was that shimmer in her eyes from joy or sorrow?

"Not as beautiful as its new owner. Come on." He turned, and with her right hand in his, moved toward the bar once more. "This calls for champagne."

"Give me a second, will you? I'll meet you in the lounge."

She escaped into the bathroom before he could stop her.

Paul watched the door swing closed. This was way beyond what was necessary to bring Mark to his knees. He was being selfish, essentially trapping her in this situation, taking advantage of her vulnerability.

He didn't love her—he was incapable of that—but he liked her more than anyone he'd ever known and had for as long as he could remember. There was no denying he wanted her, too, but that was off the table. The longer she stayed with him, the greater the chances were he could keep his ghosts at bay. When she ended this, all he could do was hope they could remain friends.

CHAPTER TEN

MJ stopped trembling, unable to take her eyes off the ring on her left hand. She swiped at the tears creeping down her cheeks. What the hell was wrong with her? The man she'd dreamed about for years was offering her what she'd always wanted, had given her the most incredible ring, and here she was carrying on as if there'd been a death in the family.

Splashing cold water on her face, hoping it would obscure the damage from her tears, she stiffened her spine. Instead of bemoaning what she couldn't have, she should be grateful for what she would. If this engagement did result in a loveless marriage, she wouldn't be the only one caught in it.

Presentable once more, she entered the lounge. Paul stood at the bar chatting with Lucette. Was he flirting with the barmaid just minutes after proposing to her?

He turned toward her, and MJ's jealousy melted. Paul wasn't Mark. He had honor and integrity. She'd seen the look on his face when he'd fixated on her nipples last week. Just because their marriage would be a loveless one didn't mean it had to be a lustless one, too. There was nothing in the deal that said she couldn't try to seduce her husband, right? And if she succeeded, who was to say what else might happen?

"Congratulations," Lucette said when MJ stepped up to the bar. "May I see the ring?"

MJ extended her hand.

"*Magnifique*. It matches your eyes."

"Glad to see you're feeling better. What matches your eyes?" Lindsay asked, coming over to stand beside her.

"My ring," MJ said. "I've agreed to marry Paul."

She blinked. "You what?" The woman's voice rose two octaves.

MJ flashed her ring and removed her glasses.

"You're right; it does, and it's gorgeous!" Lindsay exclaimed.

"Congratulations," said Noel, reaching out to shake his hand. "I'm glad you guys worked things out. Lindsay was really worried."

"Paul will never let anything happen to me," she answered, knowing it was the truth. "Would you like to help us celebrate?"

Lindsay nodded, a huge grin on her face. "Damn right. I know there's a story here, and I want to hear it all."

"Two more glasses, Lucette," Paul said. "We'll sit over there."

Champagne in hand, they returned to the table where she and Paul had sat earlier. At Lindsay's insistence, between them they managed to tell her the story they'd concocted, adding details as the questions arose.

"This time, she said yes," Paul finished, reached for her hand, his eyes fixed on hers, and planted a kiss in the palm of it. "I intend to spend the rest of my life convincing her she made the right choice."

Even knowing it was all an act, MJ let herself be swept away by the gesture.

"That's so romantic," Lindsay said, putting down the camera after taking their picture once more. "Promise me you'll send me an invite so I can do your wedding pictures."

Before she could find a suitable answer, Paul stood.

"You've got it, but you'll have to excuse us now," he said, reaching to help MJ up. "We have to get back to the bungalow and give her mother the good news. We have the second seating for dinner. Maybe we'll see you both later tonight?"

MJ wanted to have Paul to herself, but she saw the wisdom of spending time with the other couple. If they accepted their relationship, then it would be that much easier to feed the lie to Mark.

"We've got the first, but maybe we can join you for drinks. Apparently, there's a big announcement about the treasure hunt between the two seatings," Lindsay answered.

"That will work. See you later."

Ten minutes later, holding Paul's hand even though no one could see them, the reality of what they were about to do struck her.

"Are you sure you really want to go through with this?" she asked as they walked along the path back to their bungalow. "We could put it off until tomorrow after we sign the nuptial agreement, or wait until Tuesday morning. Maybe we should've slept on it before we decided on this cockamamie plan."

Was that desire in his eyes? More likely it was a product of her own libido and one too many glasses of champagne.

"I don't need any more time, MJ. I'm in for the long run whether it's ten days, ten weeks, or ten months," he answered, unlocking the door. "But you'd better not Skype your mother with that sullen look on your face. She won't believe you're happy for a second, and I feel like the big bad shepherd leading the lamb to slaughter."

MJ giggled, no doubt a combination of the alcohol she'd imbibed and her nerves.

"Not that miserable, I hope. I'm just not looking forward to this. Mama will start with a lecture about my hair, and then … She may not believe me anyway. I've never been able to get a lie passed her in my entire life. Maybe we *should* wait until tomorrow. I'll look better, and I'll be as sober as a judge."

He laughed. "MJ, you're beautiful, your hair looks terrific, and that slight, inebriated glaze in your eye is from celebrating. The sooner Mama knows, the sooner she'll spread the news. Once all of Stilton is in on this, there's nothing Mark can do to her, or to us."

The compliment warmed her. "I hope you're right." If she told Mama what she wanted to be true rather than what was, it might work. "Here goes nothing."

MJ took a deep breath, plastered the smile on her face she reserved for those long parent-teacher evenings she abhorred, and dialed her mother's number on her tablet. Maybe they would be lucky, and Mama wouldn't have the computer on, or she would be out with her friends.

"MJ, I was waiting to hear from you, but I didn't expect a video call," her mother said. "Your hair! What have you done to your hair?"

"I wanted a change, Mama. I'm moving on with my life, and I wanted to get rid of the old and bring on the new me."

Instead of the lecture she'd expected, her mother dabbed at her eyes with the ever-present tissue stuffed in the sleeve of her blouse.

"I haven't seen you blonde like that since you were five years old, before your hair darkened. I should've realized how well it would suit you. Your father, bless his soul, used to call you Goldilocks. So many curls. You look younger."

MJ blinked back tears at the memory.

"Where are you? Is that your new apartment? It looks very expensive," Mama said. "Hold up the computer so I can see more of it."

When MJ didn't answer, her mother frowned. "Is everything okay?"

Realizing her mistake, MJ smiled broadly again. "It's fine, Mama. You just made me think of Dad. I miss him."

"So do I," her mother said, dabbing at her eyes once more. "Everyone I love has left me—even you." She sniffed. "I suppose that's why you made a video call, not only to show me your new hair, but your new apartment."

"No, Mama, although I'm glad you like my hair. The reason for the video call is to give you some wonderful news," MJ said, injecting what she hoped was the right amount of excitement in her words.

"You've come to your senses, and you're coming back to Stilton?" her mother asked, her voice rising on the last words.

"No. Mama. I told you that isn't going to happen." Grinning, MJ continued. "I thought it would be better to give you my news this way, rather than over the phone or in a text. First off, I have a confession to make. I'm not in Watertown. I'm on Paradise Island, off the coast of Martinique."

Her mother furrowed her brow and narrowed her eyes. "That place you were going on your honeymoon? By yourself? Are you crazy? I knew you were up to no good."

"She's not alone, Mrs. Summers," Paul said, standing so that his face was on the screen with hers, saving her from a lecture of epic proportion. "She's with me."

If this had not been such a serious moment, MJ would've loved to screen capture the stunned look on her mother's face and the joy spreading across it when she recognized Paul. Mama opened her mouth to speak, closed it, and opened it again.

"Paul? My God, Paul Davis? Is that really you?" she asked, as if she couldn't believe her eyes.

"Yes, ma'am."

"I didn't even know MJ had reconnected with you." Her pleased look turned into a scolding one. "It's so nice to see you again, but you should've called or sent a letter," she admonished. Frowning more deeply, she compressed her lips. "What's my daughter doing at a honeymoon resort with you?"

"Nothing I hope you won't approve of," he said smoothly. "Marilyn's agreed to marry me." He held up her hand so that her beautiful sapphire ring was visible. "I hope we have your blessing."

Mama screamed, praised half a dozen saints, and thanked Jesus before settling down again.

"Marry you? How? I don't understand? When did you meet again? How could you keep this secret?" The questions tumbled out of her faster than they could be answered.

With the patience of a saint, Paul related the cover story they'd created, while MJ smiled and filled in the pauses or answered her mother's awkward questions. He explained about the nuptial agreement, promising to send her a copy as soon as it was signed in the morning. He even managed to tell her they would be sharing a room because of a computer error without Mom getting upset. And when they promised to get her Louis James's signature, she did everything but purr. By the time the story was finished, Mama had bought it hook, line, and sinker. MJ felt a twinge of remorse at deceiving her mother, but knowing Mark couldn't hurt either of them soothed her guilt.

"No wonder you spent so many nights in your room and wouldn't consider dating, you little minx. I should be furious with you—with both of you—but I'm too happy to be angry now. Wait until I tell Aunt Sophia. She's been giving me such a hard time."

"Let me get some drinks, and we can have a toast," Paul said.

As soon as he left the screen, her mother's face grew serious once more. "MJ, do you love him?" she asked. "This isn't some rebound thing because of Mark, is it?"

"Do you really have to ask me that?" she answered, her fingers crossed. "You know how I've always felt about Paul." She smiled brightly.

"I predicted this would happen fifteen years ago," Mama said. "The heart knows what it wants. Papa would be so pleased. He loved Paul like a son. As soon as you get back, we'll have a big party to celebrate."

"Well, after the vacation, Paul and I both have to get ready for work," MJ prevaricated.

"Nonsense," Mama said, dismissing whatever argument MJ could've offered. "You'll come home for Labor Day, and we'll have an engagement party, followed by a Thanksgiving wedding."

MJ swallowed the panic rising inside her. "But Mama," she stammered, fighting for control. "That's only four months away. We can't possibly plan a wedding in that short a time with me living in Watertown…"

"That sounds great, Mrs. Summers," Paul said, handing MJ a glass of rum and fruit juice. "I think we can plan a couple of nights at Labor Day and a Thanksgiving wedding is a great idea. Just try to keep it reasonably small—no more than two or three thousand guests."

Mama burst into laughter, and MJ couldn't help herself from joining in. The man's idiotic comment had eased her tension.

"I promise," Mama said when she could stop laughing long enough to speak.

"I'll put in for the time as soon as I get back to work."

He raised his glass to her, and Mama raised her tea cup.

"Here's to the most beautiful fiancée in the world." He clinked his glass and took a mouthful.

MJ did the same and as soon as she put down the glass, Paul kissed her quickly, sending heat coursing through her at light speed.

"My son-in-law, a war hero, and a policeman," Mama crooned. "I'm so proud of you. MJ, you were right to follow your heart. It knew you and Paul were meant to be together. Does Carla know?"

"Not yet," MJ said, still stunned by the power of this second kiss. "We wanted to tell you first."

Mama chortled. "Don't be surprised if she hasn't figured out you were up to something. She was really cagey when I asked her about your place in Watertown. Well, since you're there, you'll be able to join the treasure hunt and maybe come home rich. I'll be watching each day."

"MJ mentioned you might," Paul said, suppressing his laughter. "But Mama with MJ in my life, I'm already the richest man here. We've got to go. We'll call after we see the notary in the morning."

"Okay. I'm so happy for you. Remember to wave at me if you see a cameraman. I'll tell everyone to watch for you. And behave yourselves," she said, giggling like a sixteen-year-old. "I can't wait to see my beautiful grandbabies."

MJ's cheeks heated. How red was she now? "Let's wait a while before we start talking about babies."

"You're not getting any younger. Maybe I need to move to Watertown, too."

"I love you, Mama," MJ said, suddenly feeling the tears pricking at the back of her eyes.

"I love you, too—both of you. Have fun."

MJ ended the call, turned to Paul.

"You're really good at this stuff, but you laid it on a little heavy at the end."

Before he could answer her, she dissolved into tears. He pulled her into his arms, and she went willingly, crying for all her lost hopes and dreams.

She would get through the next ten days if it killed her, and then, once they were back in Watertown, she would face reality. There was no way she could hold Paul to this promise because she didn't want what he was offering. She wanted it all—the love, the sex, and the babies—especially the babies. It might be unrealistic, but it was what it was.

* * *

Paul stood on the deck admiring the sunset. Sipping the scotch in his glass, he watched the gilded ball, suspended midway on the horizon, turn the water into molten gold. It was all part of the magic of this place. There had been sunsets in Kabul, ones with the sky blood orange, but what he recalled was the Maghreb, prayed from the minarets, the sound filling the streets just an hour before the attack.

He shook himself out of the memory. There were no silhouettes of soldiers marching in the distance, no veiled women rushing home, and no wails of sorrow here to mar the beauty of nature. No wonder people believed their dreams came true on Paradise Island. This was as close to Heaven on Earth as any mere mortal could get.

The patio door slid open, and he turned around.

Dressed in the brilliant colors of the sunset, MJ smiled at him, her top teeth embedded in her lower lip.

"Will I do?" She twirled.

He swallowed the sudden desire flooding him and moved behind the chair, hoping she hadn't noticed his body's response. Her long, floral skirt was paired with a bright tangerine, off-the-shoulder blouse that accented the slight tan she'd acquired during the day. She'd piled her hair loosely on top of her head, and large gold hoops hung from her ears, giving her a gypsy-like appeal.

"You look great, Kid," he answered, hoping the nickname would calm his libido. It didn't.

"You don't look so bad yourself," MJ smiled, indicating the clothes he'd donned.

He shrugged. "Just about everything I have that isn't military issue is new. I didn't have much call for this kind of get-up when I was in the service. I let the sales clerk in the men's store pick out my wardrobe—but I warned him I didn't want anything sissy."

She chuckled, her laughter as clear as a crystal bell. "Women love a man in uniform, and I'm hoping I'll get to see you in yours one day, but I doubt you would look sissy, as you put it, no matter what you wore. More champagne?" She indicated the bottle he'd just opened.

"Yeah. It was delivered with the hors d'oeuvres while you were showering. He suppressed the image of her naked once more and focused on the iced bottle. "It's part of the gold key package I mentioned earlier."

MJ looked over at the plateful of delicacies and reached for a tiny stuffed tomato. She seemed calm enough, but the slight trembling in her hands showed that to be an illusion.

"Well, at this rate, I'll be the size of a house by the time we leave here. I probably don't need any more alcohol, but the stuff's addictive. Are you going to pour me a drink or just stand there holding the glass?"

"Sorry." He poured the wine into the flute and handed it to her. Reaching for his own glass, he raised it in a toast. "Here's to us."

"To us," she said echoing his words and sipping from her glass. "You realize by now, our 'engagement' is probably all over town. No doubt that selfie Carla made us send has gone viral, too. You're stuck with me for a while, but God willing, we can get out of this without having to go through with that wedding, although how we can manage that is beyond me. You shouldn't have agreed to that Thanksgiving date. Hopefully, we can get her to put it off, but Mama's even more stubborn than I can be."

Paul frowned. "MJ, I don't consider it 'stuck' with you, and if we do have to get married on Thanksgiving, so be it. I don't have any other plans. If you want to think of someone being stuck here, it's you. I'm coming out on top."

He groaned silently at the image that flashed through his mind. "What I mean is I finally have someone to watch baseball, football, basketball, and hockey with."

She chuckled. "The sports I can manage, but we'd better be cheering for the same team or you'll regret it."

"New York, all the way, but it's Yankees and Islanders for me."

"Yankees work, but I'm a Ranger girl, through and through."

He chuckled. "I can't wait for hockey season."

"It's beautiful, isn't it?" she indicated the Caribbean sunset.

Paul blinked. "Do you always do that?"

"Do what?"

"Change topic mid-sentence."

She hissed in a breath. "Sorry, when I'm stressed I usually say the first thing that pops into my head. I'll try not to, but I've been known to jump from one topic to another in an instant."

"Don't change for me," he said, liking her just as she was. "I love a good multi-tasker. Now, what were you saying about the sunset?'

Giggling slightly, proof that some of the alcohol might indeed still be in play, she grinned. "I rarely got to stand around and watch the sun go down at home. Nine out of ten times, I was either working on something in my room or Mom had me stirring a pot in the kitchen. By the way, Carla said you make great bean soup."

"*Bazinga,* as Sheldon would say. You've done it again."

Her cheeks pinked.

"Sorry. Like I said—"

Reaching out, he touched her arm and turned her toward him, the contact making him wish he could pull her closer, but that wasn't on the agenda. He shook his head. "Don't. As for the soup, a man's got to eat, and I was pretty fed up with mess chow and K-rations. Being able to cook for myself was the greatest gift your mother ever gave me. I look forward to cooking for you." He moved away from her.

"I would like that," she said, turning back to the sunset. "We'll have to work out some ground rules in Watertown. We really can't live together if we aren't married, you do know that?" she said, her voice tinged with sorrow. "You have a great place, but I have one, too. While Mom might be okay with this for ten days, both she and the diocese will frown on cohabitation before the vows."

"I figured as much, but we can still hang out together—watch the games, have dinner, take King for walks … Carla doesn't seem to like your new digs."

MJ choked on the mouthful of champagne and set the glass down quickly.

"Ouch. That stuff feels awful coming out of your nose," She blinked her eyelids rapidly and waved her hands in front of them. "Carla's just too fussy. The place needs a good cleaning, and it'll be fine. Besides, it may only be for a few months."

She turned back to the sunset.

He covered her small hand with his. Being with her, catering to her, wanting her, treating her as if she were the most important person he knew would be easy. The problem would be controlling those desires when he was alone with her at night. Acting on them could only bring her anguish and heartache.

MJ turned away from the sunset, pulling him out of his musings.

"Shall we go?" she asked, finishing the champagne in her glass and setting it on the tray next to the empty plate of appetizers they'd unconsciously consumed. "It's almost half-past seven. Isn't that announcement coming up soon? I'm so stressed right now, I'm not sure I can eat another bite—not that I need to. I've been eating and drinking all day."

"Relax. We've thought of everything. As far as eating goes, I'm convinced these resorts spike the food so that it runs through your system more quickly." He chuckled. "We did get a fair amount of exercise in the pool and playing in the surf on the beach."

"I had a great time this afternoon. It's hard to believe I managed to go into the water without having a heart attack, even if I did squeeze your hand a little. Carla tried to get me into a wave pool last year, and I lost it."

She looked up at him, her eyes serious once more.

"Being able to forget about Mark and Melena and what's going to happen in a couple of days was the best part," she admitted. "Thank you for that." She indicated the champagne. "Can we cork that and finish it later? I wouldn't mind a midnight swim before bed. You did say I can touch bottom and that nothing dangerous comes in here, right?"

Paul choked. Visions of her glistening in the moonlight wearing nothing but the low cut/high cut swimsuit she had on earlier had him hard as a rock once more. He swallowed awkwardly, begging his body to settle down and not betray him.

"No predators, guaranteed, and a swim before bed will help you sleep better."

It certainly wouldn't help him.

MJ smiled, picked up her evening bag, and turned toward the door.

"Shall we?"

Before he could answer, her tablet chimed.

"It's from Carla. Let me see what she wants and write a quick response." Opening the message, she read it and shook her head.

"I was right. News of our engagement is all over Stilton." She frowned. "I sure hope this plan of yours works and isn't going to come back and bite me on the ass."

Paul refused to dwell on that delectable image.

"Tomorrow, after we sign the nuptial agreement, we'll take a small boat back to Martinique for the day. Lindsay and Noel are joining us. I didn't realize she was a professional photographer. Maybe you can post a few for Carla to fuel the rumor mill, but I think, once we make an appearance on *Louis James Live*, we won't have to worry about that. What I said earlier still goes. You could end up in the movies."

"You're so full of crap, your eyes should be a darker brown than they are," she said, her cheeks the brightest he'd ever seen them.

"Why is it you don't know how beautiful you are?"

"Maybe because I'm not. I'm just ordinary, and sometimes because of my eyes, barely that. Now, are we going to eat or not?"

"On one condition. Since we've done all we can until the infamous Achilles Heel and his bride arrive, I suggest we forget about them and just enjoy ourselves for the next forty-eight hours or so."

She smiled. "I like the sound of that."

"Then, my lady, dinner awaits."

Before this vacation ended, Paul intended to give MJ the best gift he could. Not only would she face her fear of the water, she would realize what a beautiful woman she was, and what a prize she would be to the man smart enough to love her and be loved by her. More than ever, he deeply regretted the fact it couldn't be him.

CHAPTER ELEVEN

MJ had only taken three steps out onto the boardwalk when Paul scooped her up into his arms.

"Put me down." The aroma of his aftershave was doing strange things to her slightly inebriated senses.

"No way. Not with the shoes you're wearing. The last thing I want is for you to twist your ankle. Relax and enjoy the ride."

He pulled her closer, and she had no choice but to put her arms around him and hang on. While she admired the man who'd come to her rescue, she liked this playful side of him. He had secrets—dark secrets—that tore at his soul. She'd seen it in his eyes when he talked about Kabul, but he'd pushed those memories aside for her. If only they could stay like this … two friends on vacation having fun.

Paul veered off the path they'd used earlier.

"Where are we going?" she asked. "The dining room is near that door, isn't it?"

"I'm taking you in through the main doors."

"I went in that way when I arrived, silly," she said and giggled, enjoying herself far too much to quibble. "You don't really have to carry me that far."

"Just settle back. I've been told that along with the information session, there's a surprise tonight."

She smiled and relaxed into his arms.

"How does that saying go? 'Eat, drink, and be merry?'"

For tomorrow we die.

The thought sobered her. Once Mark and Melena arrived on Tuesday, everything would change.

But not yet.

Tonight, she would pretend that all of this was real. Overhead, twinkling lights resembled hundreds of fireflies flitting through the canopy.

"Whoever designed this place is a genius," she said, unable to prevent the sense of wonder from filling her. Paul stepped out of the trees. The building was awash in the soft glow of multicolored floodlights, bathing the walls in rainbow colors. He climbed the front steps, set her gently on her feet, opened the main door, and stepped back, letting her walk in ahead of him.

It was like stepping four hundred years into the past. The foyer had been transformed into the façade of a small town. Wooden signs, suspended from black wrought iron bars, identified the various areas. The reception desk even boasted leaded windows similar to what one might've seen in a tavern or coach inn. The plants that had originally given the impression of the rainforest indoors, now were grouped to resemble a park in a town square, the plush couches replaced with rattan benches, the modern lamps with old-fashioned candle lamps. The exquisite doors leading to the bar had looked out of place earlier, but now fit right in.

"It's incredible," she said, taking in every aspect of the area at once.

"This way."

Paul led her toward the closed doors under the restaurant sign. MJ inhaled sharply as the dining room doors opened. The tiered room reminded her of the ballrooms she'd seen in copious historical movies. Below the mezzanine area where they stood with the other diners, the round tables covered in white damask cloths with floral centerpieces were set for six. Surrounding the exotic flowers, the tea lights in various sized crystal holders flickered. She'd never seen anything more beautiful. At the far end of the room, one long table, set for six, a beautiful three-tiered cake decorated with flowers and Paradise Island's signature plaid ribbon in the center of it, stood beyond an empty space no doubt meant as a dancefloor.

Around her, animated couples chatted and took pictures of the fairytale setting. Servers moved through the crowd offering appetizers and champagne.

"I'm speechless," she said, accepting a champagne flute. "It's so ... I want to pinch myself to prove I'm awake and not dreaming. I feel like Cinderella arriving for the ball. This is all so much more than I could ever imagine. I can't believe Mark almost took it all away from me."

Paul grinned. "Let's forget about the ugly step-groom. I don't mind playing Prince Charming to your Cinderella." He lifted his glass in salute. "Lucette mentioned the staff and the islanders had gone out of their way to make this coming week special. She wasn't kidding, but unlike in the fairytale, all this doesn't have to end at midnight."

"But unfortunately, once Mark and Melena arrive, it will," she said, sorrow thick in her voice.

Paul put his arm around her, sending waves of desire crashing through her.

"Only if we let them, but for tonight, we're two people determined to have fun, remember?"

"I'll try, but ... So many things can go wrong—"

"Stop with those negative waves," he said, repeating an old Donald Sutherland line her father used to use. He squeezed her shoulder gently and tucked her closer to him. "The next ten days will fly by, I promise, and when you get home, Mark will be only too happy to give you back every cent he took from you rather than face prosecution."

"If you say so," but that waiting for the other shoe to drop feeling wouldn't go away. "Who gets to sit up there?" She sipped the champagne which she really didn't need, and used her glass to indicate the head table.

"The bride and groom, of course."

She almost choked on the mouthful of wine. "You mean this is someone's wedding reception?"

"Raymond explained it earlier," he said. "On Saturday nights, it's customary to honor all the newlyweds. Louis James thought it would be nice to spotlight not only the treasure hunt but the resort itself. Apparently, everyone's name went into a bowl and one couple will be chosen to be the hosts for the treasure hunt. Don't worry, our names aren't in there."

"MJ."

She turned and smiled when Lindsay and Noel made their way over to them. Lindsay had a camera strapped around her neck.

"Isn't this incredible? I can't believe what they've done to the place."

MJ nodded. "I feel like I've walked into someone's fantasy."

"Well, if they pick your name, it could be yours."

Knowing that couldn't happen eased MJ's nerves.

"I like the contacts better than the tinted lenses, even if they do make your eyes more blue than aqua."

MJ smiled and shrugged. "I'm blind as a bat without lenses of one kind or another, but since bright light sometimes hurts, the tint is necessary."

Lindsay nodded. "That makes sense. Have you heard about the draw? If they were to call my name," she said, "I would faint."

Before MJ could answer, a bell tinkled, and she turned toward the sound.

"*Mesdames et messieurs.*" Raymond St Louis wore a tuxedo with a plaid cummerbund. If the grin on his face were any wider, it would split it in half. "Who does not dream of hitting the jackpot? As you know, starting Wednesday, we will host a three-day hunt for the infamous pirate Jean Lacorneille's treasure. Legend says his ship sunk during a violent storm, the Hurricane Ovine, if we name it after the witch said to have conjured it, with his ship's hold full of Spanish gold and cursed Incan treasure, originally looted by Francisco Pizarro's men from the treasure vault of Atahualpa, the last Inca emperor. The story goes on to say some of the men survived, brought here to Paradise Island by mermaids who took pity on them. Where did the ship sink? No one knows exactly. We have Lacorneille's charts and maps. Will Antoine Leroux be the one to find the booty, or will one of you uncover the secret cache? Magic and mystery have always gone hand-in-hand on Paradise Island."

As a cold breeze filled the room, MJ shivered.

"They just turned up the fan on the AC for effect," Paul whispered, but he pulled her closer to him.

"Tonight," the manager continued, "thanks to *Louis James Live*, earlier this evening, the names of those of you here were placed in this bowl. Rosette, a descendant of one of Lacorneille's men, will select the name of the first couple. These two will act as Best Man and Matron of Honor to the couple lucky enough to be the resort's official bride and groom for the week. Rosette, if you please?"

Rosette dipped her hand into the bowl and pulled out a small gold envelope.

"Monsieur and Madame Richard Larson, from Toledo, Ohio."

A high pitch squeal filled the room as a couple stepped forward. The man resembled Rick Moranis. He was short, no more than five-foot-five, wore glasses, and seemed ill at ease in his white dinner jacket. The woman beside him was a touch shorter and a little plump, but looked lovely in her black, sequin-trimmed, floor length gown. She was so excited, she trembled.

MJ smothered a giggle that the man's name should fit his appearance so well. The crowd applauded. When the clapping subsided, the manager spoke once more.

"And now, Rosette, the second attending couple."

Once more, the woman dug into the bowl, pulled out an envelope similar to the one drawn earlier, and handed it to Monsieur St Louis.

"The second attending couple are Monsieur et Madame William Smith, from Fresno, California."

A woman shrieked and dragged her husband to the stage. MJ recognized the couple who'd been standing in front of her arguing before she'd gotten off the ferry. Whatever their problem had been, they obviously hadn't resolved it. While the woman looked thrilled, the man beside her seemed annoyed.

"And now, if you would draw the name of our lucky bride and groom."

Rosette's gaze scanned the crowd before she dug into the bowl once more. Handing the envelope to Monsieur St Louis, she stepped back.

"Your bride and groom, and the hosts for this week's treasure hunt and festivities are..." A drumroll filled the air.

He slowly opened the envelope, increasing the tension in the room. He pulled out a small white card and looked at it, his eyes growing large. He held up the paper for Rosette to see and asked her a question. She shook her head, the astonishment on her face no less than his.

Voices buzzed in the room. The manager shrugged and smiled.

"Monsieur et Madame Paul Davis."

Lindsay screamed as the room erupted into applause.

"That's you," she cried.

MJ turned to Paul, unable to mask the panic on her face, somewhat mollified when the surprise on his matched hers.

What the hell just happened?

"And you said our names weren't in the draw," she hissed before Mendelssohn's Wedding March flooded the room.

"That's what Raymond told me," Paul said, his gaze begging her not to overreact. "I swear it on my mother's grave."

MJ read the truth in his eyes. Whoever had orchestrated this fiasco had done so without Paul's knowledge.

The manager bustled over to them.

"*C'est incroyable*," he said, softly enough that no one around them could hear. "Look at this."

He held up two small cards. On one, their names were written in an elaborate script that was almost calligraphy. On the other, the names 'Monsieur et Madame William Smith' were typed.

"As the Greeks would say," Raymond continued, his eyes filled with wonder, "the gods have cast the dice. I took your name out of the bowl myself just an hour ago. How this happened I do not know."

"The script looks familiar," Paul said, eying the small card.

"*Mais oui.* It's Jean Lacorneille's hand. You only have to look at his diary to see. It must be *Quimbois*."

"Or a very clever forger," Paul said.

Monsieur St Louis frowned. "But why? How could such a person know the card would be pulled?"

"I don't know," Paul answered, trying to smile pleasantly at the well-wishers.

"And we aren't married," MJ whispered, fighting not to give in to the terror flooding her.

"*C'est de rien.* Once you sign the agreement in the morning and after Monday night's *noce civil*, it will not matter. Here, on Paradise Island, you will be bound. *Que sera, sera.*"

Before she could ask what a *noce civil* was, a chant went up from the crowd.

"Kiss her, kiss her, kiss her."

MJ looked up, fear and panic making the butterflies in her stomach battle for supremacy.

"Looks like this is out of our hands now. In for a penny…" Paul bent his head and met her lips gently.

The moment his lips touched hers, she lost the ability to think. All she could do was feel. Unlike the two brief pecks he'd given her, this time, Paul made love to her mouth. Heat pulsed through her, sending wave after wave of desire rushing along every nerve she possessed. Unconsciously, she opened her mouth, and his tongue dove into her. She was on fire, a phoenix rising from the ashes of whatever existence she'd had before. The room vanished, and she floated in this new magical space where only the two of them existed. Desire consumed her, and she responded to his kiss with every fiber of her being. This was the culmination of her long-ago dream, the touch she couldn't imagine until now, and it was worth every second she'd waited for it.

"Ahem."

The sound pulled MJ back to reality as Paul raised his head, ending the kiss. Desire flashed through his eyes for a second, and with it the realization that he was rock-hard against her, proving he wasn't as immune to her as she thought he was. That was no brotherly kiss. MJ looked away, certain her cheeks were blazing.

"On the kiss meter, I'd say that was a twelve," Lindsay said and laughed. "And it looks like I captured it." She held up her camera for her to see.

MJ couldn't breathe. The image showed a couple deeply engrossed in one another. Was that really her? If Paul hadn't been holding her, she would've collapsed for sure.

"Shall we go, darling? They're waiting for us, and I'm sure these people want to sit down and eat," he said loud enough to be heard by those around them. "We can finish this later." He winked.

The gesture and words shattered the magical illusion, as if he'd thrown a bucket of ice water on her head. He'd been playing it up for the crowd. He didn't have to catch his breath because the kiss had meant nothing to him other than adding another layer to this charade, and as far as his arousal went, Mark had always been able to rise to the occasion and look what that had gotten her.

Drawing on her inner strength, she batted her eyes, not to flirt but to keep the tears away.

"Of course." She turned and smiled at the maître d. "Lead on."

As they approached the head table, MJ pasted a grin on her

face. No one here would see how devastated she was, especially not Paul.

"Enjoy your meal." The man snapped his fingers and moved away from their table.

"Bonsoir. I'm Etienne." The young Creole dressed in black tie and wearing white gloves smiled at her. "Would you care for an aperitif? The sommelier's suggestion is a *kir royale*, crème de cassis topped with champagne."

"Why not," MJ said. Could she get drunk to get through this? Probably, but it wouldn't help one damn bit, and she would most likely end up making an even bigger fool of herself.

"Make it two," Paul said, his voice clipped, causing MJ to look at him. Was he upset?

Etienne nodded and slipped away.

"MJ, about that kiss," Paul started to speak, but she cut him off, not wanting to hear him say that it had been an act.

"I think we did great, don't you? The crowd certainly bought it." She smiled despite her inner pain. "Lindsay said it was a twelve, so thank you. If we can keep this up, Mark will believe it, too."

Paul cocked his head to the left, his brow furrowed, his eyes troubled.

"Glad I lived up to your expectations." He bit off the words.

She frowned, but before she could say anything, the Larsons arrived at the table and sat on Paul's left.

The woman laughed. "Hi. I'm Cindy. Wait until the folks back home see this. We won a shot at the treasure hunt when Ricky entered an online contest. Now, we're going to be on television. Best of all, since we were chosen, on Monday, we'll be moved to an ocean-front bungalow. I'm amazed there would be one available."

MJ looked at Paul, who nodded. As emotionally stressed as she was, it took everything in her not to burst into a fit of giggles that would lead to tears she would never be able to suppress.

"I'm MJ. This is Paul. There must've been a cancelation," she said, astonished she could speak, guessing that bungalow had been intended for Mark and Melena, and he would be livid when he saw his accommodations. She almost wished she could see his face when he checked in.

First, he would turn an ugly shade of gray, and then the color would change, slowly becoming a livid red, when he would vent his anger and disdain in one of his infamous snit-fits that usually resulted in him getting whatever he wanted. But not this time.

Cindy's voice pulled her back to the table. "Can you believe it? We've never won anything in our entire lives, and here we are."

"Maybe you'll find the treasure, too," MJ said, not because she believed it, but to keep her mind focused on the here and now, away from M and M, and the hell that would ensue once they arrived.

"Wouldn't that be something? My mother's looking after the terrors for us. Wait until they see us on television."

Pain pierced MJ at the thought of the children she might never have. "You've got kids?"

"Yes," Rick said, joining the conversation and pulling out his wallet to proudly display a picture of two dark-haired, dark-eyed boys. "Ewan's five and Sean's three, and believe me, they can be a handful. This is the first time we've left them." He reached for his wife's hand. "She deserves this and so much more."

Cindy blushed and kissed her husband. Envy tore at MJ.

"You're wrong. I have everything I could possibly need back home, but while we're here ... This is a wish come true. This place is so beautiful it's as if it's touched by magic."

Magic or voodoo? If only MJ could be sure nothing else would go wrong. As it was, Mark wouldn't like this latest development one damn bit, and Mark on the warpath wasn't a pleasant sight. Added to that, he'd lost his waterfront bungalow. He would be fit to be tied. She shivered.

"Cold?" Paul asked softly, the concern in his voice genuine, touching her despite her distraction.

She smiled. Did it look natural? It felt like a plastic mask.

"Not really—one of those 'someone walked over my grave moments.' I'm fine."

Paul frowned, but before he could say anything, Cindy went on. "When we got off that boat, I thought I'd died and gone to Heaven."

"Here come the Smiths," Ricky said. "Can you believe it? Bill and I belong to the same chat group—Seekers of Treasure, S.O.T. for short. The man's been preparing for this ever since the hunt was announced. I guess you two will be on our team now, but there's a half-dozen of us among the Indiana Jones wannabes. I've never found more than a few arrowheads, but some of the others have been much luckier. I didn't think we could come because of the cost, but if Lady Fortune's smiled on us once, maybe she'll do it again." He stopped talking and cocked his head to the left. "I've seen you before, but you aren't part of the group." He frowned. "I've got it. You were on the ferry." He stared at MJ, his eyes narrowing, the intensity in his gaze making her squirm.

Cindy frowned. "You were, I'm sure of it, but you spent most of the time up on deck in the rain. Why on earth would you do something like that?"

MJ shivered once more and swallowed the panic rising within her.

"I asked her the same thing," Paul said, coming to her rescue. "Marilyn hates flying and gets airsick. I'm sure she didn't have her land legs before she got on the boat. It's the one thing about her that's never changed. We were forced to arrive separately, not by choice, I can assure you. I would never have foisted that ordeal on her if I could've prevented it."

There was no mistaking the honesty and sincerity of what he was saying even if he was speaking about something entirely different from what Cindy and her husband thought. The fact he remembered her aversion to air travel surprised her.

"Believe me," Paul continued, "this place may be beautiful, but it isn't much fun without the right person by your side."

MJ fought to hang onto her composure. This entire situation was rapidly going from bad to worse. Paul had smoothed over a gap in their cover they'd ignored. What if something else they hadn't thought of cropped up? It would only take a minor error to expose the truth, and if Mark were the one who found it...

"That explains why you looked so lost and out of place. You were feeling sick and lonely," Cindy said, satisfied with Paul's excuse. "I sure know what that's like. I'm a lousy traveler, too. I've got Dramamine if you need it ... better safe than sorry."

MJ nodded, sympathizing with someone else who didn't travel well.

"I've got lots, thanks. Besides, I won't need it again until I fly home."

The second attending couple reached the table, the man looking no happier than he had earlier.

"Hello, I'm Christy Smith, and this is Bill. Congratulations. Isn't this all so exciting?" the woman offered her hand.

"It certainly is," MJ said, reaching for it, surprised by how cold it felt.

Etienne set her cocktail in front of her, poured some of Paul's beer into a glass, and then turned to take drink orders.

Without being obvious, MJ scrutinized the newcomers. Slender, almost to the point of emaciation, wearing a tight, midnight-blue, satin dress, Christy had hazel eyes and shoulder-length blond hair, let loose to brush the tops of her bare shoulders. In contrast, Bill was bald, with a dark mustache and goatee. The heavy-set, broad-shouldered man wore a white dinner jacket and black shirt, no tie. His dark trousers hung low, belted under a belly that proved he enjoyed his food and drinks. On his left hand, he wore a wedding band and next to it, a diamond ring that would pale in comparison with some of the Super Bowl rings she'd seen.

"Is everything to your liking?" Monsieur St Louis asked stepping up to the table, his brow furrowed.

"It couldn't be better," Christy answered.

MJ noted her smile didn't reach her eyes.

"So, we'll be a team of six looking for the treasure?" Bill's voiced oozed annoyance.

"*Mais non,*" the manager answered, the same smile on his face he'd worn when she'd first arrived. "There are ten teams of six now, but twenty couples arrive Tuesday, raising the number of people per team to ten."

"I was hoping to be able to hunt with some friends," Bill grumbled.

"Perhaps you can persuade others to change places." The manager shrugged. "It is of no importance who is on which team."

Bill nodded, but he didn't seem any happier. "Christy and I are huge fans of Antoine Leroux. Will he be joining any particular team?" he asked.

"Monsieur Leroux will spend time with each group. He will not play favorites as you say." The manager turned to them. "Monsieur et Madame Davis, you will meet me in my office at nine in the morning, yes? We have a few things to discuss before you leave for your day-long excursion. It will take no more than half an hour,

I promise."

"We'll be there," Paul said, raising her hand to his lips and kissing the palm.

Heat radiated from the spot his lips touched and flooded her. It was the second time he'd done this, and despite knowing it was all an act, the gesture turned her to mush.

Ricky stood.

"That's my cue. As Best Man, I get to kick off the festivities."

MJ glanced around the room, noting everyone was seated. Her friends were on the mezzanine, Lindsay's face hidden by the camera she clicked furiously.

"Ladies and gentlemen. Bear with me. I'm really not used to doing things like this," Ricky said.

The crowd laughed softly.

"On behalf of Louis James and the Paradise Island Resort, I would like to welcome you all to the island." He raised his glass. "May the fates be kind to all the seekers of treasure."

MJ stifled a giggle. Was he really singling out his group of friends? She forced herself to sip her cocktail.

"This is really good. What's in it?"

"Black current liqueur, champagne, and a dash of *Quimbois* magic," Cindy said, holding up the small card with the information printed on it. "It is damn fine, isn't it?"

"We can all use a touch of magic now and then," Paul whispered in MJ's ear.

"Magic got us into this," she mumbled. "Maybe we should find Lucette's grandmother and see if we can get out of it. The least she could do is tell us what's next."

He chuckled. "Sometimes a surprise or two is nice." He reached for her empty hand and squeezed gently. "We've got this."

"So you say," she answered, not in the least bit convinced they did.

Paul lifted her hand to his lips once more, the gentle kiss sending shivers down her spine.

"We agreed to forget about anything that could go wrong and enjoy ourselves, remember? Tonight is ours, Cinderella."

MJ swallowed. And how many tomorrows would she have before she turned into a pumpkin?

CHAPTER TWELVE

Taking a swig of his beer, Paul smiled as MJ laughed at something Ricky said. If it were at all possible, she looked even more vibrant and desirable than she had earlier in the evening. The kiss they'd shared had filled him with a hunger unlike anything he'd ever felt before. Selfishly, he wanted this to last, not just a day or ten, but forever.

He sighed, knowing he'd probably consumed more alcohol than he should've—hell, they all had—but he refused to believe it was the booze talking. Being with her seemed to fill up the emptiness inside him.

Dinner had been superb, each course as tasty as the last, but MJ hadn't eaten much.

"I tell you, MJ," Ricky said, back on the topic of the treasure, something he'd been quite vocal about throughout the meal. "There have been too many mermaid sightings for it not to be real. You were an English teacher. I'll bet you can cite a whole pack of myths about them intermingling with men ... They know where the treasure is."

"I agree," Bill said, finishing his bourbon. "My research says the sea witch called up the storm because Lacorneille stole something from her—gold talismans of unspeakable power. His mermaid girlfriend hid the chest before the witch could find it. If one mermaid hid that treasure, another can find it. All we have to do is find a mermaid. I know what to look for. The eyes give them away. They're almost colorless. If I can catch one, either with a tail or legs, I'll force her to give it up."

MJ giggled, but Paul saw fear in her eyes. "If she's got legs, how will you know she's a mermaid?"

"I'll know," Bill said. "Don't you worry your pretty little head about that."

Paul reached out and took MJ's hand in his. If either of those guys ever found out about her eyes and the fact Lucette called them mermaid eyes, it could be a real problem. He'd stick close to her in case. Mark might not be the only predator to watch.

"Whether they know or not won't help us unlock the secret though. We'll need Lacorneille's descendant for that," Christy said, almost as interested in the treasure hunt as her husband. "I'll bet Leroux is the one. We just have to cozy up to him—once we find it, of course. Let's dance."

Rick and Cindy got up as well. The music was too fast for him and his bum knee, so they stayed at the table with Lindsay and Noel who'd joined them after dinner.

"Wow! I had no idea so many people here were into that treasure hunting stuff. Noel and I knew about it, but it wasn't a motivating factor for the vacation. So, you've got light eyes. Are you holding out on us?"

MJ choked on her drink.

"Are you alright?" Lindsay asked, patting her back. "I was just teasing."

"I know you were," Paul said. "Lucette called them mermaid's eyes. I'm pretty sure I can get her not to repeat it, but I would appreciate it if you didn't say anything. While I can guarantee my fiancée doesn't turn into a fish in the water, I'm not sure Bill and Rick would believe it."

MJ hiccupped. "I don't even like the water."

Lindsay chuckled. "Don't worry. We were all in the pool together, remember? I'll be honest with you. I think Bill's just a big blow-hard who drinks too much, but I don't trust him. It's odd that he and Ricky would be friends. Cindy and Christy certainly aren't. Those two don't have anything in common. At least they won't be underfoot tomorrow."

"I agree. That couple's strange," Noel added. "Great music, isn't it? I'd expected Caribbean, but this is a nice surprise."

"I agree," Paul said, lifting MJ's hand to his lips and watching the rose bloom in her cheeks once more.

The band had stayed partially hidden behind the diaphanous gold curtains, while the singer, dressed in a red sequined gown, stood in front of them, her sultry voice perfect for the jazz tunes she sang. He and MJ had danced several times, including to the first song as would the bride and groom at a wedding. He'd enjoyed having her in his arms, and while the ache in his leg was noticeable, he wasn't about to forego the pleasure of one more dance.

"Ladies and gentlemen," the singer said. "This will be our last song for tonight. I hope you've enjoyed this set and our tribute to the late, great George Gershwin. Here's one of my personal favorites made popular by Ella Fitzgerald, the First Lady of Song."

"Dance with me," he said, standing and pulling her up, making it impossible for her to refuse. A single, slow trumpet sounded out the first few bars of "Summertime" and then the singer's voice filled the room. MJ swayed, and he held her closer to him.

"Don't worry, I've got you," he said as she stumbled.

"I know," she answered and giggled softly. "You're my knight in shining armor. Good thing, too. Don't look now, but I think the island is moving."

Her knight in shining armor? If only it was true. He might've come to her rescue, but everything he did from here on in was selfishly for him. He pulled her closer.

"Then, my lady, hang on to me."

The dance floor filled with the last twenty or so couples still enjoying the festivities, and he held her more tightly than before. In just over twelve hours, his world had been turned upside down. If this was *Quimbois* magic, bring it on.

"Having fun?" he asked, his lips pressed against her hair.

"Yes, too much fun. Bill and Ricky are kind of creepy, fixated as they are on mermaids and the treasure, but Cindy is sweet, and Christy looks lonely to me. I think she's been really sick, too."

"Well, if her husband is always this obsessed with treasure, she probably is."

She nodded. "I keep waiting for the clock to strike midnight and turn everything back into what it was."

"Sorry, Cinderella, but that clock won't be striking tonight. We've got another two and a half days and two nights before we even have to think about anything else but enjoying ourselves."

She sighed and nestled into him. "I know. Cindy's right. There's something about this place that makes you believe all your dreams can come true. No matter what happens, I want you to know this has been the best evening of my life."

The music ended. "Shall we go back and have that swim?" he asked.

"That sounds lovely, and I promise not to turn into a fish. Let's say goodnight and go."

Paul chuckled, led her toward the table, but it was empty.

"Looks like they've all left. Must've gone while we were dancing."

MJ shrugged, tried to stifle a yawn, and picked up her bag. "Then we'd better get going, too. We do have to meet Monsieur St Louis at nine, and it's after midnight."

He led her out of the dining room and crossed to the side door leading to the lagoon and their bungalow. As soon as the door closed behind him, he lifted MJ into his arms.

"You don't have to carry me again. I can take off my shoes and walk."

"On the crushed stone? I don't think so. Besides, you might step in lizard doo-doo."

"Yuck," she said, putting her arm around his neck.

Paul walked slowly wanting to savor the moment. He was only a few feet from the door, when her hold on his neck relaxed. Looking down at her, he realized she was asleep.

Reaching for the keycard in his jacket pocket, he opened the door, carried her over to the bed, and pulled down the covers. Laying her down, he removed her shoes and covered her. He wouldn't wake her. She was exhausted, and so was he. On top of that, his leg hurt like hell.

He ignored the sheet of paper on the table, no doubt it was simply the itinerary for tomorrow. After going into the bathroom and taking two of the painkillers he still had for nights when the leg ached like it did now, he stripped down to his shorts. Eying the couch, he knew he should go over there, but sore, tired, and as drunk as he was, the bed was too inviting. Besides, the thing was wide enough for a whole damn platoon and King, too. Surely they could share it for just one night. Beat, he lay down and closed his eyes. With any luck, he could sleep a few hours without the nightmares.

* * *

MJ drifted awake, the sheets and blankets so tightly wound around her, she was suffocating. The pounding in her head, worse than any stampeding elephant migraine she'd ever suffered, nauseated her. This must be the champagne hangover Paul had mentioned.

Where was she?

Vaguely, she remembered leaving the main building. He'd insisted on carrying her once more ... she must've passed out ... Not her finest moment.

Opening her eyes, painfully dry and gritty thanks to her contact lenses, she glanced around the dark room. The nightlight in the bathroom beckoned, and admitting she needed to go in the worst way, she untangled herself from the bedlinen and sat up. The room spun, increasing her nausea. Closing her eyes once more, she waited for the movement to stop.

Since she was in the bed, Paul must've opted for the couch. Poor guy. He would have to curl up like a pretzel to fit. She should probably trade places with him, but that would mean waking him, and she wasn't ready to face him just yet. Besides, at the moment, she wasn't sure she could get that far without vomiting all over.

Could she make it to the bathroom without opening her eyes? Probably not. She stood, swayed slightly, cracked her eyes open, and stumbled toward the light. Once in the bathroom, she attended to her most pressing need and then wove her way over to the counter.

To puke or not to puke?

Despite her trembling hand, she removed her disposable contact lenses and tossed them into the trash. Peering closely at her reflection, she groaned. She should remove her makeup—raccoon eyes weren't her best look—but with the headache from hell and the taste of the bottom of a taxi cab in her mouth, she just didn't have the time, heart, or desire to do so. If she took some analgesics and something to settle her queasy stomach, she might live through the night.

Certain the contents of her stomach intended to stay where they were for the moment, she stripped down to her assless, beige silk panties, wishing she'd actually brought a few pairs of the old standards with her instead of letting Carla's, "if you feel sexy, you'll act sexy" philosophy dictate what she'd packed.

Taking two acetaminophen tablets and a dose of anti-nausea medication, she rinsed her mouth with mint-flavored mouthwash and turned off the bathroom light. She stood in the doorway, allowing her eyes to adjust to the darkness, then staggered back to bed. She plopped down belly-first, burying her face in the pillow, praying that wakeup call Paul had ordered was hours away.

Sometime later, still half asleep, MJ opened her eyes. The room was slightly brighter than it had been, but the headache was still a steady throbbing. Reaching for the quilt, she turned onto her side and snuggled up to what must be the pillows and bolster that had been on the bed earlier. Warm and toasty, the scent of Paul's aftershave tickling her senses, she drifted back to sleep, feeling safe and contented.

The ringing phone roused her from a deep sleep, but MJ refused to let go of the dream. Cuddling more closely into the warm, hard body beside her, she sighed. The bells sounded again.

"What the hell?"

Her eyes flew open. Pushing away from Paul's chest, as if it were one of the island's iguanas, she bounced across six-feet of bed, and jumped up.

Paul turned over, picked up the phone, and then hung up.

"What are you doing in my bed?" she demanded, embarrassed by the remnants of the dream which apparently wasn't a dream at all.

"I was sleeping," Paul answered and yawned. "How are you feeling?"

"That's beside the point," she snapped back.

He chuckled. "Not a morning person, I see." His glance raked her up and down. "You got undressed during the night. So, if you got up, then you knew I was here, so the question would be, what are you doing in *my* bed?"

MJ scowled. Just like a man to turn the tables on her.

"Since you put me here in the first place, let's forget it," She rubbed her temples to ease the throb still present. Nothing had happened—at least nothing she remembered. "What time is it?"

"Just after seven. I ordered breakfast for eight. We need to be in the manager's office by nine. Why don't I shower first?"

"Fine, but I … you know…"

"Be my guest." He sat up and pulled the pillow up against the headboard. "Nice outfit, by the way." His face shone with approval.

"This?" She raised her eyebrows in surprise. "I know you like the Yankees, but…" Looking down at her oversized shirt, she almost died when she realized it was caught up in the band of her thong on one side, exposing half her ass.

"Damn you," she shouted, running into the bathroom and slamming the door.

After relieving herself, she took two more analgesics and found her glasses. There was no way on earth she would be able to put contact lenses into her eyes this morning. Able to see once more, she stepped back into the room. Paul was up, dressed in a pair of shorts, waiting for the machine to brew his coffee. He held a sheet of paper.

"What's that?" she asked.

"Tonight and tomorrow's schedule of events."

She chuckled, the gesture sending a fresh wave of pain through her head.

"A honeymoon resort with a 'to-do' list? Now, that's funny. I think most people know what to do."

Expecting him to laugh, she was surprised when he didn't, holding out the sheet of paper instead.

"Just remember I had nothing to do with this."

Frowning, she reached for the document.

"I know," she admitted, curling her lip. "Since the manager says he didn't do it, it has to be one of the staff. I'm not ready to believe some pirate came back from the grave just to make our lives more complicated than they are." She huffed out a breath, grateful he was standing far enough away not to smell what she could taste. "Last night wasn't so bad. Rick and Bill are a little intense, too caught up in the treasure hunt and mermaids, but we don't have to spend every waking moment with them, do we?

After all, this dog and pony show won't start for another couple of days. This latest snafu, especially the loss of that bungalow, will make Mark livid." She imagined his face as purple as the grapes in the basket on the counter in front of them. "But we will have to tell Mama about this before the show airs on Tuesday morning."

"Try Monday night," he said, his body tense, his chin indicating the page she held. "The main event gets underway with a *noce civil* Monday night at eight, aired in a special episode of *Louis James Live*."

"Damn," she grumbled. "And the camera always adds ten pounds. The way I ate yesterday, I'll look like a little tub of lard."

"You'll look great. In fact, I recommend the eyes. They give you that zombie look—so popular these days. Bill might not even notice their color."

She laughed and winced at the pain in her head. "Very funny. The makeup will come off when I shower. By the way, what's a *noce civil*? I know what *civil* means, but *noce*?"

He chewed his lip and ran his hand through his bed-messed hair.

"It's a wedding, a civil ceremony like at city hall. It's the second step in a French marriage contract."

"What?" she asked, feeling the room tilt, and backing into the bed.

"We're getting married tomorrow night at six."

"But we can't." MJ dropped down onto the mattress. "We don't have residency…" She fought to remember what Paul had told her about French matrimonial laws.

"It won't be legally binding, but it'll seem that way to the audience," he admitted, shrugging his shoulders and sitting beside her.

Before he could touch her, she jumped up, panic sending her flying into the bathroom, where she lost whatever she'd consumed last night. Feeling more wretched than ever, she rested her head against the toilet seat.

"I can see the thought of marrying me doesn't thrill you," he said, his voice filled with sorrow. "If you think about it, it doesn't change anything. We'll sign the paper this morning, go through with the farce tomorrow night, and then get on with our original plans."

"But Mama…"

"That won't change either," he continued. "I'll go through with the Thanksgiving wedding. I know it's not quite the way we planned, but we can make it work. Look at the bright side. It'll solve any problems with the diocese, and you can move into the house as soon as you're ready. There are three bedrooms, remember? You can shower first while I get you something to settle your stomach." He helped her stand. "If you really want out of this, say the word. I'll get you to Saint Pierre and wait until you can get a flight home."

MJ nodded, and Paul left the room, closing the door behind him. She undressed and stepped into the shower, the hot water pummeling her body, the dejected look on Paul's face filling her mind.

Reaching for the bottle of shampoo, she tipped some into her hand, rubbing it into her head none too gently. This was all her fault, her mess. Getting even with Mark was important to Paul—it had to be considering what he was willing to endure for it. Maybe something else had happened between the two men, something he hadn't shared. The least she could do was play her part and see it through. Her heart told her to stay while her head begged her to make a run for it. The only thing waiting for her when this was over was more heartache.

Less than two hours later, feeling slightly better, MJ checked the room before picking up the bag she'd packed for the sightseeing tour to Martinique. The headache was still a mild throb, but she'd been able to eat and that had helped the nausea. She'd chosen to omit her contact lenses in favor of the Jackie O prescription sunglasses she loved. Feeling like a condemned prisoner, she turned and followed Paul out of the bungalow, determined to put on a happy face for his sake.

"You're going to love this excursion," Paul said, reaching for her bag and then taking her hand. "Diving is more exciting than just paddling around."

"What? Me?" she screeched. "Have you lost your mind? You can't really expect me to go underwater."

"You'll be fine. I'll be right there with you, and with a tank, you can breathe naturally. You trust me, right?"

"Trust has nothing to do with it," she argued. He had to be joking. "You're pulling my leg, but if you're trying to get me to relax, this won't do it."

"True, but I have taken your mind off what we're about to sign," he said, his eyes pleading with her. "There's absolutely nothing to stress about. Everything is out of our hands now, so relax. I will never put you in danger or let you down."

The way he said it made it seem as if he was talking about a lot more than the upcoming paperwork, the trip to Saint Pierre harbor, and the civil wedding tomorrow night.

"Are you sure you really want to do this?" she asked, knowing he would understand what she meant, grateful the dark glasses covered the confusion in her eyes.

"I am."

She hadn't realized they'd reached the main building until he held the door open for her.

Paul walked over to the desk.

"*Bonjour.* Monsieur St Louis is expecting us."

"*Mais oui.* Please follow me."

The young girl, dressed in a madras skirt and white blouse, wearing a fan-like coif on her head, led them to a door behind the desk. She knocked.

"*Entrez.*"

Monsieur St Louis sat behind a huge desk, a *demi-tasse* of coffee in his hand.

"I hope you had a pleasant night?" he asked as he stood. "*Merci, Collette. Du café pour tous, s'il-vous-plait?*"

"*Oui, monsieur.*"

"Sit, sit," the manager said, indicating the chairs across from his desk. "Unfortunately, I have not been able to figure out how your names ended up in the draw, but perhaps it is better this way since Monsieur Theopolis will not be able to dispute your relationship. Before my brother-in-law arrives, I will explain what should happen at the *noce civil* tomorrow night."

The receptionist returned with a tray of coffee and set it down on the desk. As soon as they'd served themselves, with a fair sprinkling of French words she didn't quite understand, Monsieur St Louis took them through the process.

As he spoke, MJ stifled a laugh at the irony of the situation. She'd purchased the simple, strapless, white and silver Schapiro gown she'd planned to wear for her wedding specifically because it could be worn again as an evening dress. Because the dress had been altered, she couldn't return it, and since she'd paid a fortune for it, she'd decided to keep it rather than send it to a consignment store as Carla had suggested. At the last minute, she'd added it to her suitcase.

Monsieur St Louis had just finished speaking when his brother-in-law arrived with the legal document that would make this fantasy a reality. He explained the clauses quickly, his English harder to understand than his brother's, but eventually, she signed beneath Paul's name.

Once it was done, Paul insisted the prenuptial agreement be scanned and emailed not only to her mother but to her brother, too.

"I want everyone to know this is all above board," he said, reaching for her hand again. "Now, I guess we should make that call so that when Mama is watching Monday night, this won't be too big a shock to her system."

Twenty minutes later, feeling as if she'd been caught in a twister and carried off to another reality, MJ walked beside Paul, her hand in his.

"That went well," Paul said.

MJ shook her head. Who was he trying to kid? It had been a disaster.

"Seriously? You've got to be joking. Didn't you hear her? She'll probably invite everyone she knows over to the house to watch. Hell, she may even rent a hall. She's got what? A day and a half? That's enough time to plan a whole damn reception."

Paul chuckled and led her to the main doors.

"It wasn't that bad. Look at it this way. It'll be all over town by tonight, and the Achilles Heel will be powerless to do anything about it. Now, let's get down to the dock. The boat should arrive at any time. We'll be away until late this afternoon, and we're going to have fun without thinking of anyone but ourselves. After all, this is our honeymoon."

MJ shook her head.

"You do realize you're certifiable, don't you?" She scrunched up her nose at his 'who me?' face and giggled. Maybe she was still drunk. "Fine. I give up. If you're determined to see only the positive side of this, who am I to burst your bubble?"

"Maybe I am crazy, but for the first time in months, the future looks good to me," he said, pulling her into his arms and giving her a quick kiss.

Her world tilted once more, until she realized there were other couples around them. Paul was playing his part again.

"You've given me something I thought no one and nothing ever could. I can't remember when I've ever been happier," he said softly, smiling down at her, looking so sincere that she almost believed him. Almost.

He reached for her hand once more and twined their fingers.

"Added to last night's unexpected surprise, I watched an incredible floor show, danced with the most beautiful woman in the room, and made new friends—some I probably won't add to the Christmas card list." He chuckled.

She noticed his slight limp, more pronounced now that the footing wasn't as solid as it had been.

"Your knee hurts. I'll wear flats and carry my heels tonight, and I will definitely take it easy on the champagne. We can avoid the dancing, too."

He hefted her beach bag onto his shoulder and followed the others toward the dock. "I did warn you the stuff had a kick, but carrying you was a pleasure, not a chore, and I'll gladly do it again. And as far as the dancing goes, promise you won't deprive me of that. The knee's fine. Did you put in sunscreen and a hat?"

"I did and added two towels," she answered, chewing her lower lip. "You were joking about me joining you on this dive, weren't you?"

He smiled and shook his head. "I never joke about diving. Prepare to let the ocean dazzle you. You'll have the time of your life."

"If I survive," she grumbled.

His lips met hers again, but this time, the kiss was sweet and slow, turning her legs to jelly, making it impossible for her to think straight.

Paul pulled away slowly. "You're going to love this, you'll see."

MJ, surprised to see they were alone on the path, could do nothing but nod.

CHAPTER THIRTEEN

Fifteen minutes later, she stood at the bow of a smaller boat than the one she'd been on yesterday, looking out at the turquoise ocean as she waited for Paul to return.

Reality asserted itself. Paul wasn't the one who'd lost his marbles, she was. Diving? In over twenty feet of water? What was she thinking?

"Good morning. Noel's gone down below to get me coffee. I assume Paul's done the same?" Lindsay asked, coming to stand beside her. "I must say you look a lot better than you did yesterday on the boat—a little terrified, but definitely happier."

"I am," MJ answered, "but Paul's planning to take me on this dive, and I've got this thing about deep water. He promises not to leave my side, but..."

If something did go wrong, it might be a blessing in disguise. Dying was probably the only way she would get out of this.

Lindsay chuckled. "You mentioned that yesterday, but I wouldn't worry. Paul's an expert diver, and he hasn't left your side since you wilted at his feet yesterday. I couldn't bring it up last night, but the look on your face when they pulled your name ... I wish I'd had my camera ready."

"I was surprised, that's all," MJ said, worried her new friend was far too perceptive.

"Uh-uh. Not buying it," Lindsay answered, shaking her head and frowning. "Terrified would come closer to the truth. In fact, I would say you were in a bigger panic last night than you are now."

Heat burned her cheeks, and MJ knew it had nothing to do with the sun.

"I'm not much for fanfare and being chosen 'Bride for a Week' will put me in the limelight, the last place I want to be." She removed her sunglasses. "People haven't always been kind because of my eyes. Growing up I was teased a lot, and considering Bill's determination to bag himself a mermaid, based on some cockamamie theory he has about their eyes ... I guess I'm just gun-shy."

Lindsay raised her eyebrows quizzically. "I don't know what kind of people you hung out with, but I love your eyes. You know, one of my favorite actors has the same condition."

MJ frowned. "Condition?"

"Yes. Didn't anyone ever explain to you? It's called central heterochromia. I did a photoshoot on Benedict Cumberbatch. While his irises are a deeper color than yours, you both have eyes that are two distinct colors, blue and green. Since yours are paler than his, they resemble this water. That's probably why the locals call them mermaid eyes." She chuckled. "Your ring has similar characteristics. Since Bill's been reading too many weird tales, I would keep your glasses or contact lenses on when you're around him. The man's clearly an idiot, but I don't trust him. He's got gold fever, even though he apparently has more money than I can shake a stick at. That chunk of gold on his finger has to be worth thousands, and the rocks Christy was wearing weren't paste. As far as the rest of it goes, I don't buy it for a minute. I can tell when people are lying, and while there's truth to what you say, there's more than a little bullshit, too."

MJ's blood ran cold, and she sucked in a breath.

"Hang on. Let me finish. I don't think you and Paul came here planning to get engaged, but you two have history—a blind man can see that. The atmosphere between you crackles."

"Here you go," Paul said, handing her an orange-gold concoction, ending her conversation.

"This isn't coffee." She eyed the glass.

"It's a mimosa—similar to that cocktail you had last night. Might even have a touch of Quimbois magic in it, too." He winked. "A little of the hair of the dog. Try it."

MJ lifted the glass and sipped. She licked her lips.

"They might be onto something here. I'm not used to alcohol so early in the morning, but this is delicious." She raised her glass once more.

Smiling, Paul moved closer to the rail and slightly behind her so that she was spooned against him for stability.

"The coffee wasn't ready yet," he explained. "I thought this would be better."

Lindsay chuckled. "I'll go and find Noel and get one of those pretty things myself." She indicated the champagne flute. "We should be at the dive site in half an hour. I'll see you later."

"What was that all about?" Paul asked, as soon as the woman disappeared down the steps. "You two looked so serious."

"Lindsay noticed how stunned I was last night when they called our names. I guess I didn't hide it as well as I thought." She didn't want to talk about last night. Taking another mouthful of mimosa, she smiled. "This may be giving me extra courage, but since it's possible this dive of yours will be my last, tell me all about this statue I'm risking my life to see."

Paul tightened the arm around her waist and settled her against his chest, tilting her head to meet his gaze. "Be prepared to be dazzled by my great store of knowledge."

"If I'd been smart, I could've avoided all of this and left your life in peace instead of a tangled mess."

Paul bent his head and whispered into her ear, his voice husky, and his warm breath sending goosebumps dancing along her flesh.

"But I would be alone and miserable. I may regret a lot of things in my life, but this will never be one of them. We're in this for the duration."

He kissed the top of her head. While he was only performing for the other couples around them, keeping up appearances of a man in love, being held like this felt good and, as much as it was a mistake, she wanted the feeling to last.

Resting his head on hers, Paul continued. "You already know people around here believe in mermaids. Sixteenth century sailors were a superstitious lot. Some considered the creatures to be good luck, while others believed they were sirens intent on luring sailors to their deaths. These same people believed women aboard a ship were bad luck and that fully clothed women in particular upset the sea gods. In that case, a naked mermaid used as a ship's figurehead was meant to appease them. In dire situations, if the weather turned bad, some sailors apparently tossed their fully-clothed female passengers overboard."

MJ shivered. "You aren't saying anything here to bolster my confidence."

Paul laughed. "Don't worry. No one's going to throw you into the ocean while I'm around. Besides, that bikini keeps you from being overdressed. Now, where was I? Oh yes. I'm sure Bill knows this, but apparently, if you want to find a mermaid, at least in the water, legend says you should look for her purse."

"A mermaid's purse? Seriously? You're teasing me," MJ said, leaning into him, trying to get past the heebie-jeebies she'd just experienced.

"No, not lying. They're actually the egg capsule or casing of some species of shark, but legend has it, if you find a mermaid's purse, then that lady isn't too far-off."

"I'll have to keep my eyes peeled for that. Tell me about what we'll see."

"Well, Manman dlo means mermaid in Creole," he began, his silky voice attracting the attention of those around them. "Maybe she's meant to represent Ovine, the sea witch, but unlike the Moai on Easter Island or the Olmec stone heads in Mexico, she was created by a French artist and sunk in place in 2004. She's part of an underwater exhibit that includes Yemaya, the siren. Legend claims mermaids are responsible for all the shipwrecks in these waters, including Lacorneille's floundering, and the statues are meant to remind people to respect the sea. They've become elements in a man-made reef..."

Paul continued his narrative and she relaxed, growing more and more enthralled by the minute. When they arrived at the dive site, she was so eager to see what he'd described, she didn't balk when he fitted her with a full scuba outfit.

"Without your glasses, things will be blurry, but there's just so much to see. We'll get as close as we can. It's only twenty-five feet down."

She swallowed and nodded. Did it really matter how deep it was? As long as she could stave off a panic attack and not disgrace herself completely, this might work.

Paul reached for her and pulled her into his arms. "I'll be with you every single second we're down there. Trust me. Ready?"

"Let's do it." With a trembling hand, she put the rubber mouthpiece into her mouth.

Falling backward into the water didn't bring on the panic attack she'd expected. Instead, the water enveloped her like a soft blanket. Paul reached for her hand, indicated the statues below them, and led her down.

Two hours later, she sat in the boat once more removing the equipment.

"That was the most incredible thing I've ever seen. I don't know what I was afraid of." She couldn't stop her hands from moving a mile a minute in her excitement. "The mermaid and the siren are outstanding works of art, and those wrecks ... if you can get passed the idea people died on them, are truly awesome." She chuckled. "Although that wahoo—that's what you called it— swimming out of the hole in the side of that last ship, scared the daylights out of me. He was beautiful, but my God, he had to be eight feet long."

Paul laughed. "That's about right. The fish don't usually pay any attention to the divers. The natives around here call it a *peto*. He's a great fish to catch. If we get a chance to go fishing you'll see. They put up a terrific fight, but those silver marks fade quickly once they're caught."

"You mean once they're dead," she said softly, her heart breaking for the poor animal. "He's safe from me." She put her hands up in surrender. "Besides, anything that large would pull me right off the boat, and I've no desire to make a spectacle of myself and become shark bait."

She unfastened the weight belt, handed it to the young man collecting their gear, and put on the green flowered cover-up. The matching bikini was nice, but she felt a touch too naked in it.

"Look." He pointed to the water off the starboard side.

She turned to see a school of dolphin swimming passed the boat.

"They're beautiful," she exclaimed, watching them jump out of the water, racing one another and the waves. She blinked. What the hell was that? It looked as if that last dolphin had a much larger tail than the others, and she could've sworn it was purple.

"Did you see that?" she asked.

"See what?"

"That last dolphin ... it looked like it was purple."

Paul shook his head. "Probably some rainbow effect from the water sparkling in the sun."

MJ nodded, not convinced. He was right. Her eyes had to be playing tricks on her.

"Do you remember when I used to complain when Mom or Dad wanted me to do something I didn't want to?"

"Yeah," he answered, a wide grin on his face at the memory. "You usually stomped your foot and said, 'Stop forcing me to have fun.' Your dad always cracked up at that. For years whenever the guys in my unit complained about something, I thought of that."

"I'll skip the foot stomp, but thank you for forcing me to have fun."

She leaned over and kissed him, pulling away quickly when several couples joined them.

Paul licked his lips as if to taste what she'd left there and smiled.

"You're more than welcome. I enjoyed it as much as you did. I was afraid I'd lost you down there when you tried to speak, and the mouthpiece popped out. Funniest face I've ever seen."

She giggled. "I'll bet. The last thing I expected was for all those fish to come swimming out of the mermaid's mouth and mob me. It's damn hard to make any sound with that mouthpiece in. The colors were amazing. They might not have pretty faces, but the mahi mahi's coloring is incredible."

"It is," he agreed, pulling her into his arms. "I'm very proud of you, not panicking and replacing your mouthpiece like a pro. Let's go find Lindsay and Noel and get a celebratory drink. You've earned it. By now you must be the most photographed woman here." He winked.

"I wish she would find another model," MJ said, pouting slightly. "It's too bad we didn't see one of Bill's mysterious mermaids. That would've been a photograph for the ages."

* * *

MJ sipped her champagne and munched on a shrimp canapé. Wait until Mama, Ron, and Carla heard about her day. They would never believe it.

The bathroom door opened. She turned away from the

window. Smiling, her hand paused halfway to her mouth, whatever thought she'd had gone forever. With her head tipping to the left, her gaze focused on the scrumptious man standing in front of her.

Dressed in a white dinner jacket, black shirt, white tie, and slim black trousers, Paul reminded her of Pierce Brosnan and her heart beat double-time. The coat emphasized his broad shoulders and slim waist. He walked over to her and smiled, exposing that dimple she loved but rarely saw. Her mouth wasn't the only part of her that watered.

"You look incredible," he said. He reached for his flute of champagne on the table. "To us."

She echoed his words and clinked her glass against his. "Thanks for giving me a fairytale-perfect day."

"It isn't over yet. Lindsay must think we need time alone. The way she bamboozled the other four into an early dinner almost gave me whiplash."

"She wasn't very subtle, was she?" MJ giggled. "But she did promise to show them the pictures and the videos she took today, which should appease the guys and give them a mermaid fix. Poor Cindy didn't look too thrilled though."

"I'm sure she'll get over it. Apparently, they were going to join some of their chat room friends who made it here. Not every wife can be as crazy about this adventure as the men are." He shook his head. "Bill's hoping to rearrange the team and add his fellow treasure seekers to it."

"Well, I hope we don't have to be on it, especially if they are all fixated on proving mermaids exist. I would much rather be with Lindsay and Noel, but as far as Cindy goes, I think she has a crush on you," she said, licking the champagne from her lips. "Didn't you see the way she made gaga eyes at you last night? You'd better watch yourself, or I might have to challenge her to a duel or something." She burst out laughing. "If only you could see your face. You look as if you've been poleaxed."

"You don't have to worry." He reached for her empty hand and stepped close to her until their bodies almost touched. "The only woman here who interests me is you."

MJ moved away slightly, heat rising in her cheeks. He had to stop looking at her and saying things like that before she combusted.

"Yes, well, at least with Lindsay eating early, I won't be photographed as much. After this vacation, I may never let anyone take my picture again."

The scent of his woodsy aftershave filled her with longing.

"Since I had to share you with the others all day," Paul said, "it'll be nice to have one night alone before the dog and pony show, as you call it, starts."

She nodded, reality rearing its ugly head once more. It was all a game, an elaborate trap for a rat. MJ exhaled heavily. While she was pleased he enjoyed her company, she wanted so much more from him and from this marriage—she wanted it all. How ridiculous was that?

* * *

Paul swallowed the last of his champagne and inhaled MJ's delicate floral perfume. He would gladly forgo dinner and spend the rest of the evening here with her, but the bed loomed large, and he was sober and wide awake. Staying here any longer was dangerous and foolish.

"Finished?" he asked.

"Yes. I don't want to repeat last night's overindulgence." She handed him her empty flute. "If we're lucky, maybe we can sneak into the dining room unnoticed."

"If you think you can walk into that room and not have every eye in the place on you, you're delusional. In that dress, you look ethereal, almost too beautiful and delicate to be real." The powder blue sheath left her right shoulder bare, and, with her hair loose, the curls held in place with combs, she reminded him of Aphrodite. Ron had a picture of his perfect woman on his bedroom wall years ago, but the goddess of love couldn't hold a candle to MJ.

She looked away and tucked in her chin. "We're alone, Paul. You don't have to say things like that here.

"Dismiss my words if you want to, but once you see Crazy Camera Lady's pictures, you'll agree."

MJ blushed so deeply he could feel the heat coming off her cheeks.

"You shouldn't call her that. Noel can get away with it, but you might hurt her feelings. And as far as the other stuff goes, it makes me uncomfortable."

He shook his head. How badly had the Achilles Heel damaged

her ego?

"Fine, have it your way. Come on, Cinderella. Day two of the ball awaits."

"Do you think there'll be any more surprises?" she asked, reaching for the blue shawl and silver bag on the bed.

"Maybe, but nothing like last night's whopper. According to today's itinerary, we're looking at a seven-course meal, followed by a floor show highlighting both Incan and Martinique culture to put us in the right frame of mind for the treasure hunt. The evening will end with calypso music and dancing."

"A seven-course meal? If I eat all that, you'll have to roll me home."

Taking the wrap from her, he placed it across her shoulders, his hand lingering to caress her bare skin, watching the flush rise in it. The urge to kiss her was strong, but if she objected to compliments, she would balk at that for sure. He'd already stolen more than a few today and didn't want to push his luck. Swallowing his desire, he studied her face, but she wouldn't meet his gaze, her cheeks a deeper shade of pink than ever. The moment passed.

"Shall we?" He opened the door and led her out of the bungalow. "You'd better hang onto me. Those heels could easily get caught in one of the openings between the slats of the pier. The last thing you want to do is go ass over teakettle into the lagoon." When they reached the crushed stone, he picked her up. "If those shoes are dangerous on the boardwalk, they're doubly so here. Besides, I like this part of my job."

As soon as they reached the side door, he put her down. Tonight, the lobby had been transformed into a jungle. Here and there, miniature animatronic monkeys and mechanical birds moved among the branches of large tropical plants. On the far wall, a floor to ceiling screen showed water tumbling over a waterfall.

"This is absolutely amazing," she said, rubbernecking to take in everything. "Look at the orchids. And the noises ... If I close my eyes, I won't be able to tell it isn't real. It even smells like the rainforest." She scrunched up her face. "They didn't let one of the iguanas in here, did they?"

Paul smiled, captivated by the joy and wonder radiating from her. "I doubt it."

"Good. I wouldn't want to run into one on my way to the ladies' room." A feline's yowl filled the room. "Did you hear that?"

"Probably the recorded cry of a jaguar."

"It's incredible."

"The décor represents Peru in the early sixteenth century. Check out the staff."

Instead of their usual plaid dresses and fancy knotted head scarves, the women wore ankle-length, cream-colored dresses bound at the waist by a wide, woven, multicolored sash. In contrast, the men wore white knee-length tunics, heavily embroidered with Incan designs.

"It's like stepping onto a movie set," she said.

"In a lot of ways, it is. Resorts like this hire special event coordinators to create lasting memories. Lindsay must've had a field day. She probably filled another card."

The tropical setting begun in the lobby continued in the dining room. Tonight, the tables were separated by lush plants, giving the illusion of privacy. Here and there, mock Incan statues added to the atmosphere, while murals depicting temples and ruins decorated the walls. On the table, candlelight flickered from centerpieces resembling ancient golden artifacts.

He stepped up to the desk, gave his name to the maître d who wore the regalia of an Incan official, complete with a feather cloak and headdress. The man smiled, checked their names off a list, and led them to a table beside the dance floor.

"Etienne will see to your needs. Enjoy your meal." He snapped his fingers and left to be followed immediately by the young man.

"Bonsoir," Etienne said, costumed like the others. "Would you care for an aperitif? Tonight's suggestion is a mocha martini."

Her eyes lit up at the mention of the drink, and Paul chuckled.

"Make it two," he answered.

The young man nodded and left after placing a menu card on the plates in front of them. Dinner would start with a squash soup, with six other courses to follow.

"I'll never be able to eat all of this," MJ said, "but I intend to try. It all sounds delicious."

"If there's something you really like, we can look up the

recipe online. This surprise isn't so bad, is it?"

MJ smiled. "No, it isn't. I keep wanting to pinch myself to prove I'm not dreaming."

"You aren't the only one having fun, and I don't plan on letting M and M ruin it." He reached for her hand and squeezed it gently before letting go. "Look up and smile."

Noel and Lindsay waved at them. As expected, she wore her camera. He couldn't see the other four, but they had to be up there somewhere.

Before she could comment, Etienne returned with the martinis and set them on the table in front of them. The glasses were trimmed with crushed chocolate and sugar crystals. A white chocolate butterfly, its wings dusted in gold sugar, sat on the edge of the rim.

"It's so pretty," MJ cried, reaching for her glass.

"It certainly is," Paul agreed, picking up his drink and raising it to her. "To an enchanted evening and the most beautiful woman in the room."

She looked down and chewed her lower lip.

"Thank you." She sipped the martini and closed her eyes. "I've died and gone to Heaven. This is fantastic."

"Sweetheart, this is only the beginning," he whispered. He'd never meant anything more.

CHAPTER FOURTEEN

MJ stood beside her chair applauding as the costumed *bélé* dancers took their final bow along with the *tambour* and *tibwa* players, the soloist, and the choir.

"That was absolutely amazing. Who would've thought you could get such a sound by pounding two wooden sticks on a bamboo tube? And I've never seen a man ride a drum as if it were a horse before, but it was incredible. I'm really glad Monsieur St Louis explained the history of the folk dance before it began." She giggled. "He did look rather impressive dressed as an Inca emperor."

"I agree, although all those feathers have to tickle. The Inca *tuntuna* was really something, too, but the last one was mesmerizing." He smiled. "Not sure I'm up to learning how to do it though. I prefer dances where I can hold you in my arms." He wiggled his eyebrows making her laugh.

She was about to comment when Bill materialized beside the table, ruining the moment. Damn the man for destroying the magic. He pulled up a chair and sat.

"The others will be here shortly," he said as if his presence was not only welcomed but expected.

So much for their romantic evening.

"Rick's getting some fresh air, and the girls are in the bathroom. Lindsay and Noel have packed it in. She said something about capturing the sunrise." He smiled, but it didn't reach his eyes. "I saw those pictures she took today. Quite impressive. No one would believe it was your first time diving. I thought you said you were afraid of the water. Don't you know it's not nice to lie?"

Goosebumps trailed down her back.

Paul smiled. "She wasn't kidding, believe me. I've known her more than twenty years, and until today, she never even got her face wet unless it was in the shower, but she took to diving as if she'd been born to it."

Bill guffawed. "I'll bet she did. You know what they say—just like riding a bicycle."

MJ frowned. What did bicycles have to do with diving?

"I don't know about bicycles," Paul said as if he'd read her mind. "But I was very proud of her. When she accidentally lost her mouth piece, she didn't panic."

"I noticed that. Pretty impressive. Even the most seasoned divers get upset when that happens. Most of them don't breathe well underwater. How long were you without it?" he asked, his gaze piercing her.

MJ frowned, uncomfortable with the third degree she was getting. What the hell difference did it make how long she'd been without the mouthpiece? The point was she hadn't panicked.

"Only a second or two. If you saw the video, you know that school of Creole wrasse scared the daylights out of me when they came out of the statue's mouth. It looked like she was exhaling blue smoke." She chuckled. "I didn't expect that. I gasped, and the mouthpiece fell out. I put it right back."

"I'll bet you did. Did you notice anything else down there? Anything familiar? Like the reason for those colored auras?" he asked, leaning closer to her, invading her personal space.

She frowned. "How could anything be familiar? I've never even seen pictures of Manmam dlo. As far as the auras as you call them, I thought they were underwater lights. Aren't they?" She leaned into Paul who'd moved his chair beside hers to watch the show. He put his arm around her, the gesture comforting.

"I suppose they could be." Bill's eyes narrowed. "I noticed you moved pretty fast when you went deeper to look at the wrecks. Where did you learn to dolphin kick like that? I'll bet you've got a hell of a set of core muscles. For someone who says she can't swim, you moved as fast as some of the Olympic swimmers I've seen."

MJ shrugged. "I don't know. I didn't even realize that was a swimming stroke. It just felt natural."

"I'll bet it did," he mumbled.

Etienne appeared with a couple of other servers and added three more chairs to the table just as the women arrived.

"Wasn't that a fantastic show?" Cindy asked, moving her chair closer to Paul's.

MJ smothered a giggle.

"It was," he said, shifting even closer to her. "MJ and I enjoyed the meal, too. I think my fiancée has a thing for chocolate martinis."

Rick joined them and Etienne materialized to take drink orders.

She looked at Cindy and shrugged. "I'll have another of those chocolate wonders."

While drink orders were given, Rick and Bill whispered together.

She didn't need to be a mind reader to know that whatever Rick was saying displeased him.

"Did you find anything near the wrecks?" He resumed the inquisition.

"What's with the twenty questions?" Paul asked. "There's an excursion to Manmam dlo next Sunday if you want to see it for yourself. And for the record, even if we had found something around the wrecks, we couldn't take it. Doing so is illegal—pilfering national treasures."

Bill nodded, his lips tight. "Of course, I just wondered."

"How was your day?" Paul asked. "Find any mermaids?"

Bill frowned, his jaw tight, his chin jutting out. "I didn't, but I have a feeling there's at least one around here, and she's closer than you think."

The band started playing. Paul held out his hand. "Shall we?"

MJ reached for it as if it was a lifeline.

"That guy should be working for the *National Enquirer*."

Paul pulled her into his arms. "He is a nosy bugger. For a minute there, I thought he was going to accuse you of being a mermaid."

A shiver ran down her spine and Paul pulled her closer.

"Good thing he doesn't know about my eyes," she said. "He'd never believe me if he did."

"Forget him. Let's just focus on the music."

Safely enclosed in Paul's arms, she did just that. The band played slow music and they swayed together until the series of songs ended. When they returned to the table, her tormentor was gone.

It was after midnight before they left the restaurant.

As he'd done the previous night, Paul picked her up and carried her along the path back to the lagoon.

"Isn't your knee sore?"

"A little, but carrying you won't hurt it. You're as light as a feather."

She chuckled. "Have it your way. Considering everything I ate tonight, I doubt that. I've never had bananas Foster before, but I'm definitely going to learn to make them."

He set her down outside the door.

Unlocking it, he frowned. Lights were on not only near the bed as they had been the past five nights, but also in the living room and in the bathroom. Maybe the staff had cleaned up a bit when they'd collected the appetizer plate.

"I didn't realize we'd left so many lights on," MJ said, and yawned. "I hope electricity isn't as expensive here as it is at home."

"Probably not. I'll bet they have their own system. Maybe solar panels on the roof of the main building. I saw generators when I was snooping around the other day. You want the bathroom first?"

"Yes, please."

"I'll sleep on the couch tonight."

Hands on her hips, MJ shook her head. "Don't be ridiculous. That's like closing the barn door after the horse ran away. We shared the bed last night and nothing happened." Her cheeks heated. "Now that I know you're going to be in it with me, I'll make sure to stay on my side. Besides, your knee will have a better chance to rest if you stretch out in the bed." She grabbed her Yankees' shirt and a pair of shorts. "I won't be long."

Saying sharing the bed would be fine was one thing, but sleeping with him beside her was something else. She probably wouldn't get much sleep tonight.

* * *

"Are you ready yet? Raymond expects us in fifteen minutes," Paul called from the other room.

MJ paced in front of the mirror in the bathroom, trying to convince herself she could do this.

They'd spent the morning in the village with the other members of their bridal party and Noel and Lindsay. Bill seemed intent on keeping a close eye on her. He couldn't possibly think she was a mermaid, but the man was a strange one—even stranger than Lucette's grandmother.

She'd met the woman when all of the ladies had been treated to traditional headscarves. The plaid creations were more than a piece a cloth tied in knots. The number of knots indicated a woman's availability. She and Lindsay had opted for three knots, typical of married women, while Christy had gone for the fan-like projection that could mean just about anything. Cindy had chosen four knots because as she put it, with the boys, she definitely had more than one man in her life.

It had been fun—another memory to treasure. The only thing to mar the afternoon had been Germaine's comment that all was happening as it should, not to worry, and trust her heart. She had a long, happy life ahead of her. MJ had wanted to ask more questions, but Lindsay had come in to take yet another photograph, and the older woman had clamped her jaw shut.

She shook her head. There was no more time to procrastinate. Whatever was about to happen would, and like the engineer on a runaway train, she was powerless to stop it.

"I'm as ready as I'll ever be," she said, entering the main room.

Paul reached for her hand and lifted the palm to his lips.

"I want to tell you how beautiful you are, but you take my breath away and leave me speechless."

She blew out an anxious breath. "You're exaggerating as usual, but thank you." Her tongue licked her gel-covered lips. "What if I can't do it, Paul? I've never been a good actress, and if my asthma acts up…"

"You'll be great. We've got this. Nothing else is going to happen. You'll see. The mock wedding will be a one-shot scene and then everyone will go back to focusing on the treasure hunt."

He kissed her fingertips, the romantic gesture sending heat spiraling through her.

"There's nothing to be nervous about. You trusted me with your life yesterday; this will be a piece of cake."

She nodded. "Let's hope I don't choke on it."

"I've got your back. We'll get through the *noce civil,* have another phenomenal meal, and then we'll dance the night away, just like we did last night." He gazed into her eyes. "Lindsay will be in photographer heaven. We make a good team, Marilyn. All you have to do from here on in is be yourself."

"You make it sound so simple," she said, shaking her head.

"That's because it is. Let's go get married."

As soon as they reached the stone path, Paul scooped her into his arms, holding her close to his chest as he'd done the last two nights. Held like this, she could feel his heart racing almost as fast as hers.

That spicy, woodsy cologne he favored tickled her nostrils and stirred her body. As he set her on her feet once more, she shivered.

Signing what she'd expected would be a temporary marriage contract had seemed simple enough Saturday afternoon, but then everything had snowballed. It was true nothing was legally binding, but it was just too real.

Paul smiled as if he didn't have a care in the world, while her stomach was a cesspool of nerves.

"Cold?" he asked.

"Not cold—maybe a little edgy," she admitted. "Isn't a girl supposed to be anxious on her wedding day?"

"Only if she's a princess marrying a frog," he said and winked. "There's nothing to be antsy about. It's like slicing bread. Think of that loaf they gave us at lunch. You don't like crust, but once I cut off the heel, the bread was perfect."

She burst out laughing.

"You're comparing our marriage to bread? Seriously?"

"Sure. Why not? Bread's a staple of life. Given the choice, I'll choose a sandwich for lunch any day. Before you can enjoy it, you have to take the first mouthful. The key's not to bite off more than you can chew. Mark's the tough crust, and I'm the white, fluffy interior slice people love. It works for me."

MJ cocked an eyebrow at him.

"You're crazy." She sobered. "Why are you really doing this, Paul? And don't give me anymore of that helping out an old friend or getting even with a bully crap," she said, her gaze insisting on an honest answer, not another quip or deflection. "This pseudo wedding isn't just going to transform my life; it's going to change yours, too. I know you think we can get out of it easily, but so many things have gone wrong already. To use your analogy, tell me the real reason you want me to be the filling in your life's sandwich."

"Because I can't imagine anyone else doing it."

MJ swallowed. Did he mean what she thought he meant?

Paul took both her hands in his.

"I loved being a soldier, helping people, doing what little I could to make the world a better place, but sometimes, the best intentions blow up in your face. When I woke up in the hospital in Germany, I swore that I would find a way to atone, a way to make my life count for something. My life wasn't perfect in Stilton, but I was happy when I was part of your family. I need to find that place again, so I can lay to rest the ghosts that haunt me, and having you in my life gets me there. Change isn't always a bad thing, but when it is, you've got a choice—let it beat you or do whatever you can to fight back. I've railroaded you into this marriage because I'm a selfish bastard. I'm not doing this for you. I'm doing it for me."

"Bullshit," she exclaimed, stomping her foot. "You haven't forced me to do anything. You've given me a chance to get even with a man who tried to ruin me. If you think marrying me will help you, then I will do everything I can to make that happen. I haven't been through hell the way you have, and, while I know you have secrets, for now, I'll respect your right to keep them. The only thing more I'll ask from you is that we don't lie to one another. You tell me that this relationship ends whenever I say it does. That has to be a two-way street. If ever you want the charade to end, say the word. Do we have a deal?"

Paul nodded. "We do."

There was more to his reason for wanting to marry her than he was saying, but he'd admitted he needed her and that would do for now.

* * *

Paul reached for MJ, intent on sealing this new deal with a kiss. The door opened, startling them apart.

"*Vous voilà,*" Monsieur St Louis exclaimed, his face red, beads of perspiration dotting his brow.

What the hell had gone wrong now?

MJ's gasp proved she'd come to the same conclusion. God, he was beginning to hate surprises.

"At the last minute, Monsieur James has made a few changes and, while my staff is efficient, you understand moving the festivities from here to the beach on the first lagoon is not as easy as he thinks. We are almost ready. The guests are slowly making their way there now, and there is a cart waiting for you. Since we need a bit more time, the driver will take you on a tour of the island—no more than a fifteen to twenty-minute delay."

"That's fine," Paul answered, relieved it hadn't been something worse. They'd walked along that beach earlier in the day. Unlike the others on the island's west side, it had no bungalows, left *au naturel*, with only a tiki bar, beach loungers, and umbrellas to mark the passage of time.

MJ nodded and smiled, slipping her arm through his.

"Louis James knows best. If tonight's sunset is anything like the ones we've seen, standing with a liquid gold ocean behind us will be the perfect backdrop not only for the ceremony but for the treasure hunt itself."

The pulse throbbing at the base of her throat spoke of her agitation even if her words hadn't.

Monsieur St Louis nodded. "*C'est vrai.* If you will come with me?"

The manager opened the door and ushered them inside.

Paul put his hand over MJ's as she held his arm and followed the manager. He could feel her trembling.

"This is it, Kid. We're about to become famous television stars. The mock wedding is a one-take scene. Once it's in the can, everyone will reach for champagne, toast the occasion, and then focus on the treasure—the real reason many of them are here. In a few hours, we'll be nothing more than window dressing."

She chuckled. "I hope so, but I can't help thinking this is one of those movies, where, just as the bride and groom kiss, the camera cuts to the water and an enormous Great White shark surfaces and makes a beeline for the shore."

Paul laughed, unable to erase the image of a bad B-rated horror flick from his mind as Monsieur St Louis opened the building's main door.

"You crack me up, you know that—"

"Oh my God!" MJ cut him off before he could finish. "I wasn't expecting this." The awe in her voice matched his surprise. "It's Cinderella's coach. Paul, it couldn't be more perfect."

Her eyes shone with excitement. Come hell or high water, he wouldn't let her down.

"Your carriage awaits, princess," he said softly.

The beautiful, white, antique *calèche*, designed for two passengers, was shaped like a pumpkin, its ribs festooned with greenery and ribbon. A man, dressed in the island's livery, held the carriage door open for them.

"You like it?" the manager asked, the smug look on his face telling him he knew she did. "Monsieur James brought it to the island this morning, horse and all."

"It's a dream come true," she said. "If I'm asleep, please don't wake me up."

Monsieur St Louis chuckled. "Madame, as I have said before, on Paradise Island, all your dreams come true. Enjoy your carriage ride."

Paul glanced at his bride to be. If he lived to be a hundred, he would never forget the look of pure joy on her face. No matter what was to come, this moment made it all worthwhile.

"Where are you taking us? he asked the driver.

"*Au bain des sirènes*," he answered, closing the door. "It is customary on Paradise Island for the bride and groom to make a wish before their marriage."

MJ cocked her head. "What does that mean?" she whispered. "*Sirène* means mermaid, but what about the rest?"

"*Bain* is bathtub." He shrugged. "I don't think we're expected to take a bath, but this should be interesting. It isn't mentioned in the brochure, that's for sure. The island may only be three miles wide at its center, but it's ten miles long. The resort occupies only the southern tip. The village is five miles to the north, but it's that way. We're in unchartered territory here."

Lush vegetation grew wild and thick on each side of the road, giving way to fields of tall green stalks that could only be sugarcane. Had the island been a plantation at one time?

"It looks like tourism isn't the only industry here," Paul said. "That's sugarcane. We're headed beyond the village, toward the back of the volcano."

"Oh my God, what happened here?" MJ asked, her hands coming up to cover her cheeks, her mouth gaping open.

On the right side of the road stood a forest of blackened stalks, some twelve feet tall.

"They've started the harvesting, Madame," the driver said. "It is customary to burn the plants to get rid of the leaves, weeds, and other pests. If you look over on the left, you will see our processing plant. By next year, we hope to offer tours and explain our history. There is more to Paradise Island than pirate treasure and mermaids."

Paul nodded. "Before the resort, I would guess this was the islanders main source of income."

"Now, yes, but at one time only the rich benefited from the bounty of our land."

MJ's brows rose, and Paul opted not to comment. Sometimes discretion was necessary. Paradise Island wouldn't be the only place where someone had gotten rich off the sweat and labor of others.

As they drove along, the lush vegetation and sugarcane fields disappeared, replaced by scrub grass.

"Based on the change of scenery, my guess is the mermaids' bathtub is a volcanic pool. Looks like it's time to make a wish." He knew exactly what he wanted. What would she?

The driver stopped the carriage in front of the white picket fence. He got down and opened the carriage door.

"Here." He handed them each a Spanish doubloon. "It is tradition for both the bride and groom to make a wish and toss one into the water."

"Where do these come from?" Paul asked, examining the coin. It had to be several hundred years old. Someone had polished it to perfection.

"Many of the island families have such coins, handed down from one generation to the next for this very purpose. Your coins come from the priestess's cache. Don't worry, every coin tossed in the well is returned in time by the spirits themselves, or perhaps the *sirènes*." He grinned, showing off near perfect white teeth. "Follow the wooden sidewalk to the end. You cannot miss it." He turned away.

MJ frowned. "I'm sorry, but I don't see mermaids putting these under pillows like some kind of Tooth Fairies," she whispered. "Someone's got to be diving and retrieving these suckers. They're probably from Lacorneille's treasure and after all these years, there's nothing left of it. Bill's in for a hell of a disappointment."

Paul chuckled, opening the small gate for her to precede him.

"I agree. Lucette mentioned that some of the previous guests had found doubloons. Maybe the whole damn treasure was hidden at the bottom of this tub. Over the years, the chest has broken down and the coins washed away. If this is a volcanic pool as I suspect, it no doubt has underwater access to the ocean."

Paul took her hand in his and followed the wooden sidewalk as instructed. Within a few yards, even the scrub vanished, replaced by a barren landscape similar to the lava fields he'd seen in Iceland a few years ago.

"It looks like we're at the gates of Tartarus," MJ whispered, gripping his fingers tightly enough to cut off the circulation. "Hell of a place to make a wish for a happy future. It's so black and barren, and it stinks." She wrinkled her nose. "It smells like rotten eggs."

"Sulfur dioxide, a common but potentially dangerous volcanic gas," he answered frowning. "There must be a vent nearby. They often mine sulfur in active volcanoes. I thought this one was dormant, but maybe not. Let's not push our luck and hang around too long."

The sidewalk turned left and MJ gasped.

Before them, amid the black rock was a large pool maybe twenty feet in diameter. A pier had been constructed to allow people to get closer. Below them, milky aqua water steamed.

"I've never seen water that color before," MJ whispered. "It's so beautiful."

"There's a place very similar to this in Iceland. It's called the Blue Lagoon. The geothermal water has a unique composition I didn't expect to find anywhere else in the world. Its color comes from the silica, algae, and minerals it contains. The sun reflecting off the silica is what makes it appear this shade of blue. People come from all over the world to bathe in that water, but judging by the fence around it and that sign, I would say bathing in the mermaids' bathtub isn't encouraged."

He pointed to the sign printed in six different languages and read aloud.

"Danger. Do not enter the water. Depth unknown. Temperatures fluctuate between 100 and 150 degrees Fahrenheit. High sulfur levels may create potentially toxic gases. Prolonged exposure can be hazardous. Beware."

"At 150 degrees, a person is looking at third degree burns in as little as two seconds. And they come here hoping for good luck with their marriages?" MJ asked, her eyebrows raised.

"Maybe if they can survive this, they can handle anything. But that fluctuating temperature tells me there is definitely an opening into the ocean. No doubt the water at high tide cools the pool. Too bad the sulfur prevents it from being used as a spa. Ready? We need to make our wishes and get back to the carriage before the scent of sulfur sinks into our clothes."

MJ nodded and reached for his hand. "On three, okay?" She closed her eyes. "One, two, three."

He flung his coin into the water, knowing she had as well when he heard two plops. His wish had been simple. He'd asked for MJ's happiness always.

"Shall we? It's time to get married."

Taking her arm in his, he led her back to the carriage and into what he hoped would be a happy future for them.

CHAPTER FIFTEEN

During the carriage ride to the beach, MJ sat quietly, pretending to take in the scenery, mulling over the wish she'd made. A real marriage. Who was she kidding? This wasn't even a real wedding, for heaven's sake, and here she was dewy-eyed over the future.

Within a matter of minutes, the vehicle rolled to a stop. Most of the hotel's sixty guests stood around chatting and enjoying champagne or one of the other cocktails provided.

She and Paul had been here less than four hours ago. When had the staff found the time to do this? Waiters dressed in tuxedos with plaid cummerbunds moved through the crowd. Women, in plaid gowns and matching headdresses, offered canapés. Large cameras on tripods scattered throughout the area reminded her this was a television set.

"Hello," a man in a dark shirt and pants stepped over to them and opened the door to the carriage. "I'm Giles. If you'll come with me, Mr. James is waiting to go over things with you."

MJ allowed him to help her out of the coach, but as soon as Paul was beside her, she reached for his arm.

"I think I'm going to be sick," she whispered, the butterflies in her stomach in full revolt.

Paul squeezed her hand. "We're in this together, remember?"

She smiled, her mouth barely opening, and reached for the glass of champagne that materialized beside her, downing it in one gulp, and grabbing another.

"Take it easy," Paul admonished and winked. "You don't want to stumble down the aisle."

"If I could pass out and wake up to discover this was all a nightmare, I would."

But she heeded his advice and sipped more slowly.

As soon as they entered the tent on the far side of the carpet-covered sand, a familiar man stepped over to them.

"Mr. Davis, Ms. Summers, welcome." Louis James extended his hand to each of them in turn. "Congratulations."

"Mr. James," Paul said. "It's an honor to meet you, sir."

Louis James laughed. "The pleasure's all mine. Millions of Americans are waiting to share this special moment with you." He turned to the woman beside him. "This is Kate. She's going to be translating everything for the audience at home. Ms. Summers, if you'll go with her, she'll fix your makeup. There's a lot of white here, and we don't want you to look washed out."

"Thank you," she answered, not feeling in the least bit grateful. She would have to let go of Paul and that was the last thing she wanted to do.

"It's okay," Paul said. "I'll be right here when you get back."

"Actually, you won't. Makeup's waiting for you, too, and then we've got a pre-wedding interview. The bride will join you when the officials are ready to start. There's plenty of champagne."

Fear gripped MJ, but the look of concern on Paul's face—and the two glasses of bubbly she'd just swallowed—eased her worries.

"I've got this," she whispered shakily. "I won't let you down." She turned to the woman. "I'm all yours."

Ten minutes later, MJ stared at the face in the mirror. Was that really her?

The makeup artist had deepened the slight tan she'd acquired and had rearranged her hair, pulling her loose curls up behind her left ear, securing them with a sprig of island greenery complete with a beautiful, red gumamela, better known as a double-petal hibiscus. A matching bouquet sat on the table in front of her.

"I'd originally chosen white based on the picture your mother showed me. It's a good thing the manager gave us a head's up," Kate said, fussing with the hair ornament. "Given the color of your hair, white would've washed you out under the lights. Red works much better, and we were able to get gowns to match. How are you feeling?"

"Nervous, scared—no make that terrified. Didn't I read somewhere that the camera adds ten pounds?" she joked.

"I don't think you have to worry about that," Kate said. "You look fantastic, and that gown was made for you. Honestly, you're the most beautiful bride I've seen in a long time."

Giles stepped into the room, the curtain swishing closed behind him.

"Wow! Kate, you've done it again."

The girl shook her head. "Nothing to do here but add a little color and waterproof as the boss requested."

Waterproof? Why the hell did her face need to be waterproofed. If there was one thing she didn't plan to do, it was cry.

* * *

Louis James ushered Paul over to two barber-style chairs. He indicated the dark-haired man on his left.

"This is Malcolm. He's going to do your makeup while Tony does mine."

"I'm not going to end up looking like a circus clown, am I?"

"No, not at all. He'll just tone down the shine. You don't really need color since you've got a decent tan. How long have you been here?"

"Since Tuesday," Paul answered. The man probably knew that already. "I got away before MJ could. What happens after Malcolm finishes?"

"I have a surprise for you, and then you and I will go over to the sofas and have a little chat."

"About what?"

He tried to sound casual. A surprise? Damn. Since he'd arrived on Paradise Island, it had been one surprise after another, and he definitely had had more of them than he wanted or needed.

"The usual—how you and your wife met, what you've been doing the last few years, where you'll be living once the honeymoon is over. Nothing too complicated."

Once the shine on his complexion was gone, Paul nodded to Louis James.

"Doesn't look bad. What now?"

"I just love happy endings and high ratings," Louis admitted.

"When Raymond sent me the names, the first thing I did was interview your future mother-in-law. She explained about this civil ceremony and how it wasn't legal, so I decided to fix that for you."

Paul's heart dropped into his stomach, and he swallowed the bile it produced.

"Fix it how?" he asked, amazed he could speak.

"With a little help from the White House—it pays to have the president as a friend—we've persuaded the French government to allow the military chaplain from Puerto Rico to perform a legal wedding after the *noce civil* as they call it. I can tell you Mrs. Summers is thrilled. She's quite anxious for grandkids."

Paul stared at the television host, not sure his heart was still beating. The man had to be joking, right? No one could pull that many strings.

"I made a few other calls," Louis continued. "The friend looking after your house got your uniform for me."

Malcolm stepped over to the chair, a garment bag in his hand.

"It would be great PR for our forces if you wore it instead of the tux. We see so many negative stories about our men coming home and the challenges they face, it would be nice to have a feel-good story to share. That being said, I spoke with your CO, and I realize you've spent the last few months getting back on your feet. The decision is yours."

Paul felt cold and clammy. The last thing he'd expected was a frigging background check. If Louis James had looked into things that closely, he could blow apart their carefully built house of cards.

Reaching for the clothing bag, Paul pulled down the zipper. His dark blue uniform was there, complete with his white shirt. His two black ties, the four in hand and the bow tie and his headgear as well as his cufflinks and studs were in a plastic bag attached to the hanger. He'd always been proud to wear his uniform, and it hadn't been the uniform that had let him down. It had been his own inability to do the job he'd had to do.

"Why not? It's what I would've worn state-side," he said, hoping this wasn't going to backfire, too. "Where can I change?"

"This way, Lieutenant," Malcolm said.

Ten minutes later, in dress uniform, complete with the medals and ribbons he'd earned during his years in the service, Paul returned to the impromptu set where a technician waited to mike him.

"Here," Louis James handed him a glass as soon as the tech was finished. "It's scotch. You may be in uniform, Lieutenant, but you aren't going into battle. You look scared to death." He chuckled. "I realize this comes as a surprise, but hopefully it's a pleasant one. Don't worry about the mike. If they need to turn up the audio, the guys in the sound booth will take care of it."

Paul took a mouthful of scotch and allowed the amber liquid to burn away some of his nervousness.

"Now, this is just a casual interview. Eyes on me. Ignore the cameras. We're just two guys talking. It's show time."

Lights came on and a disembodied voice shouted, "Quiet on the set. We're on in five, four, three, two, one. Go."

"Good evening, ladies and gentlemen," Louis James spoke into the camera. "Welcome to a special edition of *Louis James Live.* Tonight, you're guests at a very special wedding ceremony, one that will join Lieutenant Paul Davis, a soldier who's served his country proudly in Afghanistan, and Marilyn Jean Summers, a school teacher from Stilton, New York. Paul, I had the pleasure of talking to your mother-in-law earlier, and she was telling me that your romance with MJ, as she called her, started years ago. Why don't you tell us a little about that?"

Paul smiled. Was he a good enough actor to pull this off? There was a chance Mark and Melena might see the broadcast as well as Mama. If there was ever a time to be convincing, it was now.

"I've been in love with MJ from the first moment I saw her..."

Paul sat back, warming to his topic. He described growing up in Stilton and spending time at his best friend's home.

"The day I left Stilton was one of the worst days of my life. Reconnecting with her through the pen pal program was something I didn't expect, but I'll be forever grateful for it. There were times back then when MJ drove me crazy, but I would've done anything for her. Now, it looks like I'll finally get my chance."

Louis chuckled. "Well, I've seen your bride, and I can attest that tomboy has grown into a beautiful woman. Judging by the way your face lights up when you say her name, I would say you've fallen hard."

Paul's face heated and sweat trickled down his back. It had to be the lights.

"We still have a few minutes before the ceremonies begin. Can you tell us a little about your military service? From the bio I accessed, you've done several tours in the army. How does it feel leaving that life behind?"

Paul smiled. He'd expected this. Why make him wear his uniform otherwise?

"I enjoyed my years in the service, protecting our country and its assets on foreign soil," he said, "but I'm ready to get back to my old life."

"What was your assignment overseas? Or is that violating some security protocol?"

"I wasn't involved in any clandestine operations if that's what you mean," he lied and chuckled nervously. "For the most part, I spent my time working with the military police, and on my last tour, I was assigned to the embassy in Kabul."

"You decided to leave the service after that posting."

Paul kept the smile pasted on his face. He didn't want to talk about Kabul, not now, not ever.

"I was wounded and decided to get out while I was still in one piece. I wouldn't have been able to serve in the same way, and I'm not really cut out for a desk job."

"Your record states you were ambushed on duty and that the civilians with you were killed. Can you tell us about that?"

"I'm afraid I can't," he said, weighing his words carefully.

Irritation flashed in Louis's eyes. "Can't or won't?" he asked.

"I can't tell you what happened because I don't remember it all," he lied once more, hoping no one would read anything into his sudden nervousness. "I was escorting the U.N. teacher and two of her students, and we were attacked by snipers. I was shot three times, passed out, and don't recall anything else. The first bullet hit me in the right shoulder, the second creased the left side of my head, while the third one blew out my knee. The memory loss is slight and confined to the events surrounding the ambush itself. Sorry." He shrugged.

"I don't suppose you could explain how escorting those civilians was part of your embassy responsibilities?" Louis asked, leaning forward, looking for blood.

"It wasn't. I'd just gone off duty when the ambassador's wife asked me to do her a favor. She and Fiona Lake were friends. Fiona visited the embassy at least once a week to collect bread, milk powder, and other non-perishable food for the girls at the school. That particular night, she had two of her students with her and the three stayed for dinner. The streets of Kabul can be dangerous at night, especially for women and girls. I was escorting them back to the school. That's all I remember."

"Thank you for your candor, Lieutenant. Now, I have another surprise for you, one I know you'll enjoy."

Paul smiled and nodded. If he'd survived Kabul and this interview, what was one more shock to the system?

"Look who's here to join in the festivities."

The curtains parted and out walked Mama Summers.

Paul stood and opened his arms to the woman who'd been more of a mother to him than his own.

"How did you manage this?" he asked, seconds before the reality struck him. "Does MJ know you're here?"

Louis chuckled. "Not yet, but Mrs. Summers is here to walk her daughter down the aisle."

Paul swallowed. MJ might've managed to avoid an asthma attack so far, but if anything was going to put her over the edge this was it. To hell with *Quimbois* magic. Enough was enough.

* * *

"Are you ready to become Mrs. Davis?" Giles asked, picking up her bouquet.

MJ nodded. Hadn't she'd wished for this at the mermaids' bathtub? But she'd wanted it to be real, not a mockery to tantalize people hundreds if not thousands of miles away. Standing, she swayed. Maybe she shouldn't have had that third glass of champagne.

"Kate, better follow along in case she needs a touchup. We've got five minutes of commercial time, and then we're live."

What kind of touchup? Her headpiece wasn't going anywhere, and Kate had said the makeup was waterproof. What were they planning to do? Toss her into the ocean when the ceremony was over? She was warm enough right now, that might actually feel good.

"Shall we?" Giles offered her his arm. "As soon as you step through the curtain, you'll be on camera. You've got a few minutes before millions of viewers see you. Paul's microphone will pick up your exchange of vows or whatever the French call this *noce civil's* answers. You do say something, right?"

"Yes, but it isn't much. Basically, he speaks and we tell him we understand. Monsieur St Louis went through it with us earlier this morning."

"Good. Kate will translate that so the audience knows what's happening. Afterwards, the padre will perform the wedding—"

"Padre?" she asked, the Earth suddenly spinning out of control. Her eyes grew large and her heart pounded in her chest. She gripped the back of the chair. "Padre, as in church official?"

"Yes. The boss pulled a few strings. He's arranged for the chaplain from Puerto Rico to perform a marriage ceremony that the United States' government will honor and accept."

"Why?" The word was the only one she could utter.

What the hell kind of power did the spirits have around here?

"Louis talked to your mother yesterday, and we found out your actual wedding wouldn't take place until Thanksgiving. That's anticlimactic for the show, so he's making it happen now. It'll be so much more satisfying for the millions of viewers out there." He frowned and turned to Kate. "I think she needs a touch more blush. She's too pale under these lights." Focusing on her once more, he chuckled. "Judging by the look on your face, Ms. Summers, I take it this is a bit of a shock."

A bit? This was a disaster of epic proportion.

"Does Paul know about the padre?" she asked, grateful her voice worked. She exhaled slowly, feeling the tension moving into her chest.

I will not have an asthma attack in front of millions of people.

Giles grinned. "I'm sure he does by now. Come on. We only have a few moments left."

Striving to school her face the way she did for those, "Oh my God, shoot me now moments," she stepped away from the chair, wishing the earth would open up and swallow her. Where was a sinkhole, earthquake, or volcanic eruption when she needed one?

"My mother will be disappointed. Waiting until Thanksgiving for her to be there is why Paul and I didn't elope," she answered, putting her arm through Giles's. Would her argument sway him enough to avoid the second part of the ceremony?

Of course, if she had any backbone, she would put her foot down, say no, and end this farce, but she'd made a promise, one she had to keep. Besides, an amicable divorce was probably easier to get than an annulment. On the bright side, she could skip several months in the sleazy motel.

Giles put his hand over hers on his arm. "We knew you'd feel that way, so…"

The curtain opened, and MJ blinked at the lights shining on her, almost blinding her. Almost…

"Mama?" she whispered, wondering if the champagne was making her hallucinate, grateful Giles was holding her; otherwise, she would fall flat on her ass. "What are you doing here?"

"What do you think I'm doing?" Mama said and laughed. "My only daughter is getting married. I'm here to walk you down the aisle." She blinked her eyes, trying to stem the tears, but the shine gave her away. "You look so beautiful ... Your father would be proud of you."

It had been years since she'd seen her mother so happy. Swallowing her anxiety, MJ grinned. Like it or not, she and Paul were in this for the long run, and would have to make the best of it. She wouldn't break Mama's heart again.

"I'm so glad you're here," she said, tearing up. What girl wouldn't want her mother at her wedding?

"I brought you something." Mama opened her small purse and pulled out a linen handkerchief embroidered with pale blue forget-me-nots. "My mother gave me this when I married your father. It's your turn to have it."

"Thank you," MJ said, tucking the tiny family good luck piece inside her bra.

"Mrs. Summers? They're ready for us."

"Yes, of course."

Giles handed her the bouquet, and Mama put her arm through hers just as the music started. Christy and Cindy came in from the wings, both dressed in red, the color an almost perfect match to her bouquet, a contrast to the white flowers they carried, and stepped in front of her.

MJ took a deep breath and looked ahead. Rick and Bill, dressed in tuxedos, stood next to Paul, looking incredibly handsome in uniform. As she walked toward him, her arm in Mama's, she realized that this was her forever wedding, the one she'd wished for, the one she'd dreamt of all those years ago. She would make this marriage work because she believed in love and happily ever after even if Paul didn't.

Once the official French formality was over and they'd signed the village's register, the padre stepped forward and began a shortened version of the traditional wedding ceremony.

"Do you, Marilyn, take this man, Paul, to be your loving husband?" the minister asked.

Praying the earth wasn't going to open up and swallow her after all, she croaked out an answer, grateful there hadn't been an obey line in there.

"I do."

Paul smiled down at her, the glow on his face too genuine to be faked. Moments earlier, he'd repeated his vows loudly, without hesitation. She had to be dreaming, and yet she wasn't.

Beside her, Cindy held her bouquet and beamed. Rick, as Best Man, had done his job well, and the beautiful wedding band designed to complement her engagement ring now adorned her finger.

"In as much as you, Marilyn, and you, Paul, have openly declared your desire to be united in marriage, have joined hands, given and accepted a ring, and stated your vows, by the powers vested in me by God, the United States of America, and with the special permission of the Secretary of State for Overseas Departments and Territories, and the Minister of the Interior of France, I now pronounce you man and wife. You may kiss the bride."

Paul pulled her into his arms and bent his head. "Looks like we've pulled it off," he whispered seconds before his lips captured hers.

The kiss should've been a quick peck, a formality to seal the deal, but instead, the heat from his mouth had her melting. If he hadn't been holding her, she would be a gooey puddle on the sand. He raised his head and smiled once more.

"Hello, Mrs. Davis. As Sherlock would say, 'The game's afoot.' We'll be fine."

MJ nodded. Had he noticed how his kiss had affected her?

She moved out of his arms and turned to her mother who almost smothered her against her ample bosom.

"I'm so happy for you, *agapiménos*," she said, releasing her and kissing her first on one cheek and then the other. She did the same to Paul. "He loved you like a son. He would be very happy. I know you'll take good care of her."

"That's the nicest thing anyone's ever said to me, Mrs. Summers. I'll protect her with my life."

Mama stood between them and put an arm through each of theirs.

"What Mrs. Summers? It's Mama. I wish Ron could've been here, but I know he's watching." She sighed, her eyes still bright. "I can't wait for more grandbabies to fuss over."

MJ gasped, her cheeks flaming. "Mama!"

Paul burst out laughing. "Slow down. We haven't even started the honeymoon yet. You need to give us some time as a couple before we become a family."

Mama narrowed her eyes. "Nine months is more than enough time. She isn't getting any younger, and neither are you."

"Please," MJ begged. Were the microphones still on? "I'm not that old, and neither is Paul."

"Well done," Louis interrupted the disastrous conversation. "We need to borrow you for some publicity shots before you get into the carriage for the ride back. Mrs. Summers, I've arranged for you to travel with me. That'll give the newlyweds a few minutes alone. I think we surprised the hell out of them. Let's give it time to sink in, shall we?"

"Of course," Mama said, letting go of their arms and stepping toward him, preening like a sixteen-year-old out on a date with the football quarterback.

"Here," he handed them each a flute of champagne from the tray the waiter beside him held. "Let me be the first to toast the new bride and groom." He raised his glass. "Congratulations."

MJ sipped from her flute. How much wine had she had? She really needed to watch herself and keep her wits about her. There were television cameras everywhere.

Paul leaned down and whispered in her ear. "Are you okay? You look scared to death."

"I feel like a goldfish in a bowl with everyone looking at me and no place to hide."

"You don't have to hide, not now, not ever. As long as you're with me, you'll be safe."

The conviction in his voice was unmistakable. How could she doubt him?

CHAPTER SIXTEEN

MJ, still stunned by Paul's words, gazed into his eyes, unable to think of anything to say in response to his oath when the technician approached.

"Excuse me, sir. I'd like to remove your mike."

"Is it still on?" she asked, covering her mouth. Had everything Mama said been heard by the audience?

"No, it went dead after the ceremony."

She exhaled heavily. Thank God for that.

"We'll give Joe a few seconds to collect his equipment, and we'll move over there," Louis said, his grin proving he knew what she'd been thinking. "Our photographer is waiting." Louis turned to Mama. "Mrs. Summers, if you could join us, too? We'll have a few mother-daughter shots taken for you."

"Mr. James, call me Maria, please."

"Then, I insist you call me Louis." He offered her his arm. "The sand isn't quite as trampled over there."

As soon as the technician removed the last of Paul's wires, he turned to her and winked.

"Looks like Mama's enjoying herself. Shall we, Mrs. Davis?"

MJ finished the champagne in her glass, hoping it would give her the strength to make it through the rest of the evening, and praying she wouldn't fall flat on her face later. She chuckled sheepishly.

"Mama's always had a crush on the man. Mrs. Davis. That will take some getting used to."

"You can always keep Summers or use Summers-Davis," he offered as they joined the older couple. "I won't mind."

"She'll do no such thing," Mama cut in, horrified by the idea. "A married woman takes her husband's name."

"It's the twenty-first century," MJ interjected. "If I want to be married to Paul and keep my last name or even hyphenate it, I can. That's between Paul and me."

Keeping Summers might be for the best since she wouldn't have to change any of her identification. If she took Davis, then once they filed for divorce she would have to change it all back.

"Actually, I'm planning to keep my maiden name for my professional career. If someone calls me Mrs. Davis, I won't go ballistic, but for now, unless the school board has some objection, I'll remain Ms. Summers."

Louis nodded. "A lot of women do that these days. I've even heard some use Mx. now, since it neither implies sex nor marital status."

Mama screwed up her face, the action warning of a "talk" to come, but she stayed silent.

Within a minute or so, they reached the area Louis had selected for the photo shoot and Kate waited to freshen her makeup.

After what felt like an hour, the photographer signaled the end. MJ's face hurt from smiling, and she was certain the spots from the flashbulbs dancing before her eyes would never go away.

"That's it for now," Louis said, coming to stand beside them. "Your driver has instructions to take the long way home to give you two time to talk. Once we get back to the main building, you'll accept the sponsor gifts—that'll be on tomorrow's show along with the tour of the island and the resort we filmed earlier. Then we'll eat, cut the cake, and have the first dance, before we wrap up for the night. I'll escort your mother back to the airport and New York in the morning—we're sleeping on the yacht tonight along with my crew and the rest of the cast. Tomorrow is all yours, although Joe will be there for Leroux's presentation. The treasure hunt starts Wednesday morning, and a crew will follow you around. Don't worry. You'll have plenty of time to relax and enjoy yourselves off camera. I'll be back Friday night for the closing ceremonies. Hopefully, someone will have found treasure."

"I already have," Paul said, raising her hand to his lips. "Thank you for everything, sir. Neither Marilyn nor I expected any of this."

"The pleasure was all mine. It's been a long time since I've attended a wedding where the couple fits so well together. Maybe we can do a follow-up special when that first baby is born."

MJ fought to keep the panic off her face and then calm filled her. There would be no follow-up for the birth of a child, and unless Louis decided to publicize their divorce, this would be the end of their involvement with him.

"MJ, wait up," Bill Smith called before she and Paul could enter the coach. "Can I speak to you for a second?"

She nodded. What choice did she have?

Paul moved away to have one last selfie taken with Cindy and Christy.

"I checked online," he bit off, his teeth clenched. "There are no lights at the bottom of the reef in the harbor that could account for those auras in Lindsay's pictures. Who did you see down there?"

Something in the intensity of his gaze made her skin crawl.

"Nobody. What are you talking about? There were fish and other divers ... if those auras weren't lights, I don't know any more about them than you do."

His gaze narrowed. "Bullshit. What did you see?" He gripped her arm to stop her from moving away. "I need the truth."

"What's wrong with you?" she hissed, trying to pull her arm away, but his grip tightened. "I told you I don't know anything."

"I don't believe you. You saw mermaids—they made the water glow around them, something else I confirmed online. One of them spoke to you, didn't she? Maybe when you disappeared behind that last wreck. If I find out you're holding out on me, you'll regret it. That treasure is mine."

"You're insane." MJ pulled her arm out of his grasp, her heart pounding so hard she was afraid he could see it beat. "I don't know where the hell you're getting your 'online' information, but mermaids don't exist anymore than the Easter Bunny, Santa Claus, and Iron Man. They aren't real. For God's sake, grow up."

"Is everything okay?" Paul asked, stepping closer to her.

"Bill's had a little too much to drink," she answered. "He seems to think I've been chatting with mermaids and that I'm holding out on him." She turned to Bill. "Get this through your head. I have no idea where your precious treasure is, and even if I did, it doesn't belong to you or to me. An international court would decide that."

"Smith, if I ever see you touch my wife again, you'll leave this place in casts," Paul uttered the threat softly and smiled. "Darling, I think it's time for us to go."

MJ nodded, but the look Bill gave her made her blood run cold.

* * *

The sun set, leaving the area in darkness other than torches lining the road. While they'd been in picture-taking hell, most of the guests had left the beach. The rest of the wedding party was probably in the golf cart behind them. Bill was lucky he hadn't punched out his lights.

Paul put his arm across the back of the seat pulling MJ closer to him. It wasn't cold, but she trembled. Shock, maybe?

"How are you holding up?" he asked, unable to see much of her face in the glow of the carriage's twinkle lights. "I know it wasn't what we expected, but your mother was in seventh heaven."

"Did you know about the padre? Was it one of the things I didn't understand?" she asked, her voice catching on the last words.

"Raymond didn't say anything about this. In fact, I don't think he knew until later and that might've been why the man was sweating up a storm. Louis James probably swore him to secrecy. I didn't find out until just before he handed me my uniform. What was I to do, MJ?"

"There wasn't anything you could've done that wouldn't have made things a thousand times worse, especially with Mama here."

"He didn't warn me about her, either. I almost choked on my tongue when the curtain opened." He leaned his chin on her head. "I've only seen his show a few times, but I should've remembered how he liked to 'surprise' his guests with the impossible."

She pressed herself deeper into his shoulder. "Yeah. That's one of his trademarks. I knew there would be another snag. When I saw her, I thought I was hallucinating. I can't imagine what my face looked like. Then, I saw you in uniform. You look great. I'm sure all the lady viewers were drooling, but how did he manage that?"

"I can't hold a candle to you." He brushed his lips across her hair. "Louis arranged to have someone from the post go into the house and get it. If the man can influence the White House and foreign governments, there isn't much we lowly peons can do to stop him. And then, there was the interview."

"Interview? You mean he questioned you on camera?"

"Yeah, but it wasn't too bad, at least not at first. He asked about us, when we met, how we fell in love—the kind of stuff we agreed on, including the pen pal program and emails. He blindsided me with questions about my last tour, but I managed to deflect them. A flawed memory comes in handy at times."

She exhaled heavily. "What are we going to do, Paul? We're married, really married. This changes everything."

"Does it? The way I see it, things have just gotten better. Unless your mother insists, we can skip a second wedding. Considering this one was on national television, it would be anticlimactic, but I'll go through with that baptism if I have to. Of course, there'll have to be a party ... You can move into the house right away, the way you'd planned. We can split costs and household duties, but the big expenses are mine."

"Pulling rank, Lieutenant?" There was a slight edge to her voice.

"I didn't mean it like that," he said. He probably sounded as controlling as the Achilles Heel. "You're my wife now, maybe in name only, but I want to protect you, take care of you, and make you happy for as long as it lasts. When I saw Bill..."

"I don't know why, but that man scares me." She shook her head. "How can he be so fixated on imaginary creatures? He's not a child, yet he believes mermaids exist and that they're in these waters. It makes no sense."

"Noel and I were talking about that earlier when we were at the beach. He's listened to the man, but he agrees he's one sandwich short of a picnic. I don't believe in Zeus, Thor, or Superman, but millions of people are fascinated by them, just as they are by ghosts, demons, and zombies. The fountain of youth doesn't exist, and yet Ponce de Leon isn't the only one who searched for it. We've met the other wingnuts in Bill's Seekers of Treasure group. They've all got one foot in the loony bin as far as I'm concerned, but these are smart people, CEOs, lawyers, doctors ... Rick may be a mechanic, but he owns his own business, and he's as committed to this treasure hunt as the others. You mentioned Mark was involved with chat groups, too. Let's hope it wasn't this one."

She shuddered as the carriage halted and shook her head.

"I doubt it, but since nothing has gone as planned, I wouldn't be surprised if he was, although his approach to treasure hunting is more logical and math-based." She stood. "You do realize this marriage might have to last longer than either of us anticipated. When it does end, Mama will be devastated."

Reaching for her hand, he held it with both of his.

"Let's not anticipate the worst. I've often heard the expression, 'if life gives you lemons, make lemonade.' My last few years have been lonely ones, filled with sorrow and regret. I want to wake up in the morning and know I deserved to survive. With you in my life, I just might."

"Of course, you do. As far as the lemonade goes, I arrived a jilted bride with no place to stay, nowhere to go, and you rescued me. I don't think I can ever thank you enough for that." She kissed his cheek.

Pulling her into his arms, his lips found hers and changed her simple thank you into another kiss that filled him with desire. Lifting his head slowly, he gazed at her, saw her tongue dart out and lick her lips. He smiled.

"We've learned this weekend that we don't have much say in what happens to us. I'm looking forward to listening to you tell me about your day, knowing it won't involve the number of casualties suffered by both sides. The thought of not sitting down to dinner with sand in my food and another hundred guys, each one lost in thought remembering loved ones far away, thrills me, especially when I'll get to sit across from you and watch your face as you sample my cooking and I enjoy yours. The last thing I expected to do on this vacation was get married. I know it isn't logical, and I don't deserve someone as wonderful as you, but I want this to work, MJ. When it comes right down to it, love is just another four-letter word, and we both know what people say about those.

We have respect and companionship. Those are stronger, more reliable words. This place is filled with magic. Let's take some of it home with us."

In the glow from the veranda lights, Paul could see the shimmer of tears in her eyes. His heart fell. Was the thought of a future by his side that upsetting?

Surprising him, she raised her head and brushed her lips across his. When she pulled back, she was smiling. "Okay, Mr. Davis. Lemonade and magic. Let's get this show on the road."

He helped her out of the carriage.

Several hours later, with most of the guest including Mama and the cast and crew of the show gone, the last song ended. Paul released MJ and stepped back.

"Time to say goodnight."

"I don't expect we'll be seeing you two before noon," Lindsay said, coming to stand next to them, Noel just a step behind her. "I know I intend to sleep in." She yawned. "It was an absolutely wonderful wedding—except for Bill. When you look at one another, it's magical, but you know that. What time are we meeting the great Antoine Leroux?"

"Not until two-thirty or three," Paul answered. "Let's hope he's playing with a full deck, unlike the Seekers of Treasure. The last of this week's guest will be here at noon, so they need to check in before we do."

MJ shivered.

"Cold?" he asked, putting his arm around her.

"No, just tired. I want to get to bed."

Noel laughed. "Of course you do. It's your wedding night. Come on, Lindsay, let's leave the lovebirds to their thing."

Lindsay chuckled. "We'll see you tomorrow."

MJ's cheeks reddened.

"Shall we?"

"Shall we what?"

"Go back to the bungalow. The staff need to clean up," he said, his brow furrowed at the 'deer in the headlights' look on her face.

MJ licked her lips. "Of course."

Paul frowned down at her. "MJ, you aren't afraid to be alone with me, are you? I will behave myself, so if you're worried about me trying to claim conjugal rights, relax."

"It isn't that. It's just Mark and Melena will be here. I'm not looking forward to adding more complications to this mess. I wish we could just get on that boat and go home."

"We will, but for now, we're just two friends on an adventure. Let me scoop you up and get you to bed."

There was nothing he would like more than making love to his gorgeous wife, but he'd promised to keep his distance and he would. Who knew what the future might bring? Magic and lemonade. It would have to do.

* * *

MJ rolled over and opened her eyes. The bed beside her was empty, but the indentation in the pillow proved Paul had slept there. Had he wanted to claim those conjugal rights last night, she would have cooperated only too gladly. Why was it getting her wish never quite turned out the way she wanted it to?

Reaching for her glasses, she glanced at the clock.

Yikes! It was almost noon. Getting up quickly, she hurried into the bathroom to shower and take care of her morning needs. A knock on the door startled her.

"I heard you get up. Brunch will be here in half an hour. I'll be out on the deck when you're done. Do you want tea or coffee?"

"Tea, please," she answered, hoping she sounded as relaxed as he did.

Fifteen minutes later, dressed in yellow capris and a black and yellow gingham sleeveless blouse, she stepped out onto the deck. Paul sat in one of the loungers.

"Thanks for letting me sleep in," she said, nervous about her role now. She was his wife, the old ball and chain. Did he feel trapped?

Paul looked up and smiled.

"I figured you needed the rest after all of last night's surprises. It was after ten when I got up. How do you feel this morning?"

Married.

"Surprisingly well," MJ lied, shoving all her fear and anxiety deep inside. "My body must be getting used to the alcohol."

He laughed, the sound of his genuine pleasure relaxing her. Maybe things between them really hadn't changed.

"It probably has something to do with all the water we drank last night, too. Nate Jeffries might be part of the nut squad, but the doctor's advice works," he joked. "I don't think we met the one drink, one glass of water rule, but we came pretty close. Bill sure as hell didn't, but he deserves whatever hangover he has. Are you hungry?"

"Starving, actually, and you must be right about the water because I did feel a lot worse Sunday morning and even yesterday, but I figure my nervousness didn't help. How did you sleep?"

"Like a baby, and believe me, that's a wonderful feeling. Having you around is good for my peace of mind."

MJ beamed. It wasn't a declaration of undying love, but it was a place to start. If she could calm his soul, then perhaps she could win his heart, and maybe this marriage of convenience could become the real thing—babies and all.

Before she could answer, the doorbell rang indicating brunch.

"I'll get it." Paul jumped up and headed indoors.

Within minutes, he was back with a waiter pushing a heavily laden cart.

"*Félicitations, Monsieur et Madame Davis*," the waiter said, expertly popping the cork on another bottle of champagne.

Whoever had the wine and alcohol contract on the island must be making a fortune.

"Would you like the champagne plain or as a mimosa?"

"Mimosa sounds good to me," she answered, "but heavy on the orange juice, please."

"Make it two," Paul added.

The waiter made the drinks and bowed. "There's a note for Madame." He handed her the small white envelope. "Enjoy your meal. Monsieur St Louis asked me to remind you that you'll meet in the main dining room at two."

"Thanks."

Paul escorted the waiter to the door.

MJ glanced at the message on the small card, shook her head, and tossed the note aside before staring out at the water. Clouds were massing on the horizon—not an auspicious start to the first day of her marriage, but what did she expect? Melena and Mark were arriving at this very moment. Was it wrong to hope they'd had a rough crossing?

She didn't hear Paul until he was right behind her.

"Here," he said, handing her the mimosa. He raised the glass. "To the future."

MJ clinked her glass on his. "To us." She sipped the drink and licked her lips. "Damn, these are good."

"What's the note about? Another surprise?"

"No, thank God. It's an apology from Bill. He claims he was drunk and misinterpreted something in his research. He hopes I understand that he means me no harm." She shook her head. "Notice he doesn't say he's given up on mermaids and his other crazy ideas, but he's the least of my problems today."

"Yeah, but we'll deal with M and M together. At any rate, he had the decency to apologize."

"True, but I'm not sure how sincere he is. You didn't see his eyes."

A long blast, similar to that of the train whistle as the locomotive pulled into the station, startled MJ, and she almost dropped the crystal glass she held.

"What the hell was that?"

"The whistle to tell the guests that the ferry to return them to the mainland has arrived. They have an hour to make it to the dock." Paul sat. "Let's eat."

MJ stood there, suddenly unable to pull the air into her lungs as panic filled her. They were here now. They were really here.

Paul looked up and jumped to his feet.

"MJ, what is it? What's wrong?"

She couldn't stop shaking as she gasped for air.

Paul pulled her into his arms, the fear on his face stunning in its intensity. "It's okay. I'm here, but I can't help you if I don't know what's wrong, honey. Are you choking? Do you need your inhaler? Speak to me. MJ, for the love of God, speak to me."

Gasping out each word, tears welling in her eyes, MJ looked up at Paul. "Oh God, Paul. They're here—they have to be. He'll kill me when he discovers what we've done."

Paul exhaled as his color returned to normal, and he pulled her into his chest.

"Is that what this is about? Relax, and take a deep breath. I'm here. If he so much as looks at you sideways, he'll answer to me. You're my wife, MJ and I will stand by you in all things and defend you from all dangers. Now, do you need your inhaler?"

She shook her head and forced herself to calm down. Gradually, the tightness in her chest eased, and she sipped the water he offered her.

"I'm sorry," she said, looking up at him. "I thought I had it under control, but..."

Paul bent his head and touched his lips to hers, spiraling her back into the awe and wonder she'd experienced during their wedding when he'd kissed her and later in the carriage. Clinging to this lifeline, she threw caution to the wind and returned his kiss with everything in her.

When he broke the kiss, she saw the passion in his eyes, quickly followed by confusion.

"We'd better eat, or we'll be late."

MJ nodded. He was right, and as much as she insisted on being punctual, this was one meeting she'd love to ignore.

CHAPTER SEVENTEEN

MJ followed Paul to the main building still not sure if her feet were actually touching the ground. After the kiss, they'd finished breakfast, and the meal had been as magical as the rest of this place. As if by mutual consent, they didn't mention anything that could disrupt the idyllic setting. Stopping under one of the trees whose leaves formed a canopy blocking out the sun, Paul pulled her into his arms again.

"This is it. The battle lines are drawn, and the enemy's waiting. We'll win, MJ, and not only this skirmish, but the whole damn war."

"Spoken like a soldier," she said, smiling nervously.

"Hey, as long as we stay together and act naturally, Mark will have to sit on any questions he has until another time, and we've agreed not to give him that opening."

She nodded. It would be easy to fall so deeply in love with this man who was protecting her and her reputation that there would be no going back. Who was she kidding? She was more than halfway there now. She gazed down at the rings she wore, stage dressing for the role she would play for the next few months.

Paul opened the door to the dining room, redecorated once more to resemble the interior of a wooden sailing vessel.

"How do they do this?" she asked, looking around, awed by the authentic detail. "Someone must've stayed up all night."

Etienne, dressed like a mid-eighteenth-century sailor, came over to them.

"*Bonjour,* Monsieur et Madame Davis. If you would come with me? The other members of your party are waiting. We have a rum punch prepared which I am sure you will enjoy. Monsieur Leroux should arrive shortly." His excitement was palpable, making MJ smile.

Following the young man to what had to be one of the best tables, she was thrilled to see Lindsay and Noel sitting there with the Smiths and the Larsons. As usual, Bill didn't look pleased, but he had the grace to acknowledge them. He probably had a King Kong sized headache, too. Served him right.

"I thought you were on a different team," MJ said to Lindsay, choosing to focus on her friend rather than the taciturn man.

Her friend shrugged. "So did we, but they had to rearrange things for some reason."

Bill was about to speak when Christy shook her head. "Give it a rest. What's done is done. Live with it."

Before the man could comment, a drum roll sounded silencing everyone in the room. MJ didn't dare look around for Melena and Mark. The last thing she wanted was for him to know she was looking for him.

Monsieur St Louis took the stage.

"Bonjours Messieurs et Mesdames. It's a pleasure to welcome all of you who are participating in the Lacorneille Treasure Hunt. Monsieur Leroux will be her shortly to go over the rules. Merci."

"That's my cue to go to the ladies' room," MJ said as Monsieur St Louis descended from the stage.

"I'd better go with you," Cindy said. "Lord knows if I don't, I'll have to go the minute he starts talking."

MJ chuckled. "That's why I'm going now." She grinned at Paul. "Be right back."

"I've never had anything to eat like what they brought us this morning," Cindy gushed as they entered the hallway. "My friends back home won't believe it. I always laugh when people post pictures of their meals, but that was amazing. My apple was cut into a swan, the banana was all chevrons, and the other fruit—some I'd never even seen or tasted before—were cut up and shaped into flowers. The strawberries were dipped in white chocolate and the oranges in dark, the very tips covered in gold-colored sugar. It was just so decadent." She giggled. "It was like having candy for breakfast."

MJ laughed, pushing open the door to the powder room. "You'll be taking lots of pictures before you're done."

As soon as they finished, MJ followed Cindy out of the lavatory.

"MJ?"

She turned toward the voice, a smile she prayed looked natural on her face.

"Mark. I heard you were coming," she said.

He held himself as if he were made of steel, his face devoid of all expression. "This is quite a surprise."

"Go ahead, Cindy. Tell Paul I'll be there in a minute."

Cindy hesitated, nodded, and hurried away.

MJ swallowed her discomfort, grateful to see so many people milling about. Mark didn't like audience participation unless the focus was on him, so he would keep his distance—for now.

"Why should it be a surprise?"

As soon as Cindy entered the dining room and closed the door, he grabbed her arm, his fingers sinking deep into her flesh and pulled her abruptly behind a wall of miniature trees. She gasped, knowing she would have a bruise when this was over. What was it with bullies? Leave an imprint wherever you could? She'd already used coverup to hide Bill's fingermarks on her other arm.

"What the hell are you playing at?" Mark demanded through gritted teeth, his fingers clenching her arm more tightly as if he expected her to try to escape. "Bride of the week? A fake wedding on national TV?"

"You're hurting me," she hissed. Her heart pounded against her ribcage, and her lungs tightened. This wasn't the time for an attack. She fought to keep her fear hidden and looked him in the eye, bravado coming to her rescue. He'd tried to ruin her life, and she wasn't going to let him know how close he'd come. If it hadn't been for Paul ... "I'm not playing at anything. Let go of my arm." She tried to pull away. If anything, Mark squeezed harder, the bone starting to ache under the pressure.

"Bitch, answer my question. What the hell are you doing here?"

Spittle exploded from his mouth, speckling her face. Her stomach churned.

"I told you I was coming here—I just didn't mention that it would be for my honeymoon," she answered defensively, cowed by his fury. "Let go of me."

"I saw your so-called wedding pictures in the lobby when we checked in. The girl at the desk went on and on about the cameras ... What did you do? Buy some poor shmuck and get him to play the doting lover? This whole set up is a scam, and I'll prove it, and when I do, that talk show host you conned into sponsoring the event will have you thrown in jail. You'll get exactly what's coming to you."

"Darling, is something wrong?" Paul materialized next to them, and Mark released her arm.

Her fingers rubbed the tender spot.

Paul frowned, putting his arm around her and pulling her to his side.

"Buzz off, buddy. The lady and I are having a conversation."

"The lady is my wife," Paul said, his voice deadly calm.

"So, you're the gigolo she picked up for this charade. You've been had. She may seem sweet and loving, but the bitch has ice water in her veins and between the two of us, whatever she's promised you for this little gig is a lie. Why don't you cut your losses and crawl back under whichever rock she found you?"

Paul stared at Mark, the muscle jumping in his cheek the only sign of his fury, something she recognized from when they'd been children. He tucked her protectively against him. Smiling down at her, he winked, no doubt to tell her he was in control, but she wasn't so sure of that. He kissed her, sending pleasant shivers down her spine.

He turned to her aggressor, the steel in his voice unmistakable.

"I suggest you apologize to my wife right now before I make you eat your words," he whispered barely loud enough for MJ to hear. "Otherwise, I have no compunction against taking you outside and beating the living shit out of you. I've done it before, and I can do it again."

All the color drained from Mark's face.

"Who the hell do you think you are?" Mark blustered. "You can't threaten people like that. It's illegal."

"So is identity theft," Paul answered. "As to who I am, I'm your worst nightmare. The fact you don't recognize me doesn't ruin my day in the least. I'll only say this once. Never come near my wife again. I know you, and I know exactly what you've done. We went to school together. You never did know when to shut up. Just to refresh your memory, I'm Paul Davis."

She watched the color rise in Mark's face. "I remember you." He reached out his hand, expecting Paul to snub him, but Paul grasped his outstretched hand and shook it, squeezing his hand more tightly than Mark had expected, since he winced.

"Oh, sorry about that," Paul said releasing Mark's hand and turning to her. "They'll be a few minutes yet, darling, shall we go out onto the veranda?" he asked, dismissing Mark as if he didn't matter.

"We need to talk, MJ," Mark said, his face red, his jaw locked.

Paul smiled, his lips compressed, his eyes cold. "I can't imagine what you and Marilyn have to discuss," he said, "unless it's how you plan to repay her the money you stole from her."

He nodded and escorted MJ out onto the veranda through the open French doors leaving Mark sputtering like a faulty engine.

"I think that should give him something to think about." Paul handed her a mojito from the tray the waiter carried.

She took a drink, almost emptying the glass in the process. "You have perfect timing. I'm glad you showed up when you did." She rubbed her arm.

"Did he hurt you? I'll kill the bastard if he did."

She reached up and touched his cheek. "It's nothing. See, the marks are almost gone." He bent his head and kissed her arm making it tingle.

"When Cindy came back to the table alone and said you'd run into some guy you knew, I saw red. He's lucky I didn't rip his arm out of its socket."

"Well, you're my hero," she said, standing on tip toe and kissing his cheek again. "This makes it four days in a row that you've come to my rescue."

Paul took her glass and placed it next to his on the cocktail table closest to them. He bent his head and captured her mouth filling her with desire. His lips were soft and tender, and when his tongue teased at them, she opened and let him carry her away on a sea of sensation only he could create. This wasn't simply a kiss. He was making love to her mouth, and she was enjoying every second of it. The kiss was full of passion and desire, and she reveled in the unexpectedness of it. Paul raised his head slowly, his gaze fixed on hers.

"You're my wife, MJ, and I'm very protective of what's mine. If he knows what's good for him, he'll keep his distance. Now, ready to join the others?"

MJ nodded, too confused by Paul's words and actions to say or do anything else.

* * *

Paul led MJ back into the main room and over to their table, fighting to keep his jumbled emotions hidden. When Cindy had returned alone, he'd known exactly who MJ had met, and then when he'd seen the bastard manhandling her ... well, had he been anywhere but here, he would've made good on his offer to beat the shit out of the son of a bitch.

But as troubling as Mark's presence was, it was the kiss and the need for more of them that had him completely off kilter. He'd spent hours last night just watching her sleep, staying as far from her as he could, terrified by the strength of his desire for her. Somehow what had started as a wish to help a friend, had exploded into a physical and emotional hunger for the woman at his side. This thing with Mark took a backseat to that, and maybe that's why he'd given everything away the way he had.

From the moment his lips had touched MJ's on Saturday night, he'd been lost, his emotions a jumbled mess. He'd kissed plenty of women in his days, but never once had a kiss affected him the way touching her lips did. At first, he'd been hurt when she'd dismissed it as play acting, but last night and today proved he wasn't imagining it. Whatever he felt, she felt it, too. It was probably only lust—after all, he hadn't had a woman in months— but whatever it was, it was an itch he had to scratch in the worst way. MJ was his wife, and knowing full well he didn't deserve any of it, he no longer wanted to keep this a marriage in name only. He wanted the whole enchilada.

MJ stopped before they entered the dining room.

"Why did you tell Mark you knew he'd stolen this vacation from me?"

"I don't really know," he admitted. "I guess I don't want the bastard ruining a single second of this for us. Getting it all out into the open seemed like a good idea. There've been more than enough surprises already."

She nodded. "Well, you certainly surprised him. Who knows? Maybe it'll work and keep him away from me, and if it stops him from badmouthing me, I'll be satisfied."

"If he intends to deny it and not make restitution, I'm certain he'll keep his distance." And that's what he wanted—that man as far away from MJ as possible.

Pulling open the door to the main room, he escorted her to their table, keeping his eyes peeled for Mark. He spotted him half a dozen tables away from theirs. The man's face was still red, and he was arguing with the brunette at his side. No one at his table looked impressed. Once a jerk, always a jerk.

They'd just sat down when Antoine Leroux stepped up to the microphone.

"*Bonjours, mesdames et messieurs.* It's my pleasure to welcome you all to join me on this hunt for Jean Lacorneille's treasure. On your tables, the lemon-colored sheet of paper is the legal document you must sign to participate. While you may find the treasure, you cannot keep any of it."

A chorus of grumbles greeted that announcement, and Bill's "What the hell do you mean by that?" was among the loudest.

"Hear me out," Leroux interrupted. "There is a finder's fee available, 10 percent of the value of whatever we find, but as is usually the case in these matters, the treasure belongs to the residents of Paradise Island, the descendants of Lacorneille and his crew. No doubt the Spanish and Peruvian governments will want some of the artifacts, but the bulk of it belongs here and must stay."

Paul looked over at Mark whose face was as thunderous as Bill's.

"Take a few minutes to read the document before you sign it," Leroux continued. "Once you do, we'll finalize the teams, get you a grid area to search, and start the treasure hunt first thing in the morning. I'm on my way back to Saint Pierre to finalize the dive permits. I'll see you tomorrow. Remember: no signed document, no treasure hunt."

"That's bullshit," Bill said. "If we can't keep any of the treasure, this is all a big waste of time."

Paul smiled at him. "Do you think so? This is a honeymoon resort. The treasure hunt should come second to that." He stood. "If you'll excuse us."

"Wait," Rick grabbed his arm. "Sign the paper. Louis James expects you to."

He glanced at MJ.

She nodded. "Why not?" and signed her name—Marilyn Davis.

Paul smiled. "Looks good. Let's get out of here. I think the tour to the volcano is leaving shortly."

MJ put her hand in his. He could feel Mark's gaze boring into his back, but he didn't care. He'd spent enough time around assholes today to last him awhile.

* * *

Watching the dark clouds mass on the horizon, MJ sipped her champagne. There would be a storm tonight. Carla had mentioned that hurricane season often started in July, the one excuse that had actually made MJ hesitate about coming here, but in the end, it hadn't stopped her. They were well ahead of the worst of it, but with the way climate change was affecting things, anything was possible. The skies did look foreboding, and she shivered.

Her nervous gaze roamed the lagoon. Until today, it had been so still it resembled blue-green glass. Tonight, the brisk wind hung whitecaps on the much darker green water. The lower deck appeared and vanished again as the waves covered it.

Memories of her brief, and yet far too long, encounter with Mark filled her. While she and Paul had avoided M and M for the rest of the day, they were bound to run into them. Perhaps they could skip the dancing for one night—not that she didn't love being in his arms—but considering the climbing they'd done today, his knee had to be bothering him.

"Ready?" Paul asked coming up behind her. "I know we don't have to be in the dining room for another hour, but Bill seems to think he's in charge and wants to go over tomorrow's itinerary for the hunt. Noel doesn't appear to care about the treasure any more than I do, so he's content to let the man continue to be a legend in his own mind. Apparently, Bill's manipulated things so that, with the exception of the four of us, he has all of the S.O.T's on his team. From what I can see," he held up the list of team members that had arrived with the canapés, "Mark isn't on it."

"Good. I wish we could just forget about the treasure and focus on other activities like we did today." Maybe it was cowardly, but wasn't avoiding bad situations an accepted survival strategy?

Paul pulled her into his chest. "If it were up to me, I would say yes, but Louis needs us on this, and it is only for part of each day. If you're worried about Mark, don't be. I can take care of my own, and don't sell yourself short. I seem to remember you had a mean left hook."

MJ bit her lip. "That was an accident, and you know it." She chuckled. "But you never snuck up on me again."

Paul laughed. "I'm a quick learner." He bent his head and kissed her once more, sending all thoughts of Mark out of her head.

"Come on, Cinderella. There's a party going on, and we're still the guests of honor."

She nodded. "If you say so. Let's just hope the ugly stepbrother doesn't make an appearance." But given the choice, she would much rather stay right where she was.

It was almost ten when Etienne cleared away the last of the dishes from yet another sumptuous meal. She hadn't noticed Mark and Melina in the dining room, so the two must've had the early sitting. Of course, the way he'd been drinking earlier, he could simply be passed out cold in his room, and that would be fine with her. Another wish come true thanks to Quimbois?

"Shouldn't the music have started by now?" Cindy asked, her voice slurred. "You did promise me a dance, Paul." She batted her glazed eyes at him.

"Smarten up, Cindy," Rick growled. "You've had too much to drink."

"Well, if you and Bill hadn't left Christy and me alone all day, I might not have had as much." She hiccupped.

MJ stifled her laughter. Come to think of it, Christy had been quieter than usual tonight, as had Bill. What were those two cooking up now?

"*Mesdames et messieurs, pardon.*" Raymond's voice boomed in the room, followed by screeching speakers. The man's face was red, and his combover stood on end, reminding her of an angry rooster. "I'm sorry," he continued, "but due to factors beyond my control, tonight's entertainment has been canceled. An unexpected tropical storm has materialized off the east coast, and while we do not expect it to hit the island, it is always best to be prepared."

MJ frowned. The clouds she'd seen had been in the west. Two storms converging couldn't be a good thing. Hadn't there been a movie about that? Something called *The Perfect Storm*? She shuddered.

"For those of you who wish to continue to enjoy the evening, there will be music in the lounge until eleven. For guests on the ocean side, hurricane shutters have been installed, and while those of you on the lagoons shouldn't face the brunt of the storm, we have secured the bungalows and patio furniture."

"Are we in any danger?" Rick asked. Cindy, suddenly sober, clung to him. "We're on the ocean side."

"You are as safe here as you would be in your own bed," the manager answered.

"That's not saying a hell of a lot," Bill grumbled. "We were in Florida when Matthew hit."

Noel smiled. "Look on the bright side. There was a freak storm the night Lacorneille's ship sank. Who knows, another one might reveal it."

Lindsay laughed. "My husband, the eternal optimist. If you don't mind, we'll skip the drinks and go out to the cabin now. We're on the ocean side so it should be an interesting night, and I may be able to get some awesome storm pictures. Hopefully, the brunt of it will pass us by and be over by breakfast. At this time of year, these storms normally blow themselves out after they make landfall." She stood. "Goodnight."

One by one the other couples left.

"Do you want a drink?" Paul asked, "Or do you want to go back."

Torn between not being certain she wanted to be in that bungalow during a storm and the fear of running into Mark again, she chose the lesser of two evils.

"Let's go back, but in case you've forgotten, I don't do well in this kind of weather. You remember the night lightning split the oak tree, and it crashed into the Miller's house next door?"

"Yeah. I was sleeping over." Paul smiled. "Don't worry. I've weathered a storm here already and can guarantee those buildings are stronger than they look." He stood. "Come on. No swim tonight; the water's too rough, but we've got a bottle of champagne and can watch the fish play around the reef."

Paul held her hand as they walked along the path to the lagoon. Even sheltered in the trees as they were, the wind was powerful, raining leaves and other debris down on them.

"Looks like the dinosaurs have all run for cover, too."

Paul nodded. "As the saying goes, it isn't a fit night out for man or beast, but we'll be safe. Don't worry. Didn't your mother have a Greek myth that covered unexpected storms?"

They'd just reached the dock when the first rumbles of thunder could be heard in the distance. She shivered.

"Not Mama. She was the 'toss holy water around the place and light every candle she could find' type. Aunt Maria, Antonia's mother, was the one who would regale us with mythology. She used to say storms like these were Hades arguing with Zeus and tossing dice for the souls heading to the underworld to see who went to Tartarus and who would get to go to the Elysian Fields. It never made me feel any better."

"I can understand why. I thought Tartarus was for the wicked," he said. "I didn't realize it was all decided on a throw of the dice. Maybe Mark has a shot at better digs despite his unsavory character."

"Possibly, but I doubt it," she giggled. "That man's rotten to the core, but there are cases where a beautiful outside hides a wicked inside. No matter what face you show the world, the gods' dice can see into your soul."

"That should be comforting but isn't," Paul said. "Come on. Let's get inside before the rain starts."

MJ nodded. Another crack of thunder had her moving a little faster toward the lagoon.

Several hours later, she awoke to darkness, vicious wind and rain pummeling the bungalow. A flash of lightning lit up the room like midday and the explosive thunder made everything tremble as if the Earth itself were shivering.

MJ quaked under the blanket, not from cold but from fear, as every bad thing she'd ever heard about tropical storms raced through her mind. When they'd finished the bottle of champagne earlier, pleasantly drowsy and slightly inebriated, she'd joined Paul in bed and drifted off despite the wind and rain, but now, it was as if Mother Nature was hitting them with everything she had.

Reluctant to get up, she climbed out, grateful Paul let her sleep on the side closest to the washroom, and hurried as another crack of thunder shook the building. Closing the door, she felt for the light switch and flipped it on. Nothing.

The power was out, but that was only a mild inconvenience. She might be afraid of storms, but the dark didn't bother her. Allowing her eyes to adjust, she found her way to the toilet, the sink, and then opened the door.

Mother Nature's light show made her shiver, reminding her of another Greek myth Aunt Maria used to tell, the one where Zeus had almost destroyed the world of men by throwing thunderbolts at the Titans who'd escaped from the underworld. For what it was worth, right now, she'd put her money behind Zeus.

CHAPTER EIGHTEEN

MJ debated the wisdom of simply riding out the storm in the bathroom when another sound all but obliterated the most recent crash of thunder. Opening the door at the very moment a flash of lightning lit up the room, she saw Paul thrashing on the bed, agonizing moans and cries escaping him.

"Don't," he shouted, caught in a nightmare.

Without hesitation, MJ climbed into bed and whispered, hoping to wake him without startling him. The next boom of thunder sent her scurrying across the tangled sheets to his side.

"Paul, wake up," she said, her voice catching in her throat as the bungalow shuddered again. Something slammed against the windows, and panic filled her. Would the pane of glass hold? Every petrifying memory of that childhood storm filled her.

She reached out and touched Paul's bare shoulder, needing his comfort. His skin burned beneath her palm. Praying he wasn't sick, she shook him, stunned when he sat up.

"Fiona, stay behind me. Stay down," he cried, pushing her face into the pillow. "Don't get up! Don't give him a target." He removed his hand from her shoulder as if he were moving away from her. In a flash of light, she saw Paul's eyes were open and filled with fear. Wherever he was, it wasn't here with her. He was with Fiona. Jealousy replaced her earlier panic, but the agony on his face shamed her, grounding her as nothing else could.

Knowing she had to wake him, MJ grabbed both sides of his face, forcing it to stay still, willing him to see her, although she doubted he saw anything but Fiona and the horror going on inside his head.

"Paul, it's me, it's MJ."

He was still deep in the throes of the vicious dream. Pulling herself up close against him, she put her arms around him and held on. Paul's flesh was sweat-covered, his heart beating rapidly. She lifted her hand to his cheek and his jumped up, gripping her wrist so tightly, he could snap it.

"Paul, you're hurting me. It's MJ. Please wake up."

Lightning blazed once again, illuminating the room, and Paul blinked, releasing his grip.

She moved away and rubbed her hand.

"MJ?" he asked, staring at her as if she were some kind of apparition. Thunder crashed once more, and the bungalow shook.

"Yeah, it's me. You were having a bad dream."

He blinked again, looked down at the way she was rubbing her wrist, and jerked away from her.

"I hurt you, didn't I?" He stood and began to pace near the bed. "This is what I was afraid of. Why I should have stayed away from you. I knew it could happen. I've put you in danger. This time I grabbed your wrist, but what if the next time I grab your throat?"

"Paul Davis, you stop talking stupid right now," she said, getting out of bed and standing in front of him, fisted hands on her hips, her teeth clenched. "You let go as soon as I said you were hurting me. I'm fine. Mark did far worse this afternoon. You may not want to do it, but you need to talk to someone about what happened to you."

He moved to turn on the bedside lamp.

"The power's out. There are candles on the table I can light, but sitting in the dark—if it would stay that way—is fine with me." She sat back on the bed and moved over to give him room to join her, not sure he would.

He settled beside her and surprised her by reaching for her wrist.

"I guess this isn't the best kind of night for you either, is it? I'm sorry I hurt you," he said, kissing her flesh. "I haven't had that nightmare in months."

"Who's Fiona?"

Without warning, he stood. "I need to go."

Moving quickly despite the dark, the room illuminated by nature's fireworks, Paul disappeared into the washroom.

MJ wrapped her arms around herself. How much longer could this go on? Something struck the window once more. At this rate, by the time the storm let up, there would be nothing left of Paradise Island.

* * *

Paul swallowed the bile in his throat and turned on the tap, splashing cold water into his face. He'd hurt MJ, far more than she was letting on, and the guilt burned holes in his already damaged gut. Could he tell her about Fiona? She deserved to know what kind of broken, dangerous, haunted man he really was, and why their marriage didn't stand a chance.

Exiting the bathroom, he made his way back to the bed where MJ sat up against the headboard. The wind screamed outside, the sound eerie, like the cries he'd heard in Kabul. Maybe her aunt had been onto something and those were tortured souls on their way to hell. He settled beside her, and when the thunder boomed again, and she started, he pulled her into his arms.

"Not exactly a restful night, is it? And after the day you've had ... The shrink made me talk about that night, but maybe I didn't get it all off my chest. I mentioned some of this in the interview before the wedding. That could be what set off the nightmare." Or it could've been facing Mark and defending her like he'd tried and failed to do for Fiona.

She nestled into him. "I'm wide awake and since this storm seems intent on staying around, I won't be able to sleep anyway."

He nodded. "Fiona was a UN teacher working in Kabul. She and the ambassador's wife were old college friends, and I got to know her when she dropped by the embassy to visit. There was a system in place in Afghanistan similar to the underground railway in the United States during the Civil War. I don't know who ran it, but Fiona was heavily involved. The goal was to smuggle vulnerable young women and children out of the country. It wasn't a government sanctioned activity, but more often than not, those in power turned a blind eye to it."

"It should've been," MJ said, the indignation in her voice reminding him of Fiona once more. "I've read about the atrocities committed against women and children there."

"For obvious reasons, including not causing problems for the ambassador, Fiona usually kept her activities to herself, but one case in particular really got to her. It was a high-risk scenario, but she was stubborn and turned to the ambassador's wife for help. According to Fiona, Anoosha was brilliant and had hopes of becoming a doctor. The ambassador's wife agreed to help and offered to hide the children in the embassy until they could get them out of the country. The girl's uncle, a warlord with Taliban connections no one could prove, had arranged her marriage, which would effectively put an end to any dreams she had. MJ, she was only ten."

MJ pushed away from him, and even in the dark he could see her flaring nostrils and jutting chin.

"My God! That's a crime. Not only shouldn't one person have that kind of power over another, but Paul, she was just a child. How could that society condone such a thing?"

He pursed his lips. "It's a tough thing to swallow by our standards, but it happens quite often and to girls even younger than Anoosha. It isn't so bad if the groom is a child as well and the marriage is meant to cement an alliance, but this time, the groom was a man old enough to be her grandfather."

"Oh God. What happened?"

"Fiona made plans to sneak them into the embassy until they could join another group of girls leaving the country in a private plane. The day it was scheduled to happen, the two didn't show up at school. Fiona was worried, and asked me to go with her to see what had happened. They could've been sick. The old woman who usually brought them to school answered the door, and I could tell she was scared. She and Fiona argued back and forth in Farsi, I caught a couple of words here and there, but they were going at it a mile a minute. In the end, the old woman let us into the house. Apparently, the uncle had insisted they stop attending school, and the girls had argued the matter. Justice is swift, and men rule with an iron fist."

MJ gasped, and nestled into him more deeply.

"Within seconds, she came out with Anoosha in her arms," he continued. "She was too injured to walk. I carried her out to the embassy car while Fi carried the six-year-old. Those poor girls had been beaten so badly, it was amazing they were still alive. The grandmother was crying, no doubt because she figured she'd get beaten too, but when I looked at her without a mark and down at those kids ... I swore I would do whatever it took to get them to safety."

Against a backdrop of howling wind, booming thunder, and flashes of lightning, the room disappeared, and he was back behind the wheel of the embassy car.

The sun had set, and the street should've been deserted, but they weren't. It was hotter than hell and people had escaped the confines of their homes, lazing about on their roofs or in the street near the doorways. Driving slowly, he watched for pedestrians, uncomfortable with how long it was taking. He looked up, certain the shadow he'd seen against the wall was that of an armed man, but the roof was deserted. An overturned cart forced him to make a right turn. He hadn't gone more than a block or two when he noticed that these narrower streets were empty. Where was everyone?

"Stay low, Fiona. I don't like the looks of this place. Don't give them a target. We're about three blocks from the gates."

The crack of gunfire sounded loudly and the pull on the wheel told him he'd lost one, maybe both, front tires. The next bullet shattered the windshield, embedding itself in the back of the seat where Fiona would've been sitting had she not gotten into the backseat with the children. Another bullet hit the glass, sending shards toward his face. He ducked, but felt the sting and burn on his brow.

"Are you alright?" Fiona asked.

"Stay down. I don't know where the shots are coming from, but we're sitting ducks like this. There's some cover under the awnings near the edge of the houses. We're going to have to make a run for it."

He turned on his radio, but the static was strong. Calling for help was a "Hail Mary" play, but it was all he had.

He stopped the vehicle, got out of the car, but before he could open the door for Fiona and the girls, the sniper's bullets hit him—one grazing his head, another in the chest, the third shattering his knee. He fell to the ground beside the car. Fiona jumped out to help him, but suddenly there were legs all around them, stepping on him, kicking him. Blood in his eyes blinded him, but he heard Fiona's screams, the sound of it something he would never forget.

"I must have drifted into unconsciousness. When I awoke, the two girls were kneeling on the ground beside Fiona's body. A man, his face covered by a blue and white scarf, yelled at them. They bowed their heads, and he stepped behind them and fired point blank into their skulls. He stepped back and spat on them. After lowering his mask, he looked straight at me, the hatred in his eyes palpable. I recognized him. He kicked me hard in the ribs and walked away. I couldn't understand why the bastard hadn't killed me, but now I realize he thought he had. It was touch and go for a few days. Once I was out of danger, I told the MPs what I'd seen, but the man was long gone. They told me that, three days after the incident, one of the embassy housekeeping staff and an old woman had walked into the girls' school, wearing suicide vests, and killed fifteen students and four UN workers. The school hasn't been rebuilt. That's why I don't deserve to be happy. I'm the one responsible for all of those deaths. I got them killed. It was my decision to ask Jasim to help us. I suspected we had a mole in the embassy, I just never thought it would be the man I'd befriended. I should've died on that street with them."

He moved to pull away from her, but her grip tightened.

"Oh, Paul," she said, her throat clogged with tears he felt running down her cheeks onto his chest.

How long had she been crying?

"You didn't fail anyone. You tried to save them from a fate worse than death, and you did. As awful as it sounds, a bullet in the head was far more merciful than the life they would've had at the hands of lecherous old men. Even the grandmother, who was probably one of the two people who blew up the school, had to know that. You were taken in by a man who pretended to be something he wasn't, and we've all been down that road. My heart bleeds for all the innocent victims, but you almost died, too. The animal who killed Fiona and executed those girls will burn in hell for what he did. Not you."

She put her arms around him and pulled him close to her.

He held her, powerless to push her away, knowing he should, and unable to do so, just as he couldn't stop the tears running down his cheeks. As they sat like that, weeping for girls she'd never known, Paul realized the lightening wasn't as bad as it had been and while the wind was still fierce, the thunder was farther way as well.

"It looks like the storm's blowing itself out," he said, knowing he should let her go, but terrified that if he did, he would be sucked back into the memories and the blackness once more. "We should get some sleep."

"Okay," she answered, but made no move to leave his side.

Paul awoke to the sound of rain beating against the window, pushed there by the winds that had yet to calm. MJ was spooned into him, while his hand was wrapped around her stomach under the oversized t-shirt she wore. Her back pressed to his front felt like molten lava and his body reacted to her heat and scent.

He might not be worthy of her, but he couldn't deny he needed more from her than friendship. Whatever this was had to be nurtured and fed. Done right, it could grow strong and endure, but one false move, and he would destroy it forever. He exhaled heavily, not wanting to move away, but knowing he had to before she recognized the strength of his desire for her. As he eased away, she matched his movement, snuggling even more. She moaned softly.

"God, MJ, there's nothing I want more than to make love to you right now," he whispered, thinking she was still asleep.

"So, what's stopping you?" she asked, looking at him over her shoulder, her eyes open in the dim light.

Unable to hold off any longer even though he knew he should, he trailed kisses down the side of her neck and shoulders. She turned toward him and raised her arms to encircle his neck. It was all the encouragement he needed. Without another word, he captured her lips. She returned his kisses with a passion that spurred him on. Slowly, afraid this might be just another dream, he removed the T-shirt, exposing her breasts to his hands. His mouth moved down to lick and caress each nipple, imprinting their taste and texture on his tongue and in his mind. He wanted to touch all of her, taste all of her, and savor each delectable bite. His lips moved along her stomach to the edge of her panties, which he quickly removed.

Panting, Paul lifted his head and looked into her eyes.

"Are you sure, MJ? Once we do this, there's no turning back."

"Make love to me, Paul. Make love to me now."

Quickly divesting himself of his underwear, he caressed her lower abdomen. Gently, as if he were opening a precious, rare gift, he spread her legs and gradually buried himself inside her. As he moved in and out, she clenched around him and held him tightly. Soft yet firm, her sweat-slicked body was everything he expected and more. He wouldn't last long, but it didn't matter. Her ragged breathing indicated she was on the verge of shattering and with one deep thrust, she went over the edge, her cry of ecstasy bringing on his release. Together, they climbed to Heaven and slowly free-fell to Earth.

Chest heaving, Paul rolled off MJ, not wanting his weight to crush her, turned on his side, and pulled her to him. Outside, the wind continued to howl, the rain lashed the windows, but for the first time in years, he was content and at peace. He kissed the side of her neck, and she snuggled into his arms. Words weren't necessary. They'd crossed a bridge and burned it behind them. There was no going back to the way things had been, and they would have to carve a new path together. She was his wife, and he would do whatever was necessary to make her happy. He closed his eyes and let sleep claim him.

Several hours later, a gentle shove in the ribs woke him.

"Release the death grip, sleepyhead," MJ said and chuckled. "I need to pee."

He grunted—it seemed the best thing to say—and let go of her.

"I think the storm's finally over." The creak of the closing door ended her comment.

Paul opened his eyes and rolled over, noting his body was still eager for his bride, but maybe he needed to slow things down just a little. Once MJ realized the implications of last night, she might not be ready to continue with this new phase of their relationship. After what had happened between them, there would be no annulment, but there couldn't be any children either. Genetically, he was flawed, and that was one bridge he wouldn't cross.

After last night's gale, the silence was eerie. Getting up, he donned his underwear and walked over to the window, pulling open the drapes. In front of him, the lagoon was strewn with floating debris, looking like some strange blue-green witch's brew.

"Oh my God," MJ said coming to stand beside him. "Where is everything?"

"I don't know," he answered, turning to pull her into his arms, pleased when she didn't resist. "Good morning."

"Good morning," she said shyly and stood on tiptoe to kiss him. He met her halfway. The moment their lips met, it rekindled his need for her, and all thought of caution flew out the window. Sweeping her off her feet, he carried her to the bed, shed his underwear, and removed the t-shirt she'd put on.

"I don't think I will ever get enough of you," he mumbled into her neck before losing himself in her once more.

* * *

Shared showers. What a wonderful idea. MJ's back had never been this clean, and as far as her hair went, that shampoo Paul had given her had been an almost orgasmic experience.

Despite having made love twice, Paul's erection grew again as he moved his hands from her back to her chest to soap her breasts. He was insatiable, but so was she. She'd never been this wanton and giving in bed before and as Carla had put it, Mark had never rung her bells, but with Paul, she had a whole damn carillon going. His hands moved down her stomach to the apex of her thighs and set her body on fire. She turned to him anxious for more.

It was several minutes later before sated and clean, Paul turned off the water in the double shower. No words of love had been spoken, but he'd given in to his physical need for her, and that would do for now. The spirits around here were working on fulfilling her wish the way she'd intended it. All she needed was a little bit more patience; sadly, that quality wasn't her strong point.

Her stomach grumbled.

Paul laughed. "Does someone need to be fed?"

"I do. All this exercise has left me starving," she said, wrapping herself in one of the two white robes from the back of the door. She grabbed the last piece of fruit from the bowl on the table. "What's for breakfast?"

"I know what I'd like to eat." He wiggled his eyebrows.

She smothered a giggle, her skin flushing at the image in her mind.

"Maybe later, but right now I need something more substantial."

"Let me call the kitchen and see what I can do." Paul picked up the receiver, but the line was dead. His brow furrowed. "The phones are down. It looks like we're going to have to go to the lounge if you want anything more than that banana. It's after ten, but I'm sure they've arranged something. There may be tons of melting ice cream we can finish off."

She pinched her lips together, striving for the look she gave a class of unruly students, but couldn't stop the snicker this time.

"Ice cream for breakfast? You wish. We're not at *Jurassic Park* on Isla Nublar. The power went down last night, but it's back. I'm sure all the ice cream cartons are safe and sound in the freezer."

"You mean both your delectable body and ice cream are off the breakfast menu? Damn." Paul pouted, sticking out his lower lip, and making her laugh so hard her sides hurt.

"You're crazy."

"So you keep saying, but I'm convinced I'm a genius." He moved around to nibble her neck, his hand reaching inside the robe to caress her breast. "Mmm. You taste so good."

He moved away, leaving her wishing for more of his touch, and handed her a cup of coffee, doctored the way she liked it.

"This will have to do for now."

He kissed the tip of her nose.

They should probably talk about what had happened, but she didn't know what to say other than she wanted it to continue.

"Let's get dressed before I change my mind and take you right back to bed. Besides, I suppose we should check on the others. If it was this bad here, it must've been brutal on the Atlantic side. Room service might not be the only thing affected."

"What do you mean?" she asked, opening the drawer to select some of the sexy underwear Carla had insisted she buy and then picking out the rest of her clothes.

"There are a number of activities that could be canceled depending on the damage. Room service might just be one of them. This could affect the treasure hunt, too." He grabbed a pair of underwear and started to dress.

"Well, if it has, the almighty Seekers of Treasure won't be happy," she said, and neither would Mark, but he was the last thing she wanted intruding on her morning.

Ten minutes later, wearing black shorts and a turquoise tube top, the turquoise pendant Carla had given her once more around her neck, contact lenses in place, MJ slipped her feet into black sandals and grabbed her non-prescription tortoiseshell sunglasses and her fanny pack. The only things in it were her lip gloss and emergency puffer, but she never went anywhere without them. Earlier, Paul had applied sunscreen to her shoulders, reminding her of all the lovely sensations his touch could bring.

When he opened the door, she couldn't stifle her cry of dismay. All around them, branches from palm trees and other tropical plants littered the wharf. The water level in the lagoon, which had been a good two feet below the walkway, was mere inches under the boards, and up ahead, along the beach, half a dozen of the majestic Roystonea trees, better known as royal palms, had been uprooted. Two of them blocked the path leading to the main building.

"Oh my God! I've never seen anything like this."

The silence was deafening. Where were the birds?

"And we weren't on the Atlantic side," Paul said. He huffed out a breath. "I hope everyone is okay."

As they neared the shore, the beach far narrower than it had been yesterday, MJ noted all the unusual shells, bits of wood, and other debris littering the far edge of it. She wrinkled her nose at the scent of rotting vegetation and who knew what beneath it.

"Look at this stuff. Maybe the ocean disgorged something to lead us to Lacorneille's ship. With all this damage to repair, the islanders could use a little unexpected money."

Paul smiled. "Ever the optimist, aren't you? But you're right. There's unusual stuff here, but I'll bet you'll find even more on the other side of the island."

She chuckled. "I should look for a mermaid's purse."

"We'll have to check on the Atlantic side. Most oviparity sharks—egg-layers—call the Indo-Pacific home, but anything is possible. Maybe Bill's mermaid likes to travel."

He bent his head and touched her lips. After what had happened between them last night, how could a simple kiss set her afire once more?

Desire flared in Paul's eyes. "We'd better get going or I'll take you right back to the bungalow, and we'll be lucky to see the rest of the day."

Licking her lips, quite ready to do just that, her stomach grumbled again, shattering the moment.

"I get it. Food first."

They'd reached the edge of the wharf.

"Here, let me help you."

Picking her up, Paul stepped over the trunks of the downed trees before setting her down on the path. Nearby, a few of the island's iguanas were munching away.

"Looks like those guys will have plenty of food for days to come," she said, nodding toward the reptiles eating their way through the heads of the downed palms. "If they get to feast like this after every storm, it's no wonder they're the size of dinosaurs."

As they approached the main building, MJ noted the many people clearing away the debris and damage left in the storm's wake. Overhead, the canopy seemed thinner, and here and there, bits of broken wire dangled from nude branches. The building itself, like the bungalows in their lagoon, had withstood nature's fury. She hoped for Lindsay and Cindy's sake that their cottages had fared as well. Since the Smiths were in another lagoon, she expected they'd been fine. Her stomach grumbled once more. Time for breakfast.

CHAPTER NINETEEN

Entering the main building, MJ grinned from ear to ear. The lobby had been transformed into a magnificent buffet, the heavily laden table covered in fresh fruit and French pastries.

"Not ice cream, sorry, but just what I need," she said, looking up at Paul. "Mountains of carbs for energy."

He threw back his head and laughed, engulfing her in his arms and nuzzling her neck.

"Eat as much as you like. I know just how we can use that energy," he whispered, releasing her slowly.

"*Monsieur et Madame Davis*, I hope the storm did not disrupt your night," Rosette said. "We have had to make adjustments. The phone lines to the bungalows are down but should be restored soon. The power is back to normal. If you would like an *omelette* or something hot, simply tell one of the servers; otherwise, we are providing a continental breakfast this morning. Monsieur St Louis will explain the changes later today."

"Okay, and this is fine with me." MJ indicated the table. "How bad was it?"

"None of our main structures were damaged, but our dock will be out of commission for some time. We will be using the village harbor instead. Thankfully, no guests are scheduled to leave on Thursday, although some wish they could, since Monsieur Leroux's participation in the treasure hunt has been canceled." Her lip curled. "Martinique was hit harder than we were, and his vessel was severely damaged as was our ferry. By Saturday, alternative arrangements will be in place." She chortled, but her eyes didn't reflect her humor. "It appears the mermaids are not ready to release their treasure."

"I doubt this storm had anything to do with them," MJ said. Sooner or later, these people had to grow up and forget about imaginary creatures, didn't they?

"Madame, many including some of the guests, would disagree with you," Rosette answered, her back stiff as if MJ had offended her.

"Yes, and I know a few of them," she mumbled. "I didn't mean to upset you. I'll need to contact my mother and let her know we're fine." She shook her head. "I can't imagine anything worse than what we got." Glancing out the window to the veranda, she gazed at the mess. "Was anyone hurt?"

"Not in the village. As you know, it is situated on the leeward side of the island near the base of the volcano, which protects it from the worst of the weather."

"I don't know how you manage, year after year, never knowing how bad it will be."

Rosette smiled, her lips compressed.

"It is our home. Where else would we go? Some storms bring more destruction than others. People were injured in Saint Pierre, but no one died ... this time."

MJ shuddered. But people had in the past and no doubt would in the future.

"Other than Leroux and the treasure hunt, has anything else been canceled?" Paul asked.

"No, but I suggest you go fishing. Fish are plentiful after a storm. If you like, I can secure a spot for you aboard my cousin's boat."

"What do you think?" Paul asked. "You did want to give it a try."

"Sounds good to me."

"Very well," Rosette said. "I will arrange it immediately. Lucette has mimosas in the lounge. Fill your plates and then go inside. There are quite a few people there already."

MJ carried a plate full of fruit and a champagne flute over to a table for two. Paul sat down across from her.

"Speaking of storm survivors," he indicated a table in the far corner. "Looks like they made it through the night."

Mark sat with Bill, Rick, and the rest of the Seekers of Treasure. Melena and Cindy weren't around, but Christy was at another table with a few of the other wives. MJ scowled and shook her head. Regardless of what they were plotting, nothing was going to spoil her day. Rosette went over to the table and said something to Bill. He followed her out of the room. What was that about? She shook her head and picked up a chunk of pineapple.

"The last time I went fishing was when I was sixteen," Paul said, reaching for the chocolate croissant he'd chosen. "Your dad took the three of us on that camping trip upstate, and as I recall, you caught the biggest fish."

She popped the golden cube in her mouth, savoring its sweetness, and swiped at the juice trickling down her chin.

"You seem to remember more about my childhood than I do, but now that you mention it, that three-pound trout was a minnow compared to the fish we saw on Sunday. If I do get a bite, I sincerely hope it won't be one of those giant specimens." She dug her fork into a slice of banana.

"If it is, you'll land it like a pro. I just hope we get back in time for a few more calisthenics before we have to attend that meeting."

MJ chuckled. So did she.

It was just after one when she stood on the deck of the fishing boat, shifting her weight from one foot to the other, waiting for the remaining passengers to board. She and Paul had spent more than an hour walking along the Atlantic shore, collecting shells, rocks, and sea glass. They'd left their booty in the bungalow where they'd grabbed a little afternoon delight before catching the shuttle to the village.

Lindsay had opted to stay back at the resort and take pictures of the storm's aftermath. Noel had remained with her as they planned to indulge in a couples' massage later, something MJ hoped she and Paul could do, too.

She scanned the shore. How long did it take to buy a fishing hat? Turning away from the boarding process, she stared out to sea.

On the western horizon, the clear, cloudless sky wasn't blue. Instead, no doubt picking up on the water, it reflected an interesting shade of blue-green almost identical to that of the emerald in her ring.

"MJ Summers, I see you're taking your chances on a boat once more," a man said coming up beside her. "Good for you."

She recognized the crewman from the ferry and chuckled.

"It's Jack, isn't it? I'm terrible with names, but mine's Davis now." She held out her ring. If he was flirting, that should get rid of him quickly. "Boats have never made me sick. It's flying I can't abide. Don't worry. You won't have to clean up after me today."

"Good. Congratulations. I'd heard there'd been a wedding at the resort. As a certain Vulcan would say, live long and prosper."

"I didn't take you for a sci-fi buff. Are you fishing, too?" she asked. Where was Paul? There was something about the man that still set her teeth on edge. He stood too close, and his breath—stale cigarette never impressed her.

"In a manner of speaking. I moonlight on the fishing fleet when I don't have a ferry run. I'm part of the engine crew."

"Here you go," Paul said coming up beside her, handing her the handwoven hat she'd chosen from the array on sale at the dock. "This should keep the sun off your face while we're fishing. Hi. Paul Davis.' He held out his hand.

"Jack Crowder, pleased to meet you. I have to get below. Enjoy your afternoon aboard *l'Étoile de la Mer*. I have a feeling fishing is your sport." He winked before turning away.

"Where did you meet him?" Paul asked, frowning, his chin thrust upward.

Was he jealous?

"On the ferry. He came out on deck for a smoke when I was there. He moonlights in the engine room on this boat."

"Good morning, MJ, Paul," Bill Smith said, standing behind her, startling her. He smiled as if he were the cat who'd swallowed the canary. "Couldn't convince Cindy and Rick to come along, but I believe you know Mark and Melena Theopolis. Mark mentioned the two of you had history."

MJ shivered. How the hell had these four gotten aboard without her seeing them?

Paul laughed. It would take a machete to make a dent in the tension surrounding them.

"Did he mention that he and I are old friends, too? I believe that little bump in your nose, Mark, is from when I laid you out cold in the boxing ring." He turned to Bill. "We all grew up together. MJ and Mark were an item for a while, but that's ancient history now."

Bill chuckled, but his eyes remained fixed on her, making her skin crawl.

"Good. I'm glad it won't be an issue since Mark and Melena are joining our team," he said. "Mark has interesting information he's willing to share."

MJ gaped. M and M on their team? How the hell had that happened? The boat hit a wave, sending her crashing into the gunwale, crushing her side against the wood, and she gasped. Paul reached for her and pulled her into his arms.

"Are you all right?" he asked, his gaze conveying his concern. "You hit hard."

She nodded. One wonderful thing happened and then—bam! So much for thinking *Quimbois* was on her side.

"I don't seem to have my sea legs yet. I thought the treasure hunt was canceled."

"Officially, Leroux's out and Louis James won't be reporting on it, but any guests who want to continue to look for it can. Mark isn't a member of the S.O.T., but the team believes his perspective can come in handy, as will yours."

"I don't have one," she stammered.

"Yeah, right." He glared at her. "What are you expecting to find out here?"

Paul grinned, but MJ saw the muscle jump in his jaw showing he was no more pleased with this latest screwup from Fate than she was.

"Seriously, Bill? It's a fishing boat. What do you think we'll find?" he challenged. "Atlantis? Maybe Shangri-La?"

"Would anyone like coffee? They've got some below in the galley," Christy interrupted, glaring at her husband.

"Coffee sounds great. What about you, darling?" he asked, pulling her closer into his body.

"That's fine," MJ answered, although right now, if the galley had a cup of hemlock, it might be more to her liking.

"I'll have the same," Mark said, his compressed lips and two spots of deeper red on his complexion telling their own story.

What had his shorts in knots? He should be thrilled to be on a team with bona fide treasure hunters.

"Water for me," Melena said, her face pale.

"Five coffees and a bottle of water coming right up," Christy said. "Come on, honey. I'll need your help."

MJ wished she had an excuse to leave, too.

"Melena and I caught the rerun of your wedding last night," Mark said, sneering. "How *did* you manage that?"

So that was his problem. He was jealous.

Paul shrugged. "Just lucky, I guess."

He turned away from Mark and smiled at Melena. "I don't believe you're from Stilton, Melena."

"No," she said softly, licking her lips. "My family's from Philadelphia," she continued, looking directly at Paul and not the horizon. "Mark and I used to meet in the summers when he visited his grandparents in Cape May, but it wasn't until I moved to Stilton that we connected again. You two know how that works. Things just happened."

Melena was pale—no, she was green—and the boat had just left the dock.

"I do, and if you and Mark hadn't reconnected, I might've made the biggest mistake of my life," MJ answered. "Thank you."

Paul bent his head and kissed her softly. Turning to Melena, he smiled, "I'll add my thanks to hers."

Mark cleared his throat noisily, but it sounded more like he'd said "bullshit" than coughed.

Melena tried to smile, but she looked terrible, and MJ felt sorry for her.

"I have some Dramamine," she offered.

Melena nodded. "I'll be fine. I took some a few minutes ago. It just needs to kick in. If I'd known we were going on the water, I would've taken it earlier."

Mark leaned closer to them. "How do you intend to continue this little charade when we get back to Stilton?" His eyes narrowed while his chin jutted out. "I checked the laws. American citizens can't legally marry here."

"They can with special permission from the French government," Paul answered, his lips tight. He puffed out his chest like an angry gorilla. "You might've watched the rerun, but you couldn't have been listening to it. As far as Stilton goes, we'll go back to visit, but we'll be living in Watertown."

Mark's brow furrowed, the lines between his eyebrows deeper than ever.

"Watertown? What about her job? She's in line for department head."

While this might be a testosterone-induced pissing contest, this conversation was about her, and MJ was determined to be part of it.

"Not that it's any of your business, but I resigned my position three months ago when Paul and I started talking about marriage. As a wedding present, he's bought me a house down the street from my new school."

"No one throws away a promotion to move to some backwater community," he said, stepping closer to her, invading her personal space. He shifted his gaze to Paul. "I saw that prewedding interview, too. Man, did you lay it on thick. No one knew where the hell you went after your loser father beat your mother to a pulp and the two of you slunk out of town. Since MJ never left Stilton, I don't buy this touching reunion miracle romance of yours. Pen pals? Bullshit. You may have conned Louis James, but I'm going to get to the bottom of this and expose you for the frauds you are."

MJ put a restraining hand on Paul's arm, felt the tension in him, and watched the muscle jump in his jaw once more.

"Mark, think before you say something you'll regret," she said. "Paul and I are married. There's nothing you can do to change that. Just leave us alone. If you do, I may decide not to prosecute—"

"Prosecute?" He snorted. "As if you ever would. You haven't got the balls to follow through on something like that. I don't believe getting even with me is why you're here. You're after the treasure. You'd made the decision to keep the vacation before I asked for it, forcing me to get creative. Bill's been going on and on about imaginary sea creatures and their unusual eyes. Does he know about yours? About the contact lenses?"

She gasped.

"No? I thought so. Maybe I should enlighten him, pardon the pun. I don't believe his assertions that mermaids exist, but there has to be a reason for creepy eyes like yours. They're the same color as this water. Do you expect them to let you see things the rest of us can't? Is that your edge?"

"You're nuts," MJ said, turning into Paul.

Mark grabbed her arm. "Don't hold out on me MJ. I can make your life a living hell."

"Let go of my wife," Paul said softly, the steel in the words surprising Mark. He released her, and Paul pulled her tightly to him. "If you ever lay a finger on her, or make a disparaging comment about her, any member of her family, or my mother, I will finish what I started fifteen years ago, and no one will come to your rescue this time. Get this through your head. Neither Marilyn nor I are interested in that damn treasure, and we know nothing about it. If we did find it, it would be a moot point since none of us can keep it as you well know."

"That might be the song you're singing, but the tune's bullshit. Do you know how much that treasure's worth? Millions. No one's going to settle for a measly 10 percent. If we get our hands on that gold, don't count on us giving it up. Bill's only interested in a few Incan pieces, but I'll take whatever I find." He snorted. "As far as prosecuting me, you want to talk fraud, I'll meet you, tit for tat. You haven't got any proof that I did anything illegal. It'll be her word against mine."

Paul released MJ and stepped closer, putting himself in Mark's face, his nostrils flared, his face red, his fists clenched at his side.

She shivered. She'd never seen him like this.

"Really? Let me lay a few facts out for you. If this team finds the treasure, one tenth of that finder's fee is all you'll get. If you try to smuggle so much as a doubloon back to the United States, you'll end up doing hard time in a French prison, and I'll gladly help them throw you in a deep dark hole and toss away the key. As far as proof of what you've done? I'm a police officer and I have far more than I need. This place keeps excellent records. They've got your emails, even the tape and transcript of that damn telephone call you made to get the reservation changed. I listened to it—all of it. Your coconspirator is in even more trouble than you are, since she impersonated MJ. If I were you, I'd consider an apology and restitution."

Melena seemed to shrink and try to efface herself into the gunwale.

Mark's face paled. "Don't threaten me, soldier boy. For the right price, evidence can disappear, and even if it doesn't, it'll be her word against mine. People in Stilton know she 'offered' it to me months ago. She'll come off as a sore loser." He shook his head. "You and the slut deserve each other."

Paul's face turned deadly white. He reached for the collar of Mark's shirt. "What did I say? I suggest you apologize right now, or you'll be swimming back."

"Please, Paul, let him go. You're making a scene," MJ begged, conscious of the attention they were getting.

In a flash, Paul changed his hold on Mark into a bear hug. "And I can still take you now," he said loudly and laughed, releasing the man. "Your wife doesn't look so good. Here come the Smiths. Why don't you grab your drinks and find her a place to lie down?" He lowered his voice. "If you ever do anything that harms my wife, you will regret it. This isn't a threat, it's a promise. I suggest you give careful consideration to what you plan to tell Bill."

"Here you go," Christy said, offering Paul and MJ the cups she held, her eyes wide. "I've got cream and sugar."

"I'll take ours to go. Mel needs to lie down," Mark said. "I'll see you all later."

"Thank you," MJ said, taking the cup and moving out of Paul's protective arms. Another bully vanquished. She had this now. "Okay. Who's ready to catch a really big fish?"

* * *

"Oh, my God!" MJ screamed, almost deafening Paul, and bouncing up and down in her excitement. "I did it! I caught a really big fish."

He laughed. "You certainly did, and landed it all on your own. Well done!"

Ramon, the crewman assisting them, removed the hook from the large, blue-green fish and lifted it up by the gills, holding it in front of MJ. The mahi mahi was more than half her height.

"You know Lindsay's going to kick herself for missing this," he said, pulling her to him and hugging her tightly. "I have most of the battle on video."

MJ laughed, her face glowing. Seconds later, she sobered. "What's going to happen to it?" she asked Ramon.

"It will go to the kitchens with the others caught today and be served as the fish course at dinner tonight. Congratulations," He stepped away from the scale. "Your fish weighs twenty-one pounds, seven ounces. That's the biggest one taken today."

Paul grinned. Until MJ landed her fish, Mark had been in the lead with a twenty pounder. Sometimes, payback worked in your favor.

"Looks like you win the pool, too," Bill said, handing her two ten-dollar bills. "Damn shame when a man doesn't even get a decent bite. Everyone else did. It's as if I were cursed."

"Beginner's luck, I guess," she said.

"Yeah, like you of all people are a beginner." He scowled. "Just remember. What goes around, comes around."

Mark frowned, mumbled something under his breath and handed his pole to Ramon.

"Did you say something, Mark?" Paul asked, choosing not to comment on Bill's cryptic remark.

"You must be hearing things, Davis. Congrats, MJ," he said, his tone implying otherwise as he placed the ten in her hand. "Since Melena didn't fish, she shouldn't have to pay. I'd better go and see how she's doing. She's pissed at me for not telling her we were coming on this excursion until the last minute."

Melena had been below deck most of the trip. Between the scent of a working fishing boat and the craft's slight, continuous movement, she hadn't done well.

"Looks like the course of love isn't running smoothly," MJ said once Mark left them. "I'm going to the head."

"Do you want me to come with you?" he asked. The water wasn't rough, but the rolling deck made walking difficult.

"I think I can handle it." She cupped his cheek. "I'll be fine. I'm getting my sea legs and, so far, other than a few cutting remarks, Frick and Frack haven't been an issue. It's not like one of them's going to toss me overboard because of ten bucks. I'll be right back." She handed her gear to Ramon, stuffed the thirty dollars in the pocket of her shorts and handed Paul her hat. "Hold on to this for me, will you?"

Paul reached for the hat and nodded, watching her follow in Mark's wake.

He scowled. Mark had been civil after his earlier blow-up, but Paul didn't trust him for a second. He was convinced the man and Bill were up to something. They kept stealing furtive glances at MJ. What the hell did they think she knew?

Christy handed Paul a beer. "To the victors go the spoils; the losers can console themselves with alcohol. Bill's gone below deck, looking for champagne. She's really something, isn't she?"

"I think so," Paul answered watching MJ disappear around the side of the boat. "I can't believe how my luck has changed since I got here. Having her in my life will make all the difference."

Christy frowned, her eyes narrowing. "But I thought she'd been in your life for some time. You make it sound like this just happened."

Paul choked on his mouthful of beer. He'd almost blown it and on such a casual comment. "I was referring to the wedding and the fact that we'll be together for the rest of our lives. For a while, I wasn't sure she was going to take a chance on me. The rest of you can have my share of the reward for finding Lacorneille's treasure if we do. I have everything I could possibly want."

"You're a lucky man. There was a time I thought I'd made the right choice, too. Now, I'm always in second place to some treasure hunt or another. I'm sure he loves me in his own way—he did bankroll my cancer treatments—but instead of being with me when I needed him, he was in Africa looking for King Solomon's Mine." She rolled her eyes. "Since the doctor gave me a clean bill of health, it's been better. At least he brought me with him this time, but it is a honeymoon resort. A man alone would stick out like a sore thumb."

"That's for sure."

Before he could add anything else, the waters around them grew rough even though the wind didn't seem to have risen, and the deck shifted violently. He grabbed Christy to prevent her from falling.

"Thanks," she said, her face pale. "What the hell was that? Did we hit a whale or something?"

"I'm not sure."

He'd barely recovered his own balance when an alarm shrieked. He had a bad feeling about this. He looked around for MJ. Hopefully, she'd gotten below without smashing her ribs again.

CHAPTER TWENTY

Moving as quickly as they could on the heaving vessel, Paul and Christy reached the port side where passengers and crew stood beside the gunwale.

"What happened?" he asked.

"Someone left one of the starboard freeboard doors open and a woman tripped and pitched headfirst into the water," a crewman answered. "I hope she's a good swimmer."

Paul looked out at the water. "I don't see anything? Could it be a false alarm?"

"Monsieur, there's no mistake. I saw her fall, but I was on the top deck and couldn't reach her. I sounded the alarm. We're launching the lifeboat now, but I haven't seen her come up."

Paul's gut burned. Where was MJ?

"There she is," someone yelled, and Paul turned to look.

His heart skipped a beat when he recognized MJ, her head bobbing momentarily above the water before sinking once more. Adrenalin pumping through him at light speed, he kicked off his shoes and dove into the sea. Surfacing, he got his bearings, and with the ship at his back, headed for the place where she'd appeared.

Paul cut through the water, more turbulent than it had been all day, swimming faster than he would've believed he could, lifted by each rising wave, watching for MJ's head, and letting terror fill him when she didn't surface again.

The lifeboat closed in on MJ's position as did he. Diving deeper, he opened his eyes, ignoring the burn of the salt water. As always when underwater without a mask, everything was fuzzy and distorted, but the water was amazingly clear. He looked below him into the darker depths and saw her drifting down, a strange iridescent purple shadow beneath her, almost as if it was supporting her.

Fear unlike anything he'd ever known filled him. Surfacing to catch his breath, he forced himself back under, kicking powerfully to follow her down. Where was she? Striking out with every ounce of strength he had, he headed deeper until he saw her, hovering over a dark oddly-shaped reef. Lungs burning, he forced himself to kick harder. He was within a few feet of her when the luminescence vanished.

By the time he reached her, her eyes were closed, and her mouth gaped open, admitting the killing water. His lungs screaming for air, Paul kicked hard, propelling them upward. She had to survive.

Breaking the surface just a few feet from the lifeboat, he gasped, black spots floating before his eyes, and grabbed the life ring someone tossed him. With his last bit of strength, he pushed MJ's pale, limp body onto it.

He watched the boat crawl toward them. As soon as she was aboard the vessel, he climbed the ladder, hurrying to her side.

"*Monsieur*, you did well to save her, but let the *médical* look after her now," the fisherman who'd helped him aboard said, wrapping Paul in a blanket. "How do you feel?"

Paul glanced over at MJ. How did he feel? As if the best part of him was being torn from him as each second passed.

"I'm fine," he lied, ignoring the searing pain in his leg, the agonizing ache in his lungs, and the acidic burning in his eyes, watching for some sign of life.

One of the sailors handed him a wet cloth. "*Pour tes yeux*," he said. "I can see how sore and red they are."

Paul accepted the cloth and pressed it to his eyes, the soothing coolness relieving some of the stinging.

"She isn't breathing," he said, tears dribbling down his cheeks.

"*Je le sais*," the *médical* answered, beginning CPR.

With each breath and compression, MJ remained the same, and Paul's heart ached more. This was his fault. Leaving her side even for a second with that son of a bitch aboard had been beyond stupid. There was no way she'd taken a header into that water unless someone had helped her, and he knew exactly who. He shivered not from cold but from fear. If MJ didn't make it, there would be no coming back from this pain.

How long had it been? Seconds? Minutes? If there was *Quimbois* magic around here, now would be a good time for it to do its job. The medic raised his head. He couldn't be quitting.

"Don't stop! For God's sake, don't quit," he cried.

"*C'est fait.*" The medic leaned back on his heels.

It's over? It can't be over.

Tears streamed down his cheeks.

MJ's body spasmed, and she coughed up water.

Heedless of his pain, Paul rushed to her side and pulled her up into his arms, holding her as she spat up more brine and her body convulsed again.

"I've got you," he said, holding her tightly, raining kisses down on the side of her face and on her head. "Don't ever scare me like that again."

MJ looked up into his eyes, her own filled with wonder.

"Did you see her?" she asked.

He frowned. "See who, darling?" He noted she'd not only lost her shoes and sunglasses, but the chain around her neck was missing.

"The mermaid, the one near the boat."

The men surrounding them gasped. One went so far as to cross himself. Why? Didn't everyone around here believe in mermaids? It wasn't as if MJ had died and been resurrected.

He gazed into her troubled eyes once more. Could hypoxia have occurred? All that nonsense of Bill's was responsible for this. Mermaids? She'd hallucinated.

"Honey, I didn't see anything."

That wasn't true, he'd seen the weird purple glow, but that had been a trick of the light and the water, the same thing no doubt responsible for the glows they'd seen when diving. Paul noted the gash on her forehead. How had he missed that?

"You've got a nasty bump." He pressed his lips against hers, encouraged to find them warm and pulsing with life beneath his. He raised his head. "For now, just rest."

MJ nodded and closed her eyes.

Paul held her in his arms as the engine on the small craft coughed to life. The fishing vessel bobbed on the horizon. How had they drifted this far from it? He couldn't imagine having swum that distance in the turbulent water. He blinked. The ocean was now as smooth as glass, the sun's reflection turning it once more the same color as MJ's eyes.

What the hell?

He exhaled, his heart still beating frantically in his chest, his knee throbbing from the exertion. He would be limping for a day or two, but that wouldn't matter as long as she was okay.

The reassuring rise and fall of MJ's chest as she took each steady breath should be calming him, but the adrenalin rush from the rescue and the fear he'd lost her wouldn't be appeased. People around here and Bill's merry band might believe in mermaids, but he worked with facts, not myths and legends. Mermaids weren't real, but sleazy ex-fiancés were.

As soon as the smaller craft came alongside the larger one, hands secured the vessel while others eased Paul away from MJ so that they could lift her onto the deck. He followed the basket up the ladder.

Bill and Mark stood at the gunwale, Melena holding her husband's arm, while Christy stood next to Bill. If anything, Melena was almost as white as MJ had been when he'd pulled her from the water. Seeing the man responsible for all this standing there snapped what little control Paul had. His hands fisted.

"Is she okay?" Jack, the crewman he'd met earlier, asked, his forehead creased. "I warned her last time. The freeboard isn't high on these boats."

"Yes, no thanks to him," Paul said, reaching for Mark, grabbing his shirt with his left hand, yanking him out of Melena's arms, and pulling the man to him, his face only inches from his. "I warned you what would happen if you hurt her. How could you do it?" He raised his right arm and pulled back his fist. "You know she can't swim."

"Stop! For the love of God, stop," Melena cried, stepping between his fist and Mark's face.

"Are you frigging nuts?" Mark asked, losing what little color he had. "Look, I know MJ and I have had problems, but I would never do something like that. I was downstairs with Melena. Other people saw me."

Bill grabbed his arm before Paul could deliver the punch. "Back off, Paul. He's right. The three of us were together when the ship lurched and the alarm went off. Besides, your wife wasn't in any real danger. I've seen her swim, remember? She moves through the water like a freaking dolphin."

Releasing Mark so suddenly that the man almost fell to the deck, Paul ran his trembling hand through his hair, shaken to the core by what he'd almost done. If Melena hadn't stepped between them, he might've killed the bastard.

"I'm sorry," he said, turning away from Mark to look at Bill. "She can't swim. Ask him. The only reason she did on Sunday was because of the flippers she wore, and she had a tank. Without them, she doesn't stand a chance. She hit her head before she went in. I watched her drift helplessly down to the bottom." He shuddered. "When I brought her up, she wasn't breathing."

Paul looked down at MJ.

Her eyes were open wide.

"MJ, I—" He rubbed the back of his neck. He what? Had overreacted? Had behaved like a psycho fool?

Mark straightened his shirt. "No hard feelings," he said, holding out his hand, dropping it when Paul couldn't bring himself to shake it. "Given what's happened between us, it's a logical conclusion." He knelt beside MJ. "No matter what you think of me, I would never have done that. I've been an ass, Melena's pointed that out to me, and I'm sorry ... about everything."

MJ nodded.

"Let me by; I'm a doctor." One of the members of the S.O.T. pushed his way through the gawkers, forcing Paul, Mark, and Bill aside. He knelt beside MJ still strapped into the rescue basket.

How many of those nuts were aboard? Maybe one of them had decided to test Bill's mermaid theory, but to do that, they had to know about her eyes. Had they overheard Mark earlier?

"Hi, MJ. Recognize me?" Nate Jeffries asked.

She nodded.

"How do you feel?" He unbuckled the restraints so that she could sit up. "Any pain anywhere?"

"My head aches, and my chest is sore," she answered, her teeth biting into her lower lip. Her eyes darted around the deck. "Can I get out of these wet clothes?"

"In a minute," Nate said, reaching for her wrist. "You have a hell of a bump on your head, but the cut isn't deep enough for stitches." He glanced up at Paul. "You gave your hubby a damn good scare." He helped her sit up and placed his ear against her back. "Take a deep breath for me."

MJ did and coughed.

Would she have an asthma attack? Where was her inhaler?

The doctor nodded. "You've come through your ordeal remarkably well. Your lungs are clear, but keep doing that, even if it hurts. You've probably got slight bruising from the CPR."

"CPR?" She gasped, her gaze finding his. "I stopped breathing?"

Paul nodded.

"Yes, and swallowed a lot of water." The doctor held up a penlight and flashed it in her eyes. "I see you managed to keep your contact lenses in. You might want to toss this pair and give your eyes a rest tonight. Sea water isn't quite the same as sterile saline. Have someone clean and dress the wound and, if you haven't had a tetanus shot lately, you should get one." He stood. "Take it easy for a couple of days until your chest stops aching." He winked and stepped aside.

MJ's cheeks pinked.

Paul watched for signs of an imminent asthma attack. Surely if anything was going to bring on an episode, this was it, but she was surprisingly calm.

"My sincerest apologies, Madame," Captain Saucier said, stooping beside her. "I don't understand how that gate was left open. It isn't one we usually use and should have been bolted shut." His brow creased. "I haven't seen turbulence like that in all my days on *l'Étoile de la Mer*. It came from beneath us. The wind gauge was barely registering." His eyes narrowed. "We may have hit a humpback—they are not strangers to these waters and do surface quickly. I've radioed for information on underwater quakes, and given them our position at the time. After last night's storm, anything is possible." He shook his head, looking out at the now calm water, wringing his hands.

Paul scowled. If the man was telling the truth, someone had opened that door on purpose.

"Captain, I'm fine," MJ said, pulling Paul's attention back to her. "Please, don't blame anyone else. It's my own fault. I thought I saw something—maybe a dolphin or a small whale. I leaned over to get a better look ... It was just an accident. I'm prone to them." She shrugged. "In my wild imagination, I was sure it was a mermaid."

"Perhaps you did see one of our mysterious ladies," Captain Saucier said and chuckled. "Many believe they live in these waters. While there have been few sightings in recent years, last night's storm may have disturbed them, too. Now, you must excuse me. We need to weigh anchor and head to shore." He stood and left the deck.

Most of the people aboard the vessel had drifted away, going back to their own business. Melena wasn't as pale as she'd been, but Bill looked shaken.

"You saw a mermaid?" he asked, his eyes glazed. "I knew you were holding out on me. What did she say? Did she tell you where the treasure is?"

Paul huffed out a breath. "For God's sake, Bill, get your head out of your ass. My wife almost died. How would you feel if Christy had cracked her skull on the gunwale and tumbled overboard? If MJ saw anything, it was probably a dolphin. Hell, it could've been another mahi mahi. The only mermaids are the ones in your head. Smarten up. Now, if you'll excuse us, she needs to go below and lie down."

Bill opened his mouth, but the glare Christy gave him shut him up. Score one for the wife. Life with that man couldn't be easy.

Paul moved over to MJ once more and squatted awkwardly beside her, his knee barely strong enough now to hold his weight. "Ready to try and stand?"

"Yes," she answered, taking his hand and rising as he did.

He pulled her into his side, turning to look down at her. That had been too close.

"Nate Jeffries was right about one thing. You scared the living daylights out of me." He pressed a gentle kiss to her mouth, releasing her much sooner than he wanted to.

"I'm sorry," she said, her eyes bright with unshed tears. "I probably should lie down, but what I would like right now is something to drink. All I can taste is salt and whatever else was in that water."

Christy handed her a bottle. "Here. Ignore my idiot husband. He's like a kid who's just been told there's no Santa Claus."

"Thanks," MJ reached for the bottle. She drained it and turned to Paul. "Can we go now?"

He nodded and helped her over to the ladder, afraid to let her out of his sight again. Something or someone was responsible for her fall into that water, and he wouldn't stop digging until he figured out who.

"At least no one was here to get this debacle on camera. I'm grateful for that. Promise me Mama will never hear so much as a murmur about this."

"You have my word. The last thing I want to do is relive that moment." He pulled her tightly against him once more, and leaned his chin on her head. "I'm sorry, MJ. I should never have let you go off on your own. I knew the footing was iffy at best."

She pushed away and frowned. "Oh no you don't. Get over yourself, hero. I was going to the bathroom. No one knew the sea was going to bubble up and boil or whatever you want to call it. You think that if you'd been with me you could've saved me from falling? Think again. Chances are we would both have been knocked out, and we would now be at the bottom of the sea. You can't keep me in bubble wrap or cotton wool. I'll go crazy. Now, let's get below so I can change."

What she said made sense, but opened doors when they should be bolted shut? Inexplicable underwater turbulence? The memory of the strange mauve glow flashed through his mind. What the hell was going on here?

* * *

"Maybe you should go back to the bungalow and lie down," Paul said, his frown deep, his worried gaze on her.

"I'm too keyed up to rest," MJ answered, trying not to let her irritation show. She felt claustrophobic, despite the fact the room they were in was bright and airy.

Paul hadn't left her side since the rescue and his hovering increased her anxiety. The bandage on her head proved she'd struck it, but while she'd almost died, she didn't remember feeling distressed, not even when she'd fallen in. The fear had come later, lying on deck, seeing the murderous look in Paul's eyes.

That mermaid had to be real. There was no way she could've imagined such a dazzling creature.

"I'm fine, Paul, really I am, but you're hovering like Mama and Carla all rolled into one, and you're driving me crazy. Back off a little, please? I probably look like hell, but what I really need is a drink, and I don't want more water." She scowled. "Did you really think Mark had shoved me overboard? I don't remember being pushed, just landing in the water."

He scratched his head. "You probably lost your footing when the underwater earthquake or whatever it was happened. But still, somebody opened that gate..."

She raised her hand and caressed his chin.

"I'm pretty sure Mark wasn't packing a toolkit in his back pocket. It was just me being clumsy again." Had there been a slight shove? She couldn't remember.

"I guess I overreacted," Paul admitted, "but I still think he and Bill are up to something, and I don't trust either one of them."

He picked her up and carried her from the village infirmary to the waiting golf cart.

"I'll agree Mark's a cad, and as far as his apology goes, that and two bucks might buy me a cup of coffee back home, but Bill's got tunnel vision when it comes to this treasure and mermaids. He thinks I'm his ace in the hole. Lindsay may think I have this weird medical condition, but if Mark mentioned the color of my eyes, and he's heard Lucette's comment about them, the last thing Bill wants to do is hurt me." She shook her head hoping things would line up and make sense.

When they reached the main lodge, Paul picked her up again.

"You can put me down."

"What if I don't want to?" he argued. "That's a big bump. The doctor did say you could have a concussion."

She huffed out a breath. "He also said I could be fine. I know I scared you, and I'm sorry about that, but it's over. Besides, you're limping."

"Let me worry about my knee. I'll ice it when we get to the bungalow, but right now, I need to hold you a little longer."

Heat suffused her at the smoldering in his eyes.

"And you don't have shoes," he added, breaking the spell.

She scrunched up her nose. "Fine. You win. I could probably manage the rocks, but there's always a chance of that iguana doo-doo you mentioned the other night. The way they've been eating today, the piles might be bigger than ever."

He nodded, a glint of humor in his eyes, replacing the fear and anxiety that had made her antsy.

"The last thing you want between your toes is iguana poop."

She giggled and settled into his arms. The way he'd reacted to her accident had to mean something, but what?

As soon as they reached the steps, he put her down, and MJ missed his arms around her. She needed to get her act together. Sex with Paul was a wonderful thing, but falling hopelessly in love with him was another.

She stepped into the lobby, the stone floor cold beneath her feet.

"I wish I hadn't lost my shoes. The pendant I can replace, but those were the only flats I had."

"What about those?" he pointed to a sandal in the gift shop's window. "They look a lot like the ones you were wearing."

MJ's eyes widened. "Are you insane? Mine were knockoffs. Those are real Ferragamos. Do you have any idea how much they cost?"

"Not really, and I don't care." He pulled her into his arms again, his lips brushing the bandage on her brow. "The only thing that matters right now is that you're safe. When I pulled you out of the water and you weren't breathing ... I couldn't have gone on without you. I never want to feel that powerless again. Come on. You're getting those shoes and since you lost your sunglasses, you'll need a pair of those, too."

She let him pull her into the shop. He hadn't said the "L" word, but why else would he be so upset? Sure, she was a friend, but friends didn't talk about not going on without you.

Ten minutes later, wearing her five-hundred-dollar shoes, a pair of Dolce & Gabbana sunglasses worth more than she spent on groceries monthly, and a necklace to replace the one she'd lost, MJ stepped into the bar. There'd been no arguing with Paul over the price of the items, and she'd simply given up. After everything else that had happened today, why not shoes that cost a week's pay and sunglasses and a necklace that were worth more than she made in a month?

Paul followed her into the lounge.

"*Vous voilà*," Lucette cried. "I heard about the accident." She placed a glass of scotch on the bar in front of Paul. "Something stronger than beer is in order, *non*?"

"Definitely," Paul said, "but Marilyn should stick to juice."

MJ frowned. "If it's all the same to you," she said, "I can speak for myself. I would like one of those rum drinks. I can still taste the salt water." Besides, she'd already hallucinated mermaids and fantasized Paul might be in love with her. Hallucinations and fantasies—add alcohol and who knew what might happen?

Paul shrugged. "If that's what you want ... I wasn't trying to tell you what to do."

"I know," she said, lifting the corner of her mouth in a half smile. "It's just ... I really need a drink. All things being equal, this is far worse than Saturday."

He raised her hand to his lips. "I'm sorry."

Within minutes, Lucette handed her one of the rum concoctions she made.

"*Voici*. Not too strong." She winked. "I heard about your adventure," she said lowering her voice. "Young Luc has told almost everyone on the island."

MJ almost choked on the mouthful she'd taken. What had the bartender said? Not strong? If this wasn't strong, what was? It certainly was burning away the salinity and that was a good thing.

Lucette's words echoed in her head. Luc? Who was Luc, and what the hell had he said?

"Told them what?" Paul asked before she could.

"About the mermaid. Luc works on *l'Étoile de la Mer*. My *grandpère* saw one as a boy," Lucette continued. "To see one is a great honor, to resemble one, a blessing."

236

"Not sure I feel blessed," MJ admitted, suddenly feeling foolish. Why hadn't she kept her mouth shut?

"Please, can you tell me what you saw?" Lucette begged.

"Why not?" She shrugged. It was just a hallucination caused by the bump anyway. "My mermaid didn't look like the underwater statues in the harbor. She had pale skin, eyes the same color as mine, dark hair that hung down to her waist, and these incredible purple scales and a marvelous tail. She didn't speak, just held up her hand and reached for my pendant." Her hand went to her throat now sporting a gold heart with a ruby in it on a matching gold chain. "It looks like she has my favorite sunglasses and sandals, too, not that those will do her much good. There were hundreds of fish and blurs of color and a strange reef, but then she vanished. The next thing I knew, I was on the lifeboat." She shuddered.

"Purple?" Paul repeated, his frown deeper than ever. What he'd seen had been purple, too, but it had been her lifeless body that had imprinted itself on his memory. "When I saw you ... I never want to see anything like that again."

Before she could comment, Lucette whispered. "What did she give you?"

"Give me? Nothing, why?" MJ asked, her voice as low as the bartender's.

"Have you checked your pockets?"

MJ reached for the strap of the bag she'd dropped at her feet. "I'm sure there isn't anything in them I didn't put there."

Pulling opened her backpack, she removed the shorts she'd been wearing. In one pocket, she found the three soggy ten-dollar-bills and placed them on the bar.

"These are my winnings for catching the biggest fish. I'll consider my new things as your payment," she said, smiling at Paul. Of course, he was welcome to settle his debt in other ways.

Paul shook his head and pulled out a ten-dollar bill.

"Oh no. Those were gifts. A bet is a bet." He placed his bill on top of the wet ones. "By now, I probably owe you interest." He winked.

MJ's stomach fluttered. How could he turn her on with just a look?

Glancing down at her wet shorts, she resumed her search, but found nothing in the other front pocket. When she put her hand into the back one, she discovered a small round disk. She held it up for Paul and Lucette to see.

"This isn't mine," she whispered, opening her eyes wide.

The object was a thin, gold coin the size of a silver dollar. The outer rim was about a quarter inch wide and solid, while the inside of the circle resembled gold netting. In the very center was a small round turquoise stone. There were no other markings on the object, its reverse side identical to the top one, minus the gemstone. Where the hell had this come from?

CHAPTER TWENTY-ONE

Paul gazed at the object in MJ's hand. He'd never seen anything like it.

"It is beautiful," Lucette said, examining the coin. "But what is it?"

MJ shook her head. "I don't know. I've never seen it before. Perhaps your grandmother would know."

"What have you got there?" Bill asked, stepping over to them.

His eyes were bright, his eyebrows raised, the tip of his tongue sticking out slightly between his lips. He reminded Paul of a kid looking in a candy store window. Why would this interest him? Mark, his face full of curiosity, stood next to him.

"Glad to see you're okay," he said to MJ, looking away from her before she could acknowledge him.

Paul frowned. Why was he afraid to make eye contact? What did he have to hide?

"Despite what Paul thinks, I didn't push you in. I would never do that."

MJ nodded. "I know."

Paul followed her gaze around the room. Melena and Christy sat on the far side of the lounge. Melena's color was back to normal.

"Your wife looks better than she did earlier," he said.

"Yeah. If she takes her medication before she goes out on the water, she's fine, but this was a last-minute decision." He shrugged. "I should've known better than to take her along. Now, I've got two women pissed at me and no treasure in sight."

Paul almost felt sorry for him, but considering he'd brought this down on himself, he'd save his pity for someone who deserved it.

"It isn't over yet, Mark. Have faith." Bill said. Turning to MJ, his voice grew angry. "I asked if I could see the coin."

MJ frowned and looked up at him. Paul nodded. Unless she wanted to be rude, she had no choice but to give it to the jerk.

"Keep your shirt on," she mumbled before handing it over.

Bill examined it. "Did the mermaid give you this?" he asked, his face animated. His eyes glowed, and his jaw hung open. He licked his lips.

He was salivating? Over a coin? Obviously, the man thought he knew what it was.

"Geez, Bill, when are you going to get with the program? I told you earlier. There's no such thing as mermaids. We found it along the shore of the Atlantic this morning after breakfast," Paul lied. "What do you think it is?"

Eyes narrow, his face flushed, Bill handed the gold disc back to her. "It's a nice forgery."

Mark moved closer to them.

"A forgery of what?" he asked.

"Just some old Incan coin," Bill said, shrugging as if the object meant nothing to him. "Maybe something from the other night when they had this place rigged to look like the jungle, but it's well-made. And you found it along the beach?"

"Yeah, near the southern tip of the island. We collected all kinds of stuff." Paul turned to MJ. "I've had enough excitement and adventure for the day. Ready to head back to the bungalow?"

"Yes," she agreed. "I want to lie down before dinner."

Paul squeezed her to him. "You never have to ask me twice to take you to bed." He winked.

"Wait," Bill said, biting the inside of his cheek, the muscle in his jaw jumping. "Why don't you leave the coin with me, and I'll look it up online? Mark here can help. The Internet's up and running again."

Paul smiled. "Have you got your phone?"

Mark frowned. "I do, why?"

"Take a couple of pictures. It'll be easier to search with an image, right? If it turns out to be something interesting, we can discuss it at dinner."

MJ placed the coin on the bar and waited as Mark took his photographs, his hand trembling when he touched it. Once he was done, Paul pocketed her coin.

"Shall we?" he asked, leading the way out of the lounge. Whatever that coin was, Bill wanted it, and he intended to find out why.

* * *

Someone had cleared all the debris from the stone pathway. MJ could see new wires wrapped around the top of the tree trunks, just below the branches. Here and there crunching sounds indicated the iguanas were still feasting. Well away from the main building and alone, she stopped.

"Why did you lie to Bill and Mark about the coin?"

"I don't know," Paul admitted, "but Bill seemed just a little too interested in it. He's been behaving strangely, accusing you of holding out on him. What if one of his buddies believe that crap about you being a mermaid and pushed you in to see if it was true? I don't trust any of them. I was certain Mark was to blame, but now I'm not so sure. Until I can narrow the pool, I want to do a little investigating of my own. If we'd given it to him, I'm not convinced he would've returned it."

"Good point." She yawned, no longer trying to hide her exhaustion. "I want to visit Germaine, but first, I need to rest. It's all so confusing. One minute, I can't believe it happened, the next it's too real not to have. Let's hope the priestess can give us some answers."

Arm in arm, they walked along until they arrived at the bungalow and she moved away to let him unlock the door. Once inside, he locked it behind them and reached for her.

"When I realized you were the woman in the water, I almost died." He bent his head and kissed her.

The emotions stirred by her near-death experience combined with a need she couldn't seem to satisfy fueled her ardor. She returned Paul's kiss with all the passion she possessed, and when he carried her to the bed and undressed her, she was eager for more than a kiss. He entered her, claiming her body as his, and fireworks exploded in her head, bringing with them a kaleidoscope of colors. Spent, she closed her eyes and rested nestled safe in his arms.

* * *

"Hey, sleepy head," Paul whispered into MJ's ear, feathering kisses along the side of her jaw. "There's nothing I would rather do than keep you in this bed for the next six days, make love to you until we were both too exhausted to do anything else, but if you want to see Lucette's grandmother before we meet the others for dinner, we have to get dressed now. It's almost six."

MJ opened her eyes and smiled at him.

Remnants of the fear that had gripped him earlier lingered. He liked her, admired her, and was more than a little aroused by her phenomenal body, but there was more to it. It wasn't as if he'd never bedded a woman before—he was no saint—but none of them had made him feel the way MJ did. He couldn't imagine spending one day of the rest of his life without her.

"I was having the most unusual dream," she said, her eyes still sleepy, her voice husky.

"Was I in it?" he asked.

She nodded, her tongue licking her lower lip, arousing him once more.

"You were a handsome pirate and I was a mermaid, but like Daryl Hannah in *Splash*, when I stepped ashore, I had legs." Shaking her head, she sighed. "It's all gone now. Let me take a quick shower, and then we'll go see Germaine. I want to show her the coin."

"Want me to wash your back?" He wiggled his eyebrows as he'd done earlier.

Laughing, she got out of bed, leaving him there.

"If I let you do that, we won't make it to the village let alone dinner," she said, looking down at him over her shoulder, her teeth biting her lower lip. "Why don't you ice your knee and look to see what you can find out about the coin?" She screwed up her face. "I know you don't believe I saw a mermaid—hell, I don't believe it myself. I must have an even wilder imagination than I thought, but that coin definitely isn't mine and wasn't in my pocket when we left here this morning. If she didn't put it there, someone else did."

He reached for her, kissed her gently, savoring her mouth. Reluctantly, he pulled away. She was right. They needed information and as much as he enjoyed having her in his arms, he let her go.

"I don't know what you saw, but I'm not ready to give up on the idea you were pushed. If I figure out what this is," he held up the coin, "maybe everything will fall into place and make sense."

"I'll be as quick as I can." She shut the bathroom door.

Paul grabbed his tablet before sitting down at the table. Using one of the small bar towels, he created a makeshift ice pack with cubes from the mini-freezer and placed it over his knee. With the tablet up and running, he typed "lost Inca treasure" into the Internet search engine and clicked on images.

"Well, I'll be damned."

MJ's disc was featured on the page along with other Incan artifacts supposedly from the missing treasure of Paititi, the city of gold the Inca's had hidden deep in the Amazonian forest in hopes that it would not fall into Spanish hands. So far, they'd succeeded since no one had found it. He ran his hand through his hair.

"And there lies the crux," he said aloud, his voice echoing in the empty room.

According to the information he had, Lacorneille's ship had been carrying treasure looted from Pizarro's men who had executed Atahualpa, the Incas' last emperor in 1533, a full forty years before this article implied.

How would a Caribbean mermaid, if such a creature even existed, get her hands on something like this? Bill was right. It had to be a forgery, and if that was the case, who had slipped it into MJ's pocket and why the hell had they done so?

"Find anything?" she asked coming to stand beside him.

How long had he been reading?

"I did, but I'm afraid Bill might be right. I doubt this coin came from Lacorneille's ship." He explained what he'd learned from the Internet.

MJ reached for the coin, examined it, and then dropped it into the pocket of the floral skirt she wore.

"It's possible the coin pre-dates moving the city, isn't it? Maybe Germaine will be able to tell us more. After assuring me that I had a long, happy life ahead of me, I almost died today. Something doesn't add up, and I want to know what it is. If *Quimbois* magic is behind this, I'm not so sure it's on my side."

"Well, I'm on your side—the left, the right, the top, the bottom, the middle—you name it," he said, licking his lips. "I like every single part of you." He punctuated each word with a kiss. "Give me a sec to use the bathroom, and we'll go. If you don't mind, we'll use one of the golf carts. My knee's a little sore. No dancing tonight."

MJ put her arms around his neck and stood on tiptoe to kiss him. "I'll think of something we can do without putting any pressure on your knee."

He smiled. "I've got a feeling the best part of the day is yet to come. Move it, Mrs. Davis. I want to visit the *quimboiseuse*, have dinner, and then allow you to use whatever creative ideas you have percolating in that pretty little head of yours."

A few minutes later MJ stepped out of the bungalow ahead of him and he pulled the door shut, locking it. Monday night, he'd told Louis James that he'd fallen in love with MJ years ago, something he realized could well be the truth. If he'd lost her ... What the hell was he going to do? She deserved a man who'd make all her wishes come true, and he still didn't believe he could be that man, but he didn't think he could ever give her up now.

Noting she'd worn her new sandals, he put his arm in hers and led her back to the main building. The cart would be waiting out front for them.

"No matter what Germaine does or doesn't tell us, MJ, we will get through this together. I may have fallen down on the job today, but you can be sure it won't happen again. I've got your back."

She nodded. "And I've got yours."

* * *

While Paul seemed preoccupied, his gaze fixed on the road ahead, MJ enjoyed the short ride to the village, determined not to dwell on what couldn't be changed, but not ready to buy a pig in a poke, either. She needed answers, and she didn't believe in magic, voodoo, or purple mermaids, even if she imagined seeing one.

Glancing around, she noted most of the debris had been cleared away, and while there might not be as many leaves, fronds, and other branches on the trees, she knew the islands had survived worst storms and would recover, but would she? It was hard to believe how much her life had changed in five short days, and this was only the beginning.

Paul stopped in front of a white stone and clapboard house. Within seconds, the elderly *quimboiseuse* came out to greet them.

"Bonjour, Madame Davis, Monsieur Davis. I've been waiting for you. I have something for your knee." She smiled at Paul.

"How did you know we were coming or that his knee was sore?" MJ challenged, her curiosity and distrust at their peak.

"You have questions. I may or may not have the answers." She shrugged. "*Les esprits* talk to me, *ma petite*, but Lucette mentioned you might come by and told me about the limp. I do not rely on *Quimbois* for everything. I heard you saw the Star of the Sea today."

"That's what my name means," MJ interrupted, her mouth gaping open. Wasn't that an odd coincidence?

The elderly woman nodded. "And meanings are often based in fact. It is what many have called the purple mermaid, Irena, but no one has seen her in centuries. Why she's returned is a mystery. Come inside. I will answer what I can."

Holding Paul's hand in a death grip, both terrified and skeptical of what she might learn and yet needing to know more, MJ followed Germaine into the small house. Her whole life, she'd relied on books for knowledge, truths and facts verified by countless authorities, and here she was, desperate to know what was happening to her and willing to take the word of a woman who thought she was some kind of priestess. It went against everything she'd been raised to believe.

Despite the heat outside and no visible signs of air conditioning, the interior of the dwelling was cool and comfortable. A large rattan fan hanging from the ceiling spun lazily. On the far wall, in a place of honor, stood an altar. Above it hung an African-styled drawing depicting many different creatures, but the most prominent was the image of a mermaid.

Several unusual objects shared the altar's small surface including a human skull, complete with teeth and its lower mandible. Hadn't Carla said the Kalinago, the original Caribs, were cannibals? Could this woman be a witchdoctor?

Swallowing awkwardly, MJ inventoried the rest of the room. Beside the altar, two bookshelves offered a variety of boxes and bottles, some empty, others filled with God alone knew what. Should she be looking for answers here? Mama might let Aunt

Sophia read her tea leaves to divine the future, but a cup of tea in the kitchen was a far cry from this. According to Lucette, her grandmother mixed potions. If she looked closely at those jars, would she find bat wing and eye of newt?

In contrast, the rest of the room could've stepped off the pages of an IKEA catalog. The elderly priestess indicated the sofa and sat on the chair across from it. As soon as they were seated, she leaned forward and lit the large white candle on the small table between them.

MJ frowned. Where had the flame come from? She didn't smell the phosphorus and sulfur of a match, nor had she seen any kind of lighter. Before she could ask, Germaine leaned back in her chair.

"I know that you have seen the purple mermaid twice."

MJ frowned. "What do you mean?"

"You saw her the day you arrived and today."

MJ frowned. "Wait. Do you mean the face in the water? How do you know about that?"

Germaine nodded. "I told you, the spirits speak to me. Irena's return was unexpected."

"What face?" Paul asked, his brow creased so tightly, his eyes were mere slits.

"I imagined I'd seen a face in the water when I was on the ferry Saturday," she explained. "It was just after I'd spoken with Jack Crowder. You met him on the boat this morning. He creeped me out then and still does." She shook her head. "I thought it was a figment of my imagination, because when I looked back, it was gone. When I checked in and all hell broke loose, I forgot all about it." She turned back to Germaine. "If the mermaid appears so rarely, why have I seen her twice?"

The priestess pursed her lips. "Because you are in danger ... and like recognizes like."

"But I'm not a mermaid; I'm human." Goosebumps danced across her skin while sweat trickled down her back. How could she be both cold and hot at the same time?

"You are, and yet you are not," the old woman said.

MJ was damn sure Germaine wasn't referring to her body temperature. She tried to swallow, but her mouth was dry.

"We are all more than we appear to be," she continued, her voice mesmerizing. "At one time, all creatures lived in the sea. Some moved to the land and stayed there, others chose to remain in the water, while a few could not choose. Instead, they created a bridge, a way to move from one form to the other and back again. You are descended from both a human and an amphibian."

"Are you crazy?" Paul cried, jumping up and pacing the small room, his limp obvious in his distress. "Look, I can buy what you said about humans evolving from the sea. Scientist have proven we share genomes with other animals including lizards, but I don't see MJ as the daughter of the Frog Prince."

"Non, Monsieur," Germaine said, her voice clipped, filled with annoyance. "Not of a frog prince, but of Irena, a sea princess, and a human, Lacorneille himself. Your wife's eyes and webbed toes are proof of that."

"Webbed toes?" He choked on a laugh. "I can assure you I've examined every inch of her delectable body, including her toes, and they aren't webbed."

"They used to be," MJ said, her voice barely a whisper. "They performed surgery to undo that when I was only days old. How did you know?"

"You had webbed toes?" Paul interrupted, his eyebrows raised.

She nodded.

"The spirits told me," Germaine said, "but they haven't shared everything with me. When black magic is involved, death often follows, and even they are blind to what may come. When I tossed the bones at Raymond's request, I discovered your husband was here to save you. Rest assured, I see a long happy future for you. Now, open your mind. You have heard many stories about merfolk interacting with humans. Literature is full of them."

"Death, black magic, spirits. I'm sorry, but the stories you're referring to are fiction or old wives' tales designed to entertain the masses and explain animals such as dolphins and manatee," MJ murmured, more uncomfortable by the minute. "Are you saying that my imaginary mermaid is not only quite real but my great-great-great-grandmother?" How many greats would she need? "That's impossible."

She reached for Paul's hand and pulled him down beside her once more, not to comfort him in his distress but to draw strength from him. Hadn't he said they were strongest together?

"I'm sure you believe all this," MJ said, choosing her words carefully, not wanting to offend the woman, but unable to accept what she said was true. "In my family, the color of my eyes isn't unusual, but it tends to skip a generation. Similarly, my name has been passed along for centuries. As far as the webbed toes go, syndactyly is a common condition affecting one in every two or three thousand births. It's no big deal. If the webbing is slight, they don't even do anything about it. Are you going to tell me that every one of those children has mermaid DNA? My family comes from Ireland and Greece, not the ocean. Any stories shared about sea creatures and humans were strictly myths. Besides, up until this week, I've been terrified of water."

"I cannot speak for those I do not know, but mermaids and mermen have walked among humans and mated with them for millennia. Children are rarely born from these unions, but those that are generally favor their human parent and seldom can transform. Many, like you, share an aversion to water."

"So, like Bill, you think I'm a mermaid?"

"No child. You are human. Ten generations have bred what little mermaid DNA you had out of you. While you retain some of the outer characteristics, what biologists call recessive traits, you cannot transform. Sadly, there are some who refuse to believe this. That is why Irena came to you today. There is evil here, one that is alien to these shores, but stalks you, believing you are the key to the power he or she seeks. The one controlling this black magic can influence others to do his or her bidding."

"Great. We're up against a man or a woman. This is all well and good," Paul said, the irony in his tone hard to miss, "but it doesn't help us."

"Doesn't it?" Germaine asked. "You have seen evil in many forms, both male and female."

"Yeah, but every one of the monsters I saw was 100 percent real and human. There was no black magic involved, no spirits, no mermaids, no whatever the hell else you think you can conjure."

"I conjure nothing. You are a Christian, Monsieur Davis?" she asked, her head tilted to the left.

Paul stiffened beside her and nodded.

"Then, as such, you were raised to believe in a triune God—Father, Son, and Holy Spirit—in angels, demons, and Satan himself. I would wager you have never seen any of them, and yet you believe they can influence the hearts of men. Did you not pray when you thought your wife might die?"

"That's not the same," Paul said, running his free hand through his hair.

"But it is exactly the same. Your faith tells you one thing, mine another. To me the spirits, good and evil, are real and the mermaids are like your angels, they are messengers. While you may not believe angels walk among us, many do. Similarly, mermaids have walked this Earth for centuries. Why wouldn't they fall in love, too? We all believe in something. Why should one set of beliefs be better than another's?"

MJ stared at the elderly lady. She sounded so sure of herself. Could any of this be real?

CHAPTER TWENTY-TWO

"Suppose I buy what you're selling, and I'm not admitting I do," Paul said, knowing he'd seen too many strange things during his life to dismiss it completely. "If I accept that MJ saw a mermaid who tried to drown her, how does that help us?"

"She did not try to drown her. As I said, she's returned to these waters because your wife needs her protection."

Paul stretched his leg and winced.

"Her methods leave a lot to be desired. Where's she been all these years?"

Germaine sighed and removed a small vial from her pocket.

"Mermaids can travel the entire ocean. She must have found a sanctuary, perhaps near Ireland—that is where your namesake originated, is it not?"

MJ nodded.

Germaine handed the small vial to Paul.

"There is no point in continuing to suffer. While you do, your mind is closed to what can be. After you pour this on your knee, you will be more open-minded."

MJ scrunched up her nose. "That scent ... I've smelled it before. What is it?"

"Just an oil to ease the swelling." She turned to Paul. "What harm is there in humoring an old lady?"

Paul looked at MJ. She shrugged, her lips tight, her eyebrows drawn together. So far, Germaine hadn't said anything useful. He needed to keep her talking, and if rubbing fish oil or whatever this was on his knee helped do that, he could put up with the unpleasant scent for a while.

"Why not?"

He rolled up his pant leg and emptied the vial into his hand, crinkling his nose. The smell wasn't the most appealing one, but he'd smelled worse. He rubbed his knee. As he did his eyes opened wide.

"What's in this stuff? Have you got more?" His voice was pitched higher than usual. "The pain's gone, completely gone. Even the scars are fading. This has to be magic."

"A good healer does not reveal her secrets, but this potion is not mine. Mermaids have the ability to heal. That potion is from Irena. She left it on my doorstep not two hours ago."

"You don't live near the water. How did she bring it here?"

Germaine chuckled. "Mermaids have legs when they are on land. Many live peacefully among humans, but because they age at a very slow pace and must return to the ocean regularly, they do not stay in one place long. That oil is identical to the one used to mend Madame Davis's lungs." She smiled smugly. "Now that her chest is clear, her asthma will no longer trouble her, nor will the knee bother you."

"My asthma's gone?" MJ exclaimed, taking a deep breath as if to test the theory for herself and grinning from ear to ear when she didn't cough.

Paul gaped. Hadn't the doctor said something about her lungs being clear? He'd expected an asthma attack on the boat, but she'd been calm and relaxed. Even now, her chest wasn't tight as she'd just proven. Was it possible the priestess was telling the truth?

"I don't know what to believe anymore," MJ admitted, echoing his thoughts.

The old woman chuckled. "Now that I have proven my worth, perhaps you will listen to what I say." She turned to MJ. "Irena took something from you."

"Yes. A necklace, although I lost my shoes and sunglasses as well. My friend gave me the silver chain and an aquamarine crystal because she claimed it would protect me when I traveled over the water. Didn't do me much good."

"But it did, child. It called Irena to you when you were in danger. Aquamarine crystals are treasured by mermaids. Sailors used them to ensure good luck and safe voyages. Some claim the stones also represent eternal youth. Since mermaids age so slowly, they appear immortal. Because of your past, the signal for help was amplified. What did she give you?"

Reaching into the pocket of her skirt, she pulled out the coin and went to give it to Germaine, but the woman withdrew her hand as if MJ were offering her a hot coal.

"No. Set it on the table, please."

Paul frowned. The woman looked scared to death. What the hell was going on?

MJ shrugged and did as Germaine asked, her brow slightly furrowed.

"Paul looked it up online and discovered it's Incan, but possibly from a later period than Lacorneille," she explained. "Have you ever seen anything like it?"

The priestess frowned, pursed her lips tightly, and nodded. She closed her eyes and mumbled words in that patois he didn't understand.

"This is more than just a coin and far older than you imagine. I have never seen one like it, but its black power rolls off it like fog off the ocean. It is one of four talismans. Together, they are powerful beyond anything you can imagine, but alone, like this, they can do no harm. Legend says Lacorneille carried cursed items in the hole of his ship, items that should never have left their home. If all four discs are in that treasure as I suspect they are, it can never be found. They say the sea witch, Ovine, caused the ship to sink because Lacorneille spurned her in favor of Irena. He may well have done so, but I believe Ovine sunk the ship hoping to collect these coins."

"Why didn't she just go and get them from the wreckage?" MJ asked before he could.

"Before the storm ended, broken-hearted and furious, Irena took her lover's body to shore where he would receive a proper burial, and then hid the treasure, cursing it so that only herself or a descendant of the child she carried in her womb could find it again."

"If what you said is true, and MJ is that person, why give her the coin? Isn't that placing her in more danger?" Paul asked, fear gripping his stomach like a vice. He'd faced many different enemies but mermaids with magic powers and evil coins ... how the hell could he protect MJ from that?

"You have all the weapons you need," Germaine said, her smile tight.

Could she read his mind? He swallowed.

"As to why Irena has done what she has, there are two reasons. The first, to shield her from its power. Think of it as a vaccine. A little of a bad thing to prevent something worse. Throughout history, people have sought apotropaic magic to ward against evil. I am certain you have seen a rabbit's foot, a four-leafed clover, amulets, and crystals. Even jack-o'-lanterns are believed to ward off evil. There are many legends about objects said to contain power. The Greek's Golden Fleece could heal, Excalibur made Arthur king, the Holy Grail gives eternal life, Buddha's Bowl guarantees whatever is needed, and the Seal of Solomon imprisons demons. Just as objects can contain good, so can they contain evil. Maori warrior masks, a witch's grimoire, jujus from Africa, even voodoo dolls, have been feared for centuries because of their power. This coin, when it joins its sisters, is as strong an example of black magic as I have ever seen. They must not fall into the hands of those who seek their power."

"If that's the first reason," MJ said, her voice trembling, "what's the second?"

"To lure the one seeking them out into the open."

"She's using my wife to bait a trap? No damn way. You call her and tell her I said no. We already know who's looking for them." Paul turned to MJ. "Earlier today, Mark said Bill didn't want the whole treasure, just a few specific Incan objects. I'm not sure how you define alien, but he's definitely not from around here."

Germaine shook her head. "You may think you know who is behind this, but evil rarely reveals itself directly until cornered. This charlatan is nearby, manipulating things, but remaining in the shadows. He forced her hand today. Irena needs to return the favor while there is still time."

MJ trembled.

"It's okay," he whispered, sensing her fear. "I told you I've got your back. I'm not going to let a bunch of spooky stories scare me." But they did. In fact, they terrified him.

She nestled closer to him and nodded, gripping his hand. Turning back to Germaine, he swallowed his surprise. Whatever this was, it was one hell of a parlor trick as MJ would say.

While there was nothing special about the long white dress that hung on her thin body, nor the plaid kerchief covering her white hair, her dark unblemished skin, not a wrinkle in sight, now glowed as if lit from beneath, giving her an ageless appearance. She appeared to be in some kind of trance, but her gaze bore into him, evaluating him, digging into his very soul, seeing all the darkness there. Was she an ally or a threat?

Perhaps they should make a run for it. MJ was quaking beside him. The *quimboiseuse* claimed he had all the weapons he needed, but as far as he could tell, two fists and a nail clipper weren't much of an arsenal, especially not if he was fighting the forces of evil. Where was Batman when you needed him? How about Wonder Woman? If there were mermaids here, why not a nearby island of Amazons?

Before he could suggest they leave, whatever glow he'd seen had vanished. What the hell was going on?

"I wish I could tell you more," Germaine said, looking far older than she had moments ago. "As I said earlier, the spirits here are not the ones behind this. I must toss the bones and see what they want from me. I fear the price will be steep. For now, Irena will do all that she can, but you, Monsieur Davis, will save your wife. Have faith. When the time comes, you'll know what to do."

Paul nodded. Germaine had said he would save MJ. She hadn't said he would save himself.

"If I leave the coin with you, will it be safe?" MJ asked.

Paul watched the woman's face. She wrestled with demons he couldn't see. Would she want this power if she could get it?

"No, my child. He or she will come looking for it here, but unless the spirits will it, they cannot harm me. You must take the coin to the *bain des sirènes*. You went there before your wedding. The pool of water is said to be bottomless, but Irena can retrieve the coin from there if she needs it."

"Will it be safe there?" MJ asked.

"As safe as such an object can ever be. There will always be someone seeking its power."

Paul frowned. The woman was an expert at speaking in riddles.

"Thank you," MJ said before following him out to the golf cart.

Walking without pain, not even the slightest limp after so many months exhilarated him.

"That certainly wasn't what I expected," she said once he sat behind the wheel. "Do you believe her?"

"Honestly, some of it was a little hard to swallow, but I can't deny that my knee doesn't hurt for the first time since the attack."

She nodded. "And breathing has never been easier. I thought it might be because I was so relaxed." She smiled, her eyes full of mischief. "I'd heard sex was the best medicine."

Paul roared. "And all this time, I thought it was laughter."

Following the road away from the village, he parked the cart in the lot next to what he'd believed was nothing more than another weird island tradition. Hand in hand, they walked the distance to the lava pool. The last time they'd been here, he'd been concerned about the future. Now he was terrified by it. He was a soldier, but no one had prepared him to fight a supernatural enemy.

"Do you think we should just toss it in or make a wish?" She pulled the coin out of her pocket and handed it to him.

"A wish can't hurt. How about this? We wish to get back to Watertown safe and sound."

And stay together for the rest of our lives.

"That works," she said.

Paul tossed the coin. It landed in the milky turquoise water with a soft plop.

"Goodbye and good riddance," she said. "Let's get out of here."

"You don't have to ask me twice."

"So, what will we tell the others if they ask?" She settled herself onto the seat once more.

Paul shrugged. "Honestly, I don't know. We're walking medical miracles. Someone's bound to notice that, and good old Bill must know about the healing qualities of mermaids." He shook his head. "Let's stick with the hallucination, at least until I talk to Captain Saucier about that turbulence and the open door." He started the cart and headed back toward the main building of the resort. "As far as the coin goes, since Mark and Bill have seen it, we'll stick with the story that we found it on the beach."

"What if they want to see it again?"

"We'll tell them the truth. We tossed it in the volcano's wishing well."

MJ chuckled. "As much as Bill seems to want that coin, I doubt he's stupid enough to try diving for it in there."

Paul glanced at his watch. "We've got almost an hour. Let's go back to the bungalow and clean up. We may even have time for another round of medicine."

She nodded. "Maybe we do."

Paul increased the speed of the golf cart.

* * *

"Where's Cindy?" MJ asked when they joined the others fifteen minutes later than expected. Mark and Melena were at the table, too. So much for enjoying her dinner.

"She's sleeping. Last night's storm had her so upset, it brought on a migraine. She's been in bed off and on all day, but she should be fine for tomorrow." Rick smiled, pushing the bridge of his glasses up on his nose. "Bill was just telling us about your harrowing afternoon. Man, that must've been scary."

"Which part?" Paul asked, jumping in before she could think of an answer. "Was he referring to her valiant fight with the fish we'll be eating shortly, the fact she won the bet for catching the largest fish, or that I almost broke Mark's nose?"

"None of that," Rick answered, "although I would love to hear about her battle with dinner and Mark's close call. He was telling us about her tumble into the ocean. That must've scared the daylights out of you. If that had been Cindy..."

"It sure as hell made me age a decade," Paul admitted. "She's promised to stay away from open freeboard doors, but I doubt I'll let her out of my sight for a while."

"Don't be silly. You can't watch me all the time. That tumble into the water was an accident. They happen," MJ said, sitting down next to Lindsay. "Thanks to my clumsiness, I have this lovely fashion accessory." She pointed to the steri-strips on her forehead. "I could blame it on the champagne, but I hadn't had any yet."

Lindsay frowned and leaned forward, lowering her voice. "Come on. There's more to it than that. I heard someone mention a mermaid."

Etienne approached the table, preventing her from answering.

"*Bonsoir Monsieur et Madame Davis*. We heard about your mishap and all of us are happy you were not seriously injured."

MJ nodded, wishing she could blend into the tablecloth. Was there anyone on this island who didn't know what a klutz she was?

"Tonight's cocktail is a citrus martini."

"Sounds good to me," she answered.

"I'll have a Blonde," Paul added. "I can't seem to get enough of them."

He reached for her hand and nibbled her fingers.

Her lower body tingled, and she licked her lips.

As soon as Etienne moved away, Lindsay brought her chair closer to MJ's.

"Did you really see a mermaid?" she asked, her voice betraying her excitement. She shook her head. "Damn it. I should've gone with you. If I could've gotten a picture of that, I would be a shoe-in for a Pulitzer prize."

Paul chuckled. "You're as bad as Bill. There was no mermaid. I went in after her, remember? If there'd been one, I would've seen her, too."

"Rats," Lindsay said, her lip curling up on the left. "I was hoping those stories were real, and I could cash in."

Noel chuckled. "You'll have to prove the existence of some other fey creature." He reached for his wife's hand. "I've always wanted to visit Ireland. Maybe we could go next year and search for a leprechaun."

"Don't tease her," MJ said, reaching out her hand, touching her friend's arm, offering sympathy, and feeling guilty. She would love nothing better than to tell Lindsay the whole truth, but if Irena had stayed away for hundreds of years, she probably wasn't ready for the cover of *Time*. "You must've gotten some impressive storm pictures last night. With the wind and the lightning, I'll bet there are some doozies."

"I did get some incredible shots, and then the aftermath pictures I took today..." Lindsay went on warming to the topic and monopolizing the conversation throughout the first two courses.

"I'm sure your pictures are great, Lindsay," Bill said, his voice laced with sarcasm, "but we have more important things to discuss."

"Such as?" MJ asked, not impressed by the surly man's lack of respect.

"The coin for one."

"Coin? What coin?" Lindsay frowned.

"Show it to her," Bill ordered.

"I would if I could, but I can't, so I shan't," she answered, sipping the wine she'd ordered with dinner.

"Then, finish your fish and get it. It's not that far back to your bungalow," he demanded.

"If you want to order women around, I suggest you stick to your own wife. What MJ means is she doesn't have it any longer," Paul explained, his chest expanding as he glared at the man.

Christy coughed, her face an ugly shade of puce.

"Are you okay?" MJ asked, hurrying over to her seat and slapping the woman on the back.

"I'm fine," she choked out an answer. "That mouthful went down the wrong hole."

"What do you mean she doesn't have it?" Rick asked, turning to her. "Did you lend it or give it to someone?"

Rick seemed quite interested all of a sudden ... odd considering he hadn't seen the coin at all.

"I didn't give it to anyone ... well, not anyone living." She giggled nervously, her gaze scanning the people at the table, all of them rapt. "Paul and I went back to the island's volcanic wishing well, made a wish, and tossed it in."

"You did what?" Bill shrieked, attracting the attention of other diners. "Do you have any idea how valuable that coin was?"

MJ blinked and assumed the dumb blonde look she'd seen on so many television comedies.

"But you said it was fake," she accused. "Now, you're telling me it was real?"

"You stu—"

"Be very careful how you finish that word, Bill," Paul growled softly. "That *is* my wife you're speaking to."

Bill reddened. "I meant it was a good reproduction and could've been worth something."

She cocked her head to one side. "You don't think the volcano god will be angry because we tossed him a slug, do you?"

Christy laughed bitterly. "And here I thought you were smart. If Bill told you it was a fake, and is this upset about it, then you can bet your ass, it was real." She turned to her husband. "Easy come, easy go, lover. What are you going to do now?"

Bill grinned, but his eyes were cold. "If she found one coin, there have to be others around. We'll just keep looking for them. And I know there's a mermaid around here. I just have to force her to reveal herself."

His gaze pierced MJ, and she struggled not to flinch. If he wasn't the evil person after her, the man could certainly be controlled by him or her, fixated as he was on his mermaids.

"Why don't we get some diving equipment and go after the coin she had?" Noel asked. "It seems to me to be the obvious solution."

"Good luck with that," Paul said. "It's a volcanic pool with a high sulfur level. Not only is the water so milky you can't see anything in it, depending on the time of day, the temperature's hot enough to cook you alive. Even in a wet suit, you probably wouldn't stand a chance."

MJ looked up, stunned by the fury she saw in Rick's eyes. What was he so angry about?

"I see," Rick said, putting down his fork and pushing his plate away. "I guess we all lose out because of your selfishness. I saw the picture, and it sure as hell looks authentic to me. It might've led us to the treasure. Cindy deserves better than the life she has with me right now."

"I'm sorry you feel this way, Rick, but I wasn't being selfish," MJ argued. "Besides, if it was fake, it doesn't matter, and if by some miracle it was real, I couldn't have kept it. I would've had to turn it in. Now, it belongs to the island. Besides, from what I can see, Cindy is happy."

"She says she is, but who would want to be married to a grease monkey when they can have this?" He indicated the room.

"I'm sure she means exactly what she says. Don't beat yourself up over this. Money doesn't buy happiness," Christy said, not bothering to mask the bitterness in her voice. "I should know. Bill has plenty of money, and he's still miserable."

Rick scoffed. "Yeah, but I would rather be rich and miserable than poor and miserable. Who wouldn't?" He rose. "I've lost my appetite. I'll see you in the morning. What time again, Bill?"

"Around nine. Stan thinks we should start near the volcano. We can take a look at that lava pool at the same time. Let me see you out."

"I'll come, too, I need to go," Christy said, following them.

"I guess they're still going to look for the treasure." Paul shook his head, his mouth tight.

"Yeah. While Antoine Leroux can't participate this year, the guests are welcome to continue searching the island for it," Mark answered, speaking for the first time.

He and Melena had been so quiet throughout the meal, she'd almost forgotten they were there.

"I see, so it'll be business as usual then?"

"Not really. The resort is giving everyone a five-hundred-dollar voucher toward a future visit, courtesy of *Louis James Live* and taking reservations for next year at this time when he'll try again. Even management doesn't think anyone will find it. I think most people are packing it in, doing other things, but Bill and his friends want to press on. They've invited me to continue looking with them. Melena isn't too keen on it, and considering what an ass I've been ... Besides, my calculations are similar to Leroux's. I put the treasure somewhere near where we went fishing today, not on the island. By the way, here." He handed her an envelope. "Don't worry. It won't bounce. Melena insisted I do the right thing. We should be square now. I'm truly sorry for everything, and I promise if you don't do anything, neither will I. Honestly, I don't know what got into me. Finding that treasure consumed me, but when Melena threatened to leave me, the desire just vanished." He shook his head.

MJ stared at the envelope she held. Where was the real Markos Theopolis, and who was this imposter?

Melena smiled, but her eyes were cold. "I had assumed he'd already settled with you for the room. Now that he's accepted there's no treasure to be had, Mark's promised to spend more time with me. Since we have to leave Saturday, we only have a couple of days left, and I would like to enjoy as much of the island as I can. We'll be three by this time next year," she said, her cheeks pinking. "This will be the last romantic getaway we'll have for a while."

Pain stabbed MJ, but she swallowed it, refusing to go down that road now.

"The literature says your dreams come true here, and for me, they have," Melena continued. "MJ, I know you don't believe me, but I am sorry for the way things happened. I hope we can be friends."

Mark reached for his wife's hand. "This island is supposed to give you whatever your heart desires. Maybe I needed to see what a fool I was, and what I would be giving up if I didn't change."

Could he possibly be sincere? His body language implied he was, but this was the biggest about face she'd ever seen. This was Mark. He had an angle. He always did. Most likely he'd realized that Melena's fortune beat out imaginary treasure.

"I hope you'll both be very happy," MJ said. "As Cindy pointed out, this place is magical."

Paul reached for her hand and raised it to his lips.

"It is. All my wishes have come true—some I didn't even know I had." He winked.

Lindsay frowned, but didn't say anything.

MJ knew she would have questions, some she didn't want to answer, but would it matter now? At least they could cross Mark and Melena off the list of suspects. She handed the envelope to Paul who slipped it into the inside pocket of his jacket.

"Anyway," Mark went on, "that's why Bill was so interested in that coin. We didn't find any mention of it in the literature we looked up, but that doesn't mean much. If it is genuine, it's solid gold, and that alone gives it value. Despite what Christy said, even he can't be sure it's real until it's appraised. It sure as hell looked real to me, but when it comes down to it, he's the expert. But, now that it's gone, it's a moot point."

Paul squeezed her hand. "Are you okay? No headache? There was that possibility of concussion."

"I'm fine. Maybe a little tired, that's all." And more than a little worried. She might be able to scratch M and M off the list, but that didn't get her any closer to finding the person after her.

The Maître d. came over to the table.

"Pardon, Monsieur Davis. There is a call for you in the lobby."

Paul wrinkled his brow.

"I'll go with you. I need to use the bathroom anyway." MJ said, knowing he wouldn't want to leave her behind and not wanting to give the others a second chance at the inquisition.

CHAPTER TWENTY-THREE

With MJ by his side, Paul walked out to the main desk. He hadn't wanted to leave her, although how anything could happen with so many people looking on was beside the point.

"Be right back," MJ said.

Paul nodded. "I'll wait for you out here."

Moving toward the desk, his footsteps slapping against the slate floor, he stopped when the receptionist turned toward him.

"Can I help you?" she asked, her English as clear and crisp as any he'd heard in London.

He smiled. This woman was as different from the rest of the staff as day from night. Not only was her English flawless, she had pale, almost translucent skin, not a wrinkle or blemish in sight. Her dark glasses were similar to MJ's, while her pearl earrings matched her necklace whose color glowed pale pink against the pallor of her skin. He wouldn't be able to guess her age if his life depended on it. Like some of the others, she wore a low-cut white blouse and a madras plaid skirt. Her long, dark hair, heavily streaked with white and braided, trailed over her left shoulder, reaching almost to her waist, the cloth covering her head worn like a bandana. Unlike Rosette or Lucette, and the other staff working at the resort, she wore no name tag.

"Hi." He said, smiling. "I don't think I've seen you here before."

"I've been away for many years, but my family needs me, so here I am. How may I help you?"

"I'm Paul Davis. The Maître d' said I had a call?" Although he couldn't imagine who might be calling. Maybe Mama was worried about them, but wouldn't she have phoned MJ?

"Yes, sir. You can take it over there." She pointed to the house phone on one of the end tables and turned back to whatever she'd been doing earlier.

"Thanks." He hurried over and picked up the receiver. "Hello?"

"Monsieur Davis, this is Captain Saucier, from *l'Étoile de la Mer*. I received your message. While I have yet to solve the mystery of the open freeboard door, I have discovered the cause of the turbulence." The man spoke quickly, his agitation clear.

"Was it an underwater quake?" Paul asked, chewing his lip like MJ did when she was nervous. He'd heard married couples often picked up one another's bad habits.

"No. I wish it had been." He sighed. "Like many boats who take tourists out diving, we have underwater cameras beneath the ship that can record twenty-four hours of tape. My son used the boat earlier in the day to check for damage to the reef along the lagoons and turned the cameras on, but forgot to turn them off. We reviewed the tape. There is no easy way to say this. Someone tossed a flash grenade into the water. There was no danger to the vessel, but I do not know who did it. While the image is blurred by the turbulence, you can clearly see Madame Davis falling into the sea."

"Are you telling me someone deliberately made the boat lurch?" Paul asked. Had they timed it to coincide with MJ being near the open door? Whoever had done it could be responsible for that, too.

"It appears that way, yes. I thought you would want to know. I have contacted the authorities on Martinique who will take over the investigation. I do not know if the goal was to damage my ship or harm one of my passengers, but this is a serious matter. I will not let it drop. The *gendarmes* will be around tomorrow to question the guests aboard as well as my crew."

"Did you see anything else on the tape?"

"You mean a mermaid, *n'est-ce-pas?* If Madame saw one of our ladies of the sea, it wasn't when she fell overboard. The only other objects on the tape at that time were fish and a school of dolphin in the distance."

"Thanks," Paul said as MJ joined him. "Maybe those dolphins are what my wife mistook for a mermaid. It wouldn't be the first time someone did. I appreciate you keeping me in the loop. Thank you."

He hung up the phone.

"Who was that?" MJ asked, the vee between her eyebrows more pronounced, her mouth turned down.

"The captain from the fishing boat." He related what the captain had told him. "While Irena could've been hiding in that school of dolphin, I don't think she goes around tossing grenades at the fish, which means someone aboard that boat did."

MJ's color faded, the fear in her eyes more pronounced.

"Someone intentionally threw a grenade in the water?" she squeaked.

"It sure looks that way." He put his arm around her shoulder. "The police will be around tomorrow to question everyone. I know what Germaine told us, but I think we should keep that to ourselves for now. Let's finish dinner and go back to the bungalow. I don't feel much like dancing tonight, and the fact that my knee isn't sore after the day we've had could raise Bill's eyebrows again."

She swallowed, nodded, and smiled weakly.

He squeezed her shoulder. If this island could give him his deepest desire right now, it would be a gun.

"You have my word, MJ. I will keep you safe." Well, as safe as any unarmed man could facing a faceless enemy who might or might not have black magic on his side.

He held the restaurant door open for her. This meal couldn't finish soon enough for him.

* * *

"Oh my God!" MJ stood in the open doorway of their bungalow, her eyes wide, her hands covering her mouth, as if she could keep the bile churning within her from spilling out. "How could someone do this?"

"Son of a bitch," Paul cursed, closing and locking the door before stepping in front of her. "Stay here. Don't move."

She nodded and flattened herself against the entrance.

Her gaze followed him as he searched the bungalow. There was clothing everywhere, drawers pulled out, left gaping open. In the sitting area, tables were on their sides, lamps divested of their shades, the sofa and chair overturned, their cushions on the floor. The intruder had stripped the bed, and its sheets and pillow cases were heaped in the bathroom doorway. Even the duvet cover had been removed and tossed aside. As for the bed itself, the mattress leaned against the breakfast bar, the frame overturned to reveal the floor beneath it. Her suitcases and Paul's were open, the lining unzipped, the dirty laundry she'd bagged in there mixed in with everything else. On the table, the coffee cups were in disarray, the fruit bowl overturned, and the small box of souvenirs she'd collected from the beach sat empty. Standing like a sentinel, the only object untouched, was a bottle of champagne in an ice bucket, two flutes upside down in the ice. In the closet, garments had been pulled down exposing the wall safe, its door hanging open, money and documents on the floor beneath it. It would take hours to clean this mess.

"It's okay," he said, his jaw tight, his nostrils flaring. "Whoever did this is gone."

He picked up the phone, hesitated, and then slammed it down, startling her.

"I'm sorry. I didn't mean to scare you. We should probably report this, but I'm guessing that's exactly what whoever did this wants us to do. Raymond will want to know if anything is missing, and judging by the cash littering the closet floor, I doubt there will be. I could be wrong, but ... It doesn't look as if anything has been broken, only tossed around." He chuckled. "Kind of reminds me of my first apartment after a party, only it smells better."

She giggled at his feeble attempt at a joke and swiped at the tears running down her cheeks. "That must've been quite the night."

"Who said it was just one night?" He pulled her into his arms. "I'm an ass, MJ. Here I am, beating my chest, claiming I can keep you safe, and I can't even keep my goddamn underwear secure."

She hiccupped, and nestled into his arms, appalled by the chaos around them.

"This isn't your fault. Whoever did this wasn't after money," she said, indicating the cash on the floor.

"I doubt it was your jewelry, either."

"The coin?"

He nodded. "That's the only thing that makes sense. And they did it after the staff came in to turn down the bed and drop off the bottle of champagne I ordered. It's sitting right there on the table. The question is who do we know that knows about the coin and where it might've come from?"

"Well, there's Germaine, Lucette, Mark, Bill, and Rick, but I can't see anyone of them doing this."

Paul moved over to the safe to collect the money and documents.

"It's all here," he said after counting it and returning it to the envelope he used. "Wedding documents, that certificate for catching the fish of the day, and our passports, too, although yours has been cracked open as if someone wanted to take a picture of your passport photo—not a flattering one, I agree, but the real color of your hair and eyes is evident. Damn!" The edge of his upper lip forced his cheek up, causing him to squint. "There were a quite a few members of the Seekers of Treasure conspicuous by their absence in the dining room tonight. Apparently, they were in the bar celebrating or commiserating as the case might be, but it wouldn't take a group long to do this. Bill escorted Rick out, remember? He was gone at least ten minutes, long enough to organize a search, and he was quieter than usual when he came back." He shook his head, the muscle in his jaw jumping. "They didn't seem to care about hiding their tracks this time."

"What do you mean?" She hugged herself.

"Do you remember when we came back and found all the lights on the other night?"

She nodded.

"I think someone was looking for something then, too."

Frowning, she shuddered once more, feeling violated and disgusted at the thought some stranger had manhandled her personal items, not once but twice. Her stomach churned at the notion of filthy hands touching her underwear.

"Maybe. Do you think it could have something to do with what happened aboard the fishing boat?"

He shook his head and ran a hand through his hair.

"God, I hope not. That would mean whoever's involved has a personal axe to grind, and the only ones who fit that scenario are Mark and Melena, but neither of them left the dining room, and he wouldn't need a picture to know the real color of your hair and eyes." He huffed out a breath. "It takes a lot of anger to do this, and an even greater amount of self-control not to destroy anything."

Stepping over the bed linen, she entered the bathroom. On the counter, her cosmetic case had been emptied, the contents spilled into the basin. Her small bag of faux jewelry had met the same fate, but other than the blue crystal pendant she'd lost in the water, nothing was missing. As she put things away, she noted she was short one pair of contact lenses. She huffed out a breath.

Leave all the money and take two-dollars' worth of useless lenses. How lame is that?

After using the toilet, she washed her hands, and then folded all the towels. Once everything was as it should be, she returned to the room where Paul had righted the furniture.

Without a word, she joined him, and together they made the bed, a domestic chore she expected they would repeat in the months and years to come.

"What do you want to tackle next?" she asked. The room still looked like a hurricane had blown through it.

"I guess we'd better pick up the clothes. Anything wrinkled beyond wearing can go in your laundry bag, and we'll send it out to be cleaned in the morning."

"I would send everything, but that would look suspicious, too."

He nodded, drew her into his arms once more, and kissed her.

The gentle touch of his lips was reassuring and stirred fires within her suppressed by the shock.

He hardened against her. Lifting his head, he gazed into her eyes.

"I'm really sorry, MJ. If it were up to me, I would forget the rest of this and take you right to bed, the way I'd hoped to do when we got here, but we do need clothes for the next few days." He chuckled. "Or not. We could just stay in here naked."

"And starve?"

Laughing, he released her and reached for the champagne, expertly popping the cork.

"And you say *I* only think of food. Here. This should help settle your nerves." He handed her a flute. "You do know we could order room service, but our absence would be noticed, and that's something we want to avoid. So, as much as I'd love to keep you here, naked and in that bed, let's enjoy this while we fluff and fold. I can take care of your unmentionables." He wiggled his eyebrows.

"Oh no you won't," she said, reaching for the thongs he held, her cheeks burning.

He laughed and picked up one of his suit jackets.

"That does it," Paul said, almost an hour later. He emptied his glass. "We can drop this off at the front desk in the morning."

The laundry bag bulged.

"I don't get it. I've gone through everything, and the only things missing are the souvenirs I collected along the beach and one pair of contact lenses. I may be able to replace the seashells, rocks, and sea glass, but why would anyone take my lenses?"

Paul frowned. "Are you sure they were all there earlier?"

She shrugged. "Honestly, I don't know. I had sixteen pairs with me. I've worn six and should have ten, but there are only nine."

"Could they have disappeared the other night?"

"I guess, but why would anyone want them?" She raised her glass and finished the champagne. "They're my prescription and would be useless to anyone else."

"Maybe to prove they were tinted. If that was the case, they needed the passport picture to verify the color. Maybe that's the real reason for all of this. Look, I want your promise to stick to me like glue from now on. Everything you collected along the beach and when we were diving is gone, so, it's possible whoever did this doesn't even know about the coin and that makes the list of suspects way too long. If whoever made this mess didn't find whatever they were looking for, they could be back, or worse, they could come after you next."

Goosebumps marched along her flesh, but she wasn't cold.

"But why? I know what Germaine said, but who else might know that? Seriously, the story is too fantastic to believe. There are lots of things in this world that can't be explained, but I refuse to believe my tenth-generation grandmother was a purple mermaid and is here looking after me."

"I know, honey, but if these people have heard Bill mouthing off about his mermaids being the key to the treasure, or overheard Lucette talking about your eyes, and if someone caught this Luc character talking about the mermaid you claimed you saw ... Greed does strange things to people." He reached for her empty glass and set it on the table next to his. "I've seen sane men do horrible things for money." He hung his head.

"Should we warn Germaine?" she asked, rubbing her hands together. "If someone's been watching us, they'll know we spoke to her."

He looked up and shook his head, his lips tight. "We'll have to hope her spirits tell her about it. Going to see her after this, especially since we aren't reporting it, could paint a bullseye on her. Let's see if anyone shows any interest tomorrow and if the police learn anything we can use. Captain Saucier promised to keep me in the loop. I'll think about mentioning it to Raymond, but right now, the fewer people know about things, the better."

"I guess, but Paul, I'm worried about her. She's an old woman and lives alone. I know she believes the spirits and *Quimbois* are on her side, but so far that hocus pocus hasn't proven to be too damn reliable."

"I agree, but our hands are tied." He stepped closer to her. "Now, Mrs. Davis, the house is clean, and it's definitely time for bed."

MJ smiled. "Yes, it is." She stood and turned her back to him. "Unzip me?"

"With pleasure."

The touch of his hand along the sensitive skin on her lower back had her flaming, and within a matter of minutes, they were both naked in bed, their bodies seeking solace and comfort from one another. Losing herself in him like this was the only way she'd get any rest tonight or any other night until they were safely back home.

* * *

"That's all I remember," MJ said, after describing their fishing trip and her fall into the sea.

"And you are certain you were not pushed?" the officer asked once more.

MJ gritted her teeth. "I've already told you. I'm not certain of anything," she answered exhaling heavily. She touched the bandage on her forehead. "As I said, I remember hitting my head when the boat lurched, but after that everything is fuzzy."

"And you saw no one near the gunwale, no one near you? No sounds or smells that didn't belong? That freeboard door is only a few feet from the deck door leading inside the boat."

MJ closed her eyes, trying to remember. Mark had been about ten feet ahead of her and had gone down the stairs. She'd heard his shoes slap against the steps. Had there been the thud of boots behind her? Paul had been so sure she'd been pushed. Come to think of it, she'd smelled oil and gasoline, too.

She shook herself. Talk about recovering false memories. Why wouldn't she smell those things? It was a diesel-powered fishing boat, hardly a top-notch yacht. There had been many odors around her all-day long—everything from fish bait to Mark's nauseating cologne. He always did overdo it. How was she to remember if she'd smelled anything before her fall?

"I'm sorry, Sergeant, but I don't recall anything else."

He nodded, his lips pursed.

"Some of the crewman claim you saw a mermaid," he insisted.

MJ chuckled. "Don't tell me you believe in them, too?"

"*Non, Madame*, but it is a strange thing to say, especially when you claim to have few memories of the accident."

MJ bit her lip, her heart hammering in her chest at the shrewd look on the young police officer's face. She was the victim here, yet she felt as if she were the guilty party.

"My husband thinks it may have been a dolphin, or it could've been a Mahi Mahi like the one I caught. There's been all kinds of references all week to mermaids because of the treasure hunt. Not only am I accident prone, I have a vivid imagination. I'm sure I hallucinated the whole thing. I doubt I saw anything at all."

Her cheeks burned. Would the policeman realize how many lies she was spewing?

"Perhaps, but that door *was* opened, and there *was* a grenade."

"Sergeant, if you think I tossed that grenade overboard and jumped in, why not come right out and say so?" she asked, offended, shaking with righteous indignation.

"My apologies, Madame," the young man said, clearly surprised by her outburst. "I did not mean to imply any such thing—quite the opposite. We do not know whether it was you or Captain Saucier's boat that was the target of the attack. On the one hand, we must consider sabotage, but on the other—you could have died, and that is attempted murder. I am simply trying to gather as many facts as I can. I am truly sorry if I have upset you." He nodded. "I believe I've taken enough of your time. If you'll excuse me."

MJ smiled. "I'm sorry if I misunderstood. Yesterday wasn't my best day, and the idea someone might have done this on purpose ... I hope the captain gets the answers he needs." Jack Crowder flashed through her mind. He'd been on the ferry the first time she'd seen Irena. "Have you spoken with Jack Crowder, one of the crew?"

The police officer frowned and looked at his list. "I do not have that name on my list. How do you know this man?"

"He was working on the ferry when I came over. He mentioned he freelanced on the fishing boats. Maybe he's not on your list because he only works part-time."

"Possibly. I will check with the captain." He tipped his cap. "Enjoy the rest of your vacation."

MJ raised her coffee cup to her lips and watched him leave the bungalow, closing the door behind him.

Paul stepped into the room from the deck. "That took longer than I expected."

"Yeah, for a minute I thought he was going to accuse me of doing it myself." She shook her head and giggled at the fury on Paul's face. "Relax. He didn't mean it that way at all. It's either sabotage or attempted murder. No gray areas for the French. Jack Crowder's name came up."

"The guy from the ferry that I met yesterday?"

"Yeah. His name wasn't on the crew manifest. Paul, I was speaking to him just seconds before I saw Irena that first time. What if he saw her, too?"

"If he did, and he knows about your eyes—"

"My eyes! He saw my eyes. He knows what color they are. I'd taken off my glasses because I couldn't see through them."

"Then he just moved into the top spot on my suspect list," Paul said, smacking his left hand with his right fist. "Who better to smuggle a grenade aboard than a crewman, and if he wanted to verify some cock and bull theory about you being a mermaid or wanted to attract the one he thought he saw, what better way to do so than tossing you overboard? If memory serves, he was on the deck when we brought you back, and I've no doubt he heard Luc mention the mermaid. Come to think of it, he said something about warning you about the freeboards. My gut says he's our man, and it's never lied to me."

She swallowed. "Should we tell the police what we suspect?"

"How can we?" He threw up his hands and started to pace. "We don't have any proof, and we sure as hell can't talk about evil coins, black magic, and a five-hundred-year old grandmother who happens to be some mysterious, purple mermaid. They'd think we were nuts and might lock us up for our own safety." He chuckled bitterly. "No. We're on our own, but now that I know who the enemy is, I can watch for him, as can you, and the minute he shows his face, I'll take the bastard out with my bare hands. Like Germaine said, he's an alien—I'm judging Midwest from his accent."

"Do you think he's the brains behind it?" The man was certainly tall and shifty-eyed, but he'd been smoking up the day she'd first met him, hardly the behavior of a man who needed to keep his wits about him.

"Maybe not the brains, but definitely the brawn. When we find him, he should lead us to the source of this great evil we have to stop. Then, we'll call in the police, and if anyone comes off as a nut job, it'll be him."

"If you say so. I feel as though I'm trapped in some game, waiting for someone to stop pulling levers and making things go wrong." She finished her coffee. "Let's forget about this. What's on the menu for today?"

"Bill's got us beachcombing. It'll give you a chance to replace those souvenirs. Who knows? Maybe you'll find that mermaid's purse after all."

MJ nodded. "Just what I need. He'll probably say it was mine in the first place. But you're right, and besides, it'll be interesting to hear what he and Mark have to say about the inquisition."

"Mark's not joining us, but from what I heard, the police officers really grilled him."

"I'll bet they did." She giggled nervously. "A lot of people heard your accusations. That's the scariest I've ever seen you."

Paul reached for her and pulled her into his arms.

"But I would never hurt you, MJ, you must believe that."

She smiled and kissed him quickly. "I know, He-Man, I know. Let's go find the rest of our treasure hunters."

Grabbing her messenger bag and sunhat, she followed him out of the bungalow.

CHAPTER TWENTY-FOUR

On Sunday morning, clouds filled the sky. Sitting in the lounge, anxiously waiting for Bill and Paul, MJ sipped her second cup of coffee. The air was heavy and humid, the way it had been the day she'd arrived. Normally, she would have trouble breathing, but that didn't seem to be an issue any longer. Lindsay had commented on it earlier, and MJ had calmly assured her that once she acclimatized it was rarely an issue. Lying was getting easy—too easy. Still, another storm was the last thing she wanted.

Mark and Melena had left yesterday along with most of the Seekers of Treasure who'd been unable to hide their disappointment. It was just as well since Mark would definitely have noticed her easy breathing. He'd apologized, given her a fat check, but while he might be acting as if everything between them was fine, once a snake, always a snake. *Quimbois* magic might've touched him here, but once they got back to the States, who knew?

She wouldn't turn her back on him, that was for sure. If something looked too good to be true, it generally was. She had her money, and there would be no court proceedings to embarrass either of them. If he'd been here, he wouldn't let her easy breathing slip by. That asthma attack she'd had last year on the Fourth of July, a day quite similar to this one, had sent her to the ER, and they'd been late for his uncle's barbecue. She'd gotten quite the lecture. He'd even accused her of doing it on purpose. She bit her lip. Maybe she had.

Taking another mouthful of coffee, she tried to relax, but the heebie-jeebies wouldn't go away.

The investigation into her accident continued, although the police had no leads. Captain Saucier had verified that Jack Crowder was a regular replacement in his engine room, and neither she nor Paul had seen him ashore. Paul had asked Lucette about the man, but she didn't know him, nor had she seen anyone like him around the bar, so the possibility he might be their guy fizzled out.

While she was ready to pack it in and spend the rest of the vacation alone with Paul, MJ knew that wouldn't happen. Rick and Bill were still determined to find the treasure, regardless of how hopeless that seemed. Noel and Lindsay didn't care one way or another, simply enjoying the vacation for what it was. This holiday had probably brought them far more excitement than they'd expected.

"So, what's on his majesty's agenda this morning?" Paul asked, coming to stand beside her, dropping a kiss on her nose. He hadn't left her side for more than a few minutes since the break-in. "The weather looks iffy at best. Maybe Bill will ease up and give us free time." He wiggled his eyebrows.

MJ's pulse raced, and she giggled. "As much as I would like to take advantage of that with a couple's massage, I doubt he'll let up. I'll bet that if he checks his ancestry, he'll discover he's related to Simon Legree."

"That's one bet I won't take." He laughed.

"Good morning," Bill said, arriving with his much smaller entourage, Christy two steps behind the rest of them. "The weather doesn't look promising, but we're going to walk the coastline one last time. If it starts to rain, we'll move inland."

"What the hell for?" Rick asked, stepping closer to him. "You said you had something different in mind. We've been around this island three times and *nada*. I say we look elsewhere."

MJ bit her lip. Rick and Bill had been at one another's throats the last couple of days, neither wanting to admit the search was a waste of time. She knew how much the idea of giving Cindy a better life meant to Rick, and while she'd love to tell them where the treasure was, she simply didn't know. Earlier on, Bill had discussed investing in Rick's business, but that had probably just been the alcohol talking.

"And what do you suggest?" Bill snarled. "You say it's in a cave, but we've checked every damn cave we found along the way."

"Not quite. I talked to Rosette this morning," Rick admitted.

"What does the receptionist have to do with this?" Paul asked before MJ could.

"I thought maybe an islander might know something we don't. There's a cavern on the north side of the volcano that's only accessible a couple of times a year. The other day, Leroux explained that the Caribbean is one of the few bodies of water that has no tide, but he's wrong. According to Rosette, there's a tidal schedule in this area, although normally, the water rises and falls less than a foot, so it's barely noticeable most of the time. The fishermen are all aware of it and tie up their boats accordingly. Today, she says that because of the storm, there's a spring tide, and low tide will be lower than normal, revealing the cavern."

"It's not spring, Rick," Cindy said, her tone filled with exasperation.

Noel shook his head. "The name's got nothing to do with the season. It comes from the real meaning of spring—jump or rise—but tides work with the moon and its gravitational pull on the Earth. I don't see what the storm has to do with that."

"Look, that's what she told me. If you don't believe me, go ask her yourself."

Bill frowned and turned to Rick. "I didn't see anything about that in the journal, the island's literature, or my online sources."

"And we haven't found anything, have we?" he challenged, pointing a finger at the man's burly chest. "So maybe your sources aren't perfect. Rosette claims the islanders don't talk about it because it's sacred. It's where those mermaids you've been looking for come ashore or return to the sea. Evidently, islanders have seen mermaids in the past. Where's the harm in having a look?"

Paul rubbed his chin, glanced at her, and then back at Rick.

"If what you say is true, why would Rosette share this secret with you?"

"Purely out of greed—five hundred bucks up front and an equal share of the finder's fee we'll get."

"That sounds mercenary enough to be true," Bill answered, frowning.

"Wouldn't she get more finding it herself?" MJ asked.

"Apparently not," Rick continued, shaking his head. "If someone from the island finds it, they get nothing since it's classified as a national treasure, but we've been promised 10 percent of its worth. Since the damn thing's worth millions, that's nothing to sneeze at. Let's compromise. We'll walk along the Atlantic coast until we reach it. According to the schedule for tides, we've got two hours before low tide, and six hours after that before the water rises again."

"I thought tides were twelve hours apart," MJ said. "Will the possibility of rain affect anything?"

"Nope. As I said, tides work with the moon. Some coastal areas experience two high and two low tides every day. That means there are just over six hours from high to low, or from low to high." Noel said. "It also means we can't stay inside that cavern more than two hours if we want to get out again, no matter what the lovely Rosette said."

Lindsay laughed. "Thank you, professor." She kissed her husband to take the sting out of her words. "It's nice to have facts and figures you can trust. I say we go and look at this mysterious cavern and see if it's any different from the others we've visited. It could be like the Blue Grotto on the Isle of Capri, and if it is, I'll get some awesome pictures."

Faced with her friend's enthusiasm, MJ agreed.

"Why not?" Reaching for her backpack, she stood. "Let's go. It looks like the clouds are breaking up. Maybe the ocean brought us new treasures this morning, too."

Four hours later, angry and covered in slime that smelled of sulfur and God alone knew what else, MJ spat foul water out of her mouth. Nice of Rosette to send them to the gateway to Hell. This place was worse than an outhouse. Bill had hip checked her off the rock ledge—and not for the first time either—sending her flying three feet, face first into a foot of water and slimy goo.

"God damn it! That's it. I've had it. I give up." She reached for Noel's hand and crawled out of the stagnant water. "You can take the rest of your treasure hunt and shove it where the sun doesn't shine. That's the third time you've sent me sprawling into the water. I don't know what you expect to gain from it. Does anyone have anything to drink? I think I swallowed some of that crap."

"Are you okay?" Paul asked, hurrying to her side, using his handkerchief to clean her face. "I should've been here." He glared at Christy.

"Why are you looking at me like that?" she asked, her lips pursed. "I didn't push her in."

"No, but you distracted me so someone else could."

"Stop arguing for Pete's sake," Cindy said, her hands on her hips, sweat trickling down the side of her face, plastering the tendrils of her hair to her skin. "I'm with MJ. Enough is enough. This place smells worse than a week's worth of dirty diapers. I'm dying of thirst, and my water bottle is empty, or I'd offer it to you."

Bill stood beside his glowering wife. "I didn't push her in, honest. My foot slipped on the wet rock."

"Bullshit," MJ mumbled, rolling her eyes. "This taste is beyond gross. Someone's got to have something to drink."

"Lucky for you and the rest of us, Rosette gave me some lemonade from the kitchen and some of these," Rick said, holding up a small bag filled with candied orchids similar to those that had decorated the cakes they'd eaten the previous night. "Apparently, the chef had a few left over so he gave them to her, and she passed them on to me."

"Well, don't just stand there," Lindsay said. "Hand them out, but do it quietly. I don't want to upset the denizens of this wonderful abode." She shook her head, reaching for one of the six-ounce bottles Rick pulled out of his pack. "I could probably drink all eight of these." She opened the bottle and sniffed it. "Rick, I know you wanted to find something, but I'm sorry. The only things in here are bats and bat shit. After exploring this icky place, I'm done hunting for treasure, too. I plan to give that lovely lady a piece of my mind. She might think what she did was funny, but I don't. Although, when you consider we're all trying to grab a piece of her heritage, I suppose she's got the right to be spiteful about it. I intend to spend the rest of my vacation lounging by the pool."

Rick nodded sheepishly. "I suppose I should've realized it was too good to be true. Quite the deal I got for five hundred bucks." He handed out the confections and lemonade. "As P.T. Barnum used to say, there's a sucker born every minute, and this time it was me."

"Don't blame yourself, honey. We all agreed to go. I guess we all saw doubloons dancing before our eyes." Cindy shoved the candied flower into her mouth. "Oh, God, these are to die for. They're even better than they were last night—not worth five hundred bucks, but..."

Rick made a face. "Too sweet for me. You can have the other two."

Lindsay chuckled. "Noel's the one with the sweet tooth in our family, and while I don't mind sugary treats once in a while, like now, I can't eat more than one of these."

"I suggest we finish this quickly, and considered getting out of here," Noel said, emptying his bottle of lemonade and popping an orchid into his mouth. "I've been examining the walls, and I'm fairly certain when this thing fills with water it does so a good eight feet deep. Judging by the less than tantalizing aromas, sulfur dioxide probably increases, too."

"Agreed," Paul said. "Our furry friends up top must have another way in, but it won't do us much good. These walls are too slick and high to climb."

MJ moved to stand beside him at the back of the cave. She drained her lemonade. Putting the last candied flower in her mouth, she savored its sweet taste, a delightful contrast to the previous foul taste and the tart lemonade. "These are fantastic. The only thing they need is to be coated in chocolate. Kitchen magic." She giggled "Lemonade and magic. Sound familiar?"

Paul chuckled. "I'll do my best to figure out how to candy flowers for you."

She nodded. "I look forward to those." She yawned. "I'm tired all of a sudden. Must've been last night's exercise session."

"Maybe," he answered, draining his bottle. "Wish there was more of this."

"I don't feel so good," Cindy said, and suddenly dropped to the ground as if her legs had let go.

"Cindy," Rick cried, moving toward his wife but collapsing before he reached her.

"What's happening?" MJ asked, fear filling her as her tongue thickened.

The cavern began to spin. She reached out for Paul.

"MJ," he yelled, but his voice seemed to come from miles away.

Before she could answer, the cavern began to spin wildly, and everything went black.

* * *

The slap of water lapping against rock woke Paul. His chest tightened. It was pitch black. That deep fear of being buried alive, the one that hadn't surfaced since the night his father had locked him in the root cellar for sassing, filled him. Sweat beaded on his forehead, and his heart raced. Where was he?

Reaching for the penlight in his pocket, he turned it on. He was still inside the cave, lying on the rock shelf where he'd been standing with MJ. His head pounded, and the air in the cavern was more fetid than ever. A strange hum resonated off the walls, and it took him a second or two to realize it was the wind whistling through a small opening above them, no doubt the way the bats entered and left the cave. The water in the pool where MJ had fallen was only an inch or so below the rock ledge. At this rate, they'd be wet in no time, and if they couldn't find a way out, they'd drown.

He sat up slowly, tamping down the nausea. What the hell had happened? Rosette had set them up, drugging the lemonade or the orchids—maybe both. He lifted his hand to his head where it hurt most. His scalp was crusted with blood. What had she used? Rohypnol? Scopolamine? Some weird drug indigenous to the area? The last thing he remembered was feeling odd, as the rest of the group started dropping around him, falling like flies in a cloud of insecticide.

He reached behind him for MJ, but the space where she'd been was empty. He sat up, grasping his pain-filled head.

Around him, the other members of their party were awaking, and judging from the moans and groans, they didn't feel any better than he did. Where was she?

"MJ," Paul called, his gruff voice echoing off the walls. The slight sounds above suggested he might've roused some of the bats, but she didn't answer.

"What the hell happened?" Bill asked, standing and turning on his flashlight. "I feel worse than I do when I'm hung over. Christy, where are you, girl?"

"I'm here. God, I felt better after chemo."

Bill pulled her into his arms. "I'm sorry, honey. I've been such an ass."

"Don't blame yourself, Bill," Rick said, leaning toward his wife who was vomiting, adding to the cavern's less than pleasant aroma. "Coming here was my fault. This is on me."

"Do you see MJ?" Paul interrupted, panic filling him. She had to be here. "She was right beside me."

Bill flashed his more powerful LED lamp around the cave.

"I don't see her," Lindsay said, worry filling her voice. "Dear God, she didn't fall into the water, did she?"

"I doubt that," Paul answered. "She was behind me, so she would've had to get up and crawl over me for that to happen. Besides, she'd never go into that water again unless she had no choice." He swallowed the bile rising in his throat as the awful truth filled him. Someone had taken MJ and left the rest of them here to die.

Bill focused the light on the water. "What the hell? Why is the ocean milky like that?"

"Sediment," Paul answered, his heart beating out a staccato. Who had his wife?

He flashed on the mouth of the cave. Where there had been an opening, there was now solid rock.

"Holy shit! We're trapped here," Bill said, his voice petering out on the last word.

Christy started to cry. "I did not survive cancer to cash in my chips in a cave like this."

"No one's going to die," Paul said, digging deep for the courage that had sustained him in Afghanistan.

He had to keep his head on straight even though he wanted to scream, rant, rave, and kill Rosette with his bare hands. She'd sent them here. He looked at the sand beside him. He recognized the pattern in the footprints. Those were Polar Fox boots, and no one here was wearing them.

"We've been drugged, and while we were unconscious, someone came in here and kidnapped my wife. She's in trouble, but I can't help her from here. I'm not sure what role Rosette played in all this, but you can be damn sure I'll find out. What we have to do right now is figure out how the hell we're going to get out. That water's a good four feet higher than it was when we came in here, and since it's above the shelf now, I'd say we have maybe an hour before it's over our heads. Any ideas?"

Bill shook his head, seeming to shrink in size as he held his wife. "No, sir. I kind of hope you do. Why would they want MJ?"

"Because like you, they believe that cock and bull story that she's a mermaid and can lead them to certain Incan objects imbued with supernatural powers." He snorted. "How sane people can believe such horseshit is beyond me. And, in case it hasn't sunk in, they've left us here to die."

The man blanched and covered his mouth.

"You're kidding, right?"

"Do I look like I'm joking?" Paul answered, his left fist clenched at his side.

"I didn't mean any harm," Bill said, his face paler than Cindy's. "I was just following the instructions I'd been given. The signs were all there—Mark confirmed her eye color..."

"And one of your damn friends tried to drown her," he spat angrier than ever. "If they hurt one hair on her head—

"None of the Seekers of Treasure had anything to do with that," he said. "You've got to believe me.

"Where the hell did you get that stuff in the first place?" Noel asked, holding Lindsay's hand. She didn't look as sick as Cindy and Christy, but her fear was obvious. She trembled.

"About six months ago, someone sent me a message online. He claimed he had inside information on the stuff Lacorneille had plundered from Pizzaro provided by an ancestor. He couldn't go on the treasure hunt, but a friend of his—a man whose name I recognized—said I might be interested in it and offered to sell it to me."

"For how much?" Christy asked.

Bill hung his head. "Fifty thousand dollars and four Incan objects he claimed were family heirlooms. He didn't describe them, but said he'd send more information if we found the cache."

Christy gasped. "You're an even bigger fool than I thought you were."

"He sent me a few things for free," Bill said, trying to defend himself. "They all checked out, so I paid him, and he shipped me the rest of the stuff. Millions in gold in exchange for four small items seemed like a hell of a bargain to me."

"Where did you send the money?" Paul asked, shaking his head at the man's greed and stupidity.

"A bank in the Cayman Islands."

"Tell me about that information. Was finding a mermaid the key?"

"Yeah, a purple one at that." Bill hung his head once more. "That's why I was so excited about those colored auras when you went diving."

Paul nodded, but didn't say anything. Obviously, the evil behind this had manipulated Bill and the rest of them.

"We don't have time to debate the matter right now. The water's rising faster than I thought it would, and even if we could tread water for six hours, I doubt any of us would do well when the bats start to drop. Our best option is to swim out through the cavern door, but given the cloudiness of the water, it would be easy to get lost looking for the entrance," Paul said. "I'll go in first and find it."

Before Paul could remove his shoes, a blue-gray head poked out of the water, followed by the squeaks and creaks associated with dolphin sounds. The dolphin rose up on its tail, as if it were performing at Sea World. Within seconds, six more heads popped up. The animal turned its back and went under, surfacing again seconds later.

What had Germaine said? Irena would help as best as she could? She couldn't come herself, but she'd sent reinforcements. He smiled.

Thank you, Grandma.

Paul jumped into the water and the dolphin approached him, still clicking and squeaking.

"I'm all for making friends with the fish," Bill said. "Obviously, they use this cavern. Must be where the legend of the mermaids coming and going originated. I feel like the world's biggest patsy."

"They aren't fish," Paul said. "They're intelligent mammals, just like you and me. I'm not making friends. I think these guys are here to rescue us."

"Who the hell would send dolphins to the rescue?" Rick asked, holding Cindy who'd finally stopped retching.

"MJ's aunt would say Poseidon, the god of the sea. The islanders might claim the local mermaids did, and if you believe in those, I'll vote for Aquaman. I can use a superhero right now. Scientists maintain dolphins are highly intelligent creatures. Maybe they sensed we were in danger. They've been known to save people who've been shipwrecked, even fighting off sharks when they had to," Paul answered, running his hand through his hair. "It seems to me, regardless of who sent them, these boys are offering us a way out, and I'm all for taking it—that is unless you prefer to die in this godforsaken place." He straddled the mammal as if it were a horse. "Ladies and gentlemen, mount your rides, and let's blow this joint. Take a deep breath as soon as you're ready." He patted the dolphin. "Okay, Flipper, let's get this show on the road."

The dolphin squeaked and then dove, swimming much faster than Paul could have. Just when he thought his lungs would explode, the animal surfaced.

They were about a hundred yards beyond the cavern entrance, but the water was almost as rough as it had been the night of the storm. The mammal swam closer to shore. Paul got off its back in the waist deep water.

"Thank you."

As if it understood, the animal rose up on its tale, whistling and nodding, before diving into the water. Behind him, the other creatures rose each with a precious burden on its back.

Paul waded ashore. Winds whipped the trees as they had the other night, thunder and lightning splitting the early evening sky. He collapsed onto the grass.

"You cannot rest yet." The English woman who'd been on the desk a couple of nights ago stepped out of the trees, carrying a duffle bag.

"Thanks for sending in the rescuers," he said, realizing who she was. "You don't look bad for a woman your age."

"Time affects us all in different ways, Paul. I'm not as strong as I used to be, or I would've destroyed them myself." She sighed, but her face mirrored her concern. "They've taken Germaine and your wife to the lava pool," she said, handing him the bag. "There was no way I could stop them. Neither myself nor the spirits saw the betrayal. We should've, but sometimes the heart refuses to acknowledge the truth. These come from the security office at the resort. There are men combing the island for Germaine, and I've pointed them this way, but they are still too far from here. You must go now if you are to save them both. There's a golf cart at the end of the path to take the women back to the resort." She smiled and touched him, the feel of her hand filling him with strength and energy. "Take very good care of my granddaughter and the seed within her."

Before Paul could comment, she disappeared into the trees. Seconds later. A loud splash came from the right.

"Who was that?" Bill asked, dragging himself out of the water and looking around.

"A friend," he answered.

"How'd she know we were here?"

"She heard Rick and Rosette talking this morning and then the woman left her post, so she followed her. It was just a coincidence that I came out of the water practically at her feet."

Bill frowned, obviously not convinced, but Paul couldn't worry about that now.

"It seems MJ isn't the only one they've kidnapped. The village *Quimbois* priestess is missing, too." He opened the duffle bag. "She brought us these." He handed each man a Glock. "I assume you know how to use them? Just remember, you release the safety when you squeeze the trigger. Since this is a French island, and we don't want to cause an international incident, don't fire unless you have no choice." He turned to the three women. "There's a golf cart at the end of this path. Go back to the resort, find Raymond St. Louis, and have him send the cavalry."

Lindsay nodded. "Come on, ladies. Let's do our part." She turned to Noel. "Be careful, old man. I still have a few years-worth of activities planned."

Rick and Bill spoke quietly with their wives before joining him.

Noel pursed his lips. "There's a hell of a lot more going on here than you're telling us, but I have a feeling I don't want to know it all. We've got your back."

Paul nodded. "I appreciate that. We're going this way. According to Irena, they've got MJ and Germaine at the lava pool."

Paul turned right, following the path through the trees that Irena had taken. With his meager army at his back, he felt less worried than he'd been before. None of them were ready to fight the powers of darkness, but four guns were better than none.

As he plodded through the undergrowth, he let Irena's words sink in. If she was right, MJ was pregnant. She could only be a few days along, but instead of filling him with dread, the thought he'd be a father spurred him on. A blanket of protectiveness covered him. He loved his wife more than life itself. How could he ever believe he wouldn't love their child?

CHAPTER TWENTY-FIVE

The smell of sulfur gagged MJ. She was at the mermaids' bath, but how had she gotten here? The last thing she remembered was being in the stinky cave.

She tried to move, but couldn't. She opened her eyes. She was trussed up like a Thanksgiving turkey!

"I see you've decided to join us."

MJ turned her head at the familiar voice. Jack Crowder. Paul had been right after all.

"What do you want with me? My family isn't rich. Kidnapping is a crime in any country," she croaked, her throat dry, her head pounding.

Lightning split the sky followed by a crack of thunder as if Mother Nature was as upset as she was. Where were Paul and the others? The rain falling in the pool created steam, rendering the visibility almost nil.

"For that to happen, they'll have to catch us, and once this gig's up, we'll be untouchable. Besides, you're far richer than you think. Sadly, you and whatever powers you control didn't give us much choice. We're all running out of time."

"Time for what?"

"Dumb bitch. What do you think? Time to find the treasure and get the talismans. I've devoted my life to the search for those coins, and I'll be damned if I have to wait a minute longer. They can only be activated during the blue moon, the second full moon in a month, and this is our last chance. Now, we both know you've met with the purple mermaid. I saw her on the ferry, and I know you saw her when I helped you overboard. What did she give you that day? Did she tell you where the treasure was?"

"You bastard! You were high that first day and were probably hallucinating, but you pushed me off the boat? I could've died. I *did* die," MJ cried, fury replacing fear.

"Cut the crap. Imagine my surprise when, in my quest for Incan apotropaic magic, I met my partner who was searching for it, too. We both had knowledge, and when we put what we knew together, we realized the search was almost over. You weren't in any danger that day, and we both know it. You're her kin, her family, although how you've managed to repress your ability to change, even when unconscious, is amazing. Here's what we're going to do. You're going into the pond and this time, you *will* transform. Then, you will call the purple mermaid to you. Once we trap her, you're free to go. See how easy that'll be?"

"You're insane. I'm not a mermaid. I can't transform into one. I'm Marilyn Jean Summers, American citizen."

"Bloody liar," he yelled, backhanding her across the mouth. "I've seen the eyes you hide from others, and I was there when you went diving. I saw the way you dolphin-kicked through the water as if you'd been born to do it, so save your crap for someone else. If you don't care about yourself, maybe you care about others. Bring her out."

Rosette moved into MJ sightline, a gun pressed against the bloodied side of Germaine's head, proof she'd been beaten. The priestess was bound from her hips to her neck, her arms pressed close to her body by what appeared to be old iron chains.

"What kind of animals are you?" MJ cried, so angry she shook. "Rosette, for God's sake. This woman is important to you and the people living here."

"To me, she means nothing—less than nothing—and bound like this, she is without sight or power," she answered, spitting on the elderly woman. "How does it feel?"

MJ's spirits flagged. "What have I or Germaine ever done to you?"

"To me? You have done nothing, but this is a family feud, and we will settle matters once and for all," she said between clenched

289

teeth, her face an ugly mask in her fury. "You cling to your lies, but I know who you are. Just like this mambo, I too can channel the spirits, the way the great Ovine did before she was stripped of her powers and condemned to rot in prison. You will help us recover what should have been hers, or your man, your friends, and this woman will die. Even now, the water rises in the cavern. I can release them. I know a secret way out of the cave, but until I hold the four gold talismans in my hands, their fates and hers is in yours. Now, what will it be? Will you transform of your own will, or does the *quimboiseuse* need to pray to her spirits for her deliverance?"

MJ shook her head. These two were insane, blinded by a lust for power and greed. She looked at Germaine. Did the woman know she would do anything to be able to save her? *Quimbois* magic. She'd put her faith in it, and not only would she never have Paul's children, she was going to die here. Germaine and her spirits had been wrong, but she wouldn't hold it against the woman who couldn't even help herself now.

"I can't," she answered, tears pooling in her eyes and dribbling down her cheeks. "I'm not who and what you think I am." If this monster was telling the truth, Paul and the others were already dead or soon would be. "What you're asking me to do is impossible."

"Not impossible. Rosie here thinks that if we dip you into the pond, the hot water will jar some genetic memory. She claims it can't hurt you because of your mermaid DNA. I say skin's skin and flesh is flesh, and we'll boil yours right off you. Want to see which one of us is right? I'll bet that old doll will cook up in no time. Ready to help?"

"I can't, dammit, I can't. How many times do I have to say that?" MJ struggled with the ropes that bound her, well aware that Jack could swing her out over the water with very little effort. She smothered the giggle forming in her throat, as panic gripped her. Carla had come so close. Instead of being captured by cannibals, she would be boiled alive by insane homicidal maniacs.

"You deceive yourselves," Germaine said, her voice surprisingly calm and strong. "You've bound me with these chains of steel, but soon, you'll be bound for all eternity by the chains you forge now." Germaine turned to her. "Have courage, *ma petite*. All is as it should be. It will be over soon."

"Shut up!" Rosette slammed the gun against the old woman's head, sending her sprawling onto the rocks.

MJ fought to slow her breathing, more grateful than ever for the mermaid's gift. An asthma attack now would've been disastrous. Germaine wanted her to be brave? She would be. Paul wasn't in the cave. He'd found a way out. She knew it in her heart, just as she knew he was coming for her. She needed to buy time.

"Leave her alone, you bitch. Weren't you taught to respect your elders? Since I'm going to die here, why not tell me how our names ended up in the draw?"

"When Jack came to me, claiming he had seen a mermaid on the ferry, and another had surfaced if only for a second, I realized Paradise Island had finally brought me my heart's desire. You were the one who would help me get my revenge and power that should've been mine from birth. When you arrived without a room, I was confused, afraid I couldn't keep you here, but then Monsieur Davis solved the problem. All I had to do was keep a close eye on you. What better way than by placing you under the watchful eyes of the Seekers of Treasure?"

"How did you do it?"

"It was child's play, sleight of hand. I held the cards in my hand and pretended to pick them from the bowl. Jack had already conned Monsieur Smith into helping us, and he selected poor Monsieur Larson because he wanted so much to belong. I added yours of course. That fool, Raymond, thought it was Fate."

MJ almost choked on her disgust. "People like you must've inspired my aunt's favorite Greek myth. A pretty face truly does hide an evil heart."

"Now, will you cooperate, or will I put a bullet in her head?"

Germaine sat up, startling the woman.

"This one cannot help you get what you want. Only Irena can unlock the chest that holds the talismans. That ability stays with her as long as she lives."

Rosette laughed. "Stupid old woman. I know that, just as I know Irena will come if this one's in danger. If she truly cannot change in the mermaids' bath, then she will definitely be in peril, and Irena will fall into my trap."

She nodded to Jack. "Begin the process."

Yanking her up roughly, Jack swung MJ out over the water.

"Temperature's about 110 degrees," he said, checking the thermometer.

"Lower her slowly. The water will scald and burn her human flesh unless she changes. Only mermaid skin can withstand the heat of their sacred water."

Germaine began to mumble an incantation in the patois MJ didn't understand. She felt lightheaded. The world seemed to slow down around her. Inch by agonizing inch, the rope lowered. She pulled her legs up, but it was in vain.

The moment her naked flesh touched the water, she screamed, the pain beyond anything she'd ever endured. She was going to die without Paul ever knowing how much she loved him.

* * *

A scream ripped the air apart, startling the birds, and tearing at Paul's heart.

"That's MJ," he cried, increasing his speed and running along the path as fast as the rocks and meager undergrowth permitted. They were close, but not close enough.

"Paul, wait for us," Noel said, hurrying after him. "Slow down. You can't help her if you break your fool neck. I'm not an expert volcanologist, but judging by the smell, I'd say there's more than one vent around. The last thing you want to do is step on one of those."

Paul slowed his pace, allowing Bill and Rick to catch up.

"We must be getting closer," Bill said. "It stinks to high heaven around here, and the trees have all but vanished. If someone wanted to make a movie about post-apocalyptic life, this place would be ideal. It's hard to believe we're on the same island. I feel like we're standing on the brink of Hell."

Rick nodded. "Not a very inviting place, I'll give you that. I'll bet no one's searched for the treasure here."

"When MJ and I came here the first time, the driver told us the coins tossed in by the bride and groom eventually made their way back to the families. MJ speculated that the damn treasure might've been tossed in there, and thanks to the chemicals in the water, the chests have broken down, and everything's drifted out."

"Damn shame if it did," Bill said. "But, one way or another, I'm not about to try and find out. That treasure's cursed. It almost cost us our lives. Let Leroux find the ship next year—if he can. We aren't coming back to look for it."

Rick nodded. "Even if we could afford it, I'll pass on that."

"Neither will Lindsay and I, but right now, we need to focus on MJ. Our wives are safe and she's not."

A second scream slashed the silence, almost driving Paul to his knees. Even Fiona's cries hadn't been filled with that level of agony. What were they doing to her?

"The lava pool's about fifty yards to the left," Paul said, lowering his voice. "The volcanic rock is rougher here than where the islanders approach it, but I'm hoping we'll come up behind the sons of bitches who are torturing my wife."

Moving as quickly as he could, he neared the pool. As they got closer, Paul could hear the sounds of weeping echoing off the barren rocks. He would tear apart whoever was hurting her.

A loud splash sounded, followed by a keening wail.

Had they thrown her in? At low tide, the water would be at its hottest, scalding her, cooking her alive. Right now, her skin would burn and blister after even a short exposure.

"Germaine," MJ shrieked, her pain-filled voice clogged with tears. "You're monsters, both of you. In those chains, she doesn't have a chance."

"We aren't the monster's here," a woman answered.

He recognized Rosette's voice. How had she fooled them all so completely?"

"The only monster here, is you. You had it within you to save her, but you refused. Change now," Rosette continued, "and you may yet save her. Stay as you are, and she will die for sure."

"We'll have real witch's brew," a man said and laughed.

Was that Jack Crowder? It had to be. There was no one else around with that distinct Midwest accent. How the hell had he and Rosette come together?

"Good for whatever ails you." He guffawed at the sick joke.

Paul might just break the bastard's jaw to stop him from speaking for a while.

MJ whimpered.

"My, but you are stubborn. I had nothing against the priestess. Time's running out on the others. By now, the water's probably up to their necks."

Silence filled the air.

"To pe rode la gratelle dan to liki la," Rosette yelled in the patois he had trouble understanding. "Lower her some more, Jack," Rosette said.

What the hell? Was she the damn ringleader?

"That's Rosette," Noel whispered, his brows drawn together in confusion. "Who's Jack?"

"An American MJ met on the ferry. He was on the fishing boat, too," Paul answered, his voice low. "Rick, come with me. Bill go left. Noel, you take the right. Remember, no shooting unless we have no choice. It sounds as if they've killed Germaine, the priestess. These people are dead serious, and I don't want one of you ending up that way. I have enough deaths on my conscience as it is."

The men nodded and moved to follow his orders, Paul walked straight ahead, staying behind the larger boulders for cover. He almost stepped on a fissure, seeing it at the last moment. Turning the corner, he saw Jack lower MJ up to her hips in the hot water. Her cry of agony was cut short as she passed out. Her head and shoulders sagged forward.

The woman he loved and the child they'd created were being cooked alive.

"You bastard," he screamed, running full tilt at the man. He heard a gunshot, felt the burn of a bullet in his upper arm, but it didn't slow him down. He knocked Jack to the ground, relentlessly pummeling his face with both fists.

"Get her out of there,' he yelled at Rick.

"Not so fast, Monsieur Davis. You seem to forget I am holding all the cards."

Paul kicked the man he'd beaten to the side and stood, his hand reaching for the sore spot on the opposite arm. He was bleeding like a stuck pig and felt nothing. Where were Bill and Noel?

"I do not know how you escaped the cavern, but it is of no consequence now. I have not finished with your lovely wife. Once she tells me what I wish to know, I will release her."

Like hell she would. Even if MJ could give her what she wanted, she would never let any of them go now. Germaine's body bobbed to the top of the pond.

"You killed her," he stated, the loss of blood making him dizzy. Had she nicked the brachial artery? "Why are you doing this?" he asked, stumbling closer to her, having a hard time maintaining his footing.

"Ah, ah, ah," she said, moving away from him, her back to the water. "Do not come any closer. You are not necessary to my plans, but perhaps I could use you as leverage."

Veering his gaze right, he spied Noel inching closer to Rick. How long had MJ been in the water? She hadn't moved since she'd been immersed, and he was too far away to see if her chest was moving. He had to distract Rosette.

Standing, he stepped toward the woman when another bullet burned into his lower stomach, knocking him backward. Blood poured from his abdomen. At the rate he was losing it, he didn't have long to go, but without MJ, what did it matter.

He lurched forward. "Come to papa, bitch. I'm taking you with me, straight to Hell. I'm sure you'll have friends and family down there waiting to greet you." He dove at her, plunging them both into the hot water, losing consciousness as soon as he did.

* * *

Blips, bleeps, and antiseptic odors. MJ wrinkled her nose. A hospital?

Curious, she opened her eyes. A ceiling fan spun lazily overhead. If this was a hospital it wasn't the one in Stilton. Memories of the nightmare grabbed her, and she sat up.

"Paul?" she cried.

"Not so loud," he said reaching for her hand. "I still have a drug cocktail headache, and believe me, I would prefer a champagne hangover any time."

"They killed Germaine," she said softly, tears brimming in her eyes.

She gazed at him, noticing the bandage on his arm and the way he sat gingerly in the chair.

"You're hurt."

"I've had worse, although if I keep letting people put bullet holes in me, you might have to start using me as a sieve."

"How? I don't remember much."

"Rosette drugged the lemonade. When we came to in that cavern, I knew you were in trouble and raced to the rescue along with Rick and Noel. Bill and Nate probably saved my life. The good doctor operated on me right in the dining room. Took out the bullets and stitched the arteries. Rosette had a hell of an aim. She's dead, or at least they think she is. Her body wasn't recovered from the pool, but Bill managed to pull Germaine out. How her corpse floated encased in iron chains is a miracle. They buried her yesterday."

MJ nodded. She'd liked the old woman.

"Jack Crowley will need a nose job," he continued, "and be lucky to ever see the outside of a prison. He tossed Germaine into the water, still claiming it's your fault she died since you wouldn't become a mermaid. I doubt he'll ever stand trial. The authorities think he's nuttier than a fruit cake."

He pulled himself out of the chair and claimed her mouth, the kiss filled with relief and possession. Slowly he raised his head.

"That's the second time you scared the daylights out of me. No third strike, please."

She nodded. "I promise. When I woke up near the mermaid's pool, I was terrified." Her eyes widened. "My legs?"

"Your legs are fine. Somehow, when the tide came in, it cooled the water quickly, which is why you only have first and second-degree burns. I got off with next to nothing. They've got this great salve here that numbs the pain and heals quickly."

"Where is here?" she asked, holding his hand in hers afraid to let go.

"The hospital in Saint Pierre. We should be good to go tomorrow. Louis James is sending a private plane for us and wants to do a feature on the mermaid in you."

MJ's breath caught. "The mermaid in me? No, never," she answered and shivered.

Paul shook his head and pulled her closer. "It's not what you think. He wants to talk about ancestry and mental health issues— specifically how people make snap judgments as well as how obsession and delusional behavior can turn deadly. Considering what's happened to you, I thought we could weigh in on that. The color of your eyes has caused you nothing but pain and sorrow for years because people jumped to conclusions. By the way, that forest of flowers is from Bill. He hasn't stopped apologizing for his own obsessive behavior. He's convinced Rosette must've heard him ranting and raving about mermaids and used it to fuel her compulsions and insanity."

She nodded. What she wanted to do was forget all about mermaids, but if talking about genetic anomalies and manic fixations could spare one person what she'd been through, it would be worth it.

"So, what now?" she asked, wringing her hands.

"Now, we sit here, hold hands, and discuss the future," he said, what little humor had been on his face gone. He caressed her cheek. "I know this started as a plan to get even with Mark, but I love you, MJ. I probably have for as long as I can remember. I don't want this—us—to end. I want to spend the rest of my days with you." He swallowed and licked his lips. "Can we try to make this marriage work, really work?"

MJ's heart thundered in her ears as her pulse raced. This was her heart's desire, everything she could possibly want, wasn't it? And yet...

"When I thought I would die, the biggest regret I had was that I hadn't told you how much I loved you." She swallowed, licking her cracked lips, tears sparkling in her eyes. "There is nothing I would like more than to stay married to you, but I want to be a mother, Paul. Is there any chance our marriage could include babies? I know how you feel about fatherhood—"

He cut her off, pressing his lips to hers in a kiss that flamed her. He raised his head, the heat of desire in his eyes making her tremble once more, and not with fear.

"Funny you should bring that up," he said, looking down at their joined hands. "My deepest fear has always been that, when push came to shove, I'd behave badly, like my father did, but I was wrong, MJ. He may have contributed to my DNA, but I'm not like him. I'll fight to the death for those I love and that includes any child we create. We can have as many babies as you like, but I think we might've jumped the gun."

She frowned. "What do you mean?"

He explained how Irena had helped them escape from the cavern. As he spoke, describing dolphins and the mermaid's part in her rescue, she gaped.

"According to her, we might have a bundle on the way. Considering we haven't used protection, it's possible."

Pregnant? She looked down at her stomach. Was it possible? It had only been a few days. What if her dip in the pool had hurt her child?

"I know what you're thinking. Don't. The doctor says there's been no damage to any of your organs since they didn't even get wet." He kissed her once more.

She smiled, a single tear slipping down her cheek. "I wish she could've saved Germaine, too. The people here will miss their healer."

"Germaine did say her spirits might exact a heavy toll this time," he added. "But I don't think those spirits will leave the people on their own. Maybe Irena will hang around for a while and help. Who knows, the next priestess might be here and just doesn't realize her abilities. But this is here, and as much as I like the place, I can't wait to get you home, Mrs. Davis."

"And I can't wait to get there, too. It's definitely going to be a step up from the White Wolf Motel." She shuddered.

He stared at her, his eyes almost bulging out of his head.

"The White Wolf? The motel out on the highway? Don't tell me that was where you were going to stay."

She nodded and looked down at the bed.

"Damn good thing we've found you alternative digs. The police raided that dump the day before I left Watertown. Some guy was running a brothel out of it, but it was a dead drop for drugs smuggled from Canada into the United States. It seems drug dealers and horny soldiers are good for business. Why the hell would you ever consider staying in that place?"

MJ burst out laughing. "I'll tell you all about it one of these days. Let's just say that Carla's instincts are still good."

He cocked his head to the side. "By the way," he reached for the small box on the table. "The resort sent this over. It was left at the desk for you."

MJ reached for the box, split the tape, and lifted the lid. Nestled on a bed of green velvet was her aquamarine crystal, and a note that read, "Pass it on."

Her eyes opened wide, and she looked at Paul.

He burst out laughing. "I guess this is about to become a family heirloom. Got to love *Quimbois*.

MJ smiled and nodded, bending her head to let Paul fasten the chain in place.

Paradise Island had certainly lived up to its publicity. It had given her far more than her heart's desire. It had given her Paul and a lifetime to make happy memories.

The End

Thank you so much for reading **Wedding Bell Blues.** I hope you enjoyed it. Please take a few extra minutes to leave a review either on my website https://mhsusannematthews.ca/ or wherever you purchased the book.

Best wishes,
Susanne Matthews

ABOUT THE AUTHOR

Amazon bestselling author Susanne Matthews was born and raised in Cornwall, Ontario, Canada. She is of French-Canadian descent. She's always been an avid reader of all types of books, but with a penchant for happily ever after romances. A retired educator, Susanne spends her time writing and creating adventures for her readers. She loves the ins and outs of romance, and the complex journey it takes to get from the first word to the last period of a novel. As she writes, her characters take on a life of their own, and she shares their fears and agonies on the road to self-discovery and love.

Her first novel, Fire Angel, set the tone for an exciting new career. While most of her books are romantic suspense, Susanne writes stories that range from contemporary to sci-fi and everything in between. She is a PAN member of the Romance Writers of America.

When she isn't writing, she's reading, or traveling to interesting places she can use as settings in her future books or as interesting entries for her blog, Living the Dream. During the summer she enjoys camping with her grandchildren and attending various outdoor concerts and fairs. In winter, she likes to cuddle by the fire and watch television.

OTHER TITLES FROM SUSANNE MATTHEWS

Please visit your favorite online book retailer to discover other books by Susanne Matthews:

Suspense Novels:
Fire Angel
In Plain Sight
On His Watch
No Good Deed
Desert Deception
Sworn to Protect
Secrets and Lies
The Harvester Series:
The White Carnation
The White Lily
The White Iris

Light Paranormal/Suspense:
Echoes of the Past
Hello Again

Christian Romance Suspense
All For Love

Young Adult Suspense
Prove It!

Contemporary Romance
Just for the Weekend
Forever and Always (novella)
There's Always Tomorrow (short story)

Light Paranormal Romance
Wedding Bell Blues

Holiday Romance
Holiday Magic
The Perfect Choice
Come Home for Christmas (novella)
Her Christmas Hero (short story)
The Best Day Ever (short Story)

Historical Romance
The Captain's Promise
The Price of Honor (Coming in 2018)

CONNECT WITH ME!

I really appreciate you reading my book! Here are my social media coordinates:

Friend me on Facebook: https://www.facebook.com/SLMauthor
Follow me on Twitter: https://twitter.com/jandsmatt
Find me on Goodreads:
https://www.goodreads.com/author/show/7009276.Susanne_Matthews
Follow my blog: https://mhsusannematthews.wordpress.com/
Look for me on All Authors: http://mhslm.allauthor.com/
And don't forget to visit my website:
https://mhsusannematthews.ca/

SWORN TO PROTECT
By Susanne Matthews

CHAPTER ONE

Nancy Frost frowned and hitched her left shoulder higher, trying to anchor the phone in place while her fingers flew over the keyboard. The multiple screens open on her monitor displayed column after column of figures that should make sense but didn't, and a page of names and numbers she didn't recognize.

"Any idea where you'd like to eat tomorrow night?" Meredith asked, her voice coming through the phone, reminding Nancy she was at the end of the line.

She clicked on another tab, opened a new screen, adding to her frustration. More names and abbreviations.

"Why don't we go down to the marina and pick a place?" she answered. Here she was trying to make sense of the most recent changes to this clients' tax portfolio, and suddenly she had three ledger pages with titles, names, and numbers she'd never seen before. Had someone been in her file? Security was tight around here, but it was possible she'd left the file open, and someone else had slipped in.

"Listen, I've got to go. This damn file might as well be in hieroglyphics."

Meredith chuckled. "If those numbers aren't talking to you, then someone's in trouble."

"Or I've lost my edge," she groaned. "Nothing's going well today. See you tomorrow."

She ended the call and glared at the computer screen, hitting "save" without thinking.

"I will figure this out," she ground out through clenched teeth and frowned.

Rumor had it the company was rebranding itself to attract new clients. As a tax accountant, her job should be secure, but a high completion and efficiency rating didn't hurt. As the only female accountant on staff, she was constantly up against the old boys' network. Despite what everyone thought, male chauvinism was alive and well at Olsen, Jansen, and Merriweather.

Looking up in the top corner where the account number was visible, she choked on her own saliva.

387800563239.

"What the hell?" she hissed, angry with herself.

A typo? Really? Four numbers out of order? How in the world did I manage that?

No wonder nothing made sense. Moving quickly, she closed the file. The last thing she needed this morning was an affronted accountant claiming she'd broken one of the gazillion rules this place had. Hoping she hadn't inadvertently changed something, she closed the program, pulled her kitty cat USB flash drive out of the slot and dropped it into the small zippered pouch in the voluminous purse she carried.

"I need a break." Her voice echoed in the empty office. Her head was pounding, it was almost lunchtime, and there was no point in starting something else now.

She'd just slipped on her suit jacket when one of the firm's security men shoved his way into her glorified broom closet, pulled the plug on her computer, undid the wires attached to it, and tucked it under his arm.

"What the hell do you think you're doing?" she cried, reaching for her laptop.

"Come with me."

The stone-faced man, probably a gestapo extra in some WWII movie, grabbed her by the arm and marched her down the hallway, her feet barely dusting the floor given the difference in height. Heads turned as other staff members watched the gorilla manhandle her to the CEO's office, no doubt wondering what dastardly crime she'd committed.

She'd only been in Harold Olsen's office the day she'd been hired. If intimidation was part of his job description, then Olsen had it down pat. He sat behind a massive antique desk, his fingers steepled under his chin, his ebony head reminding her of a shiny new bowling ball. His thousand dollar suit fit like a glove, the pristine white shirt emphasizing his dark complexion. A pasty-faced Clive Connors, dressed in a sharkskin suit that befitted the slippery eel and her immediate supervisor, sat in a chair in front of the desk. He didn't bother standing, nor did he look at her. The security guard handed him her hard drive.

What was she? A seven-year-old dragged before the principal for throwing spit balls?

"Have it searched and then wiped clean," the man barked, every inch the company executive whose orders were to be obeyed at all costs.

"Seriously?" Her eyes opened so wide, she was sure her eyebrows were at the top of her forehead. "What do you expect to find on my computer? State secrets?"

"Yes, sir," Clive answered, continuing to ignore her presence.

Clive had hit on her when she'd first started working here, but still in mourning, she'd fended off his requests. Last year, after she'd filed for divorce, she'd finally agreed to go out to dinner with him, and the evening had been an unmitigated disaster. The man might be on his way to partnership, but he was a jerk on too many levels to count. He'd made working here difficult ever since, but OJM paid better than most, and she'd kept out of his way. Seeing him here didn't bode well.

"Ms. Frost, can you explain why you opened a restricted file?" Olsen spoke evenly, but his flashing eyes and pursed lips suggested barely controlled anger.

She exhaled audibly. "This is about that? I was on the phone and made a typo. I got out of the account as soon as I realized it. It was just an accident."

The people here were territorial, but this was ridiculous. They were acting like she'd committed a crime. That file was open ten minutes at most. Fine, tear a strip off her, but relax. No harm, no foul.

"There's no such thing as an accident," Mr. Olsen said. "Your services are no longer required."

Stunned, she looked from one man to the other. "What? You're firing me? For this?" The last word was little more than a squeak.

Clive wouldn't meet her gaze.

"You misunderstand. We aren't firing you," Mr. Olsen answered, the muscle jumping in his jaw testifying to his annoyance. "We've decided to downsize. We have to reduce our workforce and the easiest way to do that is to reorganize our assets to be as efficient as possible. In view of that, your current position is redundant."

"But, Mr. Olsen, that makes absolutely no sense," she said, frustration and confusion giving her voice an edge. "I'm a tax accountant. Even if every client this firm has goes belly-up, there are still tax forms to complete. I'm exactly the kind of employee you need. My record is exemplary."

"The decision's been made," he answered tersely, not even trying to hide his irritation. "Believe it or not, this firm functioned quite nicely before you arrived and will do so again after you've gone."

"Clive, for Pete's sake, say something. I'm good at my job, and you know it," she begged, the desperation in her voice shaming her.

He shrugged and stared at her for the first time. "Sorry, Nancy, but it's out of my hands."

But he didn't look sorry. The son of a bitch looked smug.

"In view of this decision and keeping in mind your work for the firm, a generous severance package is waiting for you in HR. Tomkins here will accompany you back to your office so that you can collect your personal items, and then he'll escort you off the premises," Olsen said, his face an impassive mask.

"You're firing me right now? Without any notice? You can't do that," she whispered, so shocked she could barely speak.

This couldn't be happening. Her heart thundered in her ears as the reality of the situation sunk in. How would she pay her bills? She'd refused alimony from Neil. Sure she had a few personal tax clients and could always do more forensic accounting work for Meredith and some of the other lawyers, but those jobs were hit or miss. Three years of her life down the drain just like that. She wasn't the low man on the totem pole, so why cut her, why let her go?

"I can assure you we can, and we have. Don't make this any harder than it needs to be. I'm sure with your abilities you'll find work elsewhere." He glared at her.

What on Earth had she done to piss him off this way?

"Will I at least be getting a letter of recommendation?" She'd need one to find another job.

"By all means. Mrs. Willis has it ready for you. You can pick it up with your check. Good day, Ms. Frost."

"I'm sorry, Nancy," Clive said, opening the door for her, his thin lips drawn in a smug smile.

"You bastard!" She spat the words at him. "Just because I wouldn't sleep with you is no reason to feed me to the dogs. I could sue you for sexual harassment."

"Don't flatter yourself." He looked down his nose at her as if she were some kind of bug. "And as far as suing me," he said, chuckling, his sapphire gaze boring into her. "It's your word against mine."

Shaken by the icy animosity in his voice, she swallowed her retort. "Who will take care of my clients?" she asked, grasping at straws. "I should talk to them and bring them up to date."

"I'll look after them, and believe it or not, I can do the job as well as you can." He dismissed her, entering his office without a backward glance.

"This way," the goon reached for her arm again, and she yanked it away.

"Touch me again, and you'll regret it," she hissed. "I know where my office is."

Mustering all the dignity she could, Nancy led the way back to the small space she'd called her own. In her absence someone had emptied her desk and packed up her photographs and other memorabilia. The partially filled box sat in the center of her blotter.

"If you'll put your arms out at your side, I'll search you."

Gritting her teeth, her cheeks burned.

"Oh no, you won't. I warned you what will happen if you put your paws on me again. There are no pockets in this skirt or jacket, and I'm not about to let you cop a feel," she ground out, her chest heaving in her fury.

Glaring at her, he mumbled into the radio he carried. Within seconds, a woman, not an employee she recognized, arrived.

"Put out your arms," the woman said brusquely.

Grudgingly, her mouth a thin line, Nancy complied, allowing the woman to pat her down, more roughly than necessary.

"She's clean."

"Satisfied?" Nancy asked, her fury and humiliation warring for dominance.

"Empty your purse," he stated baldly, while the woman crossed her arms and stood by the open door.

Clenching her teeth to hold back the scathing remark on the tip of her tongue, Nancy turned over the bag allowing its contents to fall on the desk.

"If you're checking to see if I've stolen company pens, don't worry about it. I haven't. I prefer something of higher quality."

The man rifled through the items, checking inside each small bag and pouch and finally nodded.

"Keys."

"You could pretend to have manners," she grumbled. Removing the keys and the electronic fob that opened the garage door from her key ring, she handed them to him. As quickly as she could, she stuffed the items back into her purse. He picked up the box.

"Hang on a second. Let me check to make sure whoever packed this didn't miss anything."

She opened her desk drawers, but each one was empty. Turning to her filing cabinet, the suspended files were nothing but frames. Even her trash can was gone.

Stunned by the speed with which they'd erased her presence here, Nancy grabbed her coat and followed the two security people out of her office. She didn't look back. Walking between the rent-a-cops, she held her head high, looking neither left nor right, hiding the fact she was devastated.

Sondra Willis, the HR manager, stood next to her assistant's desk.

"That was fast. Mr. Olsen called down only half an hour ago. I've barely had time to print the check." She handed Nancy the large brown envelope. "That's quite the package you negotiated. If you have any questions, feel free to contact me."

Negotiated? I've been fired.

"Is my reference letter in there?" she asked, noting the female security guard had vanished.

"It is, as well as my contact information if they would like to speak to me in person."

Nodding, Nancy left the HR office and preceded her jailor to the elevator. The walk of shame was short. He depressed the number for the underground parking garage. As soon as the doors opened, he handed her the box.

"You're not to step back inside this building. If you do, the police will be called, and you'll be charged with trespassing. Is that clear?"

"Crystal."

Stepping out of the elevator, she hurried to her parking space, the behemoth standing there watching her. What did he expect her to do? Slash someone's tires with her nail file?

After placing the box in the trunk, she punched in the code for the keyless entry, her favorite car accessory. Neil always complained she could never find anything in the bottomless pit she considered a purse, and as much as she hated to admit it, nine out of ten times, he was right. Today would be no exception. She smiled and waved at the cross-looking man waiting for her to exit the garage. What she wanted to do was stick her tongue out at him, but that action lacked dignity.

The rain was coming down as heavily as ever. If it didn't let up soon, she'd be up to her knees in mud in the morning. Signaling, she eased into the surprisingly light traffic and drove away from downtown. Within twenty minutes, she pressed the automatic garage door opener as she turned into the driveway. She should've stopped for groceries the way she'd planned, but right now, all she wanted to do was crawl into bed and lick her wounds.

* * *

Nancy pushed her hair out of her eyes, wishing she'd brought a bandana, and forced the stubborn cart down the grocery store aisle, ruing the fact she'd been stuck once again with the one with the crooked wheels that required a linebacker's strength to keep straight. In the humidity, her long, frizzy curls made her look like a cross between Lady Gaga and Chaka Khan.

Her trek to the cemetery this morning had depressed her more than it usually did. She glanced down at her hands, at her dirt encrusted fingernails, and sighed. If only it were possible to turn back time.

"Hello, Nancy," Mavis Clooney said, reaching for a pint of ice cream just as she did. "Rough morning?"

"You could say that." She smiled through gritted teeth.

Murphy's Law at work. Get all dressed up, and you see no one. Go out in an oversized University of South Carolina Gamecocks' sweatshirt and dirty, old jeans, and suddenly you run into everyone you know. How was she supposed to know the sixty-five degrees at seven this morning would morph into eighty-five by eleven?

"I heard you've had another reversal," Mavis said, her curiosity palpable. "I swear you have the worse luck."

"I prefer to think of this as an opportunity. The firm's downsizing. I've been there three years, and I was ready for a change. Tax accounting isn't my forte, although the quality of my work wasn't in doubt." And she had a beautifully worded form letter that said just that. "They gave me an excellent severance package, so I've got lots of time to decide what to do. Meredith has been after me to do more forensic work for her, so who knows?" Better a small lie to save face that having the town's biggest blabbermouth spreading innuendos.

Mavis grimaced. "Divorce lawyers are a nasty bunch, but I suppose she's one of the better ones." She shook her head and added a container of chocolate ice cream to her cart. "People give up too easily."

Nancy bit her tongue. The last thing she wanted to do was make a spectacle of herself arguing with one of the town's biggest gossips.

"It was nice talking to you, Mavis. I have to get going or in this heat, I'll have ice cream soup, and so will you."

Nancy moved down the aisle toward the cashiers. The sooner she got out of this place, the better. Smiling at another acquaintance, she selected what seemed to be the shortest line, regretting it seconds later when a sudden, sharp pain in the back of her shins made her wince.

"Ouch!" She glared at the child who'd rammed the grocery cart into her legs.

"Watch it, sweetie. That really hurts." She smiled to take the sting out of her words.

This was her own fault. She'd skipped the market yesterday to go home and commiserate with the only men in her life these days—the ones who came on a box of rice, a can of pasta, or a pint of Rocky Road ice cream. If she'd taken the time to buy groceries, she could be doing something semi-pleasant, like do-it-yourself root canal surgery, instead of standing here melting. Glancing down at the digital sports watch on her left arm, she frowned. How could she have been here an hour? She rolled her eyes as the store manager came over to straighten another snafu.

Finally at the cash register, she placed her items on the conveyor belt and waited for the cashier to punch them in. The trainee, another zing from Fate, did it so slowly that Nancy wanted to yank her away from the register and do it herself. She was on the verge of hopping over the counter to do just that when her cellphone rang.

The familiar tune identified her caller, and she opened the bag, still in complete disarray, searching for the device. The large, brown leather messenger satchel held everything she considered essential, and weighed a ton. Who needed a gym when she carried that sucker everywhere? If she ever hit anyone with it, the person was out for the count. The tune repeated itself four times before she brought the device to her ear.

"How's my favorite bloodsucking lawyer?" she asked, not bothering to say hello.

Slipping her bank card into the slot, she keyed in her pin number for the cashier.

"Wow. You're in a nasty mood." Meredith's bubbly voice came across the line.

"It's been that kind of day, and from where I sit, I don't see it getting a whole lot better. I ran into Mavis Clooney. She's not a fan of lawyers."

"She's not a fan of anything."

"Are we still on for tonight, or are you calling because you've had a better offer?"

Nancy kept her voice low. Being subjected to other people's one-sided conversations annoyed her. Even if you tried not to listen, the words infiltrated your brain and insisted you forget about everything important to you and concentrate on them.

"Would I do that to you?"

"In a shot, if the right man asked."

Meredith chuckled. "Well, he hasn't, so we're good to go."

"If you aren't calling to bail, what's up?"

"Actually, I need a favor that could be mutually beneficial given your current situation."

"Give," she said, curious in spite of everything.

"A friend of mine needs your help—wife and two kids are getting screwed by Mr. I couldn't keep it in my pants in love with a girl barely out of diapers. Larry's convinced the guy's hiding money. I thought since you had time on your hands you might be willing to have a look. He doesn't need a full forensic audit, he just needs to know if it's possible the guy's got money squirreled away."

The begging tone in Meredith's voice got to Nancy the way it always did. It wasn't as if she could say no; after all, money from these private jobs might be all she would have coming her way for a while, and whether she liked it or not, she'd gotten used to eating each day, and at the price of food and other necessities … The severance package had been generous, but once Uncle Sam took his cut, unless she added to it regularly, it wouldn't last long.

She tucked the phone between her neck and her ear and loaded the plastic bags into her cart as Meredith filled in the details. As soon as the basket was reloaded, she grabbed for the phone again, but it began to slip from her shoulder and fall. Bobbling it like a poor juggler, she failed to hang onto it, and bent over to pick it up off the floor. The child giggled, no doubt drawing attention to her bootie stuck high in the air.

"You still there?" Nancy asked, straightening, hoping the phone had survived its dive to the tile-covered concrete.

"Yes. Where are you?"

"Grocery store."

"*You?*" Meredith's voice went up an octave. "On a Saturday morning? I don't believe it. You did go to the cemetery, right?"

"I did." She wasn't ready to talk about that now. "Why this case?" she asked, changing the subject.

"Larry Jackson's an old friend."

"You haven't mentioned him before."

Meredith sighed. "He used to hang around with my older brother, Charlie. We've kept in touch. What do you say?"

Nancy frowned, nodded to the cashier—who had to be all of twelve—and force the unwilling cart out into the crowded parking lot.

"Nancy?"

"Sorry, I'm waging war here. I wanted to take a breather before I decided what to do. Can it wait a couple of weeks?"

"Unfortunately, it can't. The jerk's threatening to sue for full custody of the kids if she doesn't cooperate."

"Sounds like a stellar human being," she grumbled.

Meredith knew her too well. She'd never be able to pass up a case where kids were involved. Divorce was a fact of life. Not every relationship ended in happily ever after, but kids didn't deserve to suffer because Daddy couldn't keep his fly zipped.

"Give your friend my information. Have him send me what he has, and I'll look at it as soon as possible. My fee's seventy-five an hour plus expenses."

"Thanks, Nancy. Now, where are we meeting for supper?"

"How about Lucifer's? Say eight? I'm in the mood for crab quiche and strawberry margaritas. Your treat."

"You've got it. I really appreciate this," Meredith said.

Nancy sensed a "but" coming. "Spill it," Bad news was like a beached whale. You didn't need to be close to know it was there.

"Lordy girl, sometimes you scare me. You must have a sixth sense or something. I got your signed divorce papers this morning. Once you add your signature, I'll file them with the courts."

Wanting to curl up into a ball and hide from the pain Meredith's words inflicted, Nancy wished it were true. She would never be able to set this pain aside. If she were clairvoyant as Meredith suggested, she would've avoided Cedar Drive that day. Straightening her spine, she laughed bitterly.

"That's wonderful. Great timing. You really know how to make a rotten day worse."

"Don't be like that. This was your idea. I tried to talk you out of it, remember?"

"Let it go, Merry. Even arguing requires an emotional commitment, and there was nothing left but apathy and sorrow. I'll see you tonight."

"Have it your way. See you at eight, and thanks again."

Nancy ended the call, dropped the phone into her purse and transferred the groceries from the cart to the back seat of the car. After leaving the shopping basket in the cart parking area, she got into her vehicle and started the engine. The air conditioner took only seconds to blow cooling air in her face. She slipped her favorite CD into the player and cranked up the volume hoping the music would dispel the gloom threatening to engulf her. Not even *Sweet Caroline* could chase away her misery.

I hope you enjoyed this glimpse of Sworn to Protect available from CreateSpace and other retailers.

www.ingramcontent.com/pod-product-compliance
Lightning Source LLC
Chambersburg PA
CBHW061935170626
46813CB00006B/2407